Once again, Cynthia Ruchti has me falling in love with her characters and not wanting the story to end. From the teenager to the tiny house village people, I wanted to follow them on Instagram and read every post. Don't start reading if you need to get up in the morning because this will be an all-nighter. —Becky Turner, president KBT Consulting

Cynthia Ruchti's "hemmed-in-Hope" stories always capture my attention. In *Miles from Where We Started*, her characters grabbed me from the first sentences, and my travels with them felt much like my own personal journey. Throw in the mix of a sassy adolescent foster boy and a joyful collection of roadside characters, and you've got a book that will travel in your heart a long time. Cynthia's books remind me that when love is rooted in commitment and faith, the rest is just details. Of all of Ruchti's beautifully written novels, this is her best. —Janet Holm McHenry, award-winning author of 23 books including the bestselling *PrayerWalk* and *The Complete Guide to the Prayers of Jesus*

Road trip! Come along on a creative, thoughtful, and fun road trip with Connor and Mallory as they try to figure out what marriage should look like. A wonderful book! —Gayle Roper, author of *A Fatal Arrangement, Plain Truth*

Every Cynthia Ruchti story is an unforgettable darkness-to-light journey. In *Miles from Where We Started*, the journey is literal, inviting readers to tag along on a road trip, savoring backroads beauty across the country while experiencing every bump, detour, and breakdown in a rocky first year of marriage. Like Ruchti's vibrant characters, you will not be the same at the end of this emotion-filled journey to hope. —Becky Melby, author of Guideposts' *Family Secrets*.

Traveling love's and life's highways and byways together can be a challenge at any age or stage. Award-winning author Cynthia Ruchti brilliantly draws the reader into the main characters' road trip in a way that your own life's journey is enriched and inspired. —Pam and Bill Farrel, Directors of Love-Wise, authors of 45 books, including the bestselling *Men Are Like Waffles, Women Are Like Spaghetti*

"Just add humans and the adventure begins," goes the slogan for RoadRave's new tiny trailer. And what an adventure *Miles from Where*

We Started is—following millennial newlyweds Mallory and Connor and a troubled eleven-year-old Judah cross-country. No one wants to be there. The couple is planning to divorce, the boy is wary of yet another in a long line of rejections, and the tiny trailer is just that— way too tiny to contain all this drama! But the people they meet, the places they visit, and the God who accompanies them … all work together through both trauma and transformation. Best line? This is not how our story ends. Yet another confirmation why Cynthia Ruchti remains my favorite author for contemporary fiction. Her portrayal of millennials and tweeners is phenomenal and I especially loved the down-to-earth middle America folks who offered such wise road signs for these pilgrims. Honey, it's time to take this trip! –Lucinda Secrest McDowell, author of *Ordinary Graces*

Cynthia Ruchti, with her signature blend of warmth and wisdom, never disappoints! *Miles from Where We Started* will have you laughing out loud one moment and reaching for a tissue the next. A journey of hope and healing as unforgettable as the characters you root for and grow to love along the way. Highly recommended! –Kathryn Springer, author of *The Dandelion Field*

Sometimes a risky adventure can change your life in the best way. Road trips are never perfect, so they are perfect opportunities to ex- perience the love that meets our real needs. Cynthia Ruchti offers us all a trustworthy story of redemption. Life gets broken; redemption happens in the ways we least expect. There is great hope! *Miles from Where We Started* could be our story. Doug and I could be Mallory and Connor—if they were thirty years older! –Janet Newberry, educator and educational consultant-on-the-road

Miles from Where We Started is a beautifully redemptive tale that reminds us nothing broken is beyond healing. Ruchti is a master at making readers feel deeply and examine their own lives and relationships in the process. A highly recommended read! —Lindsay Harrel, author of *The Heart Between Us*

miles from where we started

Cynthia Ruchti

GILEAD PUBLISHING

Published by Gilead Publishing, LLC
Wheaton, Illinois, USA.
www.gileadpublishing.com

Scripture quotations marked AMPC are taken from The Amplified® Bible, Copyright © 1954, 1958, 1962, 1964, 1965, 1987, by the Lockman Foundation. Used by permission. (www.Lockman.org.) All rights reserved.

Scripture quotations marked CEB are taken from The Common English Bible.

Quoted material on page 150 is from Jerry L. Sittser, *A Grace Disguised: How the Soul Grows Through Loss* (Grand Rapids: Zondervan, 2005).

This is a work of fiction. Names, characters, places, and incidents are products of the author's imagination or are used fictitiously. Any similarity to actual people, organizations, and/or events is purely coincidental.

ISBN: 978-1-68370-147-7 (printed softcover)
ISBN: 978-1-68370-148-4 (ebook)

Cover design by Faceout Studio, Lindy Martin
Interior design by Jennifer Crosswhite
Ebook production by Book Genesis, Inc.

Printed in the United States of America.
18 19 20 21 22 23 24 / 5 4 3 2 1

"Traveling. It leaves you speechless,
then turns you into a storyteller."
—Ibn Battuta

To the young souls in older bodies
And the old souls in young bodies,
To those who can still see home
In their rearview mirror
And those who fight to see through
The fog in front of them,
Those who race to stay ahead
Of the regrets chasing them,
These pages,
These very pages
Are applause for your journey.

Dedicated to the One.

chapter one

"YOU CAN'T BAIL ON ME, Nathan."

Mallory Duncan looked up from her laptop. The unfinished spreadsheet wouldn't walk out on her. It would wait. She watched as the vein on her husband's forehead—normally hidden by one or two of the random dark curls that first drew her curiosity—pulsed its displeasure with what he heard on the phone.

"This can't happen." Connor gripped his cell phone with one hand and drove the other into the countertop. Ever the gentleman, he didn't pound. He ground his fist, as if smashing roasted garlic into a smooth paste.

What can't happen? Mallory kept her fingers on the keyboard but listened for clues. She would have crossed the room to where he stood and wrapped her arms around him from behind. She would have laid her head on his broad back and planted her hands over his chest as a sign of solidarity for whatever Connor's best friend and "boss"—as Connor teasingly termed him—was or was not doing.

She would have embraced her husband … if it hadn't been for last week's conversation. If it hadn't been for the words that changed their trajectory. Couples on the verge of separation don't declare their solidarity.

This can't happen. The words belonged plastered on the exit door of their marriage. She'd said it to him, to the mirror, to the voice inside her head that insisted love was enough to overcome any first-year obstacles. Now, Connor used the same words with Nathan.

"No! No. This can't happen. You have to get an excused absence or something. Nathan, come on!"

Connor glanced at her, then turned his back and walked deeper into the kitchen. A 700-square-foot apartment doesn't allow for a lot of privacy. Who would have thought two people who were still officially newlyweds for four more weeks—until their one-year anniversary—would need private space? Need an apartment with separate bedrooms. Need to separate.

The familiar hollowness swelled, compressing her lungs and heart. She sat up straighter. It didn't improve her breathing. She sipped her tea. Tepid. Big help.

The spreadsheet on her laptop screen stared at her with its neat lines and tidy edges. Columns. Rows. Sensible. Logical. The antithesis of their home life. Nothing fit between the lines. Nothing made sense anymore. If they separated, the columns would fall into line again, wouldn't they? Mallory and Connor simply needed time apart to sort it out. Six months at the most.

They were grown-ups. Among the most grown up of their millennial friends. They could do this amicably. Refocus. Deal with a few of their personal issues. Six months. Reset. Wipe the hard drive clean and start over. From the way Connor had been talking, six months was more like the kind of hoop a couple jumps through so they could legitimately say they'd tried everything.

Her phone pinged. Her verse-of-the-day app. It would ping again in a half hour if she didn't open it. She tapped the app, then tapped it shut. Months ago, that on/off habit made her feel guilty. She waited for guilt's nudge. It never came.

Mallory set the phone on the coffee table and headed toward the kitchen with her mug of lukewarm tea. How sensible of them to decide Mallory should retain the apartment, since she worked from home most of the week when she wasn't needed on-site as director of the Hope Street Youth Center. If Nathan agreed to let Connor temporarily set up housekeeping in the empty studio apartment above the Troyer & Duncan marketing firm, that would save his commute. The men had counted on rental income to help offset their company start-up costs. Could Troyer & Duncan hold out for six months without it if Connor camped in the studio?

The first month didn't count, since the upstairs level of the building still boasted unpainted drywall. The remodeling couldn't get done any sooner, since Connor and Nathan's dream client—RoadRave—needed all that video footage of the three-week cross-country trip for their ad campaign.

The first few weeks of their separation wouldn't be the distance across town but miles. And miles.

Three weeks of pre-separation practice. Sounded horrible. But she could make far more progress on her literacy campaign for the youth center if she could work nights too, without the constant communication collapses. Lately, it was as if the entire apartment were floored with eggshells. Every attempt at a cohesive thought derailed. When he was on the road with Nathan …

She slid around Connor's still-tensed body and pointed to the microwave in the corner. He nodded and gave her room. Maybe they wouldn't have to tell anyone they were separated until Connor and Nathan returned from the trip. So far, no one knew. Not even the people closest to them. They were that good at acting, at preserving appearances.

Connor had said, *You can't bail on me* and something about an *excused absence*. And he wasn't talking about himself or their marriage. What?

"This is the end of it, then," Connor said into the phone. "I don't understand how the courts have the right to do this to us. Or why your civic duty principles seem more import-ant than our keeping the business going. You know we can't survive without the RoadRave account. Nathan, it was our game-changing break."

They lost the account?

Connor leaned his backside against the kitchen island. "Yeah, yeah. Patriotism. American values. I get it. I do. You're not telling me something I don't know." He picked a black grape from the bowl of fruit in the center of the island but rolled it around in his fingers rather than eating it. "Man, this could not have come at a worse time."

Mallory felt an inexplicable urge to scroll back and read the verse of the day she'd ignored every half hour since breakfast ten hours ago. But she stayed rooted to her spot in front of the microwave.

Connor slid his phone—hockey puck style—across the counter and pressed his fingertips into his skull, face scrunched.

"What happened?"

He crossed his arms over his chest. Did he hesitate because he no longer thought she had a right to know?

"Jury duty. Nathan has to report for jury duty Monday morning." He uncrossed his arms and let them flap against his sides. "We were supposed to receive the RoadRave delivery day after tomorrow and head out Sunday morning. It's all set. Everything. Except we're missing half of the two-man team. One small but vital detail." He growled and popped the fidgeted grape into his mouth.

Her chest registered the blow as if it had happened to her, not him. Isn't that how it was supposed to be in a marriage? And here she stood with no advice that would help in any—

Wait. "Connor, Nathan doesn't have to serve on a jury if he's a small business owner, does he? If his business depends on him?"

Mallory's hair stylist had once begged off the responsibil-ity, without argument, for that reason.

Connor swallowed harder than necessary for an already

pulverized grape. "Says he can't, with a clear conscience. And because it would send the wrong message to RoadRave." He laced his fingers behind his neck, brow still creased. "You know what sticklers they've been about family-friendly, all-American, patriotic, get-this-country-back-to-its-small-town-roots agenda. If Nathan shirks his 'civic duty,' we're likely to lose the account anyway."

"Do they have to know?" Had she really suggested that?

Connor glared at her, then softened his look. "It's the principle of the thing. In Nathan's mind, anyway. He's crippled by a triple threat. His own convictions. RoadRave's expectations. And his gut feeling that it's what *God* wants him to do." Connor sighed and turned his head, the cords in his neck taut and pulsing. "We don't call him 'faithtimistic' for nothing."

Mallory cringed. "Can you reschedule the trip?"

"No." He ripped another grape from its stem. "Sorry. I didn't mean to sound harsh. The prestaging is already set. PR schedules don't bend that easily. You don't know this business, Mallory."

"I'm not an imbecile, Connor."

"Why do you have to take everything so personally?" He grabbed his phone and left her choking on secondhand anger.

And there it was. The completely dysfunctional communication method that had brought them to an impasse in their relationship. Bridge out. No access. Within a few short sentences, she could trace the path that had led them to the only conclusion they agreed on: This would never work. Marriage can't be built on a rapid-fire volley of reasons to apologize.

◆--------------------------------◆

With the microwaved tea now too hot to drink, Mallory left it on the counter and scrubbed at water spots on the kitchen faucet. They, too, were stubborn. She loaded the rest of the supper dishes into the apartment-sized dishwasher. Neither of them felt like cooking much these days. They'd shared chef duties, Connor the more adventurous cook. But more often than not, the dishwasher held little more than silverware and the microwave splatter cover.

Connor paced. No solutions emerged from the effort. None he voiced anyway.

"I need to get some sleep," he said at length. "Are you okay taking *that*"—he indicated her laptop—"to the bedroom so I can … ?" He nodded toward the couch.

What young couple stands at the altar—music in the air, candles flickering, hearts pounding—and imagines such cold distance so soon? They weren't heartless people. They hadn't chosen each other for the wrong reasons. The online dating service had deemed them compatible. Their initial dates had kept them talking for hours. Had they been idealistic to a fault?

Connor was a good man. Solid, which could also translate to stubborn. But Mallory admired the way his brain worked. He'd said the same about hers.

It didn't take long after their wedding day to realize their passions were fueled differently, his attentions singlemindedly devoted to getting his career off the ground.

His rogue genes weren't helping any. Or his father's recent declining health. Mallory's thoughts stalled. The way Connor pressed his fingers against his temples—it meant nothing, right?

"I have another hour or more of paperwork," she said. The laptop felt heavier than it had a few minutes earlier. Yes, maybe some of this was her fault. She'd disappeared into the foggy abyss of her responsibilities at the youth center too often. "I'll try to be quiet."

Two steps from the bedroom door, she heard Connor say, "I put my pillows back on the bed this morning. I … didn't know where to store them out here."

For six days, they'd tried sharing the bed with an imaginary concrete block wall dividing it in half. She hadn't asked him to sleep on the couch. But she hadn't asked him not to either. Mallory answered without turning. "You don't need permission to walk into our bedroom, Connor."

He hesitated but then slid past her into the room that had once represented closeness. Intimacy. "I don't know how to do this," he said. "What's the code of conduct for separation? I don't want to make a mess of this part too." His voice sounded thin, childlike.

"I never wanted to know the protocol. Still don't." The last word lodged in Mallory's throat like an oversized vitamin with nothing to wash it down. "Maybe we could look it up online." She mustered a gotta-keep-our-sense-of-humor half smile.

He mirrored her expression but with his signature furrowed brows. She waited outside the door to their—the—room. Less than a minute later, he stood in front of her, arms laden with a makeshift bed. A picture of defeat. "We may have to rethink my moving into the studio above the office. Without the RoadRave account, we won't have enough cash flow to keep operations going, much less hang on to the building."

"Maybe Nathan will think of something. You're both creative geniuses."

"Feeling less genius-like every day." His gaze held hers as if the sentence had a double meaning. They likely both knew it did. "Goodnight, Mallory."

"Even friends kiss each other on the cheek."

He paused, then leaned in and held his lips against the hollow under her cheekbone an immeasurably short second.

She retreated into the bedroom, dumped the laptop at the foot of the bed, and lay facedown where his pillows had been.

chapter two

CONNOR WAS ON THE PHONE when Mallory emerged from their bedroom a little after six in the morning. The kitchen was already light-drenched. In a couple of months, it wouldn't be. For more reasons than the autumnal equinox. Even now, she felt a wave of dread for a dark commute to work and a dark commute home on days the center needed her physical presence.

Connor had made coffee and set her favorite mug next to the coffeemaker. Habit, she supposed. Once, a thing like that had seemed romantic.

His hair lay in damp, dark swirls that even from this distance smelled of oranges and cloves. How had she slept through his showering? Not falling asleep until three a.m. might have had something to do with it.

She opened the refrigerator door and stared at its faceless contents so long the open-door alarm beeped its high-pitched, nerve-scraping sound.

Connor ended the phone call and said, "There's one more toaster waffle if you want it." He refilled his coffee mug and lifted the stainless-steel French press toward her.

She nodded and watched as he poured her first cup of the day. A simple gesture. It shouldn't have brought tears. She scrubbed her eyes as if lack of sleep were her chief concern. "Who was on the phone?"

Connor handed her the coffee—handle first—and said, "Nathan, the Magnificent." The disparity between the look his smile attempted and the question his eyebrows raised almost made her laugh, except for the ever-present throbbing pain around her heart.

"Last night, you described Nathan as a big, congealed bowl of trouble. Today, he's magnificent? What changed?" Pulling off nonchalant wasn't going to be easy if they were going to keep the separation amicable. And if Mallory's heartbeat didn't quit sounding as if it were limping rather than pumping.

The atmosphere itself felt fragile. Could they carry on an entire conversation without it imploding as so many had in recent months?

"He has an idea." Connor opened his mouth as if to say more but didn't.

She dropped the waffle into her slot of the toaster. His slot no doubt held remnants of the onion bagels he favored. "A business-saving idea?" Mallory preferred her waffles with a drizzle of raw honey, but a day like today—on the verge of a life change like theirs—required full-on maple syrup. Wherever it was.

She rummaged in the narrow cupboard they called their pantry.

Connor reached around her and pulled out the bottle of syrup. As if he knew. "Nathan is not only an advertising genius, he's …"

"Misguided? An illogical dreamer? Determined to a fault?"

"I was going to say 'brave.' He's brave." Connor's facial expression made him look like an eight-year-old boy admiring his favorite superhero. He glanced sidelong at Mallory and dropped his gaze.

"He's going to ask for an excused absence from jury duty

after all?" The pop of the toaster punctuated her question. She dug it out with a fork, against human reason and safety wisdom.

"That … wasn't his idea."

Two slow passes with the stream of organic maple syrup. "What did he come up with, then?" She didn't have to fake genuine interest. She cared—more than he realized. More than he knew he needed.

Connor rolled up the sleeves of his shirt to mid-forearm and rubbed his palm down his face, forehead to dimpled chin. "Doesn't matter. It would never work."

It came to her as slowly as the top speed of a glacier but with as much splash as a glacier calving, losing a chunk of itself to the milky aqua sea. *No. Nathan couldn't have suggested—*

"This idea. It doesn't involve me, does it?"

"You and me and—"

"There are two too many 'ands' in your sentence." Mallory's coffee rebelled against where her mind headed.

"You're crazy passionate about reaching out to at-risk youth, aren't you?"

That didn't even deserve an answer.

"Nathan has one," Conner said. "A troubled youth."

"I know. His nephew Judah." Nathan had only been Judah's guardian a few months, but the boy had caused enough ruckus to be labeled "at risk." "You can't be serious. Nathan wants you to take Judah on this adventure?"

"And … you. He wants *us* to take his nephew with *us*."

"*Us* is not a word we're using much these days."

Young lady, I don't like your tone of voice. She promised she'd never say that to one of her kids. Seemed logical to use it on herself. She might never have a chance to prevent herself from using it on the in-your-dreams children she'd assumed she and Connor would have. Together. The two of them. *That almost made sense.*

Connor took the coffee mug from her shaky hands and swiped at the caffeinated dribble on the hardwood floor at her feet. With his bare foot. "I'm keenly aware how awkward this

sounds and the weightiness of what Nathan and I are asking."
He paused. "Say it. Whatever it is, you might as well say it."

"'What Nathan and I are asking?'" They were *asking*, as if
their all-consuming business didn't depend on it. As if she had
a choice. As if Connor could tell her in one breath he didn't
love her the way he should—couldn't afford to, for her sake, of
all things—and in the next expect her to drop everything and
roadtrip with him.

He was "tripping," all right. She practiced several responses
and discarded them all.

"Mallory, this could literally save the business. And I mean
literally, literally. RoadRave is all over the idea. They're stoked
at the thought of including an at-risk kid on this inaugural
adventure."

They—all of them—had apparently talked about it already. Including RoadRave. Without her input. Mallory forced
herself to blink.

"And," Connor added, "that has to help your cause with
your literacy project."

Really? You're going to use that weapon?

"I don't have to remind you, do I, what happens if this trip
doesn't work out and RoadRave no longer is obligated to make
their promised contribution to your Literacy Takes Courage
thing? Beyond what it would mean to Troyer & Duncan, do you
want to be responsible for cheating the youth out of $100,000
worth of assistance?"

That was low. Intimidating. He used the word *cheating*?
She would be cheating her kids? *Come on, Connor. Even for
you ...*

She could say *no* in five languages. Forced to learn how
in order to communicate with the inner city underserved. Not
enough. She drifted toward the couch.

"Literacy takes *courage*. The name of your little project says
it all, Mallory. Adventure. Courage. Think about it."

Oh, I am. Trust me. My little *project.*

"Nathan has nowhere for Judah to go when he's on jury

duty. They already know the chosen jurors are going to be se-questered for the trial. Can you imagine the footage we could get with the added dimension of an eleven-year-old? And Judah can run a third camera to catch better shots of us, the … the couple." He drew a noisy breath. "It's a brilliant solution. If …"

She was the *if*. And they weren't a couple.

If Mallory were her grandmother, she would have said, "The gall of that man!" Instead, she'd claimed a sudden and overpowering need for her morning shower.

Connor had knocked on the door twice already, asking if she was okay.

"Fine. I'm thinking."

Half of that was true. She was thinking. Evil, evil thoughts.

"Mallory, I have to have an answer. I'm leaving for work. What do I tell Nathan?"

It might have been easier to answer him if he weren't talking through the closed door. Or if he'd asked if he could come in.

"I don't know what to say, Connor. How can I decide a thing like this in ten minutes?"

"It's been more than twenty."

"Not helping." She leaned her forehead against the tile under the shower head so the scalding water cascaded down her back, pummeling tense muscles up and down her spine. "I can't give you an answer right now."

"Can't? Or won't?"

Mallory reached for the faucet and stopped the wall of water. Evaporation became her enemy. It chilled her as thoroughly as if she'd set the water to cold rather than blistering. Evaporation. Her enemy. Everything she cared about had evaporated and desiccated her marriage.

If only they'd had time to—

"Look, Mallory, I have to get to work. Call me, okay? Or

text." Too few moments later, she heard the entry door click shut.

Sure. I'll just text you the solution. What did it say about his commitment to her that he assumed she could send a simple text? *I'm in. No worries. Marriage on hold. It's all good.* Marriage can't be shoved down a garbage disposal without breaking a blade or two. Or all of them.

Three weeks together on the road? Twenty-one days of Gethsemane's agonizing "let this cup pass from me"?

Or would it be a chance for them to talk it through, for her to convince Connor not to give up, to try the counseling he'd resisted?

On the trip, he wouldn't have the option of taking off for work. Staying late every night. Canceling getaways. Not that she hadn't been guilty too, if a young person was in crisis. Connor wouldn't have the option of skipping their long-ago abandoned commitment of dinner together every night. Or walking away from a conversation.

No option of sleeping on the couch. Or ignoring her.

What if this crazy camper-in-a-box was a gift-wrapped answer to her prayers?

Didn't some answers to prayer come disguised as pure misery? No, they didn't.

By the time she'd dressed and blow-dried her hair, she'd created a slogan for what remained of their tattered marriage: *Love Takes Courage.*

She'd maxed out in misery, hadn't she? The night at the linen tablecloth restaurant, she'd thought Connor had arranged the evening as the setting of a "Let's get back on track, Mallory. Let's renew our vows. Fresh start." But before they'd agreed on an appetizer, Connor's conversation diverted from the path she'd expected. All the Edison-bulb lights draped around the cozy outdoor dining area on Michigan Avenue weren't enough to pierce a darkness like that.

Instead of "Let's get back on track," he'd said, "I don't love you like I should, Mallory. I ... I can't, in good conscience. Let's admit defeat before it goes any further. Cut our losses while we can. Sometimes marriage just doesn't work out. It's exhausting us to keep pretending. Maybe we both need a reboot."

The candles kept flickering. The strings of lights overhead swayed in the breeze. Music kept playing in the background. Violins, of all things.

She'd watched his expression for a sign that he didn't mean what he was saying. She saw a flicker of something, but he held firm.

After surviving Connor's pronouncement, and the prospects of an endless horizon without the man Mallory thought she loved—she *did* love—how could a few weeks on the road drain her? She'd already been emptied. In the week since, nothing had changed except from empty to emptier. Emptiest.

Her throat tightened. Guilt wrapped its claws around her neck. The truth was, she'd have paid a higher price than three weeks of bed-of-nails discomfort and emotional torture, if necessary, to ensure funding for her at-risk youth.

The mascara wand she'd been holding fell from her hand into the sink, leaving rude black smudges on its journey. The smudges stared at her with their searing charcoal-like evidence. What was she thinking? She'd have paid a higher price for the sake of the *kids* than she would to save her at-risk marriage?

Mallory sat on the edge of their—her—*the* bed and punched Connor's number into her phone. He might still be en route, in which case she could skip the awkwardness and leave a message—

"Mallory?"

"Are you driving?"

"No. Just letting myself into the office. Look, before you say anything, please know I realize—"

"I'll do it." The words slashed at her throat on the way out, like an inexperienced sword-swallower must feel on day two of circus school.

"You're serious?"

"What did you think I meant? I'm talking about starting

the dishwasher. Let me handle it. There. Done."

"Mallory …"

She ground her teeth. "I'll do the stupid road trip. We'll"—she fell backwards onto the—her—*their* bed—" have to set some clear boundaries … for this to … work."

"Of course."

"I'll go, on one condition."

"What's that?"

Mallory bent her head forward and rocked her torso back and forth as she'd seen women do when toughing it out through a contraction. "If I go along, you'll agree to marriage counseling when we get back. Before we decide to do anything … permanent?"

"Aren't we beyond that point? Isn't separation kind of a waiting room for div—?"

"You and Judah enjoy yourselves on the road." So that's what ire sounded like.

"Mallory, that's blackmail."

She stopped rocking. "It's not $100,000 worth of blackmail."

"Point taken." He breathed into the phone. "No promises it'll change anything."

"Understood." Did hostage negotiators have to be this careful? Connor had once given her a guarantee he'd love her forever. On their wedding day. She twisted the guarantee on her ring finger.

"We'll have to pull off our best acting for the video blog." Connor hadn't sounded this distressed since that night at the restaurant.

It would require something beyond all-out survival. They had to appear to *enjoy* themselves. "Both of us." Mallory cringed at the blade-like edges of her words.

"Yes. And I might as well apologize up front for what that will put you through. The company owes you, Mallory. I … I owe you."

As if he cared.

The words tasted bitter, out of character. He cared. Showed it in so many ways. He'd been tender with her even though he claimed no hope for their marriage. He went out of his way to blame himself. Maybe someday he'd realize he wasn't running from her, but from uncomfortable odds.

Well. No sense making the challenge harder than it had to be. "I'll take payment in beef jerky and s'mores," she said, "and that solemn promise we'll see a counselor when we get back." There remained a Slim Jim chance the experience would reignite fading embers. A Slim Jim chance.

chapter three

A T LEAST SHE HADN'T GONE *postal on him.*

Connor sank into his office chair, the one Mallory called his "statement chair." Sure, it cost more than a month's rent. But it made him feel like a real businessman. Not much made him feel like a real anything lately. If this road trip didn't work, the office chair would be the first to be listed on eBay.

From his desk a few feet away, Nathan was on the phone with Judah's social worker, trying to secure permission to let an unofficial guardian take the troublemaker on an unscheduled, off-road, but highly publicized—they hoped—trip across state lines. Many state lines. What could possibly go wrong with that scenario?

Add a reluctant replacement mother figure with a broken heart and …

Connor gripped the edge of his desk. No. He couldn't afford to dwell on Mallory's misery. She would get over this. Over him. She was tough. Sadness wasn't fatal. Usually. Somewhere deep inside she had to feel a sense of relief, didn't she? The possibilities of what she would dodge if they called it quits now …

The work had always anchored him when his thoughts whipped up whitecaps of what-ifs. He opened the RoadRave file on his laptop and printed the specs for the equipment due to arrive the next day. Mallory might appreciate seeing what they would have to work with. Camper for two. Correction, microcamper. Which they'd somehow stretch to fit three. He checked off multiuser items, which left them in need of a folding camp chair and hammock bed for Judah. He'd call Road-Rave to expedite those items as soon as Nathan gave the nod that the social worker had given *her* nod.

What kind of crazy was this?

The best kind. Adrenalin-pumping crazy. He didn't dare tell Mallory how excited he was to get behind the wheel and take off, despite the relationship weirdness. They'd lived together as husband and wife for almost a year. They could tolerate another three weeks. Couldn't they?

In the process, they'd see parts of the country they'd never seen before, breathe some fresh air, get out from behind their desks, make memor—

Make memories they'd keep to themselves. Memories, but with no place to hang them.

Well, other than what they would share with the thousands—maybe hundreds of thousands—he and Nathan and the staff at RoadRave hoped would watch the live-streaming video blogs of the trip.

The ideas were clicking again. In his element. Felt good.

He and Nathan would have had so much fun together on the trip. Somewhere along the line, Connor would have had to tell him the full story about the Duncan duo demise. He'd braced himself weeks ago for how that conversation would go. Nathan didn't believe impossibilities have to maintain their "impossible" status. His one flaw. Without asking questions Connor wasn't ready to answer, Nathan had reluctantly agreed to let Connor use the upstairs apartment for a while when Connor had asked. But the man had no clue how long "a while" meant from Connor's perspective.

Now, Nathan's inevitable questions and well-intentioned advice giving would have to wait. Mallory and Connor Duncan had an image to maintain for the sake of the marketing campaign. Chalk another one in the win column. Connor wouldn't have to listen to Nathan's Don't-give-up-on-your-marriage speech. Not for a while, anyway.

Connor compiled notes for specific shots and camera angles, casual but professional-looking, capturing the small details other travelers overlooked.

Was it too much to ask Mallory to wear a Troyer & Duncan or a RoadRave ball cap during filming? He'd grab a couple of them—better than a business card for advertising—from the stack in the supply closet before he headed home.

"This isn't your packing list," Connor said. "Tell me it isn't. It's an inventory of your closet, right?"

Mallory tamped down the angry retort forming. "Three whole weeks, Connor." She folded the pizza box from their quick lunch and squeezed it into the apartment-sized garbage can. "And it isn't all clothing, as you can see."

"Curling wand?"

"You know how weird my hair gets in humidity. And we're making a video journal. Vi-de-o. Where people can *see* us."

Step One: Pack for trip. They couldn't even get past the first task without finding reason to argue. Mallory was this close to telling him he could take his trip and—

She watched as, still holding her list in one hand, Connor set his guitar case in the corner of the apartment they'd designated as a collection point. "I can't begin to tell you how little space we're going to have, especially now that we're including Judah. RoadRave's microcamper innovation is as micro as they get."

"I've seen the pictures, you know. Wait. You can take your guitar, but we can't fit in my curling wand?" She hoped her hand perched on her hip said more than her words.

"Acoustic guitar," he said.

"Your point?"

Connor dropped the list onto the coffee table. "As in, not electric. We won't have electrical hookups at most of our stops, Mallory. I thought you'd know that."

He hadn't said it unkindly. But she felt like she'd pulled a muscle. A chest muscle.

Connor sank onto the couch. "Come here."

She didn't move.

"Please?"

Probably too far away for his tastes, but too close for hers, she joined him on the couch. "We can make this work," he said. "We told ourselves we weren't going to stoop to cutting comments or attacking each other just because the marriage idea didn't pan out."

Hurt and anger seemed to tiptoe the high wire between Mallory's emotions. From opposite directions. Fighting hard to make the other fall off. Neutrality would have to draw a sword on both of them.

"It isn't *the* marriage," she said, lips barely moving. "It's *our* marriage."

"Of course, that's what I meant." Connor stretched to put his hand on her knee.

She stared at it. "And it wasn't a matter of panning out, like a prospector disappointed in the lack of sparkly things in the pan."

Her shoulders rose and fell in an unnatural rhythm—longer on the inhale than the exhale. Connor's trainer would have a name for it. *Dysbreathingphoria* or something. Maybe it was a positive, letting her breath linger a while and deliver more oxygen to her how-is-this-ever-going-to-work brain. After the div— After the trip, who knew if either of them would be able to afford a trainer anymore. Or rent. Or food.

He nodded slowly. "Something we should talk about during those counseling sessions. After we get back." He reached for her hand.

She let him take it.

For a long moment, he stared at the two inches of skin on the back of her hand where his thumb rubbed. "It's not that I don't love you, Mallory. I do."

"Just not enough to stay married to me for the rest of our lives."

"It's more complicated than that. Isn't it obvious?"

Mallory tried to pull her hand from his grip. "When talking to your wife," she said, the air chilling with her words, "'complicated' usually means there's another woman involved."

His grip tightened. "You know that's not true."

"Words matter, Connor. They matter. Words like *love*, *forever*, *vow* …"

"Do we have to get into that right now?" He turned his face toward the collection corner. "You know it's more than that. I can't promise you a future. And it's not because I don't want to."

"You already did. You already promised me a future with you, no matter what crosses our paths."

"It was a mistake."

He stared at her as if waiting for tears to pool. They didn't. What did that mean? She couldn't let herself believe he was right. Or let him sink into the inevitability that had hounded him practically since birth.

"Connor, you don't even know for sure that what happened with your father—"

He jumped to his feet. "Mallory. Off limits. We will not have that discussion again."

"Your concerns might be completely unfounded. And you

know it. I will never understand why you won't have the blood-work done and find out for sure."

←——————————————→

He'd have to stop grinding his molars. It wasn't good for the headache that pounded on his brain cells. Unfounded? Since when? But this was not the time to revisit that ever-present subject.

"We have a whole lot to get ready before Sunday morning … and … I realize that makes me sound like a heartless ogre." Connor sank back into the couch and drew her into a one-armed embrace. Did it communicate too much?

She leaned her head on his shoulder. Not tenderly, but limply. More like defeat.

"Mallory, I'm indebted to you," he said. "And I'm sorry. For all of this. I don't know what else to say right now."

"I'm a remarkable woman?"

"You are that."

"You don't deserve me?"

"Agreed."

←——————————————→

Mallory let her body relax a fraction more into Connor's half-hug.

I want to stay like this, with your arm around me, Connor, my head on your shoulder, and … a future ahead of us. She bolted upright. "And I ride shotgun."

"What?"

"On the road trip," she said. "I ride shotgun, when I'm not driving."

He laughed. It had been too long since she'd heard that sound.

She took a deep breath. "Promise me this?"

"Mallory, I already said I'd do the counseling thing when—"

"Promise me you'll laugh often on this crazy adventure.

32

I … like that sound. And promise that you'll write me a song on the road."

Connor bent his torso over his thighs, hands between his knees. "You've always been my biggest fan."

I have.

"My biggest *music* fan. That's what I meant. I dabble at guitar, hon. I'm no professional."

Hon. He hadn't called her that for weeks. "I know what you meant."

He stood. "A song. *That's* what you want in exchange for this sacrifice you're making?"

Love is all sacrifice, isn't it? "*We're* making. And that whole"—she drew circles in the air with her hands—"counseling 'thing.' That's a nonnegotiable."

"I already said I would. But don't hold out false hope it will—" He growled deep in his throat. "Okay. Counseling and a song." His smile stopped midbloom. "Any old song?"

"All I can contribute is the title."

"Which is … ?"

"I think it's catchy. 'This Is Not How Our Story Ends.'"

Mallory turned off the bedside lamp and lay on her side without concern that the action might make her seem distant from her husband. You can't distance yourself from a bed partner who is sleeping in the other room.

Nothing about the bedroom—shadowed now with night and the dimness of their almost-dissolved relationship—charmed her as it had the moment they claimed Apartment 3C as their own. Delirious in the best way, they'd taken possession of the keys within hours of returning from their honeymoon in Monterrey, short as it was. Compared to their hotel room, the apartment had seemed spacious, the bedroom almost too roomy for their small collection of fresh-from-the-box Ikea furniture.

Six months in, they were in trouble. She'd thought it a temporary glitch. They needed a weekend getaway. That would solve everything. It hadn't.

Some marriages derail. Noisy, clanging catastrophes. Theirs had—*what was the word?*—fizzled. Failed to thrive. Died of starvation, which, as anyone knows, is not a quick process. Or painless.

Her stomach rumbled, agreeing. She should have eaten more than a bowl of cereal for supper. Shouldn't have refused when Connor offered to run out for sesame chicken and spring rolls. She'd worried about having leftovers they couldn't keep.

What would be left over at the end of their three weeks of intense togetherness? With an eleven-year-old delinquent between them? And mobile cameras trained on their theatrically practiced smiles?

Extreme sports. She'd said "I do" with visions of the two of them floating on their backs—hands linked—in life's equivalent of a quiet Caribbean bay, as they had on their honeymoon. When promises meant something and the future lay before them like an invitation. Who knew their marriage would turn into a gut-wrenching version of extreme sports?

Connor had given up. He never gave up on anything.

Not true. Two things. Their marriage and his hopes of avoiding what had crippled his father and in turn his parents' marriage. Mallory had been willing to risk the 50/50 odds. Connor no longer could.

chapter four

"J UST ADD HUMANS AND THE adventure begins.'"
Mallory read the scrolling font designed to look like a two-lane asphalt highway. "Was that line your idea, Connor?"

He didn't have to peer around the camper-in-a-box to catch her eye. Most of its top came little higher than his waist. "Do you like it? RoadRave thought it sounded brilliant." His words faded as if he were no longer confident.

"This camper is smaller than our washing machine," Mallory said. "Our apartment-sized washing machine."

"Hence the need to add humans before it becomes an adventure." He kicked a tire on his side. "Think of it this way. It won't impede visibility through our rearview mirror."

"Since when did you become the optimist of the two of us?" Mallory's words plowed a furrow in her tongue on the way out. A couple of months ago, she would have broken into song over her husband looking at the bright side of a situation. She toed the tire on her side of the teardrop-shaped microcamper, as if new tires need kicking. "There's not another half camper on back order, is there?"

Connor chuckled. "No. This is it, my dear. For better or worse."

"Unfortunate choice of words."

He feigned interest in the intricacies of the trailer hitch newly installed on their Subaru Outback, not that there were any ... intricacies. "It's possible," he said, "that, as you mentioned, we'll need to establish a few communication rules if we're going to pull this off."

"That's amusing, coming from you."

"Mallory."

"Sorry. It's all a little overwhelming. Or"—she glanced at the camper-in-a-box and wrapped her arms around her middle—"underwhelming."

Connor stepped over the hitch and crossed to her side. Close. As if inviting the head-lean she couldn't resist. His familiar embrace encircled her. He breathed into her hair. "I'll never get tired of that smell."

She pulled back an inch. "What?"

"Random thoughts. My brain is full of details about this trip, Mallory. So many details. It's taking everything I've got within me to juggle the advertising side of all this. Not a lot of room left for relationship stuff. You get that, don't you?"

No. Not even a little bit.

"So," he said, brushing a wisp of hair from her forehead, "we're good? For now? Good to go?"

Pushing out the right words sometimes took what Mallory could only imagine it feels like to push a baby into the world. Strain, focus, indescribable pressure, push past the pain. More exhausted than she knew she could be, she finally said, "Did it come with an instruction manual?"

"That's my girl. Yeah, I'm sure there's a manual somewhere."

She stared at the scrolling highway lettering while Connor dug for a manual and she dug for nonexistent instructions on how they would navigate the next three weeks.

Mallory had seen barbecue grills larger than the

microcamper. She hadn't considered herself the dream-home kind of woman, the not-satisfied-with-anything-less-than-a-four-bed/three-bath/granite-countertop/all-hardwood-floors/million-dollar-view/high-end-everything woman.

But this ... this stainless-steel teardrop took minimalism to new highs. Or ... lows.

<hr>

"Easiest setup in the world," Connor said. He lowered the booklet so it dangled from his fingertips at thigh height. "By the end of our time on the road, it shouldn't take us more than six minutes, they say, to completely set up or dismantle."

What was that look on her face? How could she find fault with that sentence? Which word made her forehead crease? *End? Time? Road?*

Oh. *Dismantle.* Sheesh. He couldn't censor every syllable he uttered for the whole trip. He'd go insane. And that kind of tension would show up on the videos. No escaping it. No escaping the fact that he was her main source of tension either. She probably thought him heartless—marrying, then unmarrying. That wasn't it. He was finally doing the right thing. The unselfish thing. She'd see that eventually. Wouldn't she?

How would Mallory react if he suggested she take a crash course in poker face to get them through the trip? Yeah, no. He couldn't look her in the eyes. But he'd have to find neutral words somewhere.

"Everything has a place, a function. It fits together like a puzzle, Mallory. So well-engineered. Even if we hadn't been wooing the RoadRave account, Nathan and I would have been impressed. I think you will too."

"Not that it would matter if I weren't impressed, would it?" She held her hand six inches above the stainless-steel hood as if partly sunny in Chicago in August were enough to turn it into a hotplate on wheels.

"Get in. Try it out. It's more comfortable than it looks—

more comfortable than you'd think." Connor opened the side entrance and swung the door wide.

She bent first and peered through the opening. "It's all bed."

"And it has storage cubbies everywhere on the walls. See? Great workmanship. High quality, clear alder interior." Even he knew that sounded like a sales pitch.

"There's no floor."

Most women would have whined. She stated her observation, then added, "This is a mattress with a solid stainless-steel mosquito net over it. It's a glorified cloche."

Connor couldn't stifle his sigh. "What's a cloche?"

"The dome a chef or waiter lifts to reveal a plate of food. That's what this is. A cloche."

"Yeah. They're shiny too."

"Without the 'glorified.'"

"Just go inside, Mallory. Explore, will you?"

"I'll be back in 4.3 seconds." She tried one leg first, but failed at that attempt. She bent at the waist to crawl in head first, but apparently thought better of it. Eventually, she sat in the opening, kicked off her shoes, and swung her legs into the belly of the microcamper.

"More comfortable than it looks, isn't it?" Even to Connor's ears, the words felt forced.

"Perfect for one."

The stainless steel between them muffled her words, but he'd heard her. He'd heard.

Who needed this hassle? It would be challenge enough to juggle the responsibilities on his shoulders without worrying about how unhappy the trip made her. The trip, the cramped living conditions, the deterioration of—without her harping on their state of affairs. Not that she harped.

Marriage shouldn't be this hard.

Ending one shouldn't either.

They'd tried for almost a year. Why was it so difficult for her to let go of a nonexistent dream? Sometimes love isn't enough. He'd always love her. A breath caught sideways in his throat. But that wasn't the point. Work demanded so much of him. Couldn't she see that? Making a place for himself in the world. Making a difference.

She couldn't disagree. Mallory cared as much about the at-risk teens at the center as he did about his business. Maybe more. They'd pour themselves into their jobs and eventually discover they didn't even miss the married-no-children status. Or soon, unmarried-no-children.

Thank God, she hadn't gotten pregnant. Children complicate quiet, nonconfrontational dissolutions of marriage.

Her sympathy for the medical specter that hung over his head was clear. But she insisted it didn't matter. How could it not matter? He was no fool. He'd watched the toll the disease took on his father and heard tales of what it did to his grandfather. Fifty-fifty were not comforting odds. And this thing didn't skip generations. Reading that tidbit online had almost pushed him over the edge the week before the wedding. He should have listened to his gut. But no. For those months between his blurted "Will you marry me?" and a few hours after the ceremony, he'd listened instead to his idiot heart. Now they'd both pay the price.

Connor rubbed at a smudge his palm print had made on the teardrop camper. She might need poker-face lessons, but he was in dire need of a workshop on keeping his thoughts in check.

She was still inside. "Mallory?"

"What?"

"So, what do you think?" Marketing execs were used to persuasive rhetoric—persuading consumers to purchase products they didn't know they needed. Careful manipulation of longings, desires, and compulsions formed his life's work. He used color, video, print, radio ads, stunning images, clever language, every social media avenue available. From the expression on his wife's face, it would take more than that this time.

"It's well made," she said.

A start.

"And it's definitely engineered for efficiency."

"Can I ... come in?"

"You can try."

Connor repeated Mallory's back-end-first method, leaving his shoes on the pavement. She scooted over to give him room to unpretzel himself. He lay as she laid, on his back, head on one of the two small foam pillows, legs fully extended. Stiff as an unemployed mannequin.

"Skylight," he said. "Nice touch, don't you think?"

"It could be romantic, if it weren't for—" She reached over her head to crank open the forward window. "You know."

"Yeah. The foster kid."

She pressed her lips and eyes into thin lines. "Not what I was thinking, but that's true. This camper barely sleeps two, Connor. Where's Judah going to fit?"

"Nowhere. Like always." The small prepubescent voice sounded more cartoon-like than human.

"Hey, buddy!" Connor sat upright. "Glad you're here, Judah. Can you back up a little so I can get out of this super-awesome adventure on wheels?" Connor fought to exit smoothly for both Mallory's and Judah's sake. Connor danced on one foot, trying to step into his shoes without untying the laces.

"Why do grown-ups always call a kid 'buddy'? Maybe I want to be called princess."

Connor shot a look at the newly emerged Mallory. "Oh. Okay. If that's ... sure. Princess it is." He turned toward Mallory and shrugged. Nathan hadn't mentioned—

Mallory elbowed him. Hard. "He's kidding you, Connor."

"Millennials," the kid said. "So gullible."

"We are not," the couple answered in unison.

"Again with the gullibility." Judah spit his wad of gum onto the ground beside him. "You're almost too old to be millennials. You're aging out of the system, if you know what I mean."

"There's a cutoff date?" Connor said. "I didn't get the memo."

Judah folded his arms across his chest. "I rest my case. Millennials don't write memos. They text."

"I text."

"Connor, come on. Don't let him see your weak underbelly. Hi. I'm Mallory."

The boy clicked his heels and bowed. "Judah Milo Troyer. That's right. Mom never married. Not that she didn't pretend she did. She's got issues." He dismissed the word *issues* with a wave of his hand. "But if you ever mention my middle name, I'll kill you in your sleep."

"Young man!" Connor stepped closer. Mallory's mom hadn't married. She hadn't let it turn her into a female version of the immature imp standing in front of him.

"Connor, good grief." Mallory shook her head.

What did that say about him that Connor's first thought was the public relations nightmare of a double murder in a RoadRave camper? Nathan's sister wasn't the only one with issues. Maybe the trip would clear a few things in his mind, readjust a priority or two. Or three.

"Connor?" Mallory used that voice she adopted when petting other people's dogs in the park.

She leaned toward his ear. "High risk doesn't always mean homicidal." She smiled in Judah's direction as she spoke.

"Ah," Judah said, eyebrows dancing, "but sometimes it does."

Connor watched Mallory's face for signs of fear. None. She ought to know. He threw his shoulders back and said, "Not in the script for this trip, budd—Judah. Staying alive is mandatory. Got it?"

"Just so you know, I'm here against my will," he said.

"Me too," Mallory added.

The boy made eye contact with Mallory. Was that the first time he'd done so since he arrived? "Huh. Good to know."

"Where's your uncle?" Mallory asked.

"I told him to get me a six-pack before he abandons me to you two."

"We are going to have to have a long talk, mister." Connor took a step back this time.

"A six-pack of gum, Captain I'm-Not-At-All-Gullible. What do you think? I'm going to break every point of the law before I'm twelve? I need gum if I'm going to be on the road for three weeks without a toothbrush."

Mallory let her head tilt back until her chin pointed straight overhead. "You either brought a toothbrush or that's our first order of business when we pull out. The adventure begins at Walgreen's."

"You've got a mouth on you, Judah." Connor felt the blood surging in his throat veins.

"Why yes, I do. And I know where it is. 'And where are your ears, Judah?' 'Right here. And my eyes. And my nose …'"

The edge in Judah's voice scraped Connor's nerves into frayed ropes. His hands balled into fists. "Look, buddy …"

"Go ahead. Slug me. They all do." Judah turned toward the far side of the parking lot behind Troyer & Duncan and sat on a low concrete barricade near the dumpster. His position—elbows on his knees, chin in his hands—belied the gruff, cocky demeanor from moments ago. Connor almost felt sorry for the kid. Almost.

"Connor?" Mallory's hand on his shoulder rattled him with the way it made his heart lurch.

"You think I'm in trouble, don't you?" Connor stuck his hands in his jeans pockets, thumbs out.

"Let's just say there's a learning curve for all of us when it comes to kids who've been kicked around the foster care system."

"Do you think he was being honest when he talked about being abused? Slugged?"

Mallory touched her head to his shoulder. "I wish I had a compelling reason to doubt that."

"Me too."

chapter five

MALLORY HAD SEEN HAUNTED EYES like that, shoulders slumped like that, an invisible *Do Not Approach* sign like Judah's before. In too many of the young people she worked with at the Hope Street Youth Center. It no longer shocked her. How sad was that?

But if she were going to survive working with troubled youth, she'd had to develop a shield of unshockability. Fear, disinterest, and "I have no idea what to do with you" were easy for young people to read.

She'd learned not to push. The way past Judah's locked-and-barred doors wasn't a ramrod of kindness and love. Over time, his resistance might erode. But they shared a common bond. Neither wanted to embark on the microcamper excursion. Smiling for the camera would tax them both. A little something to build on?

Mallory had stolen away from the stainless-steel disaster on wheels to grab what she needed from her office at the center, six city blocks' walk from the Troyer & Duncan offices. One office, but *offices* sounded more professional, Connor had said.

A three-thousand-mile trip would mean lots of nothing

time between stops on the route. She could fill some of the mindless passenger time by working on the details of her Literacy Takes Courage campaign.

So many of the youth operated under a key disadvantage in the area of literacy and language arts. Nothing new. But if she and the Hope Street team could make a difference in this one area, they might be able to set the youth up for success rather than the revolving door of juvenile detention. Literacy could help some of them get their GED, step into jobs that mattered to them, start to build a future.

She stepped through the doors of the former bookstore turned youth center. A few of the shelves had been retained for games and other resources. But the ambiance had changed from a battalion of tantalizing book spines and the unduplicatable smell of printer's ink on paper to teen spines slumped in an eclectic collection of donated sofas and the unmistakable odor of long-unwashed socks or sockless, untied, ragged shoes. The youth wearing them usually sat stiffened with resistance, limp with artificial swagger, or dissolved into the world that existed only on their cell phones.

In its former life as a bookstore, the building's floors had once sagged with the weight of customers loaded waist-to-chin with stacks of books they discovered they couldn't live without. They now usually groaned under the heavy footfalls of displaced, confused, bullied or bullying, lost or listing—*God love them*—teens in search of a secret passageway to hope. Some had never seen a glimpse.

Today, the main gathering room—once the bookstore's sales floor—was as empty as it was the day after the store had shuttered its doors.

Dodging conversation proved easier than she thought it would be. There was none. What had happened? She'd noted the Center's *Closed* sign when she entered, but thought it was one of the kids messing with the sign again.

Cherise, Mallory's assistant, emerged from the back

room—a combo of their two small offices and storage—as if charging a hill. "What are you doing here, Mallory? Didn't you get my text?"

Mallory reached for her phone and clicked on the green conversation bubble. "No. What tex—?"

"We're condemned. Well, not forever. But temporarily condemned seems anticlimactic."

"What are you talking about?"

Cherise's hand motions preceded her words. "Our restroom remodeling project unearthed a major, I mean *major*, problem."

Mallory's mind scrolled through the possibilities—a dead body, crumbled plumbing, *two* dead bodies, termites in the subfloor.

Cherise shoved a clipboard her direction. "The *A* word. Asbestos."

"Impossible. The inspector would have caught that before we closed on the sale."

"It wasn't visible—or *sus*, as some of the older youth would call it—until we tore up the old linoleum." Cherise clutched the clipboard with its tattling report to her chest.

The hardwood floor creaked when Mallory stepped back, as if she could distance herself from the news. "What is that going to mean? Who do we know who does asbestos *remediation*?"

"You learned that on HGTV, didn't you? Asbestos *remediation*?"

"HGTV helps me become a more well-rounded individual. Cherise, what does this mean? Where are the kids?"

"Did you miss the 'We are condemned' part of my speech? We're closed down—as of immediately—until it's taken care of."

Mallory's brain whirred. "We can use the main room, can't we, during repairs? Maybe we can talk the tanning parlor next door into letting the kids use their bathroom."

"For one, it's a one-seater. Secondly—and I need your full attention for this next statement—"

The smirk Mallory felt crawling up her face wasn't

undeserved. Cherise was a good friend and invaluable to the center. But the woman was blessed with an abundance of snarkiness.

"We are shut down—the whole place—until we can prove the asbestos is gone. Removed. Remediated. Remedied."

"How long?" Mallory should have been paying attention to her text messages instead of testing the buoyancy of a two-inch-thick camper mattress. "And how much?"

"Three and three, from all current estimates."

"Cherise …"

Cherise set the clipboard on a donated 1970s end table and planted her hands on Mallory's shoulders. "Three thousand dollars and three weeks, for a thorough job."

Three thousand miles. Three thousand dollars we don't have. Three weeks of youth wandering the streets with no safe place to hang out. No safe place.

"I guess part of this drama works out well for you." Cherise's words echoed in the empty room.

Mallory stared at her friend's oh-so-sincere but oh-so-misguided face. "Are you using some ancient definition of 'works out well' of which I am unaware?"

"Your trip. You won't have to worry about us back here. The center won't be functioning at all while you're gone."

"You don't score high on the Gift of Mercy scale, do you?"

"You know what I mean. You're off the hook. We can't get into any trouble without you because we won't exist." Cherise punctuated her optimism with a *ta-da* gesture.

"Are you happy about this?"

Her friend dropped onto the arm of a nearby sofa. Green velour. At one time. Before the sun faded it to a tarnished brass color. "No. It's devastating. But I'm trying to look for a bright side."

"Cherise, sometimes there isn't a bright side." *Let me tell you about the separation that's waiting for me at the end of this road trip.*

"I've already started calling around to see if we could use

an empty storefront for a few weeks, or maybe a local church would let us—"

"You know these kids. Some are only here because it *isn't* in a church building."

"Yeah. I never claimed to have answers. But I'm on the case. And with Zorba on hold with the remodeling until the building has been freed from the grip of the asbestos monster …"

"Cherise, your husband hates it when you call him Zorba."

"He says he hates it. I think he secretly likes it. Zorba the Greek. The exuberant peasant. So fitting."

"As much as I doubt that, I must say I admire your command of 1960s movies."

"Everyone has a passion."

Connor used to say I was his. Mallory let her gaze trace the line of fine cracks high on the wall. Their patch job might need repatching. She had walked to the center to collect three weeks' worth of work for the journey and grab her research for Literacy Takes Courage. And maybe chat with Cherise about responsibilities Mallory couldn't handle remotely. Who knew she'd exit with the gut-punch reminder that *life* takes courage.

‹-------------------------------------›

Her mother used to say a smell like the one Mallory now inhaled "assaulted" her when she accompanied Mallory to a coffee shop. How had her mother survived her whole adult life without developing a taste for coffee or an appreciation for its aroma? Baffling. "Sketch," the kids at the youth center would say. "Sounds sketch to me."

Her mom couldn't have avoided the surgery on her knee after the bike accident. Or the blood clot in her lungs. Of everything the clot stole from Mallory, at the moment all she could wonder was if her mom would have ever developed a taste for coffee. Crazy, the journeys the mind takes under stress.

Mallory let the aroma of the coffee shop envelope her in a visceral warmth like her favorite snow-day sweater. She needed to get back to packing, but caffeine's priority refused to be denied. The current circumstances called for her it's-this-or-valium option—although valium was never an option—a grande, multilayered, ombré, swirling iced coffee the Common Grounds called a Black Tie.

"Want that skinny?" the overeager barista asked, reaching for the tall, clear, scroll-handled glass mug for the specialty drink.

"Not today." Skim anything sounded too weak to accomplish significant comforting. Or bracing. Or thought-scalding.

"And one to go for your insignificant other?"

Insignificant? There's harsh, then there's rude. "Would you repeat that?"

"The dude who comes in here with you. If he's not with you, you usually take him something. I assumed he was your significant other, I guess."

Mallory had heard wrong. No one in their right mind would call Connor *in*significant. Thoughts like that had no room to roam at the moment. Mallory had to focus on pre-trip misery. Post-trip misery would have its own day. "Yeah, sure. I'll take him coffee." About-to-be-unmarried didn't have to become about-to-be-uncivilized.

"His usual?"

Mallory fumbled for her Common Grounds perks card in the purse that registered higher on the cute factor than accessibility. "Yes. His ... usual."

The barista snatched the smallest to-go cup from a nearby stack. That was Connor's usual now? Had he taken seriously her well-worn speech about cutting back on unnecessary expenses like upscale coffee so they could save for a house someday?

No, that couldn't be it.

The truth hit her hard. He was saving money to live alone. A slow crawl toward the dissolution of their marriage, one coffee bean at a time.

Mallory sat near the window with her elegant, completely

necessary light-to-dark layered drink lording it over Connor's stubby to-go cup embraced by an unadorned cardboard sleeve. His drink was hidden by a plastic spill-proof lid. Hers glistened in the sunlight. The heavy condensed milk layer settled on the bottom. The deep brown/black of the espresso rose from that foundation. Formless ballet dancers and jellyfish of half-and-half drifted from the icy surface to the depths below.

The two drinks looked mismatched, side by side. Why hadn't she seen it this clearly before? It wasn't the price or size or gourmet distinction. It was everything about Connor and her. Different on every possible level.

She slid his cup farther from hers. Distance didn't help weaken the metaphor.

They were both strong and healthy. Connor had no symptoms. She chose hope. He chose doom, certain that he would be on the negative side of a 50/50 forward slash. Her stomach acid surged. How many conversations had they had with her begging him to set his mind at rest and get the genetic testing done? How many times had he refused? Fear only had one real stronghold in his life. This one. He was afraid to know the truth, even if it could bring him peace. She'd fired every weapon she knew against the stone wall of his resistance. Not one pebble had broken off. No sign that logic had made even a small crack in his "It's inevitable, Mallory" foundation.

"I don't care if you're an invalid someday, Connor. I'll still love you."

Even that hadn't moved him. It was probably the root of his resistance. He'd watched his mom shrink as she accompanied his dad's slow death march, as if they both carried his tumors. Why couldn't Connor see that it didn't have to be that way for the two of them, even if his body did bear the von Hippel-Lindau gene mutation?

Her phone pinged a reminder to breathe. Technology. What did it know? She slipped a straw into her Black Tie artwork and took a long sip.

She cared about the art of it. The nuance. Connor called it coffee's equivalent to a meditative screen saver.

Mallory stirred the sweetness at the bottom of the glass and watched the dark liquid change to tan. Still delicious. But not much to look at anymore. The glint of her wedding ring caught the same light that had shone through the deep coffee moments earlier.

Not much to look at anymore.

chapter six

DON'T TOUCH THAT, JUDAH." CONNOR rubbed at the boy's fingerprints on stainless steel with the tail of his shirt.

"Sorry, Your Highness." Judah fake-bowed.

"Watch the mouth."

"You're telling me we're taking this pretend camping trailer on the tollway—"

"Back roads. And it's not pretend."

Judah stuffed his hands in the pockets of his oversize, pre-shredded, army-green jacket. "—on the *back roads* for the next three weeks and you're worried about my fingerprints on it? Dude, reality check."

Connor stopped buffing. But he ground his molars again when Judah let his palm hover a micromillimeter above the teardrop camper's sheen.

"Too close, mister."

"What? This?" Judah leaned his head toward where his hand had been, tongue extended, poised to taste test the product.

"Judah!"

"*Eww.* Now, *that's* a legit metallic taste." He rubbed the flavor away on his shirt sleeve and made a half-hearted attempt to erase the evidence from the roof of the teardrop.

"He's testing you, Connor." Mallory's silken voice startled and calmed him simultaneously. "Here, I brought you coffee."

He took the cup in both hands, grateful for the reminder to unclench his fists.

"Nothing for me?" Judah said, one eyebrow raised. "I figured."

"Actually," Mallory said, "I did bring you something. Iced mocha okay with you?"

The boy pressed his lips together but eventually took the lidded cup she offered.

Tell her thank you, you little—

"I made them leave plenty of room for the whipped cream," she said, seemingly unfazed by The Delinquent's lack of manners. Odd, since hers were flawless, even in the middle of their worst disagreements. And she'd walked how far with the coffee?

"How did you know I wanted—?" Judah paused. "Yeah, it doesn't take a genius to figure out nobody drinks a mocha without whipped cream."

Connor's hand crept skyward.

"Seriously, man? No whip?" The look on Judah's deceivingly cherubic face made Connor wonder if he should read up on demon possession before embarking on this journey.

"Judah, would you help me with the groceries I bought? I need to see how many of them fit into the storage hollow under the drink coaster we're calling counter space in the camper's faux-kitchen." Mallory nodded toward the cloth grocery bags still hanging from her elbows.

"It needs a name."

"The kitchen?" Connor lifted the hatch on the back end of the camper. Smooth hydraulics, just as RoadRave had touted. "How about Gourmet Central?"

Jude palmed his forehead and drew his hand down his face, fingers wiggling as if tears were falling.

"You don't like that one?" Connor said. "How about Stainless-Steel Chef? You know, like Iron Chef, but not?"

The grocery bags now Judah's responsibility, Mallory mimicked the boy's lame tears-falling gesture. "I think he meant we need a name for the camper. The whole"—she spread her arms broadly, her delicate wingspan nearly reaching from the teardrop's stem to stern—"assemblage."

Connor would not be bested. "Mighty Chondria? Get it? Like mitochondria? Invisible to the naked eye?"

Mallory almost smiled at that one. "You do create advertising copy for a living, right?"

Did no one have a sense of humor? "Maybe we could get our followers involved in naming her."

"Her?" Mallory's facial expression hinted that she was offended for her gender.

"If you ask me," Judah said, planting the grocery bags on the fold-out peninsula counter Connor had latched into place, "it's probably androgynous."

"What?" Mallory and Connor's responses tumbled over one another.

"You think I don't know about stuff like that?" Judah lined up the cans of soup and boxes of staples according to height. "I *am* eleven. And I read a lot."

Maybe neither of his companions noticed the backwash Connor spit into his coffee. This brilliant idea of Nathan's grew less sparkly by the moment. He'd have to temper his reflex to defer to Mallory for help. She wouldn't always be there to bail him out of awkward—

Again with the phone? Could the world slow down for a few minutes so they could figure out a—

Nathan. He had to take the call. "What's up, Blister?"

"Blister?"

"You hate it when I call you Scab."

"Connor, this is serious. Can we be done with the middle school jabs?"

Connor turned his back to the kitchen crew and took a few steps toward the rear entrance of the Troyer & Duncan offices. "All crisis managers are currently dealing with other customers. Please call back later."

"We have major problems. It's Judah."

"You don't have to tell me. Some are obvious. But hidden ones are emerging as we—"

"Connor. Listen to me. The Department of Child and Family Services is throwing a tantrum."

"About our taking him with us on the trip?"

"Ding-ding-ding-ding! We have a winner."

Connor shifted his phone to the other ear. "Aren't you his legal guardian, and don't you thereby have a right to make decisions like this?" He tried to focus on the conversation, but he couldn't push down the rising hope that they might not have to take the kid.

"It's a mess. I only have temporary guardianship over him. DCFS's end goal is for him to be reunited with my sister."

"You and I both know that's not likely to happen, Nathan."

Nathan's sigh traveled crystal clear through the cell signal. "Matters not to the powers that be. Every state has its own foster care laws. DCFS is concerned about everything—the jury duty keeping me from being with him on this trip, the length of the journey with two relative strangers, the video element of it …"

"Wait? Really? What kid wouldn't want to become an internet sensation? His antics could go viral."

"Exactly."

"And that's a bad thing, how?"

"You're obviously not a parent."

"Neither are you, might I add. Technically, anyway." Connor glanced over his shoulder at the kitchen scene. Stainless-Steel Chef. Still seemed a viable option. "Nathan, what happens to your nephew if they get their way?"

"He goes back into foster care."

"Aren't we his foster care for the next three weeks?"

"Back into the *system*. He'll be placed temporarily with someone even less familiar with him and his 'antics.' Connor, that kid has been through it. He may act like he's not excited to head out with you and Mallory, but it's the first thing that has put any kind of light in his eyes for months. Years, maybe."

Light. That's what Nathan called it. "Is there anything we can do?"

"I have a call in to an advocate at DCFS now. Hoping to set up an emergency meeting, but man, this won't work unless you and Mallory can be there too."

"Nathan, of all people, you realize how much work we have ahead of us to be ready to leave Sunday morning. The RoadRave team's schedule has us pulling out at nine a.m. our time so we can catch the Pacific Coast social media crowd as they slug their morning coffee."

"I know. We have one shot at this, Connor. I know. That kid may not have even one shot left."

"I'll have to talk to Mallory." He turned to fully face the people in question. The short one looked like he was making turkeys on the side of the camper with his sticky handprints—his twisted version of "detailing" the camper's signature shiny surface.

Mallory's gaze flipped from the line-up of cans and boxes to the kitchen's storage well and back again. She was arranging and rearranging, trying to make it all fit.

Weren't they all?

One of these days he'd have to come clean with Nathan and tell him how fragile their relationship had turned, that his bunking at the apartment was not to give Mallory "space" to work on her literacy project. Nathan probably suspected as much. But they'd have to talk. Not now. Too much at stake. They'd kept the decision from everyone. Connor's parents. Their friends. It had been hardest for Connor to avoid telling Nathan the full story. It wasn't fair. He knew that. Something about the sense of one more failure deterred him from coming clean with his best friend and, technically, his boss. Nathan deserved to know that what had hit Connor's father and taken his brother would likely mean Connor would leave Nathan without a partner one day.

His life story—leaving people without partners they counted on.

Mallory said she hadn't told Cherise either. Connor figured it was because she held out this ridiculous hope not only for his medical future but also that he'd change his mind and no one would ever have to know they'd entertained the idea of dissolving their marriage. Sometimes hope could be downright annoying.

Connor took a deep breath. "I'll ... I'll talk to her."

"Appreciate it, man," Nathan said. "Gotta tell you, I'm counting on her history of working with troubled teens to save the day here."

You and me both.

Despite what his job required—his whole maybe-there-will-be-a-future riding on it—he and Mallory were going to have to fight for something they weren't sure was a good idea. Dream assignment.

As if on cue, Judah sneezed. And wiped his nose with his sleeve.

―――――――――――◆―――――――――――

"Connor, it's possible the people at DCFS are right." Mallory zipped her purse shut with enough excessive force to send the zipper pull skidding across the floor of their apartment and clinking on the toe-kick of the kitchen cabinets.

He bent to retrieve the zipper pull and handed it to her. "How could you and I be considered a high risk for that kid? We have to be a better choice than complete strangers." What makes a stranger complete? Because their reality was completely strange at the moment.

She fought way too long to reattach the pull, trying from

both ends of the zipper, tugging the purse sides together to keep the teeth aligned.

"Mallory? Mallory."

"What?"

"Some things can't be fixed."

She dumped the contents on the counter and threw the offending purse in the waste basket. "So you've been telling me."

"I'm talking about—"

"I know." Mallory disappeared into the bedroom.

What now? Nathan waited for them at Child Services. Judah waited in the car. The endless list of prep work for the next three weeks grew like a science project volcano on steroids. And Mallory was—

She emerged from the bedroom with a flat leather bag a little larger than the purse that now rested on top of last night's leftovers. She slid the innards from the countertop into the gaping mouth of her second choice. The strap secured on her shoulder, she headed for the door.

"Mallory?"

"Are you coming?" His wife—for now—held the apartment door open for him as if he were a reticent child on the way to the dentist's office.

"To … ?"

"DCFS? If we don't get to the Subaru soon, Judah will have figured out how to hot-wire it. And RoadRave will not appreciate that kind of delay."

She meant that kindly, didn't she? That she cared? She cared about all this, right?

"Can we really talk them into letting us take Judah with us?" he asked. "You can do that?"

Mallory pulled the apartment door shut behind them. "I guess we'll find out. Wish we had more to go on than your need to use him for your project."

"Ouch."

"Sorry. On second thought," she said, "not sorry."

"You do understand it's more than that. We're helping Nathan. We're trying to be a positive influence on a needy kid, which should be very appealing to you, considering what makes you tick. We're offering him the trip of a lifetime. I mean, when is he ever going to—?"

"Connor, where's the car?"

"Not funny, Mallory."

"Not trying to be humorous. I can't remember what funny feels like."

He'd probably have to address that comment later. Right now, they had to find the car. And Judah. Ah. Three parking spots from where they'd left it. How had he pulled that off? Connor knew better than to leave the keys in sight. Judah didn't really know how to hot-wire a Subaru, did he? Nah. But it might be important for Connor and Mallory to prove they could keep an eye on that kid for an hour, much less a three-week road trip.

chapter seven

MALLORY LEANED ONE HAND AGAINST the brick exterior wall of the county government building. Though hundred-year-old sturdy, it wasn't enough to keep her from shaking. "I did not expect results like that."

"*I* wouldn't trust us, if I were them."

"Connor! You'd better pray the surveillance camera over the door doesn't have audio enabled."

He shook his head. Disbelief had apparently overcome both of them.

"One thing for sure," he said. "You know your stuff." He crossed his right arm over his stomach and bowed at the waist.

"It's what I do." She checked her phone for the time. Nathan had wanted a few more minutes with Judah to rehearse the conditions of the agreement. They'd emerge from that solid building soon and head to Nathan's place for a while.

"No." An awkward pause followed Connor's response. His eyes softened. "It's more than that. It's who you are."

So, today he finds that appealing? But not for a lifetime? Mallory's inhale felt studded with gravel, but if they were going to make this work, even if it bought them only three more weeks together, she'd need to stop the internal snarkiness. "Your marketing mindset didn't hurt the cause," she said. And she meant it.

"It's all in the pitch. The sales pitch is everything. Make them think it was their idea. Appeal to their felt needs. A smart idea alone no longer holds the customer's attention. They want to know what's in it for them, how it will make their life better, easier … how it will *improve* their life. They can't just want it. They have to be convinced they have to have it."

Mallory cringed. He must have noticed. She hadn't even tried to mask.

"You have to understand, Mallory, that the consumer—or in this case, the committee—processes everything differently since the advances of the last dozen years, the last few months, in some cases."

She'd heard this before.

"Today's consumers are fast processors of information. They're adept at sifting through what is relevant and what appeals."

Connor. I get it. You know your stuff too.

"Yesterday's consumer," he continued as if practicing a presentation upon which his seven-year-old business degree depended, "paged through magazines and newspapers. Today's consumer scrolls and knows in an instant whether or not an idea or a product is worth their attention, which is why we advertisers find them so elusive. It makes our job all the tougher"—he took a breath—"and I sound as if I'm applying for a job, don't I?"

"A little bit."

"Okay. Yeah. For a minute there during the meeting, I thought I saw a hint of eye-rolling spreading through the advocate committee," he said.

"A hint?" Mallory would have described the decision-makers' reactions in different terms. How did he do that? Inject humor into the most serious of conversations and gloom into what should be lighthearted?

Hey, Connor, let's get this toaster. It has a lifetime warranty. If only I had a lifetime …

How often had recent conversations bounced from the ordinary to the morbid? He thought he was doomed. Maybe his perception was the real tragedy.

"You don't think they appreciated my referring to the trip as a perfect platform to spotlight the need for reliable respite care for foster families?"

"Connor …"

"Or my line about the family that Raves together—as in RoadRaves—stays together?"

"And the traditional meaning of 'rave' is … ?"

Connor's expression froze on his face. "Oh, buttercrunch. Why didn't you stop me?"

When they were dating—short as that season was—he might not have hesitated to use real curse words. He'd grown. "You seemed so pleased with yourself, that's why," she said.

"What's that supposed to mean?"

On the tip of her tongue sat "Connor, get over yourself." She held back. Mallory repositioned her purse strap on her shoulder and glanced at her phone again. Time was not their friend. "Look, for whatever reason, they agreed to let us take Judah with us. It may have been because the Hope Street Youth Center is affected by the project. Or because RoadRave has a great family-friendly reputation. And I don't think it hurt that it'll all be recorded." Not her favorite part. None of it could be considered her favorite part. Not one little bit.

"It may be awkward working around the requirement for Judah to check in by video call with the social worker every other day."

She stopped her traverse of the parking lot. "*That's* what you see as awkward in all this?" No mention of the toll it might take on their marriage? Or her?

"Ranks up there with no indoor plumbing." Connor kept walking.

"Wait a minute." She jogged to keep up. "We're staying in campgrounds. With facilities. As in showers and flush toilets." She watched his eyes for confirmation. "Connor, tell me we're staying in—"

"The … uh … truth is I don't know where we're staying from one day to the next. Back-roads travel. You knew that."

"Yes, but—"

"And we'll be given our coordinates day by day. RoadRave thought it would be more *in the moment* if we didn't know where we were headed."

"Well, that much is true. We sure don't."

———◆———

Twenty minutes from the government building to their apartment. A twenty-minute road trip with more potholes in it than a Chicago side street in spring. Conversation potholes. Bottoming out. Splashing mud. Hard on passenger and driver. If they couldn't relationally make it less than a half hour in the same vehicle, how were they going to survive three weeks together?

Mallory rubbed the left side of her neck. They'd have to trade off driving on their "grand adventure" so she didn't strain her neck muscles glaring out the passenger window. She checked her phone again, conscious that doing so had become a nervous tic. Looking down didn't help. But scrolling through texts and social media evidence of other people's angst had always served as a distraction.

Today, it didn't.

Everyone else's whine paled in comparison to the one building inside her. *I don't have to do this. I can say no. I should say no. There's one thing more agonizing than separation. Postponing an inevitable separation.*

Was there even a small chance she could persuade him to reconsider? She kept returning to the fact that Connor wasn't a quitter. She couldn't prevent the smile tugging at her mouth. Not a quitter in front of the social workers, that's for sure.

It would have been easy for him to call it off when his plans disintegrated with Nathan's jury duty announcement. But he was still fighting.

What would it take to get him to fight that hard for their marriage? For his health? For life, no matter what it looked like or how monumental the challenges? To fight for her?

The smile disappeared into grief. She shouldn't have to beg.

She'd tried hard to reconcile his inability to rise above what was only a fifty-percent possibility. *Only.* But if it were true, if he did have the VHL syndrome …

Mallory couldn't imagine living with the weight of an "incurable" label or the anticipation of multiple surgeries to relieve symptoms, the repeated radiation treatments, the loss of one function after another.

Connor probably used his workouts with his trainer now for more than staying in shape. Without saying so, he probably wanted to maintain some kind of control over his physical body as long as he could. And his adventuresome spirit? A psychologist might say he grabbed for experiences, believing they'd soon end and he'd be left with nothing but memories until the memories too were gone.

Her husband didn't live with a death wish. He lived with the threat of a long, slow, painful crawl, with death too long beyond his grasp. She hadn't known Cody. Connor rarely talked about his brother. When he did, he often said Cody's diabetic complications and early death saved him from turning into their dad.

Connor, I can't imagine living with a 50/50. But I also can't imagine not wanting to know, one way or the other. How could that provide anything but more distress? How are you not crazy with the uncertainty? Was that it? The uncertainty had pushed him too close to the edge of sanity? He should be leaning on her, not stiff-arming their relationship, as if it didn't matter, as if she didn't matter.

She'd be okay without him.

No. That's not what she wanted.

Connor, what made you think you could live without me? Or face what you may have to face alone?

———————◄——————————►———————

She deserves better than this. Better than me. More than I can offer her.

A year from now, she'll be grateful we didn't keep pretending we could make it work. Grateful.

Connor pulled the car into their parking spot in back of their apartment building.

"We have to have our mail delivery stopped."

"Took care of it," she said.

"Oh. Good. That's good. What about prepaying our rent?"

"Transferred enough from savings to cover it. We can send it electronically the first of the month from ... from wherever we are."

The tone of defeat in her voice clutched at his stomach. Did she have no sense of adventure? All-expenses-paid vacation. Come on. Could she find nothing to get excited about? "Wait. We had enough in savings?"

She turned toward him, her hand on the door handle. "The baby fund."

"Oh. You'd started a—"

"We started a fund. The day we got back from our honeymoon."

"Huh. I thought you were kidding about that."

Her hand dropped to her lap. "Kidding about wanting children someday?"

Connor wiped his palms on his jeans. "About ... you know ... intentionally saving for ... so soon. And what would be risky to plan for."

"Doesn't matter now."

"Mallory …"

"Doesn't matter. I have *micro*-packing to do."

She didn't slam the car door. Exactly. But it was firm. Definitely firm.

He unsnapped his seatbelt but stayed behind the wheel. This was not the most impossible thing he faced. Not by a long shot. But he had to admit it was starting to feel like it.

"God, it's me again. Apologizing for the hundredth time for missing what You must have been trying to tell us before we got married. I should have listened to my gut. I wanted her. Forever. Needed her. Forgot I didn't have a forever.

"And yes, I take all the blame for that glitch in my to-then flawless stand against long-term relationships because of … Well, You know. I let down my guard. Started dreaming. And I knew better."

When Connor had skated past his late teens and early twenties, hope sent down roots. Maybe he'd be a survivor, on the good side of 50/50. Build a career. Spend some time looking at online profiles on the dating site. What could it hurt?

Then … Mallory. The unexpected profile that became a possibility and everything he'd longed for but thought he didn't dare consider.

Cody walked him down the aisle when their dad couldn't. Two months later, Cody was gone and hope's roots shriveled. Mallory tried to convince him Cody's circumstances were exceptional, like her mom's weird blood clot.

Life is always risky, she'd said. *Those who really live aren't the problem-free. They're the ones who step into it no matter the risks.*

She didn't get it. Couldn't. It wasn't her body. She hadn't carried the stench of uncertainty on her, like the odor of garlic leaking through skin pores. He had. Did.

"Why can't two reasonable, relatively smart, good-intentioned people make a go of this? Don't say anything, God. I know the answer. It's me. It's my problem. Okay, problems, plural. Mallory can't get it into her head that she is so much better off without me and my ticking time bomb. Wouldn't most women be grateful for a smooth off-ramp now, before it starts?" He'd dodged the inevitable for more than a decade. Bombs start ticking louder when the timer's about to go off, don't they?

That was no way to end a prayer. Maybe he hadn't been praying as much as talking to himself. That would explain his never receiving an answer all these months.

Mallory, you know the stats as well as I do. Usual onset of symptoms—late teens or early twenties. Early twenties. I've outlived that prediction by close to ten years. You know what that means, Mallory. Any day now.

Vision. Hearing. Headaches. Mood shift. The unrelenting hemangioblastomas would keep searching for new organs to invade, new blood vessels to distort. Kidneys. Adrenal glands. Spine. *Mallory!* How could she not know how ugly it could get?

She said she knew. She'd forced his hand about visiting his parents, so she'd seen some of it with her own eyes. He couldn't—wouldn't—put her through that.

And the testing? Expensive. Consuming. And the best the tests would ever tell him is that the genetic trait was absent in him.

But that might be the answer that killed him.

It hadn't missed his little brother, and that was the greatest injustice. Too unfair for Connor to live with.

No, Mallory. I'm not going to let some doctor tell me I get to live a normal life when Cody didn't.

Enough of that. He thumped the steering wheel and stepped out into the late-summer heat.

chapter eight

ANOTHER NIGHT ALONE IN BED.

No other arrangement would have worked, under the circumstances. But the ache of how far they'd drifted from one another pounded at Mallory's muscles all night long. She slept so sporadically that it hardly counted as more than a fitful nap. Her eyes were wide open—dry and unblinking—when the alarm went off. Her body felt like she'd run a marathon, without training or hydration. Or shoes. Uphill all the way.

Mallory cranked the shower to its hottest setting. Physical therapy against the tension. If they hadn't had a specific deadline, she would have stayed there under the pummeling water until her skin pickled. But Connor knocked at the door before she'd fully finished toweling off.

"How much longer do you need, Mallory?"

A lifetime. I wanted a lifetime. And yes, I understand that's rare these days, even without your medical fears. I get it. But I thought we were the ones who could beat the odds.

"Mallory?"

She opened the door, her towel tighter around her than it had ever been. "Sorry for the steam. The fan isn't keeping up."

His sharp intake of breath didn't go unnoticed. Nor did the way his gaze landed on her bare shoulders. She slipped past him, clutching her blow dryer to her chest. "I can finish getting ready out here."

The bathroom door barely clicked when he closed it.

She hustled into her clothes, as ashamed of her now-towelless nakedness as Eve. The revelation rattled her. As a child, she'd giggled with the other girls in Sunday school over the "and they realized that they were naked" Bible verse. Today, it wasn't funny. She slipped into her jeans and pulled her tee over her head before she heard the water in the shower stop. *This isn't at all how You intended it to be between husbands and wives, is it, God?*

Connor exited the bathroom as he always did—fresh and fabulous and smelling of orange and cloves and ginger. Like a warm cookie.

"Are you taking that with you?"

"What?"

"Your cologne. Is it going on the trip with us?" Mallory couldn't think of a way out of the corner she'd painted herself into. Maybe he wouldn't notice.

"No room for luxuries. My last day for a while. Why?" He wrestled into his tee shirt.

"No reason. Just wondered. Your shirt ..."

"Oh, hey. Yeah. They were in the bottom of one of the boxes that arrived from RoadRave. Great branding idea. I have one for you in the other room."

"It's ... brown."

"They sent several. All different colors within the Road-Rave brand. Brown. Green. Teal. Mustard."

"Mustard."

"That's what the label says. Let me go get yours. I had to guess at the size."

Uh huh. Had to guess.

The shirt fit perfectly, which she somehow found irritating. Hers had long sleeves that she pushed up to the elbows. Maybe she could drape a scarf low enough to cover the Road-Rave logo. Decidedly more outdoorsy than she was used to wearing, except to the gym. No, even more outdoorsy than that. Her workout clothes had to have style or—

"You look … good," Connor said.

"Brown isn't my color."

"Who told you that?" He took one step closer to her. "I wish …"

Mallory waited. He didn't finish his sentence. But she could see his chest rising and falling with deep breaths. *Yeah, me too, Connor.*

"Are you"—he drew one more deep breath—"open to making room in your luggage for these tees? Jettison something else, maybe? For the cause?"

Mallory eyed her duffel in the corner. Bulging like a linebacker in a too-tight suit coat. Did he know what he was asking? "I saved a little room in one of the outside pockets for another pair of socks. Seemed important. But if I roll them tight …"

"Great. Awesome. Okay, breakfast and then we're out the door. Nathan's meeting us at the office. He'll do the first video for us so he can capture 'The Moment: Liftoff.'"

"I don't think they call it Liftoff if we're staying on the ground. Let's hope not, anyway."

"Launch. A journey of three thousand miles starts with one step of hitching up the microcamper."

"Oh. *That* famous saying." She considered one final moment of communion with her curling iron, but unplugged it and laid it down solemnly as she addressed it. "I'll see you in less than a month."

A final glance in the mirror. Brown was so not her color.

"Coffee's on the counter," Connor said. "Can I haul your duffel to the car?"

"It's as ready as it's going to get."

"Mallory, just so you know, this does mean a lot to me. I'm not taking it lightly, your willingness to do this."

"For the cause."

"Right. For the cause."

And for you. Because I can't imagine we could be finished. We can't be finished. We need to find the right kind of counselor. It's as simple as that. Not simple at all.

"What do you want for breakfast?" she said. "I can get that started." The last word stuck in her throat when she walked into the kitchen. "Connor, what have you done?"

The table was set with their good plates—wedding gifts—and goblets, also from the wedding, and cloth napkins. How did he even know where she kept them? Or remember they'd had a wedding? Okay, maybe that was a little harsh.

"I figured we'd better take a minute to mark the occasion and to have a decent meal. We'll be cooking out of the back end of a washing machine for the next three weeks." He winked.

"But we cleaned out the fridge."

"Couldn't sleep last night."

The crumpled blanket on the couch and pillow under the coffee table could have told her that.

"So," he said, "I made a run to the store. Do you know how hard it is to buy just enough ingredients for two servings of eggs Benedict? Did you know eggs come in half cartons? That's great, but we only needed two. I hard-boiled the other four. They'll keep in the cooler."

"You poached the eggs in the middle of the night? How did I not hear you?"

"The water's boiling. I'm about to poach. Sit down. It'll be ready in minutes." He turned toward the stove. "Oh, that'll give you time to read over the road rules."

She slid into her customary chair. They'd positioned the table in their small apartment so the window wasn't to either's back, but at their side. They both had a view ... of the parking spaces. Parking spaces they did not resent, considering how few people in the heart of Chicago could claim one as their own. "Road rules? I know how to drive, Connor."

"More like rules of the game. Rather, the adventure."

Mallory was starting to despise that otherwise innocuous word. And the way he used it to cover emotional pain.

Connor bent over the pan of boiling water, lowering the eggs one by one as if his steadiness of hand would make or break the experience. And it would. "Hang on."

Satisfied the eggs were safely nested in their hot tub, he turned toward her, brandishing a slotted spoon. "The Road-Rave guidelines. Nathan and I had input, but there are a few surprises. More than a few, I guess. Nothing too outrageous. But I thought you might want to be aware. I texted the pdf to your phone."

"Too many rules for you to tell me?"

"Y-y-yeah." He swiveled toward the stove.

"'Twenty dollars a day allotment for food?' What?"

"They're trying to prove how economical it can be to travel."

"Twenty dollars per person won't even get us—"

Connor rolled his shoulders. "Um, for the three of us. Total."

"We can supplement with our own funds, can't we?"

Mallory watched as he lifted the eggs from the water, let them fully drain, then carefully laid them on top of the English muffin and Canadian bacon beds he'd prepared on the smaller plates on the counter. "RoadRave would rather we didn't. They have a point to prove."

"You call twenty dollars economical, Connor? In what country can you feed three people for twenty dollars a—? We are staying in the continental US, aren't we?"

"It's all part of the adventure. Tell me if there's enough lemon in the hollandaise."

There isn't enough lemon in the solar system to cover the stink of this situation. "Connor, be serious."

"It'll be fine. We're encouraged to take odd jobs to supplement, or barter. You know, dive into the full experience. See, really *see*, America."

She stared at the perfectly plated eggs Benedict in front of her. A day's worth of calories on one plate. She thought about the man who made a run to the store in the middle of the night. Considered the decision she'd made to go along with this scheme. Thought about the youth center and having a positive impact on Judah and creating a few memories for a man who fully expected he didn't have much time left to collect them. She'd agreed to the journey.

No fault but hers that she might have to clean out a chicken coop for her next fresh egg.

"Aren't you hungry? We really should chow down. I mean, it'll be a while before we stop."

She picked up her fork and broke the perfect yolk cloaked in silky hollandaise. "You're saying we should get our caloric intake now, before we lapse into starvation mode?"

His fork clinked the tabletop hard enough to sound its discord. "We won't starve, Mallory. Can you for a minute pull yourself out of complaint mode and get a little excited about this?"

Since when was she the complainer between the two of them? He was the I'm-gonna-die-but-not-soon-enough doomsday freak. She choked on her own sarcasm. *God, don't let him be right this time!*

"Three weeks, Mallory. You'd think I asked you to give me a kidney or something."

"I would have done that in a heartbeat."

"You know what I mean."

I will do that in a heartbeat, if you'll let me. If you need it. She resumed eating. But she would never admit to him that it tasted delicious.

chapter nine

I HAVE TO BE ABLE to see out the rearview mirror." Connor pushed a tote bag off a pile stacked three-high. This would never work.

"And I have to have a place to sit," Judah countered, glaring at Connor as only an eleven-year-old could. He crossed his arms in a way that matched his scowl.

"Judah, we can work this out," Mallory said. "It'll take some math skills."

"Do not look at *me*, then," Connor said, hands raised in surrender. He had to keep the mood lighthearted or they wouldn't log mile one.

He caught Mallory glancing out the windshield at Nathan. "Really? You're filming this? Could that be more inappropriate?" Her north end was buried deep in the Subaru Outback. Her south end faced the camera as she shoved boxes and duffel bags, sleeping bags and pillows, into new positions.

"You're doing great, Mallory," Nathan said. "Carry on. Pretend I'm not here. In ten minutes, I won't be." Nathan made a "keep it rolling" gesture with his free hand.

Mallory's mouth wasn't moving, but Connor heard muffled sounds. He leaned his head toward hers. "Any way I can help, Mallory?"

Her glare rivaled Judah's.

"How about if I … make sure the trailer's secured?"

"Great idea."

"Judah, I could use your help running through the checklist."

The boy drew a wide rectangle with his fingers. "This much space is for me. I need my safe space."

Connor turned his logo-tee-shirted chest to the camera and said, "Judah and I are going to run through the safety checklist provided by RoadRave, whose tagline is"—he paused for effect—"'Just add humans and the adventure begins.'"

"Cut!" Judah turned limp marionette. "Dude!"

Nathan stepped closer. "Judah, respect your elders."

"You sound like Grandma, if I had one. And Connor can't be more than, like twenty years older than I am."

"Not quite. Elders, Nathan? I'm an elder now?"

The camera at his side, Nathan put one hand on Connor's shoulder. "My man, remember our discussion about natural, free-flowing, capturing the moment, unscripted … ? Remember all that?"

"I didn't sound natural?"

Judah straightened. "Even *I* know this can't look like a three-week-long advertisement. You're like the Pac-Man of the video world, dude." He mimed an all-mouth creature opening and closing.

"Judah." Nathan let the name stand on its own.

"Done." Mallory crawled out of the back of the vehicle. "All supplies stored and secured. What did I miss?"

Wisps of her hair clung to her sweat-dotted face. One side of her tee-shirt was untucked. Still beauti—

"You missed your husband's failed attempt at an Oscar." Judah left the huddle of males and peered into the back seat. He climbed in and extended his arm through the open window. Thumbs up.

Nathan sighed. "Guys, I … I'd abort this plan if it weren't vital for the company. Judah's not going to make it any easier. I love that kid, but he can be—"

"We know." Connor and Mallory spoke in unison for once.

"You've probably been praying about this trip, but I want you to know I'm committed to praying harder than either one of you. Yes, even while in the jury box … while listening very carefully to the testimonies and paying attention to my civic duty and …"

"We know what you mean. Thanks." Mallory gave Nathan a sideways hug.

He returned the hug, then reached to bop Connor in the arm. "Hey, man. Love you for doing this. And that woman you married? The best. Hang onto her."

One of these days, somebody was going to have to tell Nathan about the whole swan-song nature of the trip. The marriage farewell voyage.

"Can I get a picture of the two of you kissing before you take off? RoadRave will love it. The family that camps together—"

"Nathan …" Mallory drove her hands into her jeans' pockets.

"Sure." Connor would apologize to her later, but Nathan was right. They needed a shot like that. "Where do you want us?" His question was addressed to his business partner, but his eyes were on his life partner. For the time being. She averted her eyes, but nodded.

Nathan scanned the scene. "You two lean your backsides on the front of the car, facing the endless highway ahead of you. I'll pan out to encompass the whole setup. At my signal, Connor, put your arm around her and … well, you know the next part."

The couple made their way to the front of the vehicle, Connor's whispered "Sorry about this" expressed but unacknowledged. Cue the longing gaze into the future. Arm around shoulder. Bend and kiss.

How long was appropriate for a family-friendly moment? Better safe than sorry. Sorrier than he already was. Mallory didn't squirm from under his arm. She tilted her head to rest on his shoulder. *Nice one, Mallory. The perfect predeparture shot.*

Nathan moved from in front of them to catch another angle from the side. Connor lost him in his peripheral vision. Then he heard, "Okay. Got it. Including Judah's thumbs up. Nice touch, kid. I gotta get out of here so you three can hit the road."

Mallory lifted her head but didn't move. "Connor?"

"Yeah?"

She took his hands in hers. "We can do this." She kept her voice low. "We have to do it. For God and country and RoadRave and Troyer & Duncan and for the youth program and for Judah. And for us."

He couldn't lead her on. He wasn't that cruel. "Mallory, this journey isn't going to change us, what we know we need to do. Hon, don't get your hopes tied up in reconciliation or avoiding—" He glanced behind him at Nathan and Judah, no doubt engaged in their version of a father-son interchange about manners and behavior. "Avoiding separation. I wouldn't want you to think—"

She dropped his hands. "What I meant was that we are two relatively mature adults who can pull off a semblance of happiness for twenty-one days on the road, can't we? We can pretend our way through this."

"Right. Yes. Yes, we can."

But he could still feel the memory of her lips on his.

◆————————————————◆

Sunday morning. The perfect time to exit Chicago. Didn't anybody go to church on a Sunday morning anymore?

Mallory stopped the thought in its tracks. She was one of the anybodies. Conner and she had talked about making church a habit in their newlywed days. Tried a few places. Nothing seemed a good fit for them. Too noisy. Too quiet. Too friendly. Not friendly enough. Too rigid. Too casual. An unsuccessful shopping trip.

Despite their lapse in church attendance, they hadn't completely neglected their faith. Nathan was so faithtimistic, so positive about God, it wasn't uncommon for them to hear his mini-sermons scattered throughout their conversations. She hadn't objected. She was pretty sure Connor hadn't objected. The two of them were quieter about faith. Didn't make a big deal about it.

That's what made it so strange when, leaning on the car, she *knew*—somewhere deep inside—that she was being asked to drop her resistance and pour herself into the success of the—oh, okay—*adventure*. It wasn't her own determination. It was bigger than that. A calling. She didn't see a *woo-woo* vision or hear a Morgan Freeman voiceover. But she knew.

And when she agreed, the tension released as if she'd double-dosed on muscle relaxant.

Peace. She could only describe it as peace.

Weird, though. Nothing had changed. A surly preteen was ensconced behind her, grumbling under his breath. The man she loved but couldn't keep was positioned behind the wheel. And they were towing an impossible housing situation to parts unknown.

She couldn't think of a single reason for peace to have appeared on the scene. But there it was.

Mallory pulled down the visor to check her face in the mirror, then thought better of it and slipped her sunglasses in place. The video cams were packed in a metal case for now. No need to freshen her makeup until they stopped. A few days from now, she'd probably be wearing flannel and a baseball cap and embracing the makeup-free look.

Nah. Who was she kidding? A popular trend on social media, but not one she'd ever truly embrace.

Connor pointed through the windshield. "There's our mile

marker. We can open the app now and plug in for our first destination."

"Aye, aye, Captain Connor." Mallory scrolled through to the app.

A groan traveled forward from the back seat. "Cheesy factory. High alert." At least Judah had a wide vocabulary. Nathan had warned them that his intelligence almost made his issues more challenging. He could hold his own in any adult argument. He'd likely have plenty of opportunity to practice.

When Connor glanced at Mallory, she risked a smile. He turned his attention to the road, but she caught his mirrored response.

The app directed them south and east. As expected, it led them off the interstate onto a series of back roads. Within a few miles, Mallory knew her propensity for efficiency would be tested on the trip. But the mind-numbing monotony of speeding down concrete ribbons of straight roads wouldn't be a problem. Not only was their destination unknown, so was the scene around the next bend … unknown until they got there.

What was that smell? Engine trouble already? Had they hit a long-dead raccoon who left a reminder of his demise on their tires?

Connor glanced in the rearview mirror. "Judah?"

"Yes, Cap'n Crunch?"

"Did you take your shoes off?"

"Is that a felony in this state?"

Mallory shifted in her seat. Such an innocent-looking face for someone so abrasive. "It is if you didn't change your socks this morning."

"What day is it?"

"Sunday." Mallory narrowed her eyes, calculating his angle. "Then no. My policy is to change socks on Wednesdays."

"New policy," Connor said. "Daily sock change."

"See? That'll be a challenge since I only brought one other pair."

Connor's hands tensed on the wheel. Mallory took over.

"Not going to cut it. We'll stop and get more."

"You guys told me to pack light. So I did."

Mallory powered down her window, enough to let in fresh air, but not far enough to turn her hair into a tornado. "We probably wear close to the same size. At our first pit stop, I'll get you"—she swallowed harder than intended—"a pair of mine for now."

"I won't wear fuzzy socks with kittens on them."

"Yeah, me neither."

Judah's mouth scrunched on one side. "You can't make me change my socks." His voice sounded less rebellious and more deflated.

"Oh, yes we can." Connor powered down his window too.

Mallory laid her hand on Connor's forearm. "Judah, tell us what's up with the socks."

He sniffed. "They're my lucky pair. My dad never beat me when I wore this pair."

Mallory felt Connor's arm tense under her hand. "I thought you never met your dad. He wasn't in your life." An emptiness she knew well.

Judah smiled. "See how lucky they are?" He raised one foot to eye level and draped it over the console between them.

Mallory would have taken a deep breath and counted to ten, but the deep breath would have made her pass out.

"Judah Milo Troyer." The words came out ground between Connor's teeth.

"Proving my point."

"Oh, we got your point, buddy. Mallory, do you have a plastic zip bag up here?"

"Just the one with grapes for snacking later."

"So, we have a plan then?" Connor's eyebrows punctuated his question.

"Yes, we do." She distributed the grapes among three paper cups she'd tucked in their open-air-meal-on-the-road tote at her feet and handed the cups to her travel companions. Then she opened the mouth of the quart-sized zip-seal bag and pointed. "Those socks. In here."

Once safely sealed, the offenders joined the luggage and equipment behind the second seat. Out of sight, not necessarily out of mind.

"I probably should have mentioned," Judah said, "that I get car sick if I'm not sitting in the front seat on long trips."

Connor frowned. "You do not."

"I can prove it."

How many looks would pass between Mallory and Connor in the next three weeks? At least they were looking at each other. That was an improvement.

Mallory shrugged her shoulders. Less than a mile down whatever county road they were on, Connor found a spot wide enough for them to pull over. He shoved the shift stick into park and laid his head on the steering wheel.

She grabbed her purse and thermal travel mug and opened the passenger side door. Funny. Someone with a Judah-like sense of humor had posted a cardboard sign at the edge of the shoulder that read *Scenick Overlook*. Half the letters were backward. As she waited for Judah to peel himself out of the back seat, she scanned the scenery. Flatland. Looked like a sod farm that stretched to the horizon. Clever. Some overlook.

"Come on, Judah." Connor's patience showed its frayed edges.

"I have to"—he grunted—"put my shoes on first."

Mallory bent and touched her toes, stretching her hamstrings and shoulder muscles. She twisted at the waist. Clasped her palms together and reached for the sky. Traditional morning stretch, except for the scene behind her. And the road ahead of them. *God help us all. I mean it. God, help us all.*

chapter ten

CONNOR KEPT HIS FOOT ON the brake, watching the caravan of hay wagons from the field on the right cross to the farmyard on the left of the road. "So, big guy, tomorrow we start your homeschooling assignments, huh?"

"You've seen my stature. I'm obviously not a 'big guy.' Choose some other lame nickname, Captain Trying Too Hard."

"Look, Judah …"

"Yes. Judah is fine with me. But I can't read or do homework on the road. Again, motion sickness." He pressed the back of his hand against his forehead. "It's a curse."

Mallory leaned forward between the seats. "We'll find a way to work around that."

"From what I hear, we'll be riding a lot. Might have to wait on the schooling thing until the trip is done."

"Nice try, Private Not Trying Hard Enough." Aha. He *could* wrangle a grin out of that kid.

He checked on Mallory in the rearview. *With legs like hers—*

He redirected his thinking. With her height, she must be dying. "Hey, Judah. Adjust your seat ahead a little. Give Mallory some legroom, will you?"

"I barely have enough the way it is, with this huge bag of her stuff up here."

"They're provisions for all of us," Mallory said. "Hand it back. I can put it on the floor behind Connor."

"Is it all that organic, high-nutrition, low-taste stuff?"

"We're eating as healthy as we can on this trip, Judah," she said. "Be grateful for every celery stick in that bag. Our budget is crazy low for meals."

"So is it? Organic? Because I only eat organic."

"I'm sure. I recognize Cheetos stains when I see them."

Connor waved at the last tractor driver, who looked not much older than Judah. Now, there was a kid who knew the meaning of a good day's work, and—oh, good grief, he sounded just like his father when he could still carry on a conversation. He'd become Old Man Duncan. Connor shook off the comparison and searched his repertoire of personal affirmations. Nothing came to mind.

Connor arched his back as far as his seatbelt would allow. Maybe it hadn't been the best idea for him to insist on doing all the driving this first day. They'd made a couple of fuel and restroom stops, but never long enough to loosen his muscles.

The roads they were assigned through Indiana boasted few reasons to crane his neck. Judah seemed lost in a book. So much for the motion sickness. A glance in the rearview told him Mallory was either asleep or pretending. The trailer followed smoothly behind them. Connor rolled his shoulders and concentrated on tackling the hash marks on the road.

Hash marks. One after another. To his dad, hash marks on his Navy uniform—despite his medical discharge two years into his career—meant more than conquering hash marks on a highway. *Dad, I hope you'd be proud of what I'm doing here with Troyer & Duncan. I would tell you about it the next time I see you, but I won't know how you feel about it any more than you'll remember my name.*

Connor's college squad of guy friends were more interested

in hash marks on the football field these days, according to social media. He couldn't believe how many of them had settled. The routines they'd boasted they were determined to resist—steady but meaningless jobs, working too much to pay for their accumulation of too much, falling into the rut of responsibilities—had become their norm. What happened to their nothing-is-impossible mentality? They'd all had dreams. What made them give up? A mortgage? Having a family too soon? Assuming adulthood meant their dreams had to be put on hold?

They knew better than that. They'd preached it to him. To him, the dreamless one.

The hash marks took them closer to a larger metropolitan area than they'd seen since leaving Chicago. He thought about waking Mallory as they crossed the Ohio River into Kentucky. Thought about it.

"Hey, Judah," he whispered. "Look out the window."

Judah didn't close his iPad but glanced up. "What do you know. A river." Monotone. Disinterested.

"Does Mallory know you brought an iPad? I thought she said you needed to follow the RoadRave guidelines about minimal electronics for the trip."

"My books and homework assignments are on it."

"Oh."

"The woman has this thing about literacy."

"I know. But her name isn't 'The Woman.' It's either Mallory or Mrs.—" Stumbling blocks seemed to pop up in every conversation. "*Ms.* Duncan to you."

Judah shrugged and returned to his book. Connor resumed the monotony of hash marks.

Hash tags. Had Nathan gotten the word out about their hash tag for the trip?

"Hey, buddy?"

"The name's Judah."

Score one for the kid. "Can you take my phone and see what pops up if you key in #justaddhumans?"

"I'll need your security code."

"Never mind. I'll wait until Mallory's awake." *That's right. I don't trust you. Give me a reason to trust you and I might reconsider.* Or … he could manage to trust him until their next fuel stop, at which time Connor would reset his passcode. "Kidding." He rattled off the sequence of numbers.

Judah thumbed them and the hashtag info as if he'd been born with a smartphone in hand. First generation to have no memory of life before smartphones. What a world. What a world.

"Sick."

"What?"

"Sorry. I forgot I was talking to an old guy. Far out, man."

"Judah."

"They already have our departure video uploaded. And it's getting hits. Likes. Shares."

Sweet. "How many?" *How many shares equals "viral"?* He should know the answer to that question.

"So far, four. Is your mom's handle @duncandonuts?"

"That would be her. She thought it was so clever."

"Does she make donuts like Dunkin?"

"Not a baker."

"But—"

"You have to understand my mother's sense of humor."

"I'll probably never meet her."

"What makes you say that?"

"Look, it's no secret I'm only here because my uncle ran out of options. You don't have to pretend you like me."

That's a relief. "We're just starting to get to know one another. It takes time."

"You have three weeks. Think you can hang in there that long? Then I'll be out of your life. It's no big deal. Happens to kids like me all the time."

"Incoming," Mallory called from the back seat. "The app says we're turning right at the next intersection. A thousand feet. Five hundred. Four."

"Highway number?" Connor peered ahead. All he saw was more of the same nondescript road they were on.

"It doesn't say."

The crossing could hardly be called an intersection. The road onto which they turned was little more than two dirt tire tracks separated by undercarriage-brushing late-season grasses.

"How long do we follow this replica of the Oregon Trail?" He tightened his grip as the vehicle and trailer bounced over ruts and tree roots, even at five mph.

"Still uploading new info. And, yeah."

He could see her in the rearview mirror, but the road demanded his full attention.

"So …" she said.

"Would you mind sharing the information with the driver? Where do I go now?" He followed the tire tracks around an oasis of trees and over a crude bridge that barely cleared a shallow creek. "Did that sign say *Trespassers will be shot?* Mallory?"

"Dude." Judah leaned forward. "It said *Trespassers will NOT be shot.* Does that mean they'll be tortured first?"

"Judah!"

Connor stepped on the brake. Their bodies followed a split second later. "Mallory, he has a point."

"And we have arrived. Apparently." She pocketed her phone. "Our first … destina— Oh. Okay. That's a good sign."

"What is?" Connor tried to follow the path of her gaze.

"The sign. Isn't that the RoadRave logo?"

A box the size of a college dorm fridge rested against the base of a wide-branched tree. Definitely the RoadRave logo. The three exited the vehicle and huddled around the box.

"Can I open it?" Judah said.

"I guess so. Be careful." Connor stepped back to give the boy more room.

"I'll need a knife."

"Nice try." Connor was not about to give a mini-delinquent

a weapon to aid his escape and/or hostile takeover of their traveling troupe. He picked at the edge of the packing tape until it started to release.

"I got it. I got it," Judah insisted. "Maybe there's something decent to eat in here."

"I doubt it," Connor said. "Food would either spoil or attract—"

"Other hungry campers," Mallory finished, eyeing Connor. "What? Oh."

"You don't have to whisper over my head," Judah said. "I already know we're sitting duck confit for predators."

"'Con fee'?"

"It's a fancy duck dish, Connor. But how do you know about duck confit, Judah?"

"The last place I lived, with Those People, the lady watched a lot of food shows on TV."

Mallory raised her eyebrows. "Was she a good cook?"

"No. But she was real good at eating. Real good."

Connor helped peel back the last run of packing tape. "Let's see what the mystery box holds. Hey, nice. A telescoping canoe paddle. That may come in handy."

"RoadRave expects us to find space to store yet one more thing?" Mallory's excitement registered on the low scale.

"Maybe it's a clue," Judah said. "There's water in our future. Or bats. I'm a master bat exterminator. Slept in the attic at one foster home."

"A bedroom in the attic?"

"No. Just the open attic. With the bats. I used a tennis racket to keep them away from me. But a canoe paddle would work."

Connor leaned toward his wife. "How much of this are we supposed to believe?"

"In my experience," she said as Judah dove deeper into the box, "fifty or sixty percent. It can vary."

"Dibs on the parachute!"

"Parachute? That's a sleeping hammock, buddy." Connor pulled out the second of two tightly wrapped packages and an armful of aluminum tubing.

"Put it back, put it back, put it back!" Mallory yelled as if she'd seen a swarm of bees rising from the box.

"What *is* your problem?"

"Shouldn't we be recording this?" she asked. "Finding the box, opening it, discovering the treasures, 'Thank you, Road-Rave,' etc.?"

It's hard to be married to a woman who's always right. Connor let the sentence linger a moment before correcting himself. *But harder to be married to a woman who never is.* "I'll get the equipment."

Mallory and Judah repacked and retaped the box. Its plastic surface made that easier than if it had been cardboard. Cardboard scars when you rip things from it. He shook off the life analogy and set up the small tripod.

"Shouldn't the microcamper be in the frame too?" Mallory asked.

Who's always right. "Good idea."

"I'll pull it into position," she said.

"That's okay. I can do it."

"So can I."

A muscle in his neck spasmed. "Don't forget to—"

"I know," she said over her shoulder with a dismissive wave. "I read the manual."

He prepared to object to where she'd chosen to park, but Judah pointed out that the lighting would be better. The sunset visible but not blinding. *Everybody's an expert.*

"Okay, let's get this in one take, people," Judah said as he backed away from the box. "One take. I'm hungry."

When was he not hungry? But their time was limited. Connor didn't want to set up the camper in the dark, despite its ease of operation. "Good idea."

Mallory held back. "I'll man the camera," she said. "Then I can zoom in for the reveal."

Connor considered. "We can wait, if you want to put on

your makeup."

Judah nudged him and, eyes wide, mouthed, *Noooo*.

"What I meant was …"

"I'm behind the camera this time." The way she said it left no room for argument. Not that he had the energy for a discussion at the moment anyway.

"Let's go then. And Judah?"

"I know. I know. Deep-six the melodrama."

"Deep-six?" Mallory looked up from the viewfinder. "How is it you're familiar with … ?"

"One of my foster fathers was a Navy guy … who turned mafia. I'm sure you can see the connection."

Fifty or sixty percent. At most. Day One. Twenty more days stretched ahead of them.

chapter eleven

VIDEO COMPLETE AND ON ITS way to the RoadRave intern in charge of final editing and uploading to the vlog, the three turned their attention to setting up camp for the night. The instruction manual boasted six minutes setup for the experienced, "slightly" longer for first timers.

The camper itself followed those guidelines. The people had a harder time.

"Connor, it's obvious we can't have all three of us in the camper, on the mattress, off the damp ground, protected from ... mosquitoes."

"We talked about that," Judah said.

"Oh, you did?"

Connor nodded his agreement and opened his mouth to fill in the details. As always, Judah preempted, with "And we decided we probably should let you have the ..." He doubled over as if in pain. "I can't say it, Captain. You tell her." Judah turned his back on the scene.

That boy.

"What he's trying to say," Connor began, "is that no

combination is perfect here." *Obviously, you and I are not sleeping side by side and leaving the delinquent within range of hot-wiring the car.* "Obviously, it wouldn't be fair for the guys to have the camper and you sleep in the car."

"Thanks for that."

"And it isn't appropriate for a preteen and a ... someone ... like ... a woman like ... a woman to share the camper, which is little more than a mattress."

"That's how I described it to you, I believe," Mallory said.

"Yes, well, for this particular line of reasoning, I agree with you. And unless we unload all of the gear, both of us guys can't bunk in the Subaru. So, we're going to set up the hammock sleepers RoadRave sent us."

"They're like a sleeping bag and a hammock combined," Judah said. "And a swing, when you think about it."

"You're not using your hammock as a swing, Judah." Connor could picture the damage that child could do to the Road-Rave equipment.

Mallory frowned. "You're sleeping in the trees?"

Mallory seemed slow to catch on to the beauty of Connor's plan. "No. The aluminum tubing is an apparatus that hooks on to the back of the SUV. We hang from the car. Of course, we have to unhook the camper from the trailer hitch first."

They discussed a raft of other options, including, ironically enough, an inflatable raft-bed which they didn't yet have but considered purchasing if they ever passed a retailer larger than a convenience store. At least with the hammocks, the guys would be off the ground.

Mallory pulled Connor aside when Judah slipped out of sight to use the imaginary facilities. "We don't know this area at all, Connor. What if there are ... bears?"

"We left the Bears in Chicago. Get it?"

"Not funny."

"Maybe a little bit?"

"Nope."

"Okay, I understand the out-here-in-the-wide-open-wilderness-of-western-Kentucky concern. But I saw a sign that said Louisville is a little more than thirty miles from here. And you do remember that a few miles back, we were dodging farmers with hay wagons. This isn't Daniel Boone's Kentucky anymore."

"But," Mallory stretched her arms both directions, "this is someone's property. Maybe their *No Trespassing* sign really meant 'just go ahead and try it.' I think I saw a bullet hole in the sign. And ..." She paused, straightened her posture, and said, "On further consideration, I will take the camper, which also locks from the inside. Have fun in the great outdoors."

She grabbed a well-stuffed tote bag from inside the vehicle, shoved it into the camper, sat in the doorway, swung her legs in, and clicked the door shut. "Goodnight."

A moment later, Connor heard a muffled, feminine, "Rats." Mallory emerged with a flashlight and headed for the cluster of low bushes away from the flat, open spot on which the camper rested. She turned at the line of bushes. "I need ... and I can't emphasize this enough ... a brief minute of privacy."

As if choreographed, Connor and Judah saluted their "Yes, ma'am."

<hr />

By the time she returned from her "nature hike," the two hammocks hung from the framework installed on the back of the Outback. RoadRave had been right about ease of installation, apparently.

Mallory couldn't imagine hanging like a sideways cocoon all night with no protection other than the thin fabric, impenetrable as it claimed to be. She crawled back into the teardrop-shaped camper and locked the door. If he had his way, Connor would soon be fending for himself on all fronts. She was obviously no longer necessary for his life goals or worthy of sharing his life challenges. Tonight was as good a time as any for him to test his don't-need-you-anymore theories.

She sat cross-legged on the mattress. The stark interior kept distractions to a minimum. On a night like this, she would have appreciated a distraction or two. Ah, one arrived. Then two. Mosquitoes.

So small, but with so much disruptive power.

Like the word *over*.

More precisely, Connor's words, "Mallory, what's the point of trying anymore? We both know this marriage gig isn't working like we'd hoped. It's over."

That's not the family dynamic he came from. His parents had been married more than thirty years. Devoted to each other, even after his dad's brain tumors and his other von Hippel-Lindau syndrome symptoms and treatments changed their relationship. It had to be hard on his mom. Caregiving consumed their relationship now. Caregiving without hope of healing. Would Mallory have walked away in a similar situation? Was Connor walking away now to prevent having to find out?

What if Connor's need to separate himself from her wasn't about the two of them? What if it was about his dad and mom?

No. He was sharp enough to recognize misdirected emotions. The truth was he'd lost whatever passion he'd once felt for her. What held them together wasn't strong enough glue anymore to withstand what pried them apart.

She positioned the pillow under her neck and pulled the comforter to her nose. "No Mosquito Zone. Do you hear me?" she whispered into the dark.

The two small cans of tomato soup they'd split three ways plus the handful of crackers and string cheese sat heavy in her stomach as she waited for sleep to tap her thoughts on the shoulder and send them off duty. They refused to leave.

It didn't help that she could hear Judah practicing his preteen belching for national competitions. He could easily make the finals. "Connor!"

"Yeah, I got it. You should hear it from hanging right beside him. Judah, dude, deep-six the burp factory."

As well-insulated as the microcamper was, she could hear every word.

"I can't let the gas build up or I'll explode."

The stainless steel and insulation between them did muffle sound, but she thought she heard Connor say, "At least the hammock sack will expand to contain the resulting debris."

And here she'd been putting money in a baby fund, assuming Connor would make a great dad.

"This is my lovely wife, Mallory, emerging from RoadRave's newest creation—the model T900 teardrop microcamper. As you can see, she looks rested and ready for our next adventure."

"Connor, turn that thing off." Mallory slid into her shoes without stopping to tie them.

"Her manners are still sleeping, folks, but after a great breakfast made in the T900's kitchen, I'm sure we'll see that smile of hers return."

"Connor. Chill." Mallory brushed past him, heading for the makeshift facilities.

"Mallory, that area is currently … *occupado.*"

"What?"

"Judah."

"Oh."

"Can you give the folks at home an assessment of the comfort level of the T900 mattress?"

Forgive me, Father, for I am about to sin by saying three bad words in succession. Plug Your divine ears.

"Next?" Judah said, emerging from the privacy zone.

Mallory took the small camping shovel and the roll of toilet paper from Judah as she hustled past him, vowing to find a roll she could call her own before the day's end. They should have already discussed the off-limits nature of first-thing-in-the-morning hair, face, breath …

They shouldn't have had to discuss it. *Come on, Connor.* The video blog watchers were not interested in pillow lines no doubt crisscrossing her face. Maybe the vlog watchers were interested. But if so, was that the kind of advertising RoadRave wanted?

She returned to the smell of bacon. Kale smoothies last week. Bacon this week. If it hadn't smelled like heaven, she might have objected. "Need any help with that?"

"We didn't pick up any eggs before we left, did we?" Connor dug through the cooler now resting on the ground.

"No. We said we'd get those on the road as needed."

"Then breakfast is bacon with a side of bacon."

"Could you make mine a double?" Judah said from his perch on a fallen log.

"We're rationing," Connor said.

Judah pouted. He was Shakespearean-theater good at it.

Connor pointed toward the cooler. "Mal, could you get out the yogurt? I should have done that when I was in there."

"I'm no longer known as your 'lovely wife, Mallory'?"

"You're not upset about that, are you? I hadn't even pushed Record. It was a joke. You have to lighten up if we're going to make it all the way to the end of this."

"Let's go with that," Judah said.

"With what?"

"Connor's cooking bacon in the background and Mallory, you talk to the camera about what it's like to have a fully immersive experience in the great outdoors. And add that human interest 'lighten-up' stuff for those who care about emotional junk."

"Judah, I'm not going to—"

"And … action!"

He panned the camera from right to left, letting the sizzle of bacon have its fifteen seconds of fame, and then it was pointed at her. *Think, Mallory. Think.*

94

"Simple pleasures. The smell of bacon on a cool morning. A cup of fresh coffee." On cue, Connor handed her an enamelware mug. "Experiencing nature up close and personal." She bent to pick up a speckled rock. It squirmed in her hand. She clamped her hand firmly to keep the critter—probably a toad—from moving while she got through the video piece. "And waking up next to—close to—someone you love." She put her arms around Connor from the back and leaned her head on his shoulder blade as he flipped bacon with a rubber-handled set of tongs. She slid the toad between the buttons of his flannel shirt and grabbed a paper towel for her hands.

"What's this? What? Mallory!"

She stepped closer to the camera. "Life can be hard sometimes. For a moment or a season or forever." She heard Connor drop the tongs and fight to get his shirt unbuttoned behind her. Judah gave her a thumbs up as she continued.

"It's never too soon to remember, is it, Connor"—she half turned toward him—"to lighten up if we want to make it all the way to the end of the journey. Have a great one, viewers. We'll be on the road again. Don't forget to follow us at #justaddhumans." She held her coffee cup high. "Here's to creating your own adventures."

"And … cut." Judah lowered the camera and high-fived her on the way to snatch a piece of bacon from the cooling plate.

Connor's expression could have melted chocolate in Antarctica. Mallory waited, arms crossed. Slowly the iceberg shrank and his eyes glinted.

"Point taken. We could both—all—use some lightening up."

"Can I keep the toad?" Judah asked, taking it from Connor's grip.

"No." Another unison answer. There was hope for them yet.

chapter twelve

EVERYONE BUCKLED IN?" MALLORY GLANCED back at their camping spot. Better than they found it. Good life goal. "Let's hit the road then," she said, grateful for a wide area in which to swing the small SUV and camper to face the dirt path that had led them here. Connor's seatbelt was buckled, but he kept shifting to find a comfortable spot for his legs, as she had the day before.

"Judah, is there any way you can give me some more leg room back here?"

"I really wish I could, Mr. Duncan," he said, "but I need the space for my homework materials. I wouldn't want to get much farther behind in my schoolwork because of being forced to come on this trip."

"I thought you said working on homework made you carsick?" Connor's voice sounded road weary already.

Mallory kept her eyes on the rutted road and the speedometer. Who would think that five miles an hour could be too fast? The jostle over one exposed root made her front teeth clank together. "What was that?"

"Hope we didn't bottom out on that one," Connor said. "Take it slow, Mal."

"I am."

Judah peered at the side mirror. "Hey, guys?"

"What?"

"Aren't we supposed to be pulling a camper?"

Mallory checked her side mirror. "Oh, no! Whose job was it to lock the trailer hitch?"

"Not mine," Judah added quickly.

"You have to go slow over these ruts, Mallory. I told you that."

"Not our current problem, Connor."

"Well, we do."

"And I was. And the camper is back there at Rut #1, so I hardly think speed was an issue, now, was it?"

Connor and Mallory unbuckled, exited the vehicle, and stood staring back down the sorry excuse for a road. A glint of sun on stainless steel told them exactly where the camper stood. Leaned.

Under his breath, Connor said, "It may or may not have been my assignment to lock and secure the trailer ball and hitch."

"Want me to back the Subaru all the way to the trailer?" Mallory asked.

"I can do it. Unless you want to."

"Go for it, cowboy."

"What's that supposed to mean?"

Mallory's bacon soured in her stomach. "It means that I'd appreciate it if you did the backing. I'll walk. Then I can guide as you line it up."

"You don't have to walk."

"I want to walk."

"Smiles, everyone." Judah hit Record.

The two checked for damage to the trailer and its tongue. None. Connor backed the vehicle into position, attached the trailer to the hitch, and made a show of clicking the mechanism into place and locking the added protection.

"Not a great start to the day," Mallory said to the camera, "but bumps like this often form stronger mental reminders than a sticky note ever could."

If only other things that came unhitched carried the same benefits. Maybe they did, and she and Connor had missed them, missed the life lessons in their marriage's disastrous first year.

She had to stop thinking that way. It's not that every minute after "I do" had spiraled downward. They'd weathered and walked away unscathed from plenty of disagreements, including what time they should leave for the airport to catch their plane to their honeymoon destination. An hour and a half should have been enough time to get through security and find their gate. Connor was nervous about it, but Mallory assured him they'd have plenty of time.

They hadn't counted on the O'Hare-wide power outage that stalled them mid security line. Nothing like the Atlanta shutdown. But enough to keep them from making their connecting flight to Monterrey. The last flight of the day between LAX and Monterrey. A three-day honeymoon cut short by one day. Because of her.

Or so Connor claimed. Repeatedly.

Never mind that Mallory thought they needed a full week for it to count as a real honeymoon. Connor insisted he couldn't take that much time away from work. Three days to start their marriage sliced down to two ... because she chose wrong about how long they'd need at the airport. The electrical problem bore no guilt.

Mallory hadn't been late to anything since that day almost a year ago. But Connor's habit was to add "Don't be late" or "We can't afford to be late" to all event planning for the two of them.

Church, in the early months before that was no longer an issue. Dentist appointments. Christmas celebrations. An evening out. Grocery shopping. "Will you be ready to leave in ten minutes? Ten minutes, Mallory."

As if she needed the reminder.

Lately, she didn't give him the courtesy of an answer. And, truth be told, she sometimes wasted the final minute so she wasn't ready any sooner than a second before departure time.

As she climbed behind the steering wheel again, she realized how vindictive that sounded. What happened to her? What had she become?

Connor raised a "halt" hand when she asked if everyone was buckled in. He unlatched his seatbelt and climbed out. Triple-checking the hitch? Maybe some of the fallout of their relationship failure was that he didn't trust himself anymore. Mallory brushed off the thought. No. He didn't claim any blame. Real or imagined. It's as if he blamed the institution of marriage. Or genetics. Or her.

When they reached the county road, the app instructed them to turn right. She swung wide and eased their caravan onto the asphalt. Blessed, smooth asphalt. "How far for this first leg?" she asked.

"Don't know," Connor said. "It just says to drive."

"Do you think we should capitalize more on the 'See America' aspect of the RoadRave campaign, Connor?"

"What do you mean?"

"Should we be ready for 'exciting moments' like the hay wagon traffic jam? That's pretty Americana right there."

"I keep the cameras charged. I don't know what more I can do."

Mallory stole a look at her husband in the mirror. "Are you okay? I didn't mean any offense by that."

"If anyone knows what sells, it would be the ad guy. So, leave the scene mapping to me, if you don't mind."

"I'd mind," Judah said from his nest on the passenger seat.

"It's none of your business, Judah."

Mallory cringed.

"Sorry, kid," Connor said. "I got up on the wrong side of the hammock this morning. And I'm one cup of coffee shy of civil. I apologize. You too, Mallory."

"What do I need to apologize for? Oh, you mean … Thanks. Apology accepted."

"I've got skills," Judah said. "I'm only eleven, but I've got skills. We're in this together, aren't we?"

A mile of silence is longer than a regular mile.

"Turn left on 31W." Connor leaned over the front seat and pointed to his phone.

"A real highway? That'll be fun for a change." Mallory signaled as the sign approached.

Within minutes, they were leaving Highway 31W.

"Do you see a sign for Bridges to the Past?" Connor tapped Judah's shoulder to get him to join in the hunt.

"What is that? Bridges to the Past?" Mallory asked. "Have you ever heard of it?"

Judah leaned forward. "I see a flashing yellow light. Could that be it?"

"Matches the coordinates," Connor said.

Mallory took the exit at the flashing yellow light and followed the road almost a mile before Connor yelled, "Stop! This must be it."

"A parking lot?" She steered toward a double-long space with easy exit access.

"I see a RoadRave sign." Judah pointed. "It's right by the one that says"—he squinted—"'Tioga Falls Hiking Trail.'"

"We drive nine hours yesterday before we stop and only nine *minutes* today?" Mallory turned off the ignition and tossed the keys to Connor.

"Personally, I was ready for a break," Judah said, bounding off toward the RoadRave box.

"You still all in, Mal?" Connor touched her shoulder as a friend might touch a grieving widow at a funeral.

She processed several layers of what that might mean before responding. "All in. It will take more than a bad beginning to make me think the day is ruined."

"I … I appreciate that about you."

"That has more than one application."

"I know."

She left out the part about thinking God might have told her she had to come on this journey.

The RoadRave box held instructions for hiking the Tioga Falls trail, which, as it turned out, wasn't at all maze-like or challenging. The trail was an abandoned road. A steady climb, but paved most of the way, weaving in and out of the woods.

Judah stayed surprisingly close. Mallory assumed he would have tugged at the invisible leash and bolted ahead.

The trail led to a railroad trestle. They eventually crossed the set of train tracks. Judah warned them to be careful and pointed out the shine on the rails. The tracks were still in use.

"Are you always this observant, Judah?" Connor asked.

"When I want to be."

Mallory smiled. You had to give him props for honesty. When he wanted to be.

Only a handful of people shared the trail with them. They nodded their greetings as they passed. How many did that when passing on the sidewalks of Chicago? Most avoided making eye contact. Something about the outdoors made strangers feel connected.

The trailhead had started with a barricade. Mallory couldn't help comparing their honeymoon fiasco with the closed trail.

"Property of Fort Knox," Judah had read. "Cool."

"Take the detour," a fellow hiker had suggested, indicating the path that veered to the right of the barricade.

Mallory reread the sign. "*The* Fort Knox?"

"The one and only," Connor answered. "The app says this is all Fort Knox property. Hiking is forbidden during training exercises."

"We could break into Fort Knox?" Judah said. "Now, that would be an adventure. Viral footage, Connor. Viral."

Connor checked their distance from other hikers. "Crimes are frowned upon by the RoadRave corporation. By law enforcement. By me. And by the God of the Universe, if you didn't know."

Mallory hadn't heard him speak God's name for a long time. Even in jest, which she was fairly certain this wasn't.

The trail took them through a forested area that showed signs of recent rainfall. Must have been at least two days prior. It hadn't rained on them in the night. Mallory would have heard the drops pounding on the stainless-steel roof of the teardrop.

"Don't touch anything, Judah." Mallory opened her mouth again to apologize for assuming he would, but his fingers were inches from an ankle-height piece of spiked vegetation. The warning stood.

"I like textures."

"Do you like poison ivy?" Connor asked.

"Was that poison ivy?"

"Pretend it *all* is. Don't touch."

They cut back on conversation for the steepest parts of the trail.

"Are we there yet?" Judah bent, his hands on his knees.

"It's the young one complaining," Connor said.

"I still consider myself young," Mallory said, crouching as if ready to race him toward the mysterious finish line ahead.

"Instead," Connor said, readying the camera, "we could record our reactions to *that*."

They turned his direction.

"Whoa."

A cascade of water tumbled over rocky ledges from thirty feet above them, a twin falls at the top, then several additional wider cascades that spilled over cliff edges on their way down. The rock ledges looked like baklava's thin layers stacked together. The thought made her long for a side trip to the Greek bakery on Wacker Drive along the Chicago River.

"It's no Niagara Falls," Judah said.

"Have you been to Niagara Falls?" Connor asked.

"Don't be mean."

"I wasn't trying to be unkind. I wondered if you were comparing because you've seen both."

Judah sat on a rock and hugged his knees to his chest. "I've seen it on TV. And on YouTube."

"Boys, behave yourselves." Mallory couldn't take her eyes off the sight of the thin veil of water flowing over the highest point.

"I bet there wasn't even this little trickle before it rained. Seems sketch to call this a waterfall."

"Judah, it's the experience, dude. On screen isn't the same as in person." Connor kept his voice video-calm. Camera still engaged.

Judah slapped at a mosquito. "Right. On screen is better."

Mallory's skin prickled when her eyes focused on a leafed twig that rode the falls from top to bottom. It disappeared periodically as it skated across the flat plateaus of rock above her sight line before dropping over another ledge. A twig. Unaware of the dangerous drops. Riding the flow of water to a destination far from where it had started. She envied its grace, its resilience.

"Come over here for a minute, Judah," she said.

"Why?"

"For the 'experience.'"

He shuffled closer. "Yeah? Same as the view over there, only closer."

"Wait for it."

Here, at the falls, the sound of water kept life's rhythm, rather than numbers on a digital clock.

"Still waiting."

"There! Did you feel that? When the breeze is blowing harder, you can feel the mist."

"Feels like sweat."

Mallory glanced up at Connor. Camera still rolling. Could any of this footage be saved? Probably not. Could Judah be saved? More important question.

She watched Connor pan to catch the view from the top of the waterfall to where it flattened out into the simple creek it would have been if not for the obstacles. "Is that the creek we crossed last night?"

Judah sighed. "Well, we could climb to the top and walk back ten miles and see. Or, if we weren't all 'experiential,' we could google it."

Connor lowered the camera. "Great idea. You walk it. I'll google." He turned toward Mallory. "Do you want to get some still shots? For Instagram? Or a chat book? Snapchat? Any other kind of -gram?"

"I'd rather just watch for a few more minutes. Soak it in."

"Waterfall sweat," Judah said. "How romantic."

chapter thirteen

IF ROMANCE HAD BEEN THE goal of the trip, a sullen preteen would not be part of the picture.

Connor couldn't afford to let Judah know how far from romance his relationship with Mallory had fallen. A kid that chatty … and evil hearted … couldn't be trusted with information that could be used against them.

Evil hearted might be too strong a term. But the kid had issues.

Okay, he had issues. Who didn't these days? The boy had to learn how to deal.

If the kid knew what Connor faced—the possibility of blowing the RoadRave deal, which might translate into losing Troyer & Duncan, and the certainty of losing Duncan and Duncan the Marriage, losing the connection with his dad because of what the brain tumor had done to his personality and memory, the good chance Connor was next on the tumor train—he'd know what real issues were.

And, if Judah did know, he'd probably tell Connor to "deal."

Connor removed his RoadRave ball cap and replaced it at the first gnat attack. No time for his brain to breathe. The task at hand was enduring twenty more days on the road with a surly preteen and the woman to whom he'd pledged then unpledged his future.

Yeah, Judah. You *have issues.*

They retraced their steps on the trail to the parking lot. No loop to offer new scenery. An out-and-back trail. Connor didn't mind seeing the same path from the opposite angle. Things he missed before. He took a swig from his water bottle. He couldn't let that kind of contemplation take him too far, under the circumstances.

"Do we have anything to eat?" Judah asked as he climbed into the front passenger seat.

"I'd donate an organ in exchange for your metabolism, young man." Mallory stood before him. Disturbingly beautiful despite her hair tucked into her RoadRave cap and a tee she usually wore only to the gym. The woman had no metabolism concerns.

And her name wasn't The Woman.

"So, do we? Food? Starving in here."

Hands at her sides, Mallory didn't move. "Leftover grapes."

"From yesterday?"

"Mighty picky for a freeloader," Connor said. Why wasn't she getting behind the wheel?

"Connor. Am I driving or are you?" She tilted her head. The sun had colored her cheeks.

"You can drive, if you want."

"Then I'll need the keys."

"Oh. Right. Why'd you give them back when we got here?"

She bounced the keys in her palm and headed for the driver's-side door. "To support your sense of ownership."

"I do not have an unnatural sense of ownership. Or entitlement. Or whatever you meant."

"*Somebody's* hangry," Judah said. "Hungry to the point of anger. Here, have a leftover grape. We're rationing."

As they pulled out of the parking lot, Connor checked the app and relayed the directions. Heading south again.

"Another sign for Fort Knox," Judah said. "There's still time for us to—"

Connor and Mallory's unison "No!" hit the same pitch this time.

Earbuds in place, Connor previewed the footage from Tioga Falls. Rough seeing himself in some of those scenes. Hearing himself. Somehow, he needed to keep a lid on his stress. Nothing said he couldn't enjoy the journey. Three weeks, all expenses paid, back roads of America, great outdoors, sleeping under the stars ... A lot to be grateful for.

Three long weeks with two people forced to take the trip with him. Twenty dollars a day for food, unless they worked odd jobs or scavenged. Back roads with fifteen-mph blind corners and few opportunities to use cruise control. Unknown destinations. Sleeping under the—

Raindrops pelted the windshield. What happened to the sun? If this kept up, they'd need an alternate plan to the hammock hotel. He removed his earbuds and focused his attention on the road ahead. Mallory was a good driver. Her record was better than his. But still ...

"Did you know," Judah said, eyeing his phone, "that the water from Niagara Falls comes from Lakes Michigan, Superior, Huron, St. Clair, and Lake Erie? Never heard of Lake St. Clair. Do not fear. I'll google it."

"Good to know," Mallory said with a slight shake of her head.

"Those lakes drain—and I quote—'a large part of the North American continent, and all feed the Niagara River. Once the water flows down the river and passes over the falls'— still quoting here—'it then flows about fourteen miles *north* into Lake Ontario to the St. Lawrence River and eventually to the Atlantic Ocean.'"

"Is that part of your homework assignment, Judah?"

"Let's say yes," he said. "Homework and proof that what we just saw was no Niagara Falls."

Connor closed his eyes. The scene didn't change. "Why don't you work on math for a while?"

"Okay. If 150,000 gallons of water flow over Niagara Falls every second, and there are four quarts in a gallon ..."

"Isn't it time for you to check in with your social worker?"

"Are we going to have to take a detour to let Judah see Niagara Falls, Mallory?" Connor stood beside her at the mom-and-pop convenience store snack rack somewhere in Tennessee, waiting for Judah to exit the single-stall restroom.

"We can't deviate from the RoadRave agenda, can we? Besides, it's a long way from here. Have you seen any baked kale chips?"

"No. And I wasn't talking about now. I mean after this. After he goes home to Nathan. Should we somehow figure out a way to get him to Niagara Falls? He seems obsessed."

"First of all, according to your plan, 'we' won't be doing *anything* together after we're back in Chicago. Second, he's working you, Connor."

"Yeah. That's obvious."

"See any freeze-dried apples?"

"No."

"Young people like Judah will do anything to draw attention to themselves. Even negative attention is better than not being noticed. He's probably not done with the Niagara Falls bit."

"I figured." Connor reached for a Twinkie. Mallory pointed to the price. He put it back.

"But I like it that you wanted to give him a meaningful experience. Generous of you."

"I'm not wicked, you know."

She laid her palm on the side of his face and held it there.

"I know." A long pause. "You're not planning to shave at all the whole twenty-one days, are you?"

"Thought I'd take this opportunity to test my beard-growing skills."

She pressed her lips together and nodded her head. "Good thing we're done with the kissing façade." Her words were flat, but she didn't suppress a small smile.

"Wish we had more time to talk. Alone." He owed her an apology for his failure as a husband. Or at least a discussion about how to keep the divorce amicable. Separation? Come on. She had to know where that would end.

"Me too, Connor." Her smile ended in a quiver.

Can a man get a charley horse in his heart muscle? If so, he had one. His last muscle cramp in his leg was at the wedding rehearsal almost a year ago. They'd had to stop the "now kneel" part of the rehearsal until it passed. He wasn't about to tell Mallory he'd just had another one. "Kale chips." He handed her the find.

"Oh, thank you. *Ahk!* The price."

"Let me handle this." He took the hermetically sealed bag of green things through the maze of aisles to the checkout. "Are you the owner?"

The middle-aged gentleman behind the counter eyed Connor, eyebrows raised, mouth downturned. "Yessir."

One word.

"We're working with a real tight budget for meals for the next three weeks."

Connor watched the owner's hand slowly move toward the underside of the counter. Great. A "we're being robbed" button connected to the local police.

"So," Connor pressed on, "I'd like to see if there isn't a way I can work off the price of this bag of kale chips for my ... my wife. Do you need anything swept or shoveled or stocked? Can I ... ?" He gulped. Couldn't help it. "Can I clean the restrooms for you? In exchange for this bag of chips?"

"And these Cheetos?" Judah added, slapping a super-sized bag on the counter.

Mallory put a hand on his shoulder. "Connor, don't. I can live without—"

"We'll all help," Connor told the owner. "We don't mind working."

"Hey, I didn't volunteer," Judah said.

"You were drafted," Connor countered. "What do you say, sir? Can we work a barter?"

"That your camper out there?"

"Yes sir."

"Don't look like you're hurting none for money. It looks brand new."

Connor turned toward the window.

"That's our home for the next three weeks," Mallory said.

"The three of ya?"

"Yes sir."

"You got room for a couple of my grandkids?"

Mallory whispered, "I can live without kale chips, Connor. Let's go."

"I'm messin' with ya. More power to ya if y'all survive three weeks in that tuna can." His chuckle somehow reassured Connor. "Lemme see. What is it I need doin'?"

"And this can of sodee pop."

Judah had seen too many stereotyped movies. The boy needed to get out more.

The owner finally settled on their moving a stack of twenty-pound bags of ice from the back freezer to the one in front of the store. He leaned over the counter to say, "But I cain't jus' give ya that food. I have bills to pay, ya know."

"How about for your price? No markup?" Mallory appeared pleased with her compromise.

"Could work. That could work. Okay. All them bags of ice, and you can have what you got there on the counter for my cost."

Mallory said, "Connor, quick. Pick something out for yourself."

"You heard the woman," the owner said.

Connor smiled. He almost said "Her name isn't The Woman" but thought better of it.

While the three worked on hauling countless bags of ice from the rear of the store, they kept an eye on the owner. He didn't reach for the panic button, but he did make a phone call. Connor expected red-and-blue flashing lights to pull up to the building before they were done hauling.

But they finished without incident. The only other vehicle that drove in was a dusty blue pickup with white bumpers. Off-white. The woman who exited—dressed in patterned leggings and a stretched-out sweatshirt—carried a paper bag into the store and set it on the counter just as the traveling trio got ready to shell out a few dollars to cover their non-labor-related expenses.

"Thank you, Maybelle. Knew I could count on you," the owner said to the woman. "Folks, this is the finest cook in the county. I think y'all 'll like what she done for ya."

Mallory peeked into the bag. "Fried chicken?"

"Her speci-AL-i-ty."

That must have been the owner's phone call. Connor breathed a second sigh of relief. "How did you make fried chicken in the time it took us to—?"

"Oh, her's always got somethin' on the stove. Yer lucky it weren't her cabbage rolls. Nasty stuff."

"George! These people don't know you're joshin'. But you can count on my remembrin' your distaste for cabbage rolls next time I make 'em. Cute little storage trailer you folks got out there."

"It's our … home," Mallory said. "Temporarily."

"Oh," the woman crooned. "We all got our troubles from time to time."

In his peripheral vision, Connor saw Judah step closer.

The rascal filmed it all. He'd have to thank him later. And get the couple to sign releases if the footage were to appear online. "We best be getting on," Connor said.

Mallory threw him a look. He hadn't meant to slip into a southern drawl. He apologized with his shoulders.

"Best had," the owner said.

"We can't thank you enough for your kindness, sir. And ma'am," Connor tipped his hat to them both.

Mallory told them the condensed version of the RoadRave story. They were happy to sign the release forms, already discussing how they'd tell their grandchildren about their day's adventure with the people "from TV." Connor gave them the hashtag and link information for the video site.

"Well, we can get one of the youngins to help us figure that out. They all got yer technology. Have a blessed journey."

Not a safe journey. Or a good one. Not, "Good luck." *Have a* blessed *journey*. What did that even look like?

chapter fourteen

I T WON'T ALWAYS TURN OUT like that, will it."

Judah's statement tugged at Mallory's heart. "You mean, the older couple's kindness? George and Maybelle?"

"Yes. People aren't always kind. Or generous. They don't always care."

True. Judah must have seen more than his share of the harsher sides of life. "Hard things happen. And good things happen. We made a memory back there. For them and for us. We choose to celebrate the good so we can tolerate the bad, Judah."

She caught Connor's stone-like expression in the mirror. Was any of this registering with him? He turned to stare out the side window. Time for her to start thinking about herself. What was right for her? What did she need? What did she deserve? Want?

Connor. She wanted Connor and the life they'd created in their dreams.

"My mom said she cared." Judah stared out the front-seat version of Connor's view.

"I'm sure she did, Judah. Does." Mallory's senses alerted. With her attention on the highway ahead of them, she couldn't read him as well as she wanted to.

"But she chose *him*."

"Who?" How far did she dare venture into this conversation?

"Her boyfriend. The wife beater. Kid beater."

Mallory had heard similar stories at the center. Nothing shocked her anymore. "She's still with him?"

"Yes. That's why I can't be with her. The judge said so. Said she had to choose—him or me."

"And she chose him?"

"Who does that? Who chooses a creep like that over your own kid?"

"It's a hard thing to explain, Judah. I can't imagine ..." Mallory turned her head to catch Connor's reaction and enlist his help. He hadn't moved from leaning on the arm rest, watching the scenery flash by.

"Maybe she didn't think she deserved you," Connor said.

Connor, are you still talking about Judah?

"She doesn't have to deserve me," Judah said. "Just *choose* me."

Exactly. Mallory blinked hard. She needed clear vision to see through the relentless rain. "There's a lot of wisdom in what you said, Judah."

"Wisdom? Well, I didn't get it from her."

"What *did* you get from your mom?" *Diversionary Tactic #27.*

"Nothing."

"Do you have her eyes?"

"Not anymore."

"Huh?"

"Hers are always black and blue. Mine used to be."

Moving on to Diversionary Tactic #27b. "Do you have her determination?"

"I guess. But she's determined about the wrong things.

Like him. Her 'bae.'" The last word came out as a snarl.

"Her what?" Connor angled forward far enough that Mallory could catch his profile with her side vision.

"Bae."

"Connor, it means 'baby.'" Mallory should have kept her mouth shut. That sounded condescending at worst and pathetic at best.

"I know what it means. I hadn't heard it from the mouth of an eleven-year-old before."

"It's not a dirty word," Judah said.

"I hope it's a fad that doesn't stick around long."

Judah turned to face him. "It's like 'brah'—short for 'brother.' Or, short for 'bro,' like, 'Brah, that's a fire jacket.'"

"*On* fire? Did you mean fine rather than fire?"

"No. Just fire. Don't you guys know anything?"

Mallory had to say something now. "Keep it respectful, Judah."

"What she said," Connor added. Then laughed. "First, texting makes us lose our vowels. Then punctuation and capitalization. Now we have to abbreviate abbreviations?"

Connor's grammar concerns lightened the moment. Mallory suspected conversations might turn darker again before the trip was over.

"In the nick of time," Connor said. "Incoming instructions."

"Where are we?" Judah sat straighter.

"Putnam County, Tennessee, according to the Welcome to Putnam County sign. Hey, the rain's letting up." Mallory turned the windshield wipers to their slowest setting.

"Are we stopping soon? I'm hungry bordering on hangry," Judah said.

Mallory wondered how many odd jobs they'd have to work to keep a growing boy fed. And wondered when she had turned into her grandmother, worried about "keeping a growing boy fed."

"Have another piece of chicken," Connor said. "And pass

one back to me while you're at it. Please," he emphasized. "Oh, wait. More incoming. I'll have some guidance for you in a minute, Mallory."

I so wish you would.

———————◆———————

"Not a place to camp for the night?" Mallory asked.

Connor reread the latest message and checked the sign at the entrance to Burgess Park. "Day use only, it looks like."

"How long will we have to stay, then?" Judah said.

"That's not complaining I hear, is it?" Connor gave Judah's shoulder a playful nudge.

"Me? Why, sir, thou offendeth me."

"Somewhere in the back of this vehicle is a plastic bag with a pair of socks that are clear evidence thou knoweth how to offend, Judah."

"Not anymore," he said, lifting a tennis-shoed foot to nose height.

"You didn't."

"Well, you told me I had to change my socks *every* day. These are the only other ones I had for this morning."

"I hate to interrupt this fascinating conversation," Mallory said, "but could somebody give me some direction? There's a car behind us."

"Straight ahead," Connor said. "I guess we're looking for another trailhead.

"Again with the walking?" Judah said.

"I'll ignore that, young man. We are here to prove the wonders of what America's back roads hold."

"And who," Mallory added.

"What?"

"*Who* the back roads hold. Like that guy. She pointed through the windshield at a thin old man whose backpack— small as it was—seemed to curve his spine forward.

"Does that look like a good place to park?" Connor asked.

"Well, he's gesturing to us like he's helping dock a plane at the jet bridge, a flashlight in each hand. I'd say yes."

"He can't be a park ranger, can he? Don't they have age limits? This guy must be ninety." Connor's protective nature kicked in more often than it had for a while. For almost a year. He eyed the gentleman and volunteered to be the first to approach him.

"Good afternoon," Connor said, attempting to take in all the information he needed on the old man in order to make a judgment about his character without being discovered. One thing for sure—Connor could take him down without straining himself.

"Just like every day," the man said. "Curious little setup you have there."

"Every heard of the RoadRave company?"

"Nope."

"Well, we aim to change that. This is their latest camper-in-a-box microcamper. Just add humans and the adventure begins."

The older gentleman tilted his head to peer into the vehicle. "You and your wife just have the one boy? So far?"

"That's a boy we're helping foster parent at the moment."

"Well, good for you."

The two men shook hands. Connor noted strength he hadn't expected. "Do you work here, sir?"

"Slade. Name's Henry Slade, but everybody just uses Slade. It's been a moon or two since anyone asked me if I was old enough to retire. Which I did, twenty-five years ago. Before that, I worked here, yes. Nowadays, I mostly use it as my man cave."

"Excuse me?"

"You heard of a man cave?"

"Yes."

"What's a person do there?"

"Be a guy." He glanced at Mallory, still behind the wheel.

"Escape from the wife." *Only her name isn't The Wife, and escaping from her is losing its appeal.*

"Bingo. My wife has her book club today, so I took advantage of the opportunity to come get refueled."

"Oh, good. There's a gas pump here in the park? Great. We need to find—"

"Not my gas tank. Here." He tapped his chest. "And here." A gnarled hand tapped his temple.

"Would you mind saying that again for our cameras?" Connor explained their mission in sound bites.

Five minutes later, Connor had some of the best footage of the trip so far. And a volunteer guide through Burgess Park.

Slade was in his element. He'd lived in the area so long, walked the trails so often, and talked to so many tourists, geologists, naturalists, and other park rangers that he knew to point out details their cameras would have missed if it weren't for his expertise.

"You passed the Butterfly Garden on your way in. A little too late in the season for much happening there. Y'all come back in June sometime for the Butterfly Garden Celebration. Quite a thing. Too many people for my taste, but it's educational. We can stop in later, though, to see the wildflower display."

"How exciting," Judah said. "Wildflowers. *Ooh.*"

Connor nudged him.

Slade looked Judah over. "Young man, are you up for a climb? The service road is a moderate hike. The scenic route is downright strenuous."

Connor wondered if the ninety-year-old labeled it strenuous or the park brochure gave it that designation. "Judah's stronger than he looks. You choose, Slade. We'll be fine either way."

Slade's eyebrows wiggled. "Try to keep up," he said.

◆————————————————◆

Strenuous. Fitting description. In all, they saw four waterfalls along the Falling Water River, the last one the most spectacular.

Its cascade fell like a broad bridal veil into a gorge carved in the rock. The overlook was accessible, but the rustic staircase to the base of the falls was closed.

It proved no disappointment, though. Even Judah stood with his mouth gaping, taking it all in.

"We can use the service road trail on the way back. Still steep, but it'll be faster and give us a chance to cool off a little," Slade said. "A couple more weeks and these trees'll be turning. Changes the light on the trail. Kind of feel sorry for those who only see things like this in one season. Every season has its own beauty."

"We're from Chicago," Mallory said. "The white season— winter—is beautiful in its own way. But the cold grows old not long after Christmas, even for those of us who like outdoor activities."

"I was in Chicago a few years ago in winter," Slade said. "Visiting my wife's people. Turned out to be the middle of a blizzard that about shut the city down. People had to leave their cars stuck in the snow drifts on Lake Shore Drive. Had to stay three days longer than I wanted to so I could get a flight home."

"An all-too-common scene." Mallory shivered as if reliving it.

"I remember," Slade said, "looking out of my hotel room window and thinking it was as pretty as meringue."

Connor was about to ask if Slade's wife shared his opinion, but Judah stubbed his toe and face-planted in front of them.

"You okay, buddy?"

"Take your hands off me." Judah jumped to his feet and brushed at his knees.

Mallory crouched in front of him. "Lift up your pant leg, Judah. Let me see if you skinned your knees bad enough for a bandage."

"I'm fine. Get away."

"Judah." Connor handed the boy his Troyer & Duncan cap. It had cartwheeled several feet when Judah fell. "Let her take a look at your knees. Or the scrapes on the heels of your hands. Man, that's a righteous road rash."

Judah slammed the cap onto his head. "I said I was fine. Let's go. I'm hungry."

"Hungry." Connor turned toward Slade. "Happens a lot around here."

"Gotcha."

When Judah was well down the path in front of them, Slade said, "Some kids are tough because they have to be. Refuse help, no matter how kind the person offering it. Won't even let themselves feel a little tenderness from someone who cares."

Connor glanced at Mallory, whose head tilted his direction as if to say, "Are you listening, Connor?"

chapter fifteen

THE QUESTION OF WHERE THEY would set up camp hadn't been a topic of conversation until the sun drooped low in the sky and their shadows looked as if they were walking on stilts.

"Connor, it's getting late. Shouldn't we find a campground for the night?" Mallory kept her voice soft but apparently not soft enough. Slade stepped into their circle of conversation.

"You need a place to park it? Y'all can use my property. Plenty of room in the backyard."

"Thanks. That sounds ideal," Connor said.

Mallory tossed her husband a look she hoped conveyed, "Shouldn't we talk about this first?" An old man's backyard could be piled high with rusted trucks and bent lawn furniture. And pet snakes. They knew little about Slade other than that he was the most athletic ninety-year-old they'd met and that he had a dozen Google pages of knowledge stored under his faded hat.

Mallory interpreted Connor's expression to mean, "What could go wrong?"

.

"What do you think, Judah?" Connor put an arm around Judah, who quickly shrugged it off and said, "Lead the way, Mr. Slade."

Moments later they were piled into the Outback, following Slade's grass-green pickup on roads that wound through a forested area that looked like a perfect spot for whatever beasts haunt Tennessee hills. Cougar? Wild boar? From the tall grasses in the ditch along the road, a deer shot between the two vehicles. Connor braked hard to avoid it. Two smaller deer followed the first.

"You guys okay?"

Judah nodded. Mallory unclenched her grip on the back of the passenger seat and drew an intentionally deep breath. "We're okay. You're sure we should be following a stranger to his house, Connor?"

"No turning back now." He pulled their rig onto a lane behind Slade. It wound through more woods, the elevation growing steeper. Eventually, the green truck swung onto a circle drive in front of a rustic cabin with a pale glow in the small front window. A log cabin with wide gray-white chinking. Roof that sloped low over the full-width porch. Two bent willow rockers from several eras ago sat side by side on the porch. Little else adorned the simple structure.

A dog the size of a small horse lay across the threshold but galloped into action when the caravan drew closer.

"See what I mean, Connor?" she whispered. "It's a scene from a movie. And I don't mean one fit for Hallmark, either."

Slade jumped out of his truck, scratched the dog's neck and ears, and motioned for Connor to pull in on the right side of the cabin onto a dirt pad. The old man waved his arm like a flight attendant steering passengers off a smoking plane. When Slade finally closed his fist to indicate they should stop, Mallory forced herself to relax and surveyed their surroundings. "Ran visual reconnaissance" sounded a little heavy.

The backside of the "cabin" stood two-stories tall, all

windowed. The camper stood on a level pad on an open lawn that eventually sloped toward a pond the size of a football field, surrounded on three sides by forest not unlike what they'd just hiked through. A platform—dock—on the near edge of the pond gave the only indication of human intervention on the serene scene. Correction. Two rickety folding chairs seemed a permanent fixture on the dock. A faded red canoe and a small daffodil-yellow kayak leaned against the base of trees near the dock.

"This is your little bit of heaven?" Connor said as he exited the car.

"Pret' near." Slade and his equine canine faced the pond, silent for a long beat. Finally, Slade turned toward his guests and asked, "You interested in fish for supper?"

"You have fish in that pond?" Connor's excitement could have had its genesis in a reclaimed childhood memory, his endless appetite for adventure, his advertising footage mindset, or his endless appetite for fish. Connor rarely ordered a hamburger at a hamburger joint. He always opted for the fish sandwich. Fish tacos. Midwestern fish fry. Mallory hadn't minded. Did he know that? Had she told him?

Slade nodded. "I keep it stocked with bass mostly. Pan fish too. The coppernose and hand-painted bluegills grow considerably larger here than where yer from. Taste good too. There's something about pulling dinner out of yer own pond that feeds more than yer stomach."

Mallory's mouth watered. Her grandfather's fishing excursions often graced their family with a water-to-table meal of fish when he was still alive. Slade didn't resemble her grandfather in any way except for hospitality. "We need to get the camper set up before it gets any darker, though."

"Right about now's the best time for guaranteeing a catch," Slade said.

Connor waved her counsel away. "Minutes. It only takes minutes to go from roadworthy to home," he said, his gaze darting to the camera Judah rarely let out of his sight. "We can manage setup with the residual light from the cabin windows," he added. "I vote fishing first."

"Me too," Judah said, turning the camera for a video selfie. "I never pass up a chance to stick a barbed hook into a defenseless worm or leech."

Editing. Almost everything Judah says needs editing.

Almost everything I've said in the past year could have used some editing.

Was that it? Was that the root of Connor's dissatisfaction with her? That she hadn't edited herself during their conversations? Or that he hadn't? Maybe authenticity had a downside. Maybe filters weren't always flattering or the kindest approach. Should she have kept pressing when he stood firm on the subject of genetic testing? Had she been inauthentic in not putting her foot down when Connor first started talking about separation? Should she have edited her pain, leaving *in* the disappointment and editing *out* her well-practiced defensiveness?

The three men—one very old, one very young, and the one she called hers for at least a little longer—plus a galloping dog named Dawg were steps ahead of her on the way to the pond's edge.

"Wait for me," she called. *Please. Connor, wait for me to figure out how marriage is supposed to work, how I can convince you to let me stand beside you, no matter what. Will you please wait?*

Connor turned to face her. "You're going to fish too?"

"Out-fish, Connor. I intend to *out*-fish the three of you put together."

He chuckled at that. Could have been doubt. Could have been amusement. He wasn't the kind of person to mock her. No. That couldn't be it.

◆━━━━━━━━━━━━◆

Connor watched Slade work on creating what Slade called a *sweet* bed of coals in the fire pit. Mallory, who had out-fished them three-to-one, worked under LED light in the camper's kitchen, pulling together something to accompany their fish dinner and swatting at bugs that gravitated to the light over her head.

"Will your wife be home soon, Slade? I can't wait to meet her."

"She's already home."

Connor turned toward the cabin. "She's been inside all this time?" Why hadn't Slade invited her to join them? If she were as old as Slade, that might explain it. She might be bedridden, or in a wheelchair. But if so, why had Slade ignored his wife's needs? That's not what husbands do.

Not what husbands do.

"I'd like to go in and introduce myself to her, Slade. Do you mind?"

Judah squirmed and shook his head. The kid was shy about meeting people? It hadn't stopped him before.

"Come on, Judah. While we're waiting for the coals to be ready for the fish, let's go meet Slade's wife. I never heard her name."

Judah squirmed more vigorously. "Arlene."

"You've seen her? When?"

"When I went in to use the bathroom."

"Why didn't you say something? We would have all liked to say hello."

Judah mouthed something Connor couldn't hear.

"Well," Connor said, "I wouldn't mind washing this fish smell off my hands, and Mallory's tying up the camper sink right now." *There's a better way to say that, Connor.*

Slade stood from his crouched position. "Yer welcome to use the indoor facilities," he said. "You know what gets fish smell off your hands quicker than quick?"

"What?"

Judah sniffed his hands too.

"Dandruff shampoo. Don't ask me how or why. It just does. And don't ask me why a bald man would need dandruff shampoo." He lifted his hat to prove his point. "I keep it around for the fish odor."

"Judah, how about you and me go in and clean up a bit? And meet the woman Mr. Slade married."

Judah shrugged his shoulders and fell in step behind Connor. When out of range, Judah whispered, "You do know she's dead. Right?"

"Dead?"

"I'd say deader than dead."

"You're creeping me out, Judah."

He opened the screen door for Connor. "Creeped me out too."

"She had her book club earlier today. This isn't making sense."

"Yeah, that's what the old guy said. Or … did he?" Judah's voice and facial expressions grew horror movie dramatic. Connor could almost hear the first notes of the soundtrack.

Judah crossed the main room on the lower level—an outdated but comfortable-looking family room with a stone fireplace on one end. When he reached the fireplace, he pointed to the mantel as if demonstrating the features of a new car. "Say hello to Arlene Slade."

A cookie jar? In the family room?

Judah leaned conspiratorially close. "It's full of her ashes."

Connor took an involuntary step back. "How do you know?"

"I looked inside. Ashes all right."

"Maybe Slade dumps his fireplace ashes in there when he cleans it out."

Judah planted his hands on his hips. "Who names their fireplace ashes *Arlene?*" He pointed to the label on the front of the pottery cookie jar.

"She's dead, then?"

"If not, she's lost a whole lot of weight. And talk about dehydrated …"

"Judah! Show a little respect." What had Connor gotten

them into? They were spending the night on the property of a man who talked as if his deceased wife were alive and off partying while he conducted impromptu tours of Burgess Falls. Should have spent more time thinking about protecting himself—well, and Mallory and Judah. If this went south … They were in the south. If this went sour, the three of them could be in a mess of trouble.

"Coals are ready," Slade said, only his head poking through the barely open screen door.

"We'll be right out," Connor said, taking Judah's shoulders and steering him toward the half-bath on that level.

"I know the way," Judah said, shrugging out from under Connor's grip.

"But I don't," he whispered.

"Shampoo's under the sink, in the vanity cupboard," Slade said as the screen door bounced shut behind him.

When they'd reached the bathroom, Judah said, "You want me to check under the sink for you, Mr. Superhero?"

"Would you? I mean, no. I'll do it." Connor opened the door. Extra toilet paper rolls. Cleaning tools. And a blue bottle of high quality dandruff shampoo.

After they'd both washed up, they returned to the fire. No words passed between them. But they smelled better. Unlike Arlene.

chapter sixteen

CHARCOAL GRILLED FISH, HASH BROWNS from a pouch, and canned peaches. Good enough. Mallory would have liked to add a big salad to the meal, but their food allotment had been used up when they'd stopped for mid-morning snacks and a carton of a half dozen eggs. The snack habit didn't help.

But the meal shared around a campfire now smoky enough to ward off most of the smaller bugs was unlike any she'd had in a long time. It felt like family.

Judah—his lawn chair pulled away from the circle—slapped at his thigh. "Score? Judah, five. Mosquitos, zero." He slapped again. "Make that six."

"Come closer to the fire, young man," Slade said. "It's hot, but it'll keep 'em off'n you."

"Ouch! Six to one. Don't like my odds." The boy held his plate aloft and dragged his chair closer.

The reflection of the fire in Connor's eyes mesmerized Mallory. He stared, unblinking.

What are you thinking, Connor? Is it about us? Not likely. That was her obsession alone.

"I should have been filming," Connor said. "Should have captured this meal from the first spark to get the fire going. Imagine that, not only video-blogged, but in the archives to return to on—" He seemed to search for the word he wanted.

You won't find it written on my face, Connor. Look elsewhere.

"On days when there's no flame. No warm fire to ward off the night chill. No protection from the things that go *bzzzzt!* in the night."

"Judah, seven. Bzzzts, three. Wish I had a BB gun."

Mallory pulled travel-sized hand sanitizer from her pocket. "Try this. And try wearing long sleeves."

Judah accepted her offer. "These Tennessee mosquitoes will not be stopped by a mere layer of fabric. Oh, no. They're genetically altered to make me salty." Judah paused. "For you older folks, that means cranky."

Slade rubbed his knees. "Yer welcome to stay another day." His voice said it matter-of-factly, but his face seemed at war with itself—the offhanded army fighting an army of hope muscles.

Connor stiffened. What was that all about?

"I'd love an opportunity to see the sun rise over the pond," Mallory said.

"Well, that you will," Slade said. "The best way is from the middle of the pond. Sitting there in my kayak or canoe, waiting for the light. When it does come, it spills over the water like molten gold. A person could drown in that light if he weren't careful." Slade clasped his gnarled hands in his lap and stared at them.

"How long ago did Arlene die, Slade?"

She's not just late getting home? She's gone? Connor, what are you talking about?

"She was sixty-seven. I was sixty-two. She never let me forget she was older and wiser than me."

He's been alone in the world for thirty years? "You never remarried?"

"No need. Not that other people didn't think I had a need.

132

Just about everybody I know had an idea for me. One old guy at church still considers it his responsibility to find me someone. I had someone. Everything Arlene gave me while she was alive—before the cancer—is still here. I have her company and her counsel and more memories than the average person. I pour her a cup a coffee every morning."

He glanced around the circle. "I have to drink hers too, because of, you know, her being dead. But I can't stop thinking about her. If I ask her a question, I just wait a bit and what do you know? She says something. Not in real words, I suppose. An impression." He tapped his chest. "Her answer always sounds like something God would say to me." Slade smiled. "But Arlene could melt a padlock with her glare, if she wanted to."

Mallory pictured what that must have looked like when this sweet man and his wife faced off. She'd been gone thirty years, and he still felt her presence as real as he did the people he was with. In some marriages, death do us *not* part.

That's the kind she wanted.

Connor had relaxed from his stiffened position. "It's a beautiful thing, Slade. That you've kept her near all these years."

"A person could get crazy lonely way out here."

"Good thing you have her ashes, huh?" Judah said.

"Judah!" Connor and Mallory voiced the same warning.

"Her ashes? She's buried in the sentimentary next to the church. In town."

Connor leaned forward. "The cemetery?"

"Some folks call it that."

Judah stood. "Well then, whose ashes are those on the mantel? In the Arlene cookie jar?"

Slade's face erupted in firelit joy. "Son, Arlene was as predictable as they come. In all our years together, she never baked a batch of cookies without burning at least one whole panful."

"Those are cookie ashes?" Judah's head jutted forward like a turtle looking for daylight.

Slade's laughter carried far across the pond. "A year to the day she drew her last breath, I had me a little ceremony. Burned her cookbooks. Gathered up those ashes. Seemed fitting to me."

Mallory wrapped her light jacket tighter around her. *To be cherished in spite of my faults. What must that feel like?*

To be cherished despite my faults. I wonder what that feels like.

Connor used a long stick to poke at the fire. "I'm sorry you had to lose her, Slade."

"Didn't lose her. I know exactly where she is."

"I mean—" Connor swallowed. How do you comfort a man who's lived without his wife for so long?

Slade stroked Dawg's fur with a weathered hand. "I know what you meant. It's odd we talk about losing someone we love like I accidentally misplaced her. 'There we were at the mall and two seconds later, she'd wandered off.' Arlene didn't wander anywhere. She walked as deliberately as she could, even on her weakest days, toward Jesus. I didn't lose her. Eventually, I gave her away, from my hand to His, as certain as her father gave her to me on our wedding day."

Only the crackling and spitting of the fire interrupted the silence. Even Judah paid attention.

"I can still see her walking down the aisle toward me in her satin wedding dress, her small hand tucked into the crook of her papa's arm. When they got to the front of the church where I waited for her, her father took her hand and laid it in mine. Then he stepped back so Arlene and me could be one. That's about how it went when I knew Arlene was close to breathing her last. It's like I could hear a Voice saying, 'Who giveth this woman to be married to this Man?' And I said, 'I do.' We shared her, Jesus and me, when she lived here. I had to step back so they could be one."

Connor blinked. It didn't help. He wished he were the kind

134

of guy to carry a handkerchief. He could have used it about now. Instead, he used his shirt sleeve to swipe at his eyes.

So much for keeping his emotions hidden. Mallory stared right at him, her eyes so dark and beautiful and glossy in the firelight that he had to fight off the urge to wrap his arms around her. She twirled the wedding ring on her delicate hand. How could he get her to see it was no one's fault they couldn't stay married? No ROI. No return on investment. For her. In addition to the medical implications, their paths hadn't melded into one. They clashed. What he wanted vs. what she wanted.

Did he even know?

He would always care about her. But right now, all he could picture was peeling her hand from the crook of his arm and letting her go into an unknown, empty, oxygen-depleted void. The inside of his elbow felt suddenly brittle. Liquid-nitrogen cold. But at least she wouldn't be saddled to a dying man.

Slade poured a cup of coffee for his wife every day. Even now. Connor made one for Mallory almost every morning. But they drank them separately, caught in their own thoughts, lost in their disjointed passions.

They talked. Sure. Schedules. Which one of them needed the Outback. Did their workdays coincide so one could drop the other off? Was it time to upgrade their phone contract? Eat in or eat out? Not the same as Slade sharing his morning coffee with a wife who'd been gone three decades but the love hadn't faded.

And Connor and Mallory hadn't managed to figure out how to make their love last twelve whole months.

The fire sizzled. And again. Rain.

Slade stood first—the one with the oldest bones the first to react. "Time to head for cover."

His last word hadn't ended before the skies opened, the faucet cranked all the way open. A crack of lightning zigzagged across the sky.

"Grab what you need," Slade said. "You can stay inside tonight."

Connor and Mallory didn't confer, but in moments they'd dismantled and secured the camper's kitchen, grabbed theirs and Judah's duffel bags, and dashed into the lower level of Slade's cabin.

Drenched, they stood on the rug, shook themselves off, and deposited their shoes.

"This'll let up soon, won't it, Slade?" Connor brushed rain from his sleeves.

"No telling."

"Do you have the Weather Channel?" Mallory asked.

"I have the weather. Don't need a channel."

"What if there's a tornado brewing?" Connor pictured the camper being tossed like a marble in the hands of a serious storm.

"Not likely, this time of year. Besides, I'd know."

"How?" Judah asked, shivering.

"I keep my eye on the sky."

Connor dug for his phone. No weather alerts. A simple downpour. He could volunteer to stay in the teardrop to prove its storm integrity. Or … He glanced at the two worn but clean sofas and the loveseat that formed a U-shaped conversation group around the fireplace. Might not hurt to spend a night indoors.

Dawg smelled like wet dog. Slade shooed him upstairs. "You can make yerselves to home down here. Plenty of blankets in the chest over there for when the greatgrands stay with me."

He and Arlene had children. And grandchildren. And greatgrandchildren. Why hadn't Connor asked about his family earlier?

"You can make yerselves tea or coffee"—he eyed Judah—"or hot cocoa, if you want. Fixings are in the wet bar. That woman."

Mallory pressed her hand to her heart. "Who, me?"

Slade shook his head, water droplets flying. "Arlene. She called it a wet bar, even though the only thing we ever served from it was tea and coffee. She insisted both of them were wet. I suppose she had a point."

The cookie jar no longer a threat to Connor's sense of safety, he looked to his traveling companions for confirmation. "Bunk down in here tonight?"

They both nodded.

"Okay, then. Thank you, Slade. We appreciate it."

"Want me to wake you in time for dawn, Mallory?" Slade stood with one hand on the bannister.

She is not going to want to skip sleep to—

"Please. Yes. You too, Judah?"

"Not even if God Himself asked me to."

Mallory turned toward Connor. She opened her mouth, then closed it and returned her attention to Slade. "I'm looking forward to it."

"Goodnight, then."

The three took turns in the tiny half bath, changing from their rain-soaked clothes to dry. Judah chose the loveseat. That left the sofas on either side of the loveseat for the loveless.

Connor heard the rain turn noisier. "Please, God, no hail."

Did God listen to the prayers of people who paid Him little attention when the sun shone?

"Connor?" Mallory's voice carried across the expanse between them, a braided rug wide.

"Yes?"

"I'm happy we came here."

"Me too." The rain was letting up. Nice. Somebody listened.

"Me three." Judah had said nothing for the last hour. Connor assumed he'd fallen asleep, his almost-teen feet sticking over the end of the loveseat, Mallory's hiking socks sacrificed to the Judah-foot-odor cause.

"Who knows where the road will take us next?" Mallory said, her voice thick with an emotion Connor couldn't define. A mashup of anticipation and sorrow and excitement and regret.

The regret, Connor recognized.

chapter seventeen

DAWN. YAWN.

Practically the same words. For good reason. Working with at-risk youth meant Mallory often served late into the night but rarely had to be on duty and alert before dawn.

But she was awake, if not alert, before she heard their ninety-year-old host sneak down the stairs in his stockinged feet. She sat up and waved to signal that she was already conscious. A tiny woodland-themed nightlight offered enough illumination for her to see Slade nod and point toward the half bath. She nodded back, tiptoed to take care of necessities, then met Slade at the door.

Judah needed his adenoids checked out. His snoring outmatched Connor's. If they'd synchronized their purring, Mallory might have been able to sleep more than a couple of interrupted hours. She stepped into her hiking shoes and grabbed her jacket, then followed Slade through the narrowest opening the two could manage. Mallory peered back into the cabin. Neither of her traveling companions had moved.

A lean-to storage shed held a variety of life jackets, many

small enough for a toddler. By flashlight, Slade chose his favorite—obvious by its signs of wear—and one for her. He then grabbed two canoe paddles before making his way toward the water.

Slick with last night's rain, the path demanded Mallory's attention. Slade maneuvered the path as if born to it. He handed her the canoe paddles. She stood back as the old man single-handedly picked up the canoe, shouldered it, and walked it toward the dock.

"I don't usually bring a flashlight," Slade said. "There's something heroic about finding your way in the dark, isn't there? The reward? Dawn."

"How long did it take you to find your way in the dark the first time, Slade?"

"You mean, in life? Or the walk to the pond?"

How did he know what she was thinking? "Both."

"Sounds like a conversation for the waiting room. Out there. On the water. While we're waiting for the light."

She followed the sound of his voice and the small circle of light from the flashlight she'd volunteered to carry for him.

"You can turn that thing off now," Slade said.

"But—"

"Trust me."

She slid the switch to the off position. Was it possible the darkness had grown thinner in the time it took them to reach the dock? Or were her eyes adjusting better?

When she and Connor bought paint for the ebony—once a blah blonde—coffee table in their apartment, they had argued over the intensity of color they needed. The patient paint mixologist at the home improvement store adjusted the base color—a little more black tint, no a little more brown—pounded the lid onto the quart can, clamped it into the shaker machine, pried open the lid, spread a fingertip of the new color on an absorbent piece of cardstock, dried it with a heat gun, then waited.

"Mallory, I think it needs a little more brown, don't you?"

"It's practically chestnut now. We want ebony. Like an antique piano's worn black keys. Not quite black." She'd known her mind and said it.

The mixologist tried another few drops of tint. And repeated the whole routine. Shake. Pry. Sample. Disappoint.

Eventually, Mallory had walked away, feigning a fascination with angled paint brushes and stir sticks. Connor found her at the display.

"Mallory, come on. If we can't agree on this …"

"Since when have you cared that much about home décor?"

"I've always cared."

"You didn't say anything when I changed the pillows on the couch."

"Those nubby things? The ones that leave pockmarks on my face? I may not have said it aloud, but …"

"Connor, if you didn't like them, why didn't you say so?"

"If I told you everything I didn't like, it would—" He'd slammed his mouth shut tight.

She hadn't invited him to finish that sentence. They'd returned to the paint counter. Mallory had asked for one more drop of the black tint, then pronounced it perfect.

Around her now, the night-almost-morning sky lightened a single drop of tint at a time. She could see more than a moment ago. More than a year ago.

Slade climbed into the canoe first then stabilized the vessel and offered her a hand when she got in. The life jacket provided a layer of warmth Mallory didn't mind, but she could already feel the humidity that would likely be full-blown in a few hours.

It didn't take long for the two to synchronize their paddle strokes. From her position in the front of the canoe—the bow—Mallory could see almost nothing but heard when Slade switched his paddle to the opposite side.

"Far enough," he said.

She stopped paddling and rested the paddle across her lap. "Do we put down an anchor or something?"

"Won't hurt anything if we drift off center a little. When it gets lighter, we can adjust if need be. It's a pond, not an ocean. Don't worry about getting lost."

But she was. Adrift on an ocean of unmet expectations with riptides of disappointment. *I wanted him to fight for us, to dig in his heels and defend our marriage. Protect it.* Instead, Connor wanted to surf on the riptides. Not that people surf on riptides. She couldn't think. Nothing made sense. And now she sat in the dark in the middle of unfamiliar waters with an old man who might or might not have lost more marbles than he could afford to.

"Are we going to talk?" she said.

"Not much."

"I thought you said we'd have a conversation out here, in the 'waiting room.'"

"Sometimes words muddy up a conversation about life."

She couldn't argue with that.

"Breathe," Slade said.

"What?"

"You're not breathing. I can tell."

She obeyed.

"If you time it right," he said, "the sky will get noticeably lighter on every exhale."

"Seriously?"

"Might be a mental thing. I choose to believe it. Try."

She focused on her breathing. Long, slow breaths. He'd tricked her. He must have timed his sage advice to coincide with the sun's beyond-the-horizon influence. It hadn't breached the tree line, but dawn couldn't be far away now. The sky seemed lighter than she'd imagined it could be without the sun in sight.

As if Slade were instructing her rather than sitting in silence, Mallory took mental notes. She may have missed hints of light in what she thought was an all-dark emptiness. Did God intend to answer her prayer and give her husband back to her, or answer her prayer and make her strong enough to find joy in singleness? Did she have the faith to believe life could be good—eventually—either way, that dawns would come and go whether she received the answer she wanted or not?

Was she naïve in thinking her love would make a difference if Connor's worst fears were realized? Maybe she *would* cave, would fall apart. How old had Connor's mom been when his dad started to show signs of VHL? Connor had been so reluctant to visit them. He'd grown more distant from Mallory after each encounter, overcome with what could become his reality. She wasn't stupid. It would be awful to watch Connor's body fail him. She'd hate every minute of his pain, dread every surgery, ache and writhe and cry out when he did.

But she was willing to be there. Because that's what love does.

The sun didn't decide to dawn if the day promised to be decent. It came no matter what. It stayed. Even if clouds tried to mask its presence. It made the journey across the sky because that was the job God assigned it.

Somehow, she had to find a way to make Connor see that—

She wouldn't make him see anything. Couldn't. Had tried. And over-tried. She could no more change the course of his mind than she could ask the sun to move a little to the left. But she knew One who could.

At the far edge of the pond, a reflection of the fading night grew pale, then bleached blue, then tangerine. The color skated on the surface of the water until it surrounded them. Neither spoke.

The canoe floated parallel to dawn's stage. Both had a front-row seat. Mallory angled her body, careful not to literally rock the boat. Slade slid his paddle into the bottom of the canoe and raised his arms as if preparing to catch the enormous ball of molten solar gases when it peeked through the trees. He flattened his palms.

"Isn't it glorious?" he said. "Close your eyes."

"I thought we were here to watch the dawn."

"We're here to *feel* it."

She closed her eyes. And she did feel it. The subtle change in the air, the temperature, the light beyond her eyelids. The slowing of her heart rate, each beat waiting a split second longer before pulsing again.

The canoe rocked underneath her, followed by a splash.

Slade was in the water. His life jacket, shoes, and shirt lay in the bottom of the canoe on top of his paddle.

"What are you doing?" Mallory started paddling toward him.

"I felt the dawn. Now I'm going home."

Not what she needed—a suicidal widower who not only intended to end his life but leave her stranded in the middle of his watery grave. "Slade. No!"

"See you at breakfast," he said, his swim stroke surprisingly even and strong for a man his age.

He intended to *swim* back? "What about me?"

"You can get yerself home. The canoe is pointed at both ends, you know."

"I'm supposed to paddle by myself?"

Slade stopped to tread water. "If there's only one person in your canoe, then yes. You paddle *by yerself*." He bent his body like a dolphin at play and left her in his wake.

But she didn't want to. She didn't want to be alone in life's canoe, paddling by herself because she had no other choice. She wanted to scream, "Life isn't pointed at both ends, Slade!"

She watched Slade cut through the water. Dawn had become day. And it was up to her to get herself back to the cabin, to the journey she'd been drafted into, to the predawn of her unhappily ever after.

Who paddles *toward* a thing like that?

Across the expanse of water, she watched Slade climb onto the dock, reach down to greet Dawg, then sprint up the incline to the cabin. She had yet to lower her paddle into the water.

I have choices. I don't have to put myself through this. I deserve someone who will fight for me.

The dock wasn't empty for long. A lone figure stood,

coffee mug in one hand, the other shielding his eyes from the now-blazing sun. Was he watching her? If she waited, he'd no doubt turn and head toward the cabin. Or check on the microcamper. Or find Judah and suggest he brush his teeth before his breath scared off the wildlife. Or check his phone for RoadRave instructions.

She watched Connor lower himself to a sitting position, his legs now dangling over the end of the dock. His gaze remained straight ahead. Toward her.

She slid her paddle into the water and took the first tentative strokes toward their temporary home.

chapter eighteen

WHAT'S SHE DOING OUT THERE?

Connor shielded his eyes against the glare that made Mallory a silhouette. Was she losing weight? That too was probably his fault. The only way he would put distance between himself and his regrets was to get past this awkward stage, this in-between phase. They were an unfortunate stat, one of the few LoveMatch matches that didn't work out as expected.

He'd stopped blaming LoveMatch a long time ago. Their screening process had led to an enviable reputation. Ninety-five percent success rate. His marketing mindset salivated over numbers like that.

Why didn't she move? She'd wanted her dawn. She got it. They had miles to conquer. Any minute, RoadRave would update their instructions. And there she sat. How ironic. He was going to leave her, but not now. Not with the trip at stake.

Maybe all the timing was off. All of it. Maybe if he'd met Mallory later, after he and Nathan had gotten the business further off the ground …

Adulting—completely overrated.

She had to know how hard he worked to make Troyer & Duncan successful. She wasn't the only one making a difference. At-risk youth. Okay, a big deal. Life changing and all that. But he wasn't going to belittle his own contribution to the world. He shouldn't have to prove himself. Even if RoadRave were their only client, Troyer & Duncan could score points in the "make a difference" department. Getting people away from their screens, away from virtual into real life. Seeing things up close and personal. Like this. Dawn on a Tennessee backwoods pond.

Yeah.

That wasn't the heart of their problem. A wave of intense phantom pain started in his spine and landed in his gut. He couldn't hear, couldn't see clearly. His brain froze. Phantom. But too real. He felt everything his father must feel, or a shadow of it. The sensation left as soon as it had come, but it was enough to remind him what really stood—or lay—between them.

He held his coffee steady and lowered himself to sit on the dock. Sunrise, but the only thing about it that held his attention was the woman in the canoe now heading his way. The woman who reminded him every day that he'd misjudged his ability to make another human happy.

Not with words. She'd never said he was no longer the man of her dreams. Or had never been. It was obvious other ways. Who had time for that? The game plan was to get married and do life together. Not add to his workload. Double his stressors. Make him dizzy with her skewed way of looking at things, her bizarre modes of communicating. He didn't have trouble getting other people to understand what he meant. Just her.

Mallory—the deluded one who insisted his genetic history didn't change things for her. Of course it did, or would. She hadn't seen him with symptoms yet. How long would it be before she discovered she'd signed on for solitary confinement on medical death row? Even if—against all odds—he had a few more years before it hit, Connor had no confidence it would escape him. Why should it? Grandfather, father, brother, and who knows how many generations back? She said it didn't change things. Of course it did.

Mallory. He could almost smell the scent of her across the water. The smell of lavender from the lotion she used at night to help her sleep. He stifled a yawn. The scent that kept him awake last night with her so close, but so far.

They hadn't slept in the same room for weeks. If it hadn't been for Judah's presence, it would have made sense for the video-screen-only happily married couple to share the teardrop. Lavender. It might have killed him.

When she neared, he stood and steadied the canoe for her. Offered his hand, then dragged the canoe onto shore. "Slade got back a long time ago." He hoped his cringe didn't show on the outside.

"Yeah? Well, he swam back."

"What was it like, waiting for the dawn?"

She shrugged out of her life jacket. "Do you really want to know, Connor?"

Why would she ask that?

"It was glorious. And a little scary. And ... en-*light*-ening."

"I see what you did there."

"Glorious and scary. Not unlike being married to you."

She kissed him on the cheek and headed toward the cabin, brushing past Judah, who—without lowering the camera—gave a victory thumbs up.

◆–––––––––––––––▶

Slade refused to promise he'd stay in touch. Mallory wasn't surprised. A person like Slade had perfected the art of living in the moment.

She resisted the urge to tell Siri to remind her to "live in the moment." It seemed so convoluted. If the trip ended today, she'd have gained a lifetime worth of food for thought. The one person she most wanted to share that thought-buffet with was intent on dissolving his connection to her at his earliest convenience.

Slade wouldn't vow to stay in touch. But he did leave them with a "mighty fine" speech.

He'd pulled a worn book from his oversize shirt pocket and thumbed through until he found what he was looking for. "'The quickest way for anyone to reach the sun and the light of day,'" he read with flourish, "'is not to run west, chasing after the setting sun, but to head east, plunging into the darkness until one comes to the sunrise.'" Slade punctuated the end of his theatrically delivered mini-speech by turning on his heel, heading into his cabin, and leaving the three to ponder.

Judah's response was, "Huh?"

Mallory hadn't stopped pondering.

She should have passed on the second toasted pecan pancake. It seemed like a good idea at the time. Correction. It *smelled* like a good idea. Now it sat halfway down her esophagus.

Sitting in the back seat had its advantages. If she kept her head turned toward the side window, her face was hidden. Emotions, hidden.

Tears.

She cried for the beauty of all the dawns she'd missed. The schedules she'd kept, to the detriment of breathing. The battles she thought she'd won, not knowing wars can never end in a tie. The collateral damage of assuming rough spots iron themselves out.

God. The word clawed its way past the pancake stuck in her chest. *God, are You listening?* Why would He?

With you always.

Mallory shifted as far as her seatbelt would allow, curling toward the window. Always? What did that mean? Connor had made it clear he would not under any circumstances be with her always. He wasn't really with her now. The tightest of all confines, and yet he was miles away.

Blurred scenery cleared as her tears exhausted themselves.

Nondescript small towns separated by stretches of nondescript farmland, empty hills, crooked creeks that couldn't make up their mind which direction they wanted to go.

Connor slowed to a near crawl behind a horse trailer. Mallory heard the familiar sound of impatience, his palm thumping the steering wheel. But the road's curves mocked his eagerness to pass. She leaned her head against the side window and counted varieties of wildflowers in the ditches.

A white spired building not much larger than a school bus sat close to the road. A sign in front let her know it was Ebenezer Gospel Church. *Services at 10:00 a.m. on Sundays and 7 p.m. Wednesdayz.* Must have run out of plastic *s*'s. *Weekly meditation: 'Lo, I am with you alwayz.' Matthew 28:20.* They had an abundance of the letter z.

With you always.

The horse trailer turned off at the intersection. Connor floored it.

"Dude!" Judah said.

Mallory closed her eyes. She could read the sign's words clearly on the inside of her eyelids.

Connor punched the cruise control button and checked his mirrors for flashing lights. The teardrop camper hadn't balked when he'd gunned it. Good thing RoadRave didn't have a drone following them. They didn't, did they? He'd broken the cardinal rule of back-roads adventures by giving in to the temptation to hurry.

He chalked it up to stress. And the fact that the "exhaust" of a full horse trailer in late summer heat could be enough to choke a person. Time to reconnect with his traveling companions. Or try.

"So," he said to whoever listened, "that Slade guy was quite the character, huh?"

Judah chugged most of a bottle of water before answering. "I liked him. And I still think his old lady was in that cookie jar."

"Judah, come on."

"Did either of you check? Notice any bits of bone or teeth?"

"That's enough."

Mallory's first words since they'd taken off. *That's enough.* His mom's favorite words when he was growing up. He couldn't blame her. Pushing the envelope was Connor's favorite form of entertainment.

She would be so disappointed in him. "Watch who you give your heart to, Connor," she said in her semiannual lecture during his teen years. "Marriage is sacred."

Like she thought it was the Ark of the Covenant or something. An altar. He'd teased her for the way the veins in her neck pulsed when she said it. "Chill, Mom. You'll give yourself a stroke."

Sacred. This coming from a woman who'd spent the last few years caring for every need of a husband who didn't know who she was.

He clicked the cruise control down two miles an hour.

"Anybody else hungry?" Judah said.

Connor repositioned his hands on the steering wheel. "Buddy, you must be kidding."

"I know we have sandwiches. I saw Slade slip them to you, Mallory."

She stirred from her cramped perch in the back seat. "They're not contraband, Judah. They're lunch. For, oh, say, three hours from now."

"My blood sugar is getting dangerously low," he said. "Starting to shake."

"You do not have hypoglycemia." Connor couldn't help it. He rolled his eyes.

"Hy*pic*. Hypicglycemia." He held his hands out to prove they shook. "It's new. A newly discovered disorder that often affects young people like me."

Connor didn't like where that train of thought headed.

"What you have," Mallory said, "is hyper-imagination. A sandwich isn't going to cure that."

"I gave it the old technical-school try."

"What?" Connor had to admit the kid could be entertaining.

"I'm not going to college. So I can't give it 'the old college try,' whatever that means."

Connor glanced back at Mallory. She shook her head. "Judah," she said, "you're a little young to make a statement like that. How do you know you're not going to college? A lot can happen in the next six or seven years."

"For you, maybe," he said, then focused on the book he was reading, something Slade had given him.

Where would any of them be six or seven years from now? Connor tried to picture life after success with the RoadRave account. So much would change. Creds. Cash flow. Workload. He and Nathan would probably have to hire an actual staff. Profitability. Freedom.

Yeah, freedom.

Only himself to worry about. He had no intention of getting involved in another relationship.

In a few years, Mallory would probably have found someone, her real soulmate. She'd have proven she could manage quite well without Connor, and would have—

His mind tiptoed close to the cliff edge of a dangerous thought. No. Not going there. But his thoughts stepped into thin air. Free falling. She had a huge heart of love to give. And a brilliant mind. And tenderness that slayed him.

He yanked the wheel to avoid a possum pancake. Mental crisis averted too. He was back in control. Back on track with what he knew had to happen.

They weren't right for each other. If they were, the marriage thing wouldn't be such hard work. And he couldn't promise her a real life.

chapter nineteen

USING HER ALREADY DAMP SLEEVE, Mallory swiped at perspiration beads on her forehead. Ten in the morning and northern Georgia proved its power to sear flesh. Even this late in the summer.

After more miles than Mallory cared to remember, a gravel road had led to the Hemlock Falls trailhead. The ever-faithful RoadRave box that waited for them contained—to her delight—a solar air-conditioning unit for the teardrop camper. Anti-heatwave ammunition. Connor insisted on installing it before they walked the trail. He may have thought himself heroic, but Mallory itched to get on the trail, get their compulsory video footage done, and move on.

He wouldn't accept her help with the installation. Or Judah's. What was he trying to prove? That he was an HVAC hero?

Judah dutifully filmed the installation. Mallory couldn't bring herself to provide color commentary. She pulled out her laptop, found a boulder the size of an armchair, and worked on curriculum details for Literacy Takes Courage. The bullet points she'd started needed a teen-friendly edit. Kids desperate for better reading skills would stop reading at the first word that didn't make sense.

Is that what she and Connor had done? Had they stopped trying at the first standoff in their marriage that didn't make sense?

She hadn't yet mentioned to him that the Hope Street Youth Center was shut down for three weeks. And he hadn't asked about it once on the trip. Mile after mile of silence in the car, and he hadn't ever said, "Hey, Mal, what's up with Hope Center? How's Cherise going to manage without you there?" When had they stopped sharing what mattered?

Mallory scratched at a bug bite on her ankle. A month after the honeymoon. Shortly after Cody died. That's when. She'd tried to enlist Connor's counsel about the foundation purchasing the Hope Street property. He'd brushed her off, claiming to be tied up with details about a work deadline of his own. She'd tried again the next day. He'd said, "Not a good time."

A few months later, she'd asked him to help create a logo for the center. She hadn't liked his first attempt. Too stark. Too minimalist. He'd said stark was the new black. What did he know about a ministry center? All he cared about was making a decent income. He wasn't being paid to offer advice on the Hope Street logo. No wonder he wasn't invested.

Wait. He'd told her he'd try again. She was the one who'd said, "Don't bother. We'll find something on our own."

The scene played out in her mind as if it had just happened. She'd dismissed what he was good at. He hadn't trusted what was in her wheelhouse. The incident became a pattern, the pattern a habit. What if they'd—?

She shook the thought and trimmed her bullet points. But they glared at her, mocked her.

"Create new habits. Forgive yourself for what you didn't do right years ago. Start where you are. Challenge yourself. See your hurdles as victories-in-waiting. They're not tests, but quests."

Mallory closed her laptop. The heat gave her a headache. She needed to hydrate and she needed to move.

They weren't the only ones in the parking lot. One of the other vehicles—an RV the size of the McCormick Place Convention Center was parked several yards away. It boasted a rear bumper sticker that said *Drowning*. Who advertises a thing like that? What if people did? What if people were honest about— She leaned forward and squinted. Oh. *Browning*, not *Drowning*. A hunting equipment company. That made more sense. In a way.

"Done," Connor said, brushing his hands together as he approached her. "Especially while we're on the open road"—he glanced at the camera—"that solar unit should fully charge on a day like this. When we stop for the night, cool air will add a new layer of comfort to the RoadRave experience."

Had she remembered to pack ibuprofen?

Judah set the camera aside. Connor strapped the head-mounted version over his cap. "Ready for wherever this Hemlock Falls trail leads, everyone?"

"Falls," Judah said, reaching for one of the beef sticks Road-Rave had included in the destination box. "I sense a theme here."

"We won't know until we get there," Connor said, his fake video voice as irritating as the constant itch on her ankle.

The trail followed Moccasin Creek. Its water music—clear water tumbling over and around chunky boulders—and the trail itself, climbing into a cooler, mossy forest, did more for Mallory than the ibuprofen would have. Calming, despite the effort it took to walk the trail.

Judah and Connor chattered about the wooden bridge that crossed the creek, small waterfalls along the way, and wildlife that skittered on the ground or twittered in the tree canopy above them. Judah's commentary sounded like a thinly veiled attempt to prove he was more educated than his age would suggest. He rattled on about identifying birds by their song. Some of it, frankly, sounded like imagination rather than information. Maybe *that* would go viral—his pretending to know everything—#preteenconartist.

Better than the pretending she and Connor were trying to pull off—#itshouldntbethishard, #helovedmeonce, #maybeIdontknowwhatloveisafterall.

At trail's end, the primary falls boasted sandy banks from which to observe and take a mental and physical break. Judah somehow turned it into a food break too.

"Hey, Judah, buddy," Connor said. "Pick up that beef stick wrapper. We leave no evidence we've been here." He reached a hand to point to the minicam on his head.

"You're leaving footprints."

"Unavoidable," Connor said. "We're trying to leave the smallest *carbon* footprint possible."

Judah bent to pick up the wrapper and stuffed it into his pocket. Mallory could only imagine what else that pocket held. A partial answer floated to the ground when he removed his hand. A crumpled piece of lined goldenrod paper, the kind used in legal pads.

"What's that?" she asked as he quickly retrieved it, too quickly for the action not to be suspect.

"Nothing."

"May I see it?" Mallory extended her hand.

Judah didn't move. Connor took a step closer to the boy. "You might as well let her see it. You know she's not going to let up."

Was that supposed to be a compliment or a cut? "Please, Judah?"

He handed over the wad of paper. When Mallory flattened it against her thigh, she saw that it was no bigger than four by six inches. Note sized.

"It's from my Uncle Nathan." Judah kept his head down and created a rectangle in the sand with his pacing. "He hid a bunch of them in my backpack. Found this one wrapped around my deodorant this morning."

"You brought deodorant?" Connor said it, but Mallory's thoughts dovetailed. "And today's the first day you thought to use it?"

Judah stopped pacing. "I could report 'shaming' to my social worker." His mouth quirked into a near sneer. His eyes narrowed to slits.

Connor flinched. "Not shaming, Judah. This is TFPE. Temporary Foster Parental Encouragement."

Judah's sneer dissolved. "I admit it. I used deodorant today. Happy?"

"Ecstatic," Connor said.

"Thrilled," Mallory added.

"Overjoyed."

"Grateful." Mallory shifted her attention to the note. "Is it okay if I read this, Judah?"

He stared at her as if she were the first to ask his permission for a peek into his life. "I guess so. It's always some lame stuff about character or"—he assumed his stringless marionette limp stance—"love."

Mallory read Nathan's architect-like crisp penmanship. "'Love bears all things, hopes all things, endures all things. So bear, hope, and endure, Judah. I miss you already. Love, Uncle Nathan.'"

"Where does he get that stuff? A quote app? He could have just sent me the app."

"Long, long ago, in a galaxy far, far away," Connor said, "people wrote their thoughts on paper, in their own handwriting. And it meant something."

Why was he looking at her? She wrote notes. Or she did. Their first month or two of married life was a steady stream of notes back and forth. As cheesy as they came. He'd drawn a crude picture of a tree and written, *My heart will* pine *for you all day at work today.* She left him sticky notes full of lipstick kisses when she was away for a three-day youth leadership conference. And left her journal open on the nightstand where he could read her daily thoughts about what she appreciated about him.

How many empty pages did that journal hold? Where was it now?

She'd lost thirty college pounds before collecting her diploma by being intentional and consistent. She'd kept them off by making healthy choices whenever she could, not counting Maybelle's fried chicken. What kind of difference might it have made if she'd been as intentional and consistent with expressing her love, whether Connor deserved it or not?

She doesn't have to deserve me, Judah had said of his wayward mother. *Just choose me.*

"Can I have it?" For all his nonchalance about the note, it had to mean something to him.

Mallory snapped back to the current scene. Judah had his hand out, waiting for the note's return.

"Sure. This is good. You can tell he put effort into making sure you know you're appreciated, Judah."

"Whatever."

"That first part came from the Bible," she said. "'Love bears all things. Hopes all things. Endures all things.'" The words felt foreign and awkward on her tongue. Like a language she hadn't yet mastered. Like how it felt to hope the verb tense was correct but not be sure.

"That figures," Judah said. "He's addicted to his Bible."

Mallory smiled. What a sensible addiction. The thought pricked her conscience as if it had been poked with a stir stick from a campfire. What a sensible addiction it would be for her.

Judah fingered the note. "How does a person 'hope' all things? Kinda weird wording."

"I know this one," Connor said, his voice authentically Connor, not the video version. "I remember asking your uncle the same question when he wrote that phrase on the card he gave me when I told him I was … engaged to Mallory."

"Dude. He sent you a gooshy card?"

"Okay, it was a business card. But it meant a lot. And he wanted me to keep it."

"Did you?"

Connor held Mallory's gaze while he dug for his wallet. "Yeah. I did. Laminated it." He pulled out a scuffed-up card with the Troyer & Duncan logo on one side and a few lines of a note on the other. "Haven't … haven't looked at it for a while. Too long, I guess." He fingered it like a magician playing with a coin, then flipped it toward Judah.

The boy caught it. "Yeah," he said. "Same words. 'Hopes all things.' How do you hope everything?"

Connor looked up, as if he'd find the answer in the tree branches above them. "Your uncle read those verses to me from a different version. He said it meant something like 'Love's hopes are fadeless under all circumstances.' It's from 1 Corinthians chapter twelve, I think."

"Thirteen," Mallory said, instantly regretting having corrected him in front of Judah.

Connor's shoulders rose and fell, but he didn't change his focus.

Love's hopes are fadeless. First time the Bible was wrong. She had to believe that. The only other option was that the Bible was right and she wasn't.

chapter twenty

LESS THAN AN HOUR LATER, they stood in front of the second of two more waterfalls. Judah made it clear he was building his collection of non-Niagara-Falls-worthy waterfalls. But even he admitted that Panther and Angel Falls had been worth the mile hike one way.

And worth the four dollars for parking. Connor retied his hiking shoes. Something rubbed wrong. More than on his heel. On his soul, the s-o-u-l kind.

RoadRave had reported a slight uptick in views of their video blog, but nothing like the numbers they expected. "Need more drama."

Connor couldn't—wouldn't—manufacture drama. Hadn't Judah's antics provided plenty? And characters like Slade? They'd edited out the small handful of people they'd met who didn't appreciate what they were trying to do. The grumblers. The snooty.

The scenery on their recent leg of the trip had been one show-stopper after another. Lake Burton. Lake Seed. The ferns and mosses of the Georgian forests. Connor hadn't been aware

Georgia had so many scenic spots. A week ago, he'd thought Georgia's landscape was Atlanta and its suburbs.

They stood now on a wooden platform, watching the water of Angel Falls pour over narrow shelves of rock. Connor overheard another hiker complaining that the last time they'd taken the trail, the falls were little more than a trickle. Connor was grateful for the recent rains. The other hiker was stuck in the past, unaware of the current gift that should have enhanced the old memory.

It wasn't hard to see why RoadRave planned things the way they did. Nathan and Connor hadn't seen the specific itinerary but had built their marketing plan around RoadRave principles. Radio spots now played in select markets and helped drive traffic to the video blog. Troyer & Duncan had created trade show displays, and more merchandising and social media ads were designed and ready to go. Years' worth of ideas were on deck, waiting to be implemented if this test trip was successful.

Everybody on the RoadRave team was quality. From upper management to the interns now handling some of what Nathan would have been doing, they all seemed handpicked to match the RoadRave philosophies. Connor had met a few of them face-to-face and others on preliminary web calls, but he couldn't wait to visit their operations, if things went well.

Focused as he was on the marketing angle of the trip, the miles and footsteps still left Connor too much time to think. Or just enough. He saw connections he would have missed in daily life, scooting past them in a blur at a hundred miles an hour. He noticed now. The bug tugging a piece of leaf along the wooden rail of the platform. He pointed the camera at the scene and zoomed in. The leaf was four times the little guy's size. But he held on tight and traversed the length of the railing.

A pair of all too familiar fingers appeared in the frame. They flicked the bug off the rail.

"Judah! What do you think you're doing?"

"Keeping things interesting," Judah said. "You've seen forty waterfalls, you've seen them all."

"What did that bug ever do to you?" Connor peered over the railing, but a small camouflaged bug and his lunch—or his wife's lunch—were hard to trace against all that foliage.

"Excuse me for reducing your squad by one bug."

"Judah, that's unkind on so many levels," Mallory said.

"I got this, Mal." Or hoped he did. She not only stepped back but headed down the path to the trailhead.

"Judah, come here."

"Turn that off first." Judah pointed at the head cam.

Connor stopped recording. "We still have two more weeks on the road."

"Don't remind me."

"We can do this the hard way or the easy way."

"How would you describe how it's been so far? Was that the easy part? Because if it was …" Judah started down the path after Mallory.

Connor grabbed the boy's elbow. "Listen …"

"Don't touch me!" Judah shrank away as if he'd been shot.

Connor let go and took a breath. "Judah, listen to me."

"I don't have to. It's not like you care."

"We do too care."

"Mallory, maybe. You? Your caring looks a lot like tolerating to me. And just barely."

"Whose fault is that?" Connor huffed. He'd acted more maturely in his last grade school playground fight. "I didn't mean that."

"Yes, you did. But I get it. I'm a pain to be around. I should use deodorant more often. My feet stink. And you have no reason to like me. My work here is done."

If not for the sheen in Judah's eyes, Connor might have thought all hope had faded.

But *love's hopes are fadeless.*

Back to haunt him again.

"Judah, wait up. Please."

"Why don't you go chase your wife if you want to chase somebody."

"What did you say to me?" Connor slowed his approach when he saw a family of four heading their way on the trail. Judah passed them, whispering something Connor couldn't hear. But the family held to the far side of the path, arms around each other, when they made their way past Connor.

Great. I'll now be known as the serial killer of Angel Falls.

Chase my wife. That kid.

He's smarter than he lets on.

"We're here," Mallory said, pulling their rig to a stop.

"It's only been"—Judah looked at his phone—"ten minutes. If we're stopping every ten minutes, I'm going to need more sustenance."

"What?"

"These death marches," he said.

Connor thumped the console from his spot in the second seat. "They're called hikes. And they're good for us." He unbuckled and climbed out before Mallory had time to turn off the engine.

What happened between those two?

Connor took to the Minnehaha Falls trailhead, leaving Mallory and Judah to record the hike, which proved to be short and stunning. The end of the trail opened to a clearing below the picturesque falls.

"I know. It's no Niagara," Mallory said, her arm resting across Judah's shoulders.

He stiffened, but didn't slide out from under her arm as he usually did. Maybe they were making progress with him after all.

In the three years she'd been the director of Hope Street

Youth Center, she'd seen much more hardened hearts than Judah's. She could see glimpses of his good side. Peeks of the fun he could be. Insights into the old soul inside of him, the thinker, the wisdom he didn't dare admit he'd accumulated.

A cold thought hit her squarely in the sternum. It left her breathless. Could she have been wrong and Connor was right?

Maybe she hadn't been as fully devoted to her calling as she imagined. Maybe getting married had been a fantasy move. Her calling was to those young people, many of whom had no one but her on their side. Connor had made it clear he could live without her. Had her love for Connor stood in the way of what she'd been called to do? Her life's truest purpose? Others seemed able to juggle marriage and a life's passion. She must not have been gifted with that gene.

Connor wanted out. Had her insistence that his pending illness didn't matter increase his stress level rather than comfort him as she'd hoped? Had she been hanging on to an image of herself that was noble because he had no confirmed diagnosis? She'd been so sure of herself, sure she would stand by him. What if that were the opposite of what he needed?

And what if … ? What if she'd been so distracted by Connor's maybe yes/maybe no crisis that she hadn't given her whole heart to the at-risk youth she'd been handed?

Had all the fresh air and exertion cleared her thinking for once?

Dawn could come in the middle of the day, she realized. If Connor hadn't insisted on separation, she might have missed the message altogether. She had a job to do. If Connor wanted out, maybe that was God's way of getting her back on track. Single-hearted devotion to caring for at-risk youth. It wasn't failure. It was redirection.

Spinning disasters to make them sound like advantages. Now she thought like an advertising expert.

Where was he, anyway? "Connor?"

She'd keep up the ruse for the sake of his company, but it

wasn't fair for him to suffer for the next two weeks. She needed to let him know he was off the hook. She wouldn't fight the divorce. She'd give up trying to change his mind about getting the testing that would set his mind at ease or—

She'd never succeed at that anyway. He was right. The truth hit her hard and suddenly, as if she'd been walking through their marriage blind and had life-changing surgery to restore her sight. The bandages had been removed. She could see.

They'd be better off pursuing their dreams unencumbered by a limping marriage.

"Connor?"

"Over here." He sat on a flat rock, his back pressed against a tree trunk.

Judah now squatted at the water's edge, pushing a floating stick in a back eddy.

"Are you okay?" she asked Connor. He had a little sunburn across his nose, but nothing else except his demeanor seemed off.

"Yeah." He sighed. "Thinking about what you do with troubled teens every day."

That caught her by surprise. "Me too, actually."

"How you must have to steel yourself against their hostility."

"They're not all hostile. Some are too broken to muster that much energy."

"It's good work you do."

She fought the urge to sit beside him, not trusting herself to say what she needed to say if he were too close. "Thanks. You too." Hope rose. Separate but amicable looked more promising. "I need to tell you something while Judah's occupied."

"Okay."

She positioned herself so there was less chance Judah would overhear or read her lips. "Connor, you've been very patient waiting for me to get to this point. But I get it now. You're right. You've been right all along. The only smart thing for us to do is"—the words felt like shards of glass—"go ahead with the divorce. I won't fight you on it. I've been too stubborn to see what you've known for a long time. And I apologize for that. You mean—" She swallowed hard and started over. "You'll always mean so much to me. And I'll be cheering you on from a … from a distance."

Stupid tears. She wasn't supposed to cry.

"Mallory …"

She sniffed back the tears and blinked hard but didn't turn around. "What is it, Judah?"

"Ha ha."

"What? I can't hear you." She faced him.

He said it again. As quiet a voice as she'd heard him use since the trip started. "Ha ha. The falls. Mini-ha-ha? Tiny little 'ha ha.' Get it?"

Eleven. Years. Old. With rotten timing.

When she turned back toward Connor, his spot was empty. She caught a glimpse of him making his way toward the trailhead. Alone.

<hr />

"'Minnehaha,'" Judah read from his phone screen. "'Often translated as "laughing waters" or "waterfall."'" He lowered the phone. "Complete surprise. A waterfall named waterfall. Creative minds at work on that one."

"Judah," Mallory said, "get in the car."

"Technically, it's a small sport utility vehicle, aka SUV."

"Judah."

"I'm going. I'm going."

Connor had reached the trailhead before them. Where was he now? Mallory circled around the back of the teardrop camper. She found him, head bent, arms extended, leaning his palms on the stainless steel on the far side of the camper.

"Connor, are you feeling okay?" She hadn't thought through what they'd do if one of them got sick on the trip.

He stood upright. "Yeah. I'm ... good. Ready to go."

"Your turn to drive?"

"Sure. No problem."

She tossed him the keys. "Connor, nothing's changed about the trip. We can pull this off. Troyer & Duncan will make a name for itself. And I'll be cheering loudest when it does."

———————————————

Nothing's changed? Everything's changed.

Connor stood too long gripping the door handle. Both Judah and Mallory were looking at him as if he had sprouted purple acne.

He pulled himself into the Subaru. Time to knock off a few hundred more hash marks.

chapter twenty-one

JUDAH, GET OFF YOUR PHONE." Connor tried to dial back on his volume mid-sentence, unsuccessfully.

"You wanna say that a little louder?" Judah said, holding his phone toward him. "I'm texting my social worker. But I could send her a voicemail instead, if you'd like to talk to her yourself."

"Boys," Mallory said. "Apologies both ways?"

"Sorry," Connor said.

"Sorry. Not sorry."

"Judah."

"Okay, okay. Sorry, Connor. But I really am texting my—"

Connor drew a deep breath. "I know. And I really am sorry I snapped." How is it that Mallory could calm the kid, even when correcting him? But every conversation Connor had with him turned ugly. Or started out ugly and went south from there.

Not unlike—Connor repositioned his hands on the wheel—most communication with Mallory the past few months. If he blamed stress, he was still a loser. What kind of man was he if stress did all the talking for him? His personal trainer had helped him conquer posture problems he'd had since childhood. Connor had worked hard to undo the damage of a weak core. But he had no power over job stress? Sounded like a software glitch. Correctable, but you have to apply the protocol.

Especially now. Especially with Mallory agreeing with him that the only smart thing was for them to split up for good. Especially now that he was no longer sure.

Perfectly rotten timing. They had zero opportunities to be alone. He had zero idea how he would even begin the conversation. "Mallory, I've been thinking."

So many ways to finish that sentence. *I've been thinking I'm an idiot. I've been thinking I was hasty.* No. Who uses the word *hasty* anymore? *I've been thinking.* Period. Should have tried that Day One.

In his defense …

A mile's worth of hash marks ticked past before he realized that nothing following "in his defense" sounded adequate. Excuses, but not reasons. Reasons, but not reason enough for him to have given up on them.

"Hey, Connor." Judah waved his phone toward him again.

If this is another threat, buddy…. Assume the best out of that kid. Assume the best. Where did that come from? "What is it, Judah?"

"We are picking up some major traction with the videos."

"We are?" Nice to have some good news for once.

"The sunrise thing with Mallory gave us a boost." He turned to face her. "Nice work."

"It wasn't work," she said.

"People are asking questions. Trying to guess where we're headed next. And …"

Connor glanced his way at the four-way stop. "And what?"

"Nothing."

"Judah, come on. Spill the tea."

"A segment of the population of humans following us think I'm … cute. *Eww.*"

Mallory leaned forward, her hand near Connor's shoulder. "Is that a problem for us? Could it be?"

"That the world thinks Judah's adorable?" He laughed. He'd needed the break from heavy thoughts.

"No," she said. "That people may now be trying to follow us, or meet us at our next destination, or …"

"Would that be so bad?" Where was she headed with her comment?

"I'm thinking about the safety factor."

His mouth was ready to dismiss her concern. But his gut stopped him. RoadRave had taken good precautions. He and Nathan had discussed the subject at length. He didn't need another news report to convince him safety was no longer a given. "Worth consideration."

"Incoming. This is nice." Mallory's voice had relief written all over it.

"What?"

"RoadRave sent an e-gift certificate for a restaurant for later today."

"Sweet!" Judah said, fist pumping.

"An actual sit-down restaurant," Mallory said. "Local favorite, it looks like."

"Did they give the name of the place?"

"Huh. RoadRave must have been reading our minds. They'll let us know when we're a few miles out to prevent a media blast."

Connor rubbed his forehead. "But a media blast—"

"We'll work it out, Connor."

Wish that covered everything.

———————◆———————

A gift certificate. For this place? Somebody in the RoadRave offices had a twisted sense of humor.

Connor lifted and replaced his cap. On the positive side,

none of the three had to worry about their attire. They'd be completely at home among the jeans-and-tee-shirt crowd dining at Tray Sheek. Nice play on words. It sounded like the kind of marketing idea he and Nathan could have sunk their teeth into. No pun intended.

He turned toward his traveling companions. "Ready for a five-course meal?"

"Five obstacle courses?" Mallory asked, unbuckling her seatbelt.

If the exterior décor were any indication, it was a possibility. Tray Sheek's open-air dining area held a collection of tables of wood, wrought iron, plastic, 1950s chrome, and Formica, with chairs from eras tracing back to biblical times, it seemed. Each was decorated with a white linen tablecloth and a fresh flower centerpiece or fresh flowering weeds, no two vases alike.

Almost every table was occupied with one or more diners. At two in the afternoon. It said something either about the food or that this was the only restaurant in the county.

The back roads they'd been on—beautiful as they were—had wandered in and out of three states that day—Georgia, South Carolina, and North Carolina. Now on foot, Connor, Mallory, and a foot-dragging Judah made their way through the maze of tables toward what appeared to be the hostess station near a screened front door.

"Y'all have reservations?" the severely pregnant hostess asked, balancing a stack of menus on her hip.

"Reservations?" Connor looked at Mallory.

"Should we have called ahead?" Mallory asked the young woman.

"I'm messin' with ya. We got room. Two, no three tables out here is still open. Or all y'all can have a fancy table inside."

"What makes it fancy?" Judah asked, scratching his armpit.

"Silverware," the woman answered, unflinching.

"That sounds … good," Mallory said. Connor nodded.

"Follow me." The about-to-be-born baby led the way into the restaurant's interior, followed closely by its mother. "Most don't want to sit near the kitchen on account of the noise. But you can about take yer pick." She indicated five or six empty tables in the refreshingly cool room.

Mallory picked a high-backed chair at the nearest table. "We have a gift certificate." She showed the woman her phone screen.

"Well, whater ya know. Bernard!" She left them and opened the swinging door to what—from the noise level—must have been the kitchen. "It's them people from the innernet! You have got to see their son. If he don't look like our Mason!"

A thin, Tin-Man-like gentleman stepped into the dining room and addressed the hostess. "Charlene, if I might beg your indulgence, I've a bit of a conundrum brewing with the green grocer."

She giggled. "Bernard, you give me chillbumps evertime you say *grow-ser*'stead of *grow-sure*. I'm still in the runnin' for blessedest woman in the world."

He dusted his hands on the towel hanging under his chef's jacket. Then he held Charlene's shoulders and kissed her on each cheek. "It's I who am the blessed one, m'dear."

Connor watched Mallory's face. Eyes wide, lips pressed tight, she appeared to be stifling something that begged to be said.

Charlene returned to their table. "These here's the people from the innernet."

"RoadRave. Yes, indeed," Bernard said, his hand extended. "A pleasure to meet you. Miss Mallory. Mr. Connor. Master Judah."

Judah leaned close to Connor. "That is so cool. He knows our names. Connor, you can call me Master Judah from now on."

Connor stood to receive Bernard's handshake. "A pleasure to meet you too."

"Long day on the road? The last we saw, you were camped someplace in northeast Georgia."

"Yes, sir. We were."

"If I can divest myself of the dilemma currently raging in the kitchen, I would much appreciate a tour of your microcamper before you get back on the road to your next destination."

Connor smiled. "The tour doesn't take long, but yes, of course. We'd be happy to oblige. Are you considering a microcamper for yourself, your family?" He eyed Charlene, who still balanced menus on her hip.

Bernard's laughter filled the room. "I'm afraid we'd need more than one. Charlene and I are the parents of seven children."

"Don't ya mean eight?" Judah asked, pointing at Charlene's bulge.

"Judah!"

"Seven," Bernard said, his voice soft, eyes kind. "From the moment we know a child is on the way, we count it as part of our family. And now, I must attend to the matter in the kitchen. Charlene will make sure you have everything you need."

Could the two have been more unlike each other? And Connor thought he and Mallory were different as night and day! Bernard and Charlene's differences hadn't seemed to keep them from … a robust relationship. How long would Connor have to park the teardrop camper near those two while they worked, raised their kids, interacted with their customers, to discover their secret?

Mallory and Judah were already focused on the menus in their hands when Connor tore himself away from his thoughts.

"Whatchall want for a beverage?" Charlene asked. "And if it ain't sweet tea, we don't have it. Other'n water."

Judah's too-frequent pout hit a new low.

"I'm yankin' yer chain, young man. We got it all. My personal favorite's the homemade peach and ginger nectar."

Judah brightened. "That sounds good."

"Me too." Mallory high-fived Judah.

176

"Make it three," Connor added.

"Be back in a sec. Y'all take yer time with the menu. Sounds like my beloved's got his knickers in a knot back there."

After Charlene left them, Mallory leaned across the table. "I don't care what the food is like. This is so worth it."

"Well, *I* care about the food." Judah rubbed his hands together over the menu on the table in front of him. "One of everything, please."

"How much is the gift certificate, Mallory?"

"Aw," Judah whined. "Do we have to split it three ways? I'm a growing boy."

"It's a generous gift certificate, men. Enjoy."

Judah puffed out his chest. "She called me a man."

"Figure of speech," Connor said.

Mallory's shoulder drop matched Judah's, although neither responded. Couldn't a guy make a joke anymore without stepping on somebody's *feelings*? Connor knew that shoulder drop. He thought he had a corner on the market. Like every time he overheard a conversation that reminded him brain tumors like his dad's didn't skip a generation.

"We men," he said, looking Judah in the eye, "can probably polish off the man-sized 'On Tray' with room to spare. Right, Judah?"

"Entrée?" Mallory searched the menu. "Oh. 'On Tray.' Tray Sheek's On Tray special of the day. Clever. Quirky."

"Excuse me, sir," Judah said to the couple at the next table, "is that the On Tray?"

They nodded.

"Yeah, I'll have that."

Connor agreed. Brisket and ribs piled high next to a quarter of barbequed chicken? What could be better than that?

Mallory ordered the Tray Sheek house salad with grilled shrimp and a side of parsnip puree with a golden raisin gastrique. Whatever that was. And the pumpkin pear soup with crème fraiche and parsley oil drizzles. She seemed thrilled to have a food option that didn't begin with the words *canned* or *dehydrated*.

She wasn't the only one. Connor added the pumpkin pear soup to his order too when the young waitress took their requests.

"Look at that," Judah said, pointing to a spot high on the wall above the beverage station.

Mallory laid her hand on Judah's arm. "We need to talk about protocol regarding pointing in public, Judah." Her smile softened the rebuke.

"Want me to use my laser pointer on my phone?" he asked, his mouth quirked in that half-sass/half-comedic way.

"Just use words," Connor said.

"Look at that sign."

Mallory read aloud, "'We appreciate your kind comments about the food. But we're only caretakers. In our house, we pause before eating to thank God for His bounty. You're welcome to do so here. Try holding hands around the table. There's hand sanitizer in the condiments rack.'"

Judah laughed. "Hand sanitizer. Good one." He poked through the sugar and sugar substitutes and finally discovered a small baby-food-sized jar with individual packets of waterless hand cleaner.

"I think you're missing the key point," Mallory said.

"I usually do," he said.

◆————————————————◆

Two refills of peach nectar later, three trays of food settled in before them. Charlene had somehow managed all three around her protrusion. "Supposed to be hostessing today," she said. "But I wanted to be the one to serve you myself. We love your show."

Connor suppressed his correction about the difference between a TV show and a video blog. *Hmm.* TV show? "Thanks, Charlene. This all looks delicious. Do you mind if we shoot

some video of you and Bernard and the restaurant for today's …
episode? We have a release form you'd need to sign."

"Wait 'til I tell Bernard. He'll be happier than a starved
squirrel with a new acorn! Things're bound to slow down a mite
by the time y'all get done eatin'. I'll tell my beloved. Y'all enjoy."

She bounced away as if she wasn't carrying the equivalent
of a thirty-pound workout ball with her stomach muscles.

It should have been Connor, but it was Judah who flipped
them each a packet of sanitizer and extended his hands toward
the two adults at the table, grinning like he'd beat them in a
sprint. Connor took his hand and reached his other hand across
the table for Mallory's, forming a lopsided triangle. Her hesita-
tion didn't last long, for which he was grateful. They bowed their
heads over trays full of seared meat.

chapter twenty-two

I CAN DO THIS. *I can do this. I can do this.*

I'm not sure I can do this, God.

Mallory felt the release of Connor's fingers over hers with searing pain at the end of their silent prayer. It would take a while before she adjusted to the idea that they had no future together except for the next couple of weeks. It made sense. No, it didn't. But it would make life easier for him. That's what love does, doesn't it? Sacrifice?

Love. A different kind of love than she'd hoped for. Love that cared more about his success and his wishes—even his phobia-based wishes—than the longings of her own heart. It had to be that way. She'd committed to the inevitable divorce and to staying not only civil but kind and supportive for the rest of the journey.

I can do this.

I'm not sure I can do this.

"Did you find a note from Uncle Nathan today, Judah?" She forked a perfectly grilled shrimp and chewed slowly while she waited for his answer. Hoped he had an answer. Hoped it held a word or two she could cling to.

"Yeah," he said through a mouthful of the roasted garlic mashed potatoes that accompanied his mostly meat meal.

"*Hmm.*"

Judah finished chewing and stabbed a chunk of brisket. It was almost to his mouth when he said, "I suppose you want to know what it said."

"If you don't mind sharing it. Yes."

He laid his fork to the side of the platter and pulled a slip of paper from his back pocket. "You can read it. I have eating to do."

The note now dotted with forensic-worthy meat-grease fingerprints, its message rose above the grime: "Miles are no challenge for God, Judah. Or to the kind of love He gives. Wherever you are, He's there too. Watch for the signs."

"I didn't understand it either," he said.

Mallory risked looking Connor's direction. He'd stopped eating, forearms leaning on the table, facing his tray, eyes un-blinking. He rubbed the handle of the fork in his right hand and the knife in his left. His chest rose and fell with a giant breath before he resumed his meal.

Where were his thoughts roaming, now that the wrestling match was over? Was he being overly considerate of her in choosing not to bounce with joy like Charlene? He was getting his way. He'd soon be free. Someday—not today—she'd have to thank him for tamping down his exuberance over his final victory.

Watch for the signs? Like the gratitude sign above the hostess station? Or Connor's stepped-up kindness toward her? She should probably quit analyzing it and try gratitude for a change.

←——————————→

Mallory thought Bernard and Charlene were poster children for marital opposites. Meeting their children added another whole dimension.

All six—well, seven, including the one Charlene still carried—emerged from the house next door to the restaurant when their parents could get away for a video segment. They clustered around the microcamper, all claiming to be fascinated by features Mallory had begun to take for granted. The ultra-efficient kitchen. The economical use of storage space. The streamlined shape and even more streamlined setup and teardown.

Mallory estimated the children's ages ranged from three years to sixteen. The oldest was one of the waitresses from the restaurant. The next oldest held the three-year-old on her hip in a stance that mirrored the one her mother used for menus.

No two of the children had the same skin tone.

The boy Charlene introduced as the spitting image of Judah—Mason—had been adopted from Malaysia. Charlene's eyes apparently saw features beyond the physical, beyond what others noted first—the differences. She saw similarities on a plane too many others ignored.

From the moment we know a child is on its way, Bernard had said. Mallory didn't realize he'd meant either by pregnancy test or airline ticket.

Mason and Judah kept a safe distance for the first few minutes, neither saying much. Hands in pockets. Eventually, Mason pulled a lizard from his pocket and formed an instant friend.

"Judah, I don't think I need to say it, but you're hereby forewarned that we will have no lizard stowaways on this trip. Got it?" Connor's face looked stern, but he lifted Judah's Road-Rave cap so he could ruffle Judah's hair.

Mallory caught the exchange on video, including Mason's Malaysian "Y'all don't have to worry about that."

Connor knelt to the level of a four- or five-year-old little girl with skin the color of their coffee table in their Chicago apartment. "And where are you from?"

"Right over there, sir." The girl pointed toward the house,

her sweet little arm missing everything below the elbow. "And the heart a' God. We all come from the heart a' God. Din' we, Julia?"

The eldest, Julia, her hair the color of maple trees in October and her clear blue eyes sparkling, still wore her Tray Sheek apron. "We did." Her wide smile curved up in the middle, a faint scar drawing a line from Cupid's bow to the bottom of her nose.

The children interacted with the crowd of restaurant guests gathering around the activity, many of them asking questions and taking selfies with the rig. Mallory kept filming while Connor talked about the camper and their journey. Judah took it upon himself to secure electronically signed release forms from those whose faces appeared in any of the filming, with a practiced, "If your segment is included after editing."

That child had a future in public relations.

Had she really thought that?

He apologized for the lizard stains on the phone screen where the prospective video stars needed to agree to the terms and add their signature with their fingertips. Public relations? Maybe not so much.

Connor made promises to send each member of Bernard and Charlene's family a Troyer & Duncan cap after they returned to Chicago. The even mix of boys and girls seemed equally excited.

Mallory stopped filming and took in the scene. The best kind of chaos. Connor in his element. Judah discovering one of his gifts. A wild blend of ethnicities with a solid, common bond. The memories of a great meal served by exceptional people.

Connor joined her at one of the outdoor tables near the edge of the parking lot. It was set with white linen napkins on the white tablecloth—and flatware—ready for the evening crowd. Strings of small lights that draped from tree to tree came to life. "Some afternoon, huh?"

"Unforgettable."

They sat in silence. She had a long way to go before she'd

consider her new perspective settled. His nearness still made her heart misbehave.

"I suppose we'd better get on the road, huh?"

"Incoming?" she asked.

"An hour ago. I texted back that we were temporarily delayed."

"Nice to throw the schedule to the wind once in a while."

"Never thought I'd agree, but yes."

Children's laughter filled the air. Mallory sighed. "All good things must come to an … end."

"Mallory, it doesn't have to—"

"Leapin' lizards!" Judah said, skidding to a stop on the gravel in front of them.

"No lizards, Judah."

"Yeah, no. Not that. We got trouble. Well, not trouble, but— At first, I thought maybe the radiator was leaking, cuz I saw that on TV once. But no. Not that far away from the engine."

Connor stood and held Judah's shoulders. "Chill, Judah. What's wrong?"

Mason came up behind his new friend. "My sister's on her way," he said, as calm and dignified as his father.

"Which one? Julia?" Mallory glanced over the boys' shoulders. Why couldn't she remember the other two girls' names?"

Judah planted his hands on Mallory's knees and leaned in to shout-whisper, "The one that ain't born yet!"

"Isn't," she said. "Wait. What?"

Connor and Mallory were on their feet in a nanosecond, heading toward the commotion.

They found Charlene leaning against the teardrop camper, doubled over, rocking side to side, breathing impossibly slow and even.

Bernard had his fist in the small of her back and addressed the children. "Julia, can you handle the restaurant?"

"Yes, Father."

"Ramon and his wife will help you with these last few customers and closing down. Lizbet?"

The second eldest now held a small boy on each hip.

"Take the young ones to your Aunt Bertha's until—"

"She's gone, Papa. It's her chemo day."

Bernard sighed. "Yes. How thoughtless of me to forget."

Connor stepped forward. "Can we help?" He looked at Mallory.

She nodded. "What can we do? How far is the hospital?"

Charlene let out a low-pitched groan and said, "'bout twenty miles further'n we need it to be. Bernard!"

Mallory supported Charlene under one arm and Bernard took the other while they shuffled toward the house. "Connor?"

"On it. You kids come with me. We'll … Not sure what we'll do, but we'll do it."

"Can we wait inside the camper?" the littlest asked.

"Yes?" Mallory heard Connor say. "Judah, buddy. You're in charge of entertainment. I'm in charge of …"

"Everything else?" Judah asked.

The rest of the conversation faded as the pregnant woman and her two-person support team reached the front porch of their home.

"Mr. Bernard, are you prepared for a home birth?"

Charlene moaned from her toes. "We done it before. I'll tell ya … where … everthing … IS!" She dropped to all fours on their immaculate living room floor. "This un's in a hurry."

"Are you, by chance or the goodness of the Almighty, a midwife, Mrs. Duncan?"

"No, sir."

"Experienced in *any* way?"

"I watched a lot of *Little House on the Prairie* reruns in college."

"Good enough for me. Let's see if we can't make Charlene a little more comfortable."

It was half an hour before Charlene was more comfortable. With their new daughter resting on her chest.

"Just like on TV," Bernard said from his wing chair drawn close to the sofa. He stroked his wife's hair with one hand and his new daughter's cap of dark curls with the other.

Not exactly. Mallory's heart rate hadn't slowed yet. A few days ago, she'd witnessed a holy dawn. Today, the holy dawn of a new life. Unforgettable.

"I'll take these sheets and towels to the laundry room."

"Much obliged," Bernard said. "For everything."

"Charlene did it all," Mallory said. "You have a remarkable wife."

"As does your husband, Miss Mallory," Charlene said.

You don't know. And I can't tell you. "Be right back. Tell me when you're ready to have the children meet their sister. I'll give you two time alone with her for a bit."

The rest of the house, like the living room, was virtually spotless, considering it had recently been vacated by six children of all ages. Mallory found the laundry room off the spacious kitchen. After putting the load to soak, she returned to the kitchen and started an electric teapot. If Charlene and Bernard didn't need a cup of tea, she sure did.

A long hickory farm table paralleled a wall of windows in the eating area. Eight chairs. Identical. So different from the eclectic look of the restaurant. Here, sameness was the theme. How fitting.

Mallory stood at the window, looking out at a wide fenced-in yard with a castle-like playset and multiple picnic tables. An herb garden filled the area closest to the restaurant. Some of the trees on the hills behind the house had started to turn the color of the pumpkin pear soup and the red of Tray Sheek's aprons. A few trees. The young ones. Always in a hurry.

The teapot shut itself off. Given his age and his British roots, was Bernard the kind who frowned on the horrors of teabags? Was he a loose-leaf only tea drinker? She wasn't sure she could make a "proper" pot of tea. But she discovered a clear canister of teabags on the counter. They smelled of ripe peaches. A theme. Mallory filled three mugs, set them on a Tray Sheek tray propped behind the four-slice toaster, and headed for the living room.

Bernard met her in the doorway and took the tray from her. "The very thing we needed. Thank you, Miss Mallory."

"It was an honor to have been here for this. I can't describe ... the ... wonder."

"Neither can we." He pronounced it as if the first half of the word rhymed with *sigh*. "She made it."

"Charlene? She was a trooper."

"The child. You might have figured we adopted many of our children. Charlene birthed one other who lived—Julia. We've had so many who didn't."

chapter twenty-three

AFTER THE NEIGHBORHOOD MIDWIFE HAD pronounced mother and child healthy, strong, and needing nothing more than rest, one by one, the six other children tiptoed close to meet their newest sibling. Shy smiles and tender touches welcomed the little one to her remarkable family.

Judah and Connor were included.

Judah whispered, "I got a name for her. Minnehaha. You know, cuz 'laughing waters.' Miss Charlene, I laughed and laughed when I thought your waters were our radiator leaking and—"

"I could use your help in the kitchen, Judah," Mallory said.

"Mine too? Please?" Connor added.

She nodded. "How did it go keeping the other kids occupied?"

"We did great," Judah said.

Connor's eyes grew wide. "Survived. There's a reason why children usually come one at a time. Speaking of that …"

"We helped Julia get the linens off the tables and made a dope sign for in front of the restaurant and one for the corner so people expecting to eat at Tray Sheek tonight know not to bother trying to come."

Mallory wondered where all those customers would find their pumpkin pear soup fix tonight.

"And then …" Judah said, "we washed all the tables. And *then* we got to play. I think we should be paid. Maximum wage."

"That's minimum wage," Connor said, "and no. We volunteered to help out."

"Judah, would you take these cookies out to the kids?" Mallory said. "We'll need to feed them supper pretty soon, but I think having a new sister is reason enough to celebrate, don't you? But ask Mr. Bernard first."

"Will do. I get it. You two want to 'talk.'"

She hadn't intended to lean into Connor's open arms.

"Mallory, I'm so proud of you."

"You too." She tucked her head under his chin as she had so many times before.

"What was it like?"

"Beautiful. And hard. And intense. And beautiful."

"I wish …"

Mallory stepped back. He didn't resist. "Yeah, Connor. Me too."

She wasn't sure what he meant. But she was certain whatever it was, she wished it too.

"We should stay and help, at least tonight," he said.

"I agree."

"The boys want to bunk in the camper."

"All of them?" Mallory tried to picture Judah plus three crammed into that tiny space.

"I made them promise the lizard wasn't invited."

She wrapped her arms around her middle and leaned against the kitchen counter edge. "Good."

"The girls asked for a slumber party. With you."

"Oh, Connor."

"I know. You must be exhausted."

She closed her eyes. The whole day replayed itself. Some

of it had been recorded. Some of it would live forever in her heart. "I think I need to say yes."

"Why? You don't have to feel obligated."

"It's not obligation. I don't think I'm done learning from this family."

"Funny you said that."

"Why?"

He rubbed the back of his neck. "I thought the same thing."

"So we're staying?"

Connor paused a moment. "If Bernard and Charlene are okay with it."

"I have a feeling they'll be grateful for the help."

He chuckled. "They're perpetually grateful."

"A worthy reputation," she said. *A great life goal.*

"I'm … heading outside for a while. I hear the boys."

"Okay. See you later."

Mallory met Lizbet on her way to the family room.

"Miss Mallory, my mom would like to talk to you."

"Is she okay?"

Lizbet smiled. Her chin quivered. *"Hmm mmm.* Even happier than normal. I'll get some supper started."

"After I see what your mom wants, I can help."

"One thing we're not shy of here is helpers."

"I noticed that."

"And it doesn't hurt that we have leftovers from the Tray most nights."

"No," Mallory said. "That wouldn't hurt."

She found the family room virtually deserted except for Charlene and the baby.

"Miss Mallory, come closer."

"Shouldn't you rest when you can?"

Charlene rested her head against the pillow. "I do. Most certainly do. My beloved is getting the master bedroom ready for us. This room stays busy until the littles are down for the night."

"Can I help somehow?"

"Miss Mallory, you haven't even asked to hold our youngest yet."

"Not my place to ask."

Charlene tilted her head, the warm glow of childbirth still glistening on her face. "Miss Mallory, considerin' what we been through together, yer more near family than some of my kin."

Mallory's breath caught in her throat. She sat in the chair vacated by Bernard. "May I … ?"

Charlene laid her daughter in Mallory's waiting, aching arms. The infant stretched a tiny fist and rested it against one rosy round cheek. Perfection. Wonder. A world of possibilities in a warm bundle of newborn humanity.

"She's utterly beautiful, Charlene."

"I love lookin' at her from this angle too." She raised up on one elbow and rested her head in her palm. "You and Connor hopin' for children?"

Mallory knew the question would come. She'd steeled herself for it. But it still cut deep. "Most people ask if we're *planning* on children. Or *when* we're going to think about having children."

"I shouldn't be pryin'."

Charlene, I wish I could tell you everything.

"Don't y'all worry, Miss Mallory. Tears is perfectly natural when ya hold a little piece of heaven in yer arms. I just may join ya."

Natural. She waited until she could speak. "Charlene, you and Bernard have such an enviable life. Different—every one of you. But it comes so naturally to you."

Charlene started to laugh, then gripped her abdomen and grimaced. The baby squirmed in Mallory's arms. The baby yet unnamed. Mallory tightened her grip and bent her lips to the baby's ear. "*Shhh. Shhh.* You are loved little one. You are loved."

The mom laid one work-worn hand on Mallory's knee.

"Nothing about this family come easy to us. Don't know if y'all noticed, but Bernard and me got us a few differences. Don't even speak the same language most days."

Sounded all too familiar.

"This little one is only our second live birth after losing more'n I can count." She sobered. "That ain't 'tirely true. I remember ever' one. Ever' one."

"Oh, Charlene."

"None of our kids come easy. We fought for 'em. Sold everthing we had six times over for the joy of sayin' they was ours, givin' them a home they could count on forever. Some days, we wonder what we was thinkin'. Most days, we know. But it ain't natural. It's us an' God agreein' ever day, 'Okay, let's do this. The three of us.'"

The baby's fingers wrapped around Mallory's thumb. How could an hours-old child have such a tight grip? How could a year-old marriage have such a weak one? Maybe because they'd tried it as a *couple* rather than the "agreein' ever day" method.

She hadn't realized she'd been rocking side to side. No point stopping.

The hands on her shoulders rested more lightly than Connor's.

"Miss Mallory, my beloved's room is ready."

Bernard.

"Would you like to carry your daughter and I'll help Charlene?" Mallory stood to face him.

"A fine idea, if Charlene weren't asleep." He sat in the recently vacated chair. "That woman of my heart …" He shook his head in wonder.

Mallory's friends might have rebelled against his wording. *Woman of mine* would have stirred resentment. *I'm not a piece of property.* But Bernard had whispered, "Woman of my heart."

"Bernard, what's this new child's name?" Mallory surrendered the babe to his waiting arms.

"Molly's suggestion took the vote. Unanimous. You can imagine how overjoyed she was. Welcome to the family, Eleanor Rose. It was my mother's name, and little Molly didn't even know."

Convinced the Tray kids were both hungry and occupied for the moment, Connor uploaded his edited video snippets, texted a report to RoadRave about their slight change of plans, and checked in on the stats. Rapidly climbing. Nathan would be jacked if he knew. Sitting on a bench under one of the grand old trees in front of the now closed-for-the-day Tray Sheek, Connor sent a long update to Nathan's email address so he could catch up when his jury duty was complete.

Business taken care of, Connor headed back to the house. Time to figure out the sleeping arrangements for the night.

He paused on the deep porch, his hand on the door. Through the glass, he watched Mallory plant a kiss on the baby girl's head, then hand the child to Bernard. They spoke for a few moments, the closed door and whirring air conditioner masking their words. Eventually, Mallory kissed Bernard on the cheek and headed to the back of the house. At the archway to the hall, she leaned against the frame, removed the ring from her left hand, and slid it into her jeans pocket. She'd never removed her ring, that he could remember. Not even to do dishes.

Finality.

He knew where he stood.

Connor backed off the porch in favor of the kitchen entrance. Safer than walking past the spot where she'd removed the last trace of hope.

A week ago, he would have been relieved.

Connor stepped into the kitchen to the sound of plates clanging and Mallory's voice.

"Lizbet, I don't know that I've ever seen a house with six children this tidy." Mallory finished peeling a carrot and added it to a growing pile on the cutting board.

"Everyone has a job to do. We grew up expecting to have fun *and* to clean up after ourselves. For friends of mine, it's one or the other. But we learned, as Mama says, 'There's time in *every* day for three things—work, play, and Jesus.'"

"I know plenty of people who would dispute that idea," Connor said, snatching a peeled carrot.

Mallory frowned at him.

What did she think he meant?

"I'm someone who hasn't nailed that yet," he said.

"You would if you lived here, Mr. Connor." Lizbet smiled and set the last of the silverware in a short but heavy jar near the stack of plates on the end of the long table. "I told the littles we'd be eating in the backyard tonight. Give Mama a few more minutes of quiet, at least. Oh, and my parents said yes to the boys camping out and the girls' slumber party. Sounds like you two will have your hands full tonight."

chapter twenty-four

CONNOR WATCHED THE TRAY HOME grow smaller in his
rearview mirror. He and Mallory had waved from the
porch as most of them climbed into the school bus that
morning, groggy from too much fun and new baby excitement
the night before.

Even Judah had been a willing participant in cleaning
up after elbow-to-elbow boys spent the night in the camper,
watching stars through the sunroof, and swapping stories of
where they'd been before they were adopted into the Tray family. The stories Connor overheard "rearranged his innards," as
Charlene would have put it.

The boys were so young to have endured so much. Their
resilience, their tenacity, put them miles ahead of Connor in
maturity, a fact that inspired and unnerved him.

The camper sparkled again. Bernard made sure their food
storage areas were well supplied for the next leg of the journey.
But the moment had eventually come when the only right thing
was to say goodbye.

Mallory. The only right thing. Saying goodbye.

If Connor and Mallory lived closer to his parents, had witnessed the daily anguish, if she'd known his grandfather, and his great-grandfather before that, she'd understand. No woman should have to—

He took a swig of coffee from the RoadRave travel mug in the console. Nice premium for those subscribing to their channel and asking for the T900 introductory packet. The words "Just add humans and the adventure begins" were embossed into the stainless-steel outer shell of the mug. His fingers traced the indentations. *Hmm.* If they won the account, they might consider RoadRave passport covers. An interesting thought.

His humans—Judah and Mallory—were even more subdued than normal this morning. Tired, sure. The prior day had provided more than enough adventure of a different kind.

"Judah," he said, clearing his throat and mind, "do you think you and Mason will stay connected?"

"Don't know. He says he will."

"They feel like the kind of family that keeps their promises." Off just a tick. Connor's filter-before-you-say-something monitor was off by seconds. But there was no retracting what he'd said. And, it was true.

Connor waited for a brilliant revelation of something intelligent to say to cover the track marks his words must have left on Judah's young and too often disappointed heart. Waited some more. Nothing. "You awake back there, Mallory?" *Rescue me, here?*

Nothing.

"On his own" felt worse than he'd imagined it would. Saddling her with an incomprehensible burden would feel worse. She had to know that.

"Well, this should be fun," Judah said, the sarcasm dripping as it only could from an expert.

"What are you talking about?"

"Incoming gave us a destination name this time."

"Great," Connor said. "What is it?"

"Dry Falls. Now, that should be a winner. 'And to your right, you'll see the place where water would be, if there were any. Photo op, everyone. Don't miss it.'"

Midmorning, they pulled through the town of Highlands, North Carolina, on Highway 28. Judah made it a point to note that the population was under a thousand people. The beauty of the Appalachian surroundings escaped Judah, but the dog-themed hotel did not.

Just northwest of "downtown" Highlands, the road followed Lake Sequoyah to a parking lot and observation platform for Dry Falls.

Connor had to admit it. He took a little too much pleasure from the fact that the waterfall roared with water, despite its unfortunate name.

"Okay, boys," Mallory said. "We're back in the travel journal business." She unhooked her seatbelt. "Waterfalls Unlimited. Smiles, everyone."

Her words sounded sincere, with a side of not. Had she taken a semester of theater in college? Had he forgotten?

Sometimes he got a little distracted by his own concerns. More than sometimes.

"This is cool!" Judah said, beating them both to the railing of the platform.

A short switchback trail of stairs and gravel led to a walkway behind the falls. The wall of water jutted out steeply from the overhanging slabs of rock in the gorge, keeping the cliff-side part of the trail and its travelers completely dry.

Judah reached his hand as far over the wooden safety railing as he could to feel the force of the water but could do no more than tickle its spray. "Dry Falls. I get it. Cool. We're dry all right, as long as we stand here, behind the falls."

Mallory had held back, approaching slowly with the camera aimed their way. Connor waved. Cheesy. So professional. He had to get his head back in the game. Stopping Judah from climbing over the railing onto the mossy rocks centered him.

How different the trip would have been in its original form. With Nathan. Two best buds adventuring all over the place. No Judah. No Mallory. How much of what they'd experienced wouldn't have happened? The people they'd talked to. The unplanned stops. The soul searching.

One thing would have been radically different. Mallory wouldn't have been on his mind every minute, like she was now.

Seriously? He could imagine having shut off the demise of their marriage if she weren't present? The smooth stone gravel crunched under her feet as she drew nearer. Who was he kidding? Answer? Himself.

"It's at least ten degrees cooler down here," she said, camera still raised. She hit Pause. "Let me go past you two and catch the angle from the other side. The foliage framing the cliff is incredible. How many feet tall are the falls, Connor?"

"The sign said sixty-five feet," Judah answered.

Connor had been the one who didn't want to talk about it anymore. *He'd* been the one. Now, he would have given … What would he have given for an hour of alone time to talk to her? No cameras. No Judah between them. No front to keep up for the sake of Troyer & Duncan.

She'd made up her mind. But so had he. Before.

His brain hurt.

Since he'd found out what was wrong with his dad, every twinge of a headache sent his thoughts in dangerous directions, like an out-of-control semi on an Appalachian mountain road, ignoring the guardrails and the runaway truck ramps. It had taken him years of intentionality to push the thought aside and let the twinges prove themselves harmless. So far.

Judah and Mallory were interviewing a lone visitor on the trail. Connor left them to it and followed the trail to its end, taking still shots with his phone.

Maybe he did need counseling for that—the constant, hovering specter of doom. Despite the averages, most of the men in his lineage didn't develop symptoms until well into their forties or fifties. When Connor was at work, he could ignore doom's nagging. Had he thrown himself more deeply into the business than he needed to as a way to stop the voice?

In the quiet of their apartment at night, alone with Mallory, the voice screamed loudest. Made sense. She was the one who would bear the brunt of the misery if they decided to stay together that long.

He deserved the discomfort of this breakup. He shouldn't have let romance tell him it didn't matter. It mattered. It changed everything. His life sentence didn't have to be hers. Shouldn't be. Couldn't be.

He needed to call his mom and talk her into accepting the respite care her church offered. She might crumble before this was all over if she didn't. He should have been more supportive for his mom all this time. The miles between them shouldn't have dictated the silence he imposed.

Not a lot of self-love consumed him these days.

Mallory and Judah laughed over something the visitor said. That's what she deserved. A life full of laughter. Not the future he could offer her. Or lack thereof.

◆————————————◆

The incline to the parking lot wasn't long or steep, but today, Mallory found every footstep took effort. The morning hadn't allowed time for her normal stretches. Sitting in the Outback for hours didn't help. Time to change that. The waterfall hikes made a difference, but the miles were taking a physical toll.

Physical. *I hereby choose to focus on the beauty around me. I can't afford to miss the stunning.*

She straightened her shoulders and lengthened her stride. No one could deny the wonder of the sights they'd been gifted. She'd traveled at 30,000 feet above the surface of the earth many times over these same parts of the country. It was a different experience feeling the power of the water's spray, hearing the dried leaves underfoot, watching the scene change around every curve in the road.

She'd never known nights so deep or a moon as bright as those they'd shared far from the distortion of city lights. The smells of earth and rain and sun-scorched fields. Of wildflowers she'd only seen in pictures and varieties she'd never known about before. Of backyard grills and curious restaurants and fresh-cut lumber and ancient rock. The resistance of water against her canoe paddle. Water's ability to carve paths in the landscape with the crooked creeks they'd crossed, depressions in the canyons at the base of cascades with names like Dry Falls.

I can't change the path of my marriage. But I can change the path my thoughts carve. Judah's note from Nathan that morning had sent her to her Bible app. *Excellent, admirable, true, pure, lovely—think on those things,* it told her.

Think. Action verb. An exercise.

Time for some emotional cardio.

Their stop for the night had them crossing back into Tennessee, to a county park with a minimum of amenities. Without being asked, Connor helped Mallory pull Tray Sheek leftovers from the cooler, proving the quilted blanket-like insulation's boost. Despite the day's temps, all the food in the cooler felt refrigerator cold. Great system. Connor said he'd make a comment on that in their end-of-day video wrap-up.

With a minimum of supervision, Judah built a fire in the stone fire pit at the campsite, then turned his attention to a string of text messages from Mason.

"Like opening a time capsule of memories, isn't it?" Mallory said as she unwrapped the food Bernard and Charlene had sent. "I wonder what they're doing tonight."

"According to Mason, they're getting ready for Charlene's mom and sisters to arrive from Alabama to help out with the baby," Connor said.

That was an Alabama accent? No. Charlene had developed

her own unique blend, like a custom tea. Everything about their family was a beautiful, curious blend. "I have a feeling they'd do just fine on their own."

"Judah said Mason included a 'rolling my eyes' emoji."

"I'm glad those two hit it off."

Connor flipped the switch for the overhead LED lights for the teardrop's kitchen. "We should see what's in the Road-Rave box."

"A second telescoping canoe paddle would be nice, in case we get a chance to use the first one."

"Well, this is sweet."

She tore a paper towel from the roll and wiped road dust from the cutting board. "What is it?"

"A bathroom sink."

Judah looked up from tending the fire. "Dude, we don't have a bathroom, in case you forgot."

Connor removed the shrink wrap. "It hangs on a window of the car. With a little pop-up mirror. And a tiny little water reservoir. Nice."

"You could shave," Mallory said.

"Or Judah could brush his teeth more often."

"Is it large enough that I could wash my hair at a campsite?" Mallory asked. "I have to say, showering at the Tray house made me do a little happy dance. It reminded me what clean feels like."

"No longer a problem." He opened another shrink-wrapped item from the RoadRave box. "We are now the proud owners of our own shower."

Mallory stopped dinner prep. "That's not a shower stall. It's a colander. For very small vegetables."

"It's a colander," Connor said, "*and* a solar water heater bag *and* a privacy shell, according to the enclosed instructions, which I—a man—am reading, in case you failed to notice."

"Also doubles as an embroidery hoop with a plastic tablecloth attached to it."

"A *waterproof* tablecloth." Connor seemed a little too thrilled with the discovery. Ah. Judah had the camera rolling. Acting.

"Can't wait to try out the makeup sink," she said.

"Dibs on the shower," Judah called from behind the camera.

Connor smiled. A genuine smile. "We will not fight you on that count, young man. This is great. We can store the items in …"

Loss for words, Connor? Let me help. "In the floor storage compartment under the mattress."

"Yes. Excellent." He tipped his hat to the camera. "Thanks, RoadRave. And thanks for your comments on these video posts, viewers, and for taking the journey with us. Remember, just add humans …"

Mallory leaned over his shoulder, "… and the adventure begins."

"And cut." Judah lowered the camera. "Can we eat now?"

"You called dibs on the shower, Judah?" Connor said. "As if you're a neat freak all of a sudden? You're not really going to shower again, are you, buddy." Not even a hint of a question in his remark.

"What day is it?"

chapter twenty-five

DAYS OF ALMOST NONSTOP TRAVEL. They'd paused to take advantage of a farmers market one day and a small town combo Labor Day parade and county fair the next. Connor couldn't remember where. When he closed his eyes at night, he saw highway hash marks. When he opened them in the morning, he saw #justaddhumans and an ever more loyal following.

But the road dragged on.

Judah had made a *Name That Tune* game out of tapping rhythms on the dashboard. It wasn't long before Mallory, bless her, had figured out they were video game songs the two of them could never guess. Judah switched to TV theme songs. Again, none of which Connor or Mallory could figure out. Who remembers the theme song from all the summer-only pilots? That kid.

Mallory made sure he stuck to the homework schedule his long-distance-learning teachers had laid out. But that only chewed up a couple of hours a day.

Connor and Mallory had fallen into a weird truce. They needed to talk, but timing remained an issue. If they could get through the trip, finish this assignment, send Judah back to Nathan, and sit face-to-face, maybe they could work this out. Poor choice of words. Maybe they could land on a plan where they could stay together until symptoms appeared, and then Mallory could check out without obligation.

Somehow that seemed less marriage-like and more college roommate-like.

In high school, he'd thought choosing a college and career were life's most agonizing decisions. Not even in the Top Ten anymore.

Mallory seemed oddly at peace. But then he'd catch her staring out her window or hear her breath lodge in her throat. When he'd asked how she was doing, she'd answered, "Fragile." He told her, "You're one of the least fragile people I know, Mallory."

Those moments never lasted long. But they tore at him.

They'd been heading on a northern trajectory. Back roads. Always back roads. West Virginia, Pennsylvania, New York. The Adirondacks. The air cooled. How many points of interest had they bypassed? For another time. If he had that much time.

"Niagara Falls is in New York, right?" Judah thumbed his phone. "Yup. That's what I thought. New York. And Canada. We're going to Niagara Falls, aren't we?"

"It's a lot farther west than our heading, Judah," Mallory said. "For now, at least. We haven't been directed to any of the major waterfalls so far. It's the smaller ones. I think RoadRave wants people to notice what other people pass by. What do you think, Connor?"

"That's part of their push. People flock to the famous and miss a lot of wonderful along the way."

"Well said, sir."

"Thank you, ma'am."

"Love," Judah said, pinching his nose. "It's disgusting."

"You won't always feel that way, Judah," Connor answered, avoiding the mirror's view of the second seat.

"And, we have incoming," Mallory said, the relief in her voice a little too evident. "Two miles ahead. Right-hand turn. The message says we'll understand when we see it."

"Let me guess," Judah said. "A waterfall?"

Two minutes later, they had the answer. No. A community. Every dwelling was a tiny house.

"We have found our people!" Judah said, fists raised.

◆------------------------------◆

Mallory had been intrigued by the tiny home trend she saw on television and social media. Innovative ideas. Living without a mortgage also had its perks. Downsizing everything imaginable. Paring nonessentials until only the essentials remain.

But until living for almost a week and a half in a practically zero-square-foot camper, she hadn't believed it possible to endure long in even less space than their 700-square-foot Chicago apartment. A tiny house community? This could be interesting.

The tiny houses dotting the well-landscaped New Day Village community seemed huge by comparison to the teardrop camper. The camper drew instant interest. A small crowd—how fitting that it was small—had gathered before they signed in at the entrance gate and collected information about the campground on the far side of the community pool.

They were welcomed so warmly that Mallory found the pool and its promised refreshment distracting, as if it might cool even the congeniality temps closer to normal.

A man heftier and more Viking-like than Connor approached, parting the crowd. "Hey, hey, folks. Let's give these people a little breathing room. Welcome to our eclectic community. You're invited to join us for the Gathering at sundown. Don't worry about bringing anything. There's always more than enough food. Take your time getting settled in. We'll meet up with you later and hear your story."

"Our story?" Mallory wasn't sure anyone should hear theirs.

"Everybody has a story," Thor said, steering the crowd out of their path. "Some of them are set to music. You'll see."

Mallory hadn't seen Connor pull out his guitar since the trip began. He'd promised her a song. The promise grew more faded every day.

Connor climbed behind the wheel again but stuck his head out the open window. "Wait. Where is the Gathering? Where should we meet you?"

"You'll see." Thor turned his broad back to them, his arm over the shoulders of a slight woman with smiling eyes.

The RoadRave box waited for them on the picnic table at what might be considered the prime campsite of the eight available. Steps from the pool. Just the right distance from the facilities, which the New Day Village brochure claimed were fully equipped with—Mallory shot a prayer of gratitude heavenward—flush toilets and electrical outlets for curling wands and blow dryers, also provided.

Hemmed in at the back by thick, old-growth woods, the campsite had a wide pull-around space. Lush but well-trimmed patch of grass. An iron fire ring surrounded by a moat of gravel for safety.

"Dibs on the box," Judah said, heading that direction while Connor and Mallory leveled the camper and chock-blocked the wheels.

"Cute tiny houses," Connor said, extracting the aluminum tubing for the cocoon hammocks.

"Adorable. I would have thought *cute* would wear out its welcome after a while, but this community looks well established. Rooted."

"I thought the same thing." Connor frowned. "Judah? No destroying our gift from RoadRave before we get to see it, okay?"

"I'm not wrecking it. I'm opening it."

"What'd they send this time?" New Day Village was a gated community. Mallory wondered if the residents could provide intel on how RoadRave so expertly snuck around to plant their bonus box at each of their stops.

"Three smaller boxes inside," Judah said. "One for each of us."

"I commend you for not trying to claim all three were for you," Connor said.

"Yeah, well, they're labeled with our names."

"Oh." Connor winked at Mallory.

A wink. Casual. Easy, like their affection used to be.

Each of the boxes held twenty single dollar bills and a small card with instructions.

"'Use it as you choose,'" Connor read, "'but not for your own needs or wants. Find someone along the journey who needs the blessing more than you do.'"

"I know," Judah said, perking up. "You give me yours, Connor, and I'll give mine to Mallory, and she can give hers to you, and we are all twenty dollars richer. Nailed it!"

"Missing the point of giving, Judah. Other than that, your plan seems flawless." Connor laughed.

Mallory fanned through her dollar bills. This could be fun. "Does it say if there's a time limit on the giveaways?"

Connor handed her the card. "Looks like the expiration date is any time before we pull back into Chicago. End of the line." A shadow crossed his face before he returned to the last of his setup duties.

"What are you guys doing with yours?" Judah stuffed the bills in his pants pockets.

"I think the idea," Mallory said, "is for us to put significant thought into the way we use the money, Judah. Thoughtful. Observing. Listening." She drew out each word. He bobbed his head in a figure-eight as if he couldn't imagine anything more boring.

Connor stepped closer, jingling the key for the trailer hitch latch. "Judah, come on. Get over yourself and try to consider—"

Mallory laid her hand on his forearm. "He'll figure it out."

Connor followed her toward the kitchen end of the camper. "You sure about that?"

"I have hope."

"You always have had, Mallory." He pocketed the key and took her left hand.

Somehow, he'd noticed. How? When?

He rubbed his thumb where her ring had lived until a few days ago.

"Mallory, you've always known how to hold onto hope."

No, Connor. I haven't. And I don't know how to hang onto hope for us anymore.

"Please don't stop now."

"What are you two talking about?" Judah called from his spot at the picnic table. "Me? Are you talking about me? Because I can hear you. A little bit."

"Mallory, can we please find some alone time? To talk?"

Now you're willing to talk? Connor, we're so beyond talking.

She eased her hand away from the stinging pain of his touch. "Miles to go, Connor. We still have miles to go on this journey."

"If you two are going to keep yakking, I'm going swimming."

Connor turned to face their traveling companion. "Not without supervision, Judah."

"I know how to swim."

"That's not the issue."

"Then I guess you'll have to hurry to catch up, because I'm going swimming."

Connor checked the sky. "It'll cool off fast tonight, this far north."

Judah trotted backward as he said, "The pool's heated. I read the sign."

"So did I," Mallory called. "Swim trunks are mandatory."

The boy stopped in his tracks and crept back toward the campsite. "Minor detail I overlooked."

The comic expression on his face turned the tension into

laughter. They hadn't totally derailed. The three of them could still find reason to enjoy a moment.

"Beach towels," she said. They hadn't thought of every eventuality. "We only have small towels."

"You people should pay more attention," Judah said, digging in his duffel bag. "They have a stack of pool towels right by the safety gate."

"Great," Connor said, his eyes focused on Mallory's face. "Perfect. Looks like I'm going swimming. Are you coming?"

"Too cool for me. I'm going for a walk. I'll take the video camera and grab some ambiance footage."

"I'll walk with you." The shadow returned. "No, I won't. Judah—"

"He'll appreciate your taking him swimming, Connor. You're scoring more points with him every day."

Was it completely impossible to simultaneously score points with an eleven-year-old reformed—reforming—delinquent and the woman whose life Connor had messed up? He appreciated the progress Judah occasionally let them see. But …

No. Connor turned his head to avoid the tidal-wave-up-the-nose Judah worked on perfecting with his cannonballs. They were alone in the pool. Other residents of the community might have realized it was after Labor Day in upstate New York, rather than the tropics mid-summer.

He swam to the pool depth where all but his head was under water. Admittedly dangerous with the waves Judah made, at least his body stayed warm. He kept an eye out for Mallory and the camera. He'd need his screen face for that.

His screen face. The one he wore for social media. RoadRave. For the second and apparently final six months of his marriage.

And he was the guy who harped about authenticity. *Nice*

going, Connor. Your whole life is the opposite of what you care about most.

He'd finally told Mallory, "Let's get real" a few weeks ago. Then within a few days, he asked her to get fake—to "screen face" a happily married couple who nobly added Judah to their so-called family for a back-roads trip in a pocket-sized camper so he could save his reputation.

Correction. His company. He hadn't meant to say reputation.

Wasn't it yesterday he'd told himself to stop thinking so much? *Just "be," Connor. You'll live longer.* Or not. Chances were pretty good the answer was "not."

While Judah dove for the weighted multicolored rings Connor tossed, Connor stretched his shoulder and back muscles. It wasn't long before Judah suggested a how-long-can-you-float-on-your-back contest.

"Where'd you learn to swim, Judah?"

"Homeless Camp."

"What?"

As if making snow angels on the surface of the water, Judah stretched his arms and pulled them to his sides, propelling him one stroke farther toward the deep end. "Camp for kids like me without permanent homes. Your tax dollars at work."

"And where'd you learn to talk like that?"

"You mean snarky? I'd like to say it comes naturally. I'm gifted. But it might be my mom's influence."

"Ah." Connor backstroked to pull even with Judah.

"I'm an atheist, you know."

Connor practiced Mallory's unshockability. "Are you?"

"Uncle Nathan still thinks there's hope for me. Personally, I don't see it."

Connor mimicked Judah's stillness in the water, the slightest movement of hands and feet keeping them afloat. "What makes you think you're an atheist?" *Steady, Connor. Don't make ... uh ... waves.*

"The traditional definition. Don't believe in God."

"You don't believe there *is* a God or you don't believe *in* Him?"

"There's a difference?"

Young man, you should be talking to someone who knows what he's talking about. But right now, I'm all you have. "Subtle, but important." Freshman year at Northwestern. The subject of many late-night, too-much-coffee, how-high-can-we-stack-these-pizza-boxes discussions. "A person can deny the existence of God or know He exists but refuse to acknowledge Him."

"Which are you?"

chapter twenty-six

MALLORY RESTED THE CAMERA ON the top rail of the
security fence near the shallow end of the pool—
twenty yards or more from the two human otters
floating on their backs. She hit Record. Seconds later, Connor
flailed his arms and righted himself. He started to tread water.
Judah joined him.

From this distance, their conversation looked intense, but
they kept their voices too low for her to hear more than mum-
bles. Approach? Stay back? Everything in her ached to know
what they were saying to one another, which probably meant
the smart thing was to hang back and let them work it out
between the two of them.

◆————————————————◆

"Neither, Judah. I'm neither." Connor's pulse pounded in his ears.

"Huh. Interesting."

"What would make you think I don't believe in God?"
The words slipped out before he considered the wake they
would leave.

"The crickets anytime someone brings up the subject,"

Judah said. "You know. Silence, except for the crickets chirping?"

"I'm familiar with the metaphor."

"What's a meta for? Get it?"

"Judah, this is serious."

"Dude, we're floating in a pool in our swim shorts, surrounded by a bunch of people who live in fairytale houses. It's a little hard to be too serious, you know? Besides," he said, jerking his head. "One o'clock."

"What's at one?"

"Not what. Who."

"Judah."

"My one o'clock. Your … well, yeah, she's at your one too."

Mallory. With the camera. The one Connor drafted her into keeping with her at all times. No question, Connor believed in God. He prayed his guts out that the camera hadn't picked up their audio.

"This conversation isn't over, Judah."

"We're done swimming, though, huh?"

"Follow me. I smell meat on a charcoal grill. I sense sunset nearing." *And perhaps soon my untimely death by a lightning bolt.* Connor needed time to compile his thoughts. Or hop a quick flight back to Chicago and let Mallory deal with Judah's—

And that's how lame a husband can get. At least now he knew for sure where he ranked on the slimeball scale. Near the top. Or bottom, depending on one's perspective, and, good grief, how would he explain the last few minutes to Mallory?

Some husbands—not him—had to face their wives with the confession of an affair, or a gambling addiction, or an alcohol problem, or dependence on prescription drugs. Connor had to confess that he had no idea how to talk to a preteen about God, a preteen who not only thought himself an atheist but wondered if Connor was too.

"You boys done with your polar plunge?"

"What's that?" Judah bounced out of the water.

Connor climbed as if recently discovering the adverse

effects of gravity. "The water was nice and warm. The air? Not so much."

"My guess is that long pants will be a good option for tonight's Gathering. I'm heading back to the camper to grab my quilted vest."

Judah ran ahead, bare feet slapping on the asphalt path.

"Interesting conversation?" Mallory asked, fiddling with the camera strap as they walked.

Ooh. He wasn't going to skate out of it. "Oh, yeah. Yup. Interesting."

"Guy talk?"

"Technically, yes." He'd always balked at the term "the Big Guy Upstairs," but if it postponed having to admit he'd been so bad at living his faith that their younger charge didn't know he had any …

Why was he so hesitant to talk about it? Mallory already knew he was a disappointment as a husband. How shocking could it be that he was a disappointment to God too? He grunted under his breath. What was he thinking? She already knew.

"Connor?"

"Lost my ability to walk and think at the same time."

"It's like road rash for the brain," she said. "Feeling a little muddle-headed myself."

Connor wrapped the towel tighter around his shoulders. "Three weeks is a lot longer than it seems on paper."

"We passed the halfway point two days ago," she said. "If that's any consolation."

"Where do you think we're heading next? Think Road-Rave will keep up the waterfall theme?"

She sighed. "I hope so."

"You do? I'm starting to think Judah's 'you've seen forty, you've seen them all' might have merit."

"I googled waterfalls while you were driving today."

"Looking for what might be nearby?" Connor wondered too.

"No. Looking for their significance. Spiritually."

Please. Not that subject. I'm a long way from ready for that conversation.

"Did you know," she said, "that in the Lakota culture, a waterfall is a place to go for spiritual healing, soul healing?"

"Interesting."

"That sent me to my Bible app, looking for references to water, waterfalls, fountains …"

"Heated pools?" Humor had been his saving grace before. Maybe this time she'd—

"Actually, yes."

They'd reached their campsite. Judah shivered beside the lifeless campfire.

Connor flapped one "wing" of his towel.

"I know," she said. "You need to get dressed. One of these days"—she looked toward the horizon—"we'll have to try taking a conversation all the way to its end. Bizarre thought, right?"

"Outrageous."

◆--------------------◆

The blacktop drive that circled through New Day Village—and campground—was lined with ankle-high solar lights spaced at intervals. Enough light to make walking in the near dark not only safe but cozy. Mallory walked with Connor and Judah, following the lights and sounds to a shelter in the section of the gated community they hadn't explored yet.

Two long tables of potluck-style food were set up under the open-on-three-sides shelter. Surrounding the shelter was a scene that stole Mallory's breath.

"Doesn't that look so much like—?"

"I was thinking the same thing," Connor said.

Judah swung the video camera in a wide arc to catch the two dozen mismatched tables with their mismatched chairs, white linen tablecloths, wildflowers in amber jars, and strings of clear bare lightbulbs draped from tree to tree.

The food was different. The people were different. But the atmosphere felt so much like the Tray family's restaurant—like the Tray family—that Mallory felt a twinge of something. Homesickness? The woods beyond the shelter area deepened to black, but the eating area glowed with warm light and hospitality.

Thor and his wife approached. "So glad you came. I don't remember if I introduced myself earlier. I'm Leif Eriksson, and this is my wife Ericka."

"Leif?"

"I'm kidding. It's a Viking joke for history fans. I'm Vic. That's right. Vic the Viking, or Norseman, as I prefer. But my wife's name really is Ericka. We have two or three kids running around somewhere. You can meet them later."

Connor shook their hands and introduced Mallory and Judah, their foster "son."

"The community noticed the RoadRave logo on your camper," Vic said. "Some of us have been on our computers all afternoon catching up with where you've been, what you've seen. I hope you're taking in Split Rock Falls while you're in the area."

"Oh, I'm sure we will be," Judah said, his voice flat. "Mallory, the food line's moving. Can I—?"

"Like I said earlier"—Vic gestured toward the shelter—"there's no lack of food at these things."

Mallory nodded.

"Sure, Judah," Connor said. "Just, you know, stay close. Close-ish. Give me the camera."

"Anyway," Vic said, "it's quite a deal you have going there. Quite the adventure."

Connor said, "I've heard of communities of tiny house fans before but never thought I'd have a chance to visit one."

Vic glanced at his wife. "You're more than welcome to take the official home tour tomorrow. Most of us don't mind showing off what it takes to go this small. What convinced me was the innovation. I mean, I'm a big guy, but Ericka and the kids and I are surprisingly comfortable."

"I imagine," Mallory said, "that you had to give up a lot of what others might consider essentials to make a dramatic move like that."

"Thing is," Vic said, "it turns out a family can drown in more and thrive with less."

"We don't have to tell you two that," Ericka added. "Your camper ..."

"Ah yes," Connor said. "The teardrop."

"You're living in a teardrop," Ericka said. "Poetic."

And all too real. Mallory nodded her agreement, but said, "Teardrops aren't designed to be permanent homes."

"From what I hear, some people do live in them long-term. A larger model, I'm sure." Connor absently straightened the white linen napkin on the table nearest to him.

"You're welcome to have a seat at any table," Ericka said.

"I'm surprised," Mallory said, hands in her vest pockets, "that you have room in your tiny houses to store all these tables."

"We don't." Ericka lifted the corner of the tablecloth. "Most of them were family heirlooms or pieces we would have had to sell when we moved into our tiny homes. Instead, we pooled them for this purpose. They're kept in the storage unit behind the shelter during the winter. We only have a few more outdoor Gatherings this fall before it turns too cold. So happy you could join us for this one."

Mallory sat in one of the chairs offered them. Connor followed.

"Are you sure you don't want to get in line?" Vic asked.

Connor answered for them. "In a few minutes. Is it okay if we take some footage here? RoadRave and the video blog followers would love this."

Mallory watched Connor closely. He didn't make a move toward the camera now on the table until Vic and Ericka gave their assent.

"A couple of us have been talking," Ericka said. "We're all in. We were hoping you'd consider our little social and cultural experiment worth adding to your adventure."

"Do you think we could interview some of the residents too?"

"Oh, we all have stories to tell," Vic said. "I'm confident you'll find more than a few who want to share theirs."

"And we'd love to hear yours," Ericka said. "There must be more to it than what we see online."

Mallory could feel Connor's tension through where their shirt sleeves touched. "Well," she said, "our one-year anniversary is coming up in October."

"How romantic!" Ericka said, her hands splayed over her heart.

"And we'll be separated by then."

"Mallory!" Connor shot to his feet.

"You being deployed, son?" Vic asked, his face a mask of concern.

"No. Mallory, what are you doing?"

She was never, ever reckless. Never. But the sentence laid there in the air. And what was at stake if the world found out? Her at-risk youth and the literacy program. Connor's business. RoadRave's investment. Judah's tentative stability. Too much.

"What I meant was that if I don't get some of that grilled chicken because we waited too long to get in line"—she faced Connor—"it's over between us, mister."

Mallory headed for the shelter, the Viking couple's laughter ringing behind her.

Connor caught up with her. She knew he would. She did not, however, know what she would say to him.

He pulled close enough in line behind her to direct his words to the back of her head. "Mallory, that was as close to a heart attack as I hope to get. What were you thinking? Never mind that. I have to give you props for the nice save. Creative."

"Oh, look. Potato salad."

"Mallory ..."

"And green beans. You know how much I love green beans."

"Are you feeling okay?"

She turned toward him, her plate listing to the right. "I am tired and inexpressibly sad and helpless to do anything about either one. Other than that," she said, "life couldn't be better. Try the coleslaw." She licked her fingers. *"Mmm. Delicious."*

chapter twenty-seven

THE LIVE INSTRUMENTAL MUSIC ACCOMPANYING their shared evening meal—two guitars, a flute, and a drum shaped like a box—had a familiar sound to it. His fingers automatically formed the chords he heard. Connor couldn't drag up the lyrics or titles, but serving as music detective was not high on his priority list. Had Mallory's cheese slipped off her cracker? And if not, if she was serious, was everything headed for Doomsville sooner rather than later? Was she pulling the plug on the RoadRave trip?

Vic and Ericka talked and asked questions through the whole meal. Judah had found a group of kids to hang with, so it was up to Connor and Mallory to be sociable. Right. Because Judah had always been the sociable one? Maybe it wasn't Mallory's but Connor's cheese that stood on a slippery slope.

Connor explained his company and the relationship with RoadRave. He and Vic shared an interest in strength training.

When Vic heard that Mallory worked with at-risk teens in the inner city, the Viking piped up with, "Lot of admiration for you, Mallory. The inner city isn't the only place with at-risk teens. We have more than our share right here in this county. What we wouldn't give for a thing like what you have going with your Hope Street center."

"We never lack for challenges," Mallory said. Nothing more.

Vic asked, "Where did you two meet? Couldn't have been on the job."

After Connor explained that he and Mallory had met through an online dating service, Ericka applauded. "I love hearing about couples who make that work. Last I read, the statistics were something like a third of all newly married couples met online. Does that sound right?"

"About right," he said, without elaborating.

Mallory asked, "How did you and Vic meet?"

Ericka sobered. Vic laid his hand on hers on the table. "How we met isn't the important detail," he said. "It's how we stay together."

Connor didn't dare press for more information on that subject.

He and Mallory kept the conversation centered on the travel challenges they'd faced, the people who'd made an impression on them, Judah's antics both on and off camera. They asked questions about tiny house living and listened to Vic's descriptions of ladders that doubled as bookshelves and shoe storage under the couch.

"Not *Judah's* shoes," Connor had said. It brought a smile to Mallory's face. A short-lived smile. A short-lived smile is better than none at all?

Thinking too hard always got him into trouble these days.

"So, which of these houses are considered permanent?" he asked.

Ericka laid her fork aside. "Almost all of them. When we arrived, like most, we expected it was a temporary arrangement. We'd thought having a tiny house was our ticket to travel wherever we wanted to go, live wherever we wanted to live. Freedom."

"That changed?"

"Freedom," she said, "has a lot more to do with content-ment than the absence of boundaries. We found ourselves content here. Would you two excuse me for a minute?"

Ericka left the table and headed for their nearby home.

Mallory asked, "Is she okay?"

Vic downed another forkful of coleslaw. "Insulin. She's diabetic. Since she was a toddler. She'll be back before long."

"You two," Connor began, "have been dealing with her diabetes your whole marriage?"

Mallory looked up from her plate.

"Part of life. She's there for me with my erratic deploy-ment schedules. I'm there for her medical needs. Comes with the territory."

Connor didn't miss that Mallory stopped eating, leaving her dessert untouched.

Vic pushed back from the table and angled his chair toward the band when a couple about Mallory and Connor's age stepped to the microphone. Ericka rejoined them and turned her chair as well.

"Good evening, folks," the man said. "Another great Gath-ering meal, wouldn't you say?"

The crowd erupted in applause punctuated by whistles and cheers.

"Did you get some of my wife's apple crisp?" He nudged her. The group responded with more whistles. "I still insist that if she opened a bakery, the village could keep her busier than she wants to be." Laugh track. "But then, who would we hire to prepare our taxes?" More laughter.

They paid taxes. Connor's concerns that they'd stumbled into a twenty-first century version of a commune dissipated.

Ericka leaned across the table and whispered, "That's Joel and Janene. You might have heard their music on the radio. I'll introduce you to them later. After the singing."

Oh, swell. Singing. The back of Connor's neck itched. Joel and Janene? He'd never heard of them. Probably should have. Their voices were as smooth as caramel. He laid his arm on the back of Mallory's chair. For appearances. She either didn't notice or didn't want to expend the energy to flinch.

A few voices joined in right away on the first song. It was obvious Connor wasn't the only one present who was unfamiliar with it. But by the chorus, more participated, including Vic and Ericka.

And Mallory.

He'd thought it was a song about brokenness. And heartache. Two words into the chorus, and he knew it was a God song. Worship music. Back to wondering if they'd accidentally stumbled into a religious compound.

He hadn't checked for locks to keep people from leaving.

A few families drifted away from the setting as the worship music started. Others who stayed waved at them or walked over to hug them before they left. Not like any compound he'd heard of.

Mallory stopped singing. She was filming.

How were they going to use footage like this? RoadRave wasn't interested in—

Wait. They'd sent them here. Sent them to the Tray family. In all Troyer & Duncan's interactions with the RoadRave people, Connor had never felt any pressure regarding religious beliefs they might hold. Americana. Family values. High standards. Impeccable work ethic.

Nathan, the faithtimistic one of the two of them, had connected with the CEO, Marc. Marc and Nathan communicated more frequently on nonbusiness issues. But ...

The music intensified. Several people rose to their feet. Mallory stood, probably so the video wouldn't be blocked by standers in front of her. Connor stayed seated. The words. The words of the song rooted him to his chair. One song ended and the duo began another, this one more upbeat, but similar in message. Whole bunch of broken. Whole bunch of hope.

God. Jesus. Holy Spirit. Power. Peace. Presence.

He'd been here before. Not this location, but this soul

location. Empty. Needing to be filled. Unsure how that could happen. Entertaining a shred of hope that God had made promises Connor hadn't tapped into yet.

Instead of decreasing, the emptiness grew, expanded, consumed him.

Mallory hadn't known the first song, but the second one had become a favorite on the playlist she started listening to while they were on the road. The three of them hadn't figured out how to compromise—no surprise—on radio stations, so they'd agreed—small victory—they'd each listen to their own music with earbuds.

She didn't turn but could hear that Connor didn't participate. Not that she expected he would. He had a great voice, but she hadn't heard him sing for months. Not even in the shower. Or when he didn't know she was there. And he hadn't even hinted that he was following through to work on a song for her. With that much inescapable togetherness, she would have known if he'd pulled the guitar out of the back end of the Subaru.

The chill inching its way from her toes couldn't be blamed solely on the dropping temperatures. A crisp evening. An apple crisp evening. But the chill was probably one more symptom of a heart in suspended animation. Or cryogenics.

"I know the secret to survival," Judah had told her a few days ago.

"Surviving what, Judah? The outdoors?"

"No. My mom giving me away."

Mallory's heartbeat had stilled for a brief moment. It had to beat twice to catch up when it started again. "What's the secret?"

He'd looked her in the eye, completely serious, as vulnerable and unmasked as she'd seen him. "Not caring. I have to learn how to not care."

Within seconds, he'd taken off after a bug, which she had to warn him not to torture. She, however, stayed rooted in his stark, cold words.

Is that my secret too, Lord? Figuring out how to not care?

With the vocalists sliding into a third song, she maintained a steady hand on the video camera. But their words threatened her ability to remain upright.

> The chill of night, the heat of day
> No steady light to show the way
> I care too much or not at all
> I grip too hard; that's when I fall
>
> And here You stand before me
> Your arms, spread wide, enfold me
> You stand in all Your glory
> Your glory shining.
>
> God who breathed Your breath in me
> God who stilled the restless sea
> My God who felled Golgotha's tree
> Pierced with Your Love
> Pierce me.
>
> I turned my back; You waited still.
> I walked away; You stood until
> I heard the Voice that pierced me through
> Where could I run, but back to You?
>
> God who breathed Your breath in me
> God who stilled the restless sea
> My God who felled Golgotha's tree
> Pierced with Your Love
> Pierce me

Your love is patient; Love is kind
Your Love will never be denied
You satisfy the longing to be free

It was Your love that gripped my heart
It was Your love that pierced the dark
Your Love that tore my walls apart
Perfect Love

God who breathed Your breath in me
God who stilled the restless sea
My God who felled Golgotha's tree
Pierced with your love
Pierce me

Tears flowed. Erika pressed a tissue into Mallory's hand and reserved one for herself.

Mallory lowered the camera and sat in her chair. The one beside her sat empty.

———————◄——————————

Connor paced the asphalt path. Every stinking tiny house glowed. Warm. Inviting. Full. A few tiny porches were occupied. Connor waved as if he were no more bothered than someone who hadn't gotten in his 10,000 steps for the day.

Most of the village was still at the Gathering. The music carried disturbingly well across the distance. But it had lost its power to penetrate bone and muscle and soft tissues. It no longer beat its fists against Connor's soul.

It merely thrummed.

I didn't sign on for any of this, God.

Figured. The one Person he tried to avoid was the one Person he could talk to about it.

He kicked at a dry leaf. It scooted a few inches forward, begging to be kicked again. The changing colors—spotty as they were in the daylight and hidden by dark shadows now—spoke their reminders that time on the road would soon draw to an end. He'd had a spreadsheet and a PowerPoint of goals for the trip. Bullet points to prove his marketing savvy. They'd gained followers, but were the followers buying in? Ordering teardrop campers? And solar showers? And sinks that hang on a car door window like a wire tray at the retro A&W drive-in in his parents' neighborhood?

Or were they logging on to enjoy the view, meet some interesting characters, and discover a new recipe for pumpkin pear soup with a crème fraiche drizzle?

Which one are you?

Judah's question stung like a fresh tattoo. Raw, red, distorting the image. *Which one am I? The one who disputes the reality of God? No. The one who follows but hasn't bought in?*

Let's just rough up that raw tattoo with a garden rake.

He laced his fingers behind his neck but kept walking. He must have looked like a criminal walking toward a cell door. The guard pushing him forward? A dry leaf. Or an invisible hand.

When he pulled even with the swimming pool, he crossed the lawn and leaned his arms on the top of the fence. His chin resting on his crossed hands, he watched the water pulse with the light breeze, bright points dancing on the surface like aquatic fireflies. Right there, in the deep end, a preteen troublemaker had troubled the waters. Connor could swim toward the shallow end and forget the conversation. Or he could stay in the deep and commit.

Commit.

Whether Judah followed or not. Whether Mallory believed him or not. Whether he saved the business or wrecked it. Whether his genes aligned with his dad's or not.

And He came to them, walking on the water.

Connor knew that verse. He'd always pictured sandaled feet picking their way between waves on the Sea of Galilee. Or Lake Michigan. He'd never considered Jesus walking on the surface of a chlorinated pool. Or sliding down a waterfall.

chapter twenty-eight

NICE FIRE," MALLORY SAID, LOWERING herself to the picnic table bench at their campsite.

"Nice of the community to offer us free firewood while we're here."

Mallory watched Connor use a long stick the thickness of his thumb to move a log. Sparks danced their dizzying, lopsided spirals into the blackness above.

"Where did you go when you left the table?" She moved closer to the fire and tucked her hands under her arms.

"Had to stretch my legs."

"Without letting me know?"

"I needed time alone. To think."

"Connor, I would have let you have time to yourself."

"You're right. I should have told you I was leaving."

She'd grown to hate that word—*leaving*.

Connor laid aside his stir stick and scrubbed at his forehead with his fingertips. "Where's Judah?"

"Judah is collecting for the poor."

"What?"

"He's scavenging for chocolate bars, marshmallows, and graham crackers."

"For s'mores."

"Yes. And we happen to be 'the poor and needy.'"

Connor opened his mouth as if to say something, then shut it and resumed troubling the fire. "I don't need the calories."

"I think he needs the normalcy of s'mores. Families make s'mores when they're camping. He's had so little normalcy in his short life so far."

"Melty chocolate. I could force myself," Connor said.

"I'm in."

"Want me to find some other sticks for toasting the marshmallows?"

Mallory shivered. "Judah's begging for those too. We should be well supplied in a few minutes."

"Could you see yourself living in a place like this? You know. Under different circumstances?"

Mallory stretched her hands toward the warmth of the fire. "I like the sense of community. Together, but free to be individuals." She'd have to choose her words more carefully to maintain their fragile truce. "Every house different from the next one. Some stay for the Gathering. Some don't."

Connor looked up at her from his crouching position.

"I didn't mean you, Connor."

The sounds of community began to quiet around them, settled.

"It's a lot more … serene. Is that the word I'm looking for?" he asked. "Yes. More serene than Chicago."

She drew a deep breath. "It depends on whether you're looking at the inside or the outside atmosphere. It can be serene even if it's noisy outside. Or vice versa."

He nodded. "I know that better tonight than I did a few hours ago."

She waited for him to elaborate. He didn't. "Connor, what's going on?"

"I want to talk to you about it. I really do. And I will. Right now, I'm having a hard enough time defining it myself. Wrap my mind around it, as my dad used to say ... in the days before he couldn't wrap his mind around anything." His shoulders curved forward.

Without her conscious permission, her hand reached out to rub his shoulders. He didn't object. He took her hand in his and tucked it near his neck. Her hand hadn't been that warm in a very long time.

"When do we start getting concerned about Judah?" he said.

"Like we haven't been already?"

"I mean, here. Shouldn't he have completed his beggar bit by now?"

"You don't think he would have ... ?"

Connor stood. "Would have what? Stolen a bike and escaped?"

"Why would he do that? We're his food source."

A bright bluish light bounced toward them. The flashlight on Judah's phone. He held it between his teeth. His arms were full of s'mores supplies.

"We're relieved, right?" Connor whispered.

"Connor."

Mallory stood and took the phone from Judah's mouth.

"I come bearing gifts," he said. "The riches of the kingdom have been bestowed upon us. We shall feast. And we shall give thanks." He laid the supplies on the ground near the fire pit.

"Took you a while." Connor reached for the graham crackers.

"One does not merely beg for food," Judah says. "One must be polite. And listen to little old ladies' stories of the olden days, before one can abscond with their marshmallows."

Mallory grabbed the you-could-poke-an-eye-out-with-these-things metal toasting sticks. "You absconded, did you?"

"Read it in a book. Literacy isn't for cowards, you know."

"That's Literacy Takes Courage, Judah." Mallory shook her head.

"There's a difference?"

"Hand me a chocolate bar."

He obeyed. "We have to be frugal with those things. I may or may not have needed a couple of them to snack on during my ardus journeys henceforth."

"That's ar-du-ous. Three syllables." Connor broke the graham cracker rectangles into squares.

"All I know is it was exhausting. The listening part."

Connor paused in his square-making routine. "Depends on who you're listening to."

Mallory slid a marshmallow halfway onto each of two prongs, then loaded a second metal roaster. "Men?"

Connor looked at Judah. "I think she means us."

"Judah?" Connor's voice seemed swallowed by the cocoon hammock. Sleep eluded him more deftly than it normally did. Could have been the sugar in the s'mores. "Are you still awake?"

"Yeah. Why?"

"I have some answers for you."

Connor felt the aluminum tubing sway as Judah shifted in his own cocoon.

"About what? And don't tell me how to get marshmallow goo out of nylon fabric. I'll figure that out in the morning."

Connor saw the conversation exit sign blinking. It would be so easy to call it a night and ignore what he knew needed to be said. Cocoons and all. "About what you said when we were in the pool."

"Oh. That. Really, dude? Your communication safety shield is a parachute? Way to confront. You're slaying it so far, man."

"Judah, hear me out. Please?"

"You'll never know if I have my fingers stuck in my ears."

A cricket tuned up. Another joined him. "I know for sure you don't have your fingers in your ears."

"How?"

"A) You answered me. B) Your fingers are full of marsh-mallow evidence."

236

"I see your point."

Connor noticed faint bits of light through the fabric. Stars. Billions of them. Clear night. That meant the temps would drop even lower. "About the atheist thing?"

"I'm a kid. What do I know?"

"A lot. More than the average kid your age."

Silence from Cocoon Numero Dos.

"You asked where I stood. Actually, you said, 'Which one are you?' after I talked about the difference between someone who doesn't believe God exists and someone who believes He exists but doesn't acknowledge Him."

"I remember."

"Judah, that cut deep."

"Sorry."

"No. It was exactly what I needed to hear."

"Yay me. Goodnight, Connor."

"Wait." Connor was losing him. High-stakes losing him. "I know at least part of the answer to your question now."

"Yeah?" The disinterest carried well in the hushed night air.

"Neither. And I apologize for not giving you a clearer impression about my faith, which, to be honest, stunk until earlier tonight."

"Connor?"

"Yeah, buddy?" *God, help me. He's about to ask the big question.*

"Can I go sleep in the car? I'm cold."

The crickets had never sounded louder. Or cicadas. Maybe they were cicadas. Or Mallory's white noise on her phone. "Sure, Judah. We'll talk tomorrow, okay?"

"If we have to."

"There's a sleeping bag behind the—"

"I'll find it."

Connor listened as Judah crawled out of his cocoon and into the Subaru. Hanging there from the back end of the vehicle, suspended in a sleep hammock, surrounded by tiny houses with contented families in their contented beds dreaming about their contented lives, Connor felt as alone as he ever remembered.

He heard the familiar sound of the teardrop camper door. "Mallory?"

"Go back to sleep, Connor. I forgot to crack a window open. The condensation is raining in there since I ran the heater. I'm going to grab a handful of pool towels and dry off the ceiling."

"I can help."

"I've got it."

"Okay."

"Are you warm enough?"

Not even close. "I'll be fine. Toasty."

"Connor?"

"Yes?"

"Keep trying with Judah. It's something he needs to hear. Not just the words. But from you."

"He's sleeping in the SUV tonight."

"I heard. Do you want to trade places? I could take the hammock."

"Not Judah's."

"Goodness, no. Yours. You could have the camper for the night."

That woman. Would she never stop amazing him? All he'd put her through and she still looked for ways to encourage him. Who does that?

Someone like Mallory.

"No, I'll stay here. It's raining where you live."

She laughed softly. "True. I intend to fix that. But as of now, yes, that's true. I'll see you in the morning, Connor."

"Right. In the morning."

"Sleep well," she said.

Not a chance.

Mallory worked hard at keeping her tossing as waveless as possible, so no one nearby—say, someone sleeping a few feet away in a hammock pouch—would know how far she was from a good night's sleep.

Both of her traveling companions were on her mind. Plus the interior rain shower, which had improved dramatically since she cracked a window open and toweled off the ceiling and walls. Mostly her traveling companions.

Something about Connor's expression of his faith in his conversation with Judah made her swell with joy and deep, deep sadness in a completely unpalatable stew. This is the man she'd wanted. This is the man she'd relinquished. So few of their days together remained. Artificial days lived before the camera lens and Judah.

They hadn't given Judah much to emulate. A few scenes. Not a solid picture of what a healthy marriage could look like.

Mallory spent hours, figuratively, on her knees, watching through the skylight as the stars circled overhead. It was pointless to close her eyes. She was alone in her own cocoon of darkness, except for the skylight's reminder that above them all hovered a God who knew.

◆————————————◆

Connor should have packed a sleep mask, the kind people use on transcontinental flights. Those ever-lovin' stars with their reminders of an enormous universe and Connor's micro place in it. It was like having a hotel room with a neon sign outside the window shining through cheap drapes.

And the chill didn't help. He didn't blame Judah for choosing the Outback, no matter how cramped. But that left no other choice for him, unless he wanted to make Mallory more miserable by sharing her space. Or sit under the hand dryer in the facilities all night, pushing the silver button for warm air every minute until dawn.

That option sounded better and better as the night progressed. But the thought of climbing out of his cocoon hammock into the cold air was enough to make him stay put, curl himself tighter, and count bits of neon.

chapter twenty-nine

IF THEY DIDN'T HEAD SOUTH again soon, Connor would have to find something warmer to sleep in. He'd learned how to tell how far the sun had risen by the amount of light that filtered through the fabric covering his head. His heavy jacket was in the car. He wasn't about to wake Judah prematurely. Maybe a cup of coffee would—

Weird how the mind works. As soon as he had the thought, he smelled coffee brewing.

He crawled out of his cocoon, using a blend of athletic and acrobatic skills. His shoes sat lined up on the Subaru back bumper, right where he'd left them. Damp and cold.

And crawling.

He ripped off the first shoe and dumped it upside down. A spider the size of a hairy and unpleasant quarter skittered away.

He knew better than to not check for creepy crawlies before sliding his feet into his shoes. One momentary lapse in judgment …

Reshod and drawn toward the smell of coffee coming from the rear of the teardrop, he stopped first at the side door and tapped. "Mallory? I know you must be awake. I smell the coffee. Can we talk?"

No answer. For good reason.

Mallory wasn't inside. She walked toward him down the paved road with her face lifted to the sky and arms spread wide. They'd seen a lot of beautiful scenery so far on the journey. The sight of her outshone it all.

He held his full coffee mug close to his heart while he watched her approach.

She pulled earbuds from her ears when she reached their campsite. "Good morning."

"And to you. Where'd you go?"

"Chasing the dawn."

"Ah. A worthy pursuit. Did you find it?"

She poured a cup of coffee for herself. "It found me. Double meaning. Anyway, it was glorious watching the first rays of sun hit the leaves that have turned. Imagine how beautiful these hills will be when they've reached their peak in a couple of weeks."

We could come back here. He almost said it aloud. That might have been a huge mistake. Or not. How would she have responded to the idea? Her words had told him they were now "on the same page," in agreement that a permanent separation was the only wise option for them. But she had moments of what sure looked like regret. And then moments like these, when the light in her eyes seemed more like joy without a hint of remorse.

Was she trying hard to convince herself? Trying hard to convince him?

◆—————————————◆

Was she trying to convince herself or him? Mallory turned to face the woods behind their campsite to collect herself. In a couple of weeks, the trees would have fully exploded with color. And her marriage would have officially imploded. Like just-boiled tea or coffee, too hot to drink, she could only sip at her cup of strength. One day she'd take a full mouthful, but not until it didn't stir so much pain.

Swallow by swallow, she'd make it. But probably not without scalding herself.

"I'll make breakfast," Connor said. "I don't mind standing over a hot stove this morning. What'll it be?"

She turned around. "Eggs Benedict?" Like Day One of this present journey?

He didn't answer immediately. He stood with his back to her, hands braced on the miniature-sized countertop. "Feels like a long time ago since we shared that table."

"'And miles to go before we sleep.'"

Connor didn't move. He nodded his head so lightly, she might have missed it.

"Are you okay," he asked, "with pita bread instead of English muffins?"

"Sure."

"And venison jerky instead of Canadian bacon?"

"Um. I guess so."

"And mayo packets instead of hollandaise?"

"Well …"

"And hard-boiled eggs instead of poached, since we … only … have … hard-boiled in the cooler …"

She could have so easily spent every morning for the rest of her life with this man. Well, not easily, but readily.

"Want me to go beg for food for the poor?" She kept her voice far lighter than her soul felt.

"Judah has a corner on that market."

"Clean out a chicken coop in exchange for some freshly laid eggs?"

Connor turned to face her, a won-the-lottery expression on his face. "Do you know of one nearby?"

"Connor! I'll have a piece of toast and a hard-boiled egg."

"I think we have a smidgen of Bernard's peach jam left."

"Enough for all three of us?"

"We'll make it work."

A twinge of pain shot across her chest. And here she thought she'd been holding her broken self together rather admirably. She'd been wrong. "We'll make it work? I thought those words weren't in your vocabulary." If she had a nickel for every sentence she wished she hadn't said …

Connor slapped the tiny skillet onto the tiny burner. "*You're* the one who gave up on them, not me."

"You never even entertained the possibility that we could make it work, Connor. You gave up six months ago! Maybe longer ago than that." The strain of holding down the volume pinched her throat muscles.

"People change."

"Yes, you certainly did. A year ago, you promised to—"

"Mallory, a year ago I didn't know what I was doing."

"That's comforting. Every bride's dream."

"Not what I meant."

"It's what you've been saying, repeatedly, for a very long time. I don't like it, but I've come to terms with it, Connor. Skip the toast."

"Where are you going?"

"Does it really matter to you?"

Bruised. Her heart had become an unprotected sparring partner at a back-alley boxing gym. Just as the bruises began to fade, just when she thought she could handle another round in the ring, Connor proved her wrong. He was so worried about the tumors that only had a 50/50 chance of attacking him. But he wasn't concerned about the decisions and word tumors that had a 100 percent chance of destroying her.

Unfair. Yes, that was unfair. She wasn't destroyed. She would bounce back.

Bounce might be too strong a word for it. But she'd survive. Wouldn't she?

She couldn't circle the village again. It had stirred to life.

Bless all the happy little families. She headed instead for the woods.

Mallory picked her way through the briars at the edge of the woods until she came to what looked like a game trail, the kind Slade had pointed out to them. Slade. Alone and thriving after thirty years as a single man who still loved his spouse with all his heart. It could be done. With grace.

"You can do it, Mallory," he'd said. "The canoe is pointed on both ends. You can make it home."

Slade's words hadn't left her since that dawn's early light. She could. But she didn't want to anymore. And that was the issue.

"I don't know where the line is," she said, quickly realizing she'd slipped into prayer mode with no warning, no "Dear Heavenly Father" or "God Almighty" or "Sweet Jesus."

"I don't know where the line is that marks the place where my desires end and Yours begin."

It's not a line.

The words settled over her like fog on a pond, only crystal clear. Transparent fog with weight, presence, but the ability to bring things into focus rather than make them fuzzy.

Clarity didn't always mean answers, as she was finding. She stepped over a downed log and headed deeper into the wakening woods. The birdsong was disgustingly happy and light.

"What does that *mean*? It's not a line? What is it then?"

It's not that she expected to hear a Voice. Some people probably did. The most she'd ever gotten was an impression. Words, yes, but stamped on her soul rather than spoken into her ear. She walked and waited. She had only one phrase to think about. *It's not a line.*

"Does that mean what I want and what You want, God, can share common ground? Is that what You're saying?"

A branch caught the sleeve of her fleece jacket. She stopped to free the barb from the fabric.

"I suppose I don't have to tell you I'm confused. And

ticked. And frustrated. And more ticked. And love is not candy on Valentine's Day and something made of paper for a one-year anniversary. Oh, that's right, the modern version is clocks. Really? Clocks. God, that could not have been Your idea. What a ridiculous—

"Time. 'I'm giving you time.' That's what a clock says. Time to figure it out. Time to grow up. Time to reconcile. Time together."

She kept her gaze trained on the path in front of her, narrower now, with fallen leaves covering hidden obstacles. Yeah, like that analogy was hard to connect.

Without a heads up, the woods opened onto a field dotted with a few round bales of forgotten hay. The grass grew tall and wild here. The field looked as if it hadn't been worked for years.

She followed the deer trail through the grasses as if she had no responsibilities calling to her, no preteen depending on her, no business and youth center counting on her sanity.

The once-tight rolls of hay had lost muscle tone over the years. She stabbed her foot into the loose spots, making her own ladder, and climbed to the top of the nearest bale. She sat facing the direction she'd come, shielding her eyes from the sun that now showed its dominance over what had been darkness only hours earlier.

Mallory couldn't blame it on the sun's strength. Her tears had other origins. She let them fall. The watch on her wrist told her to breathe. She told it to shut up.

Could she stand? Was it safe to stand on top of her hay mountain? She risked it, raising herself higher, feet spread wide for stability. She lifted her arms, fists clenched.

"Because I love you, Connor Duncan," she shouted into the serenity, fists now waving. "I'll always love you. And because marriage isn't about avoiding discomfort. It's about *commitment!*"

Her last word echoed across the open field hemmed by trees. Her throat ached. She watched two mice scoot from the base of the hay bale as if desperate to find shelter not ruled by a crazy woman. She didn't flinch. Mice, and she didn't flinch.

She held her fists in the air until her shoulders screamed for relief. Okay, then. She'd had her say.

And only heaven heard.

Movement at the edge of the woods across the field caught her attention. What was that? A deer?

Wildlife, all right. With a video camera.

"Judah Milo Troyer!"

chapter thirty

Y OU'RE BACK," CONNOR SAID, CLOSING the hatch of the kitchen. "I was getting worried about you."

"Where is he?"

When had she gotten a sunburn? Her face was as red as the maple leaves in the woods behind her. "Who? Judah? He came tearing through here a few minutes ago. Said he had to use the facilities. Why?"

"Will you please go in there and get him?"

"Mallory, you're panting like you've run a marathon. What's wrong? I mean, other than the obvious."

She started toward the bathhouse. "Are you coming? You have to go in there and get him before he—" She stopped in her tracks and faced him. "What's 'the obvious'?"

Mallory hadn't forgotten their post-dawn argument, had she? Impossible. She didn't forget things. But she acted more cheese-and-crackers than she had last night at the Gathering. "Mallory, take a minute. Take a breath. What's going on?"

"I went for a walk."

He would have called it a stomp, but … "That much I know."

"And I … said some things." She was trembling now.

"You said some bad words? Hon, you're forgiven. I under-stand. We all need to let off steam once in a—"

"Connor. I am this close to—"

"I'll stop talking. Go ahead. What happened?"

She pressed the heels of her hands against her eyes. "I think Judah may have filmed what I said."

"We'll edit out your foul language."

"I did not use foul language, Connor. But I might soon if you don't go get Judah and delete that footage."

Nothing about Mallory's facial expression hinted she would give up this pursuit. Connor locked the camper and pocketed the key. "Let's go."

"Thank you."

He chuckled. Just a little. The absolutely wrong thing to do. Which he soon discovered. Come on. She had to know how funny it was to see this gentle woman so fired up, like a dove suddenly acting like a— He couldn't think of a fitting example. Birds don't usually frown that much.

"Judah?" Connor called as he entered the men's side of the public restroom/changing room.

"Yeah?" The question echoed in the cement block building.

"Are you about done in there?" Which stall? Which one? Ah. Familiar shoes. Connor tapped on the steel door. "Can you come out and talk as soon as you're finished?"

"I guess."

"Mallory is upset, and I'm not sure why."

"Oh? Well, you know women."

Something didn't sit right in his answer. "I do not know women, and neither do you. But the one we lo— The one we are traveling with is on the prowl, and I have a sneaky feeling it's for good reason. Would you know anything about that?"

"No."

"Less convincing than you might have wanted that to sound, Judah. Come on out, will you please?"

"Give me five?"

"Minutes?"

"Yes."

"Five, Judah. Not six."

"Got it."

Mallory paced outside the building. Connor joined her, grateful for the extra steps but trying hard not to notice.

"Can you tell me what you said on the video in question?"

"No. Don't ask again." She stopped pacing. "Connor. Oh, Connor."

"What?"

"Did Judah hand you his camera when he went tearing through camp?"

"No."

"Then it's in there with him! He's uploading the video."

"What? In there? Mallory, isn't that a little paranoid? Besides, he can't upload our videos. I do that. He would have to have the … passcode. Here he comes. See? No camera in hand. I think maybe your imagination—"

"Not one more word, Connor. Judah, did you follow me this morning?"

Judah put on his protective mask of innocence. She recognized that shade of plastic. "Follow you?"

Mallory sighed. "Everyone knows that if you repeat the question instead of answering it, that's a sure sign of guilt." She circled the two.

"I don't mind admitting I followed you," Judah said. "I was … concerned for your safety."

"See?" Connor said. "Way to be protective, Judah. Thanks, buddy."

"Judah," Mallory said, "are you packing heat?"

"What? No." He covered the back of his waistband with both hands. "Oh, and we have … incoming!" He took off at a dead run.

Connor checked his phone. Not that he didn't care about the unfolding drama, but because … career.

Their travel instructions awaited. But they couldn't—technically—leave without Judah, no matter how many times Mallory suggested the idea.

The two of them had returned to the campsite to wait for Judah to realize he would have to have to face the music sooner or later.

Ten minutes ticked by. Twenty. Mallory's facial expression began to soften into concern. Leaving the campsite again to search was the surest way to miss him when the prodigal returned.

"This one yours?" Vic said, his bear paw hand on Judah's shoulder. "Found him trying to slip through the gate. I had a feeling that didn't fit in with your plans. Am I right?"

"Thanks, Vic. We need to get on the road. Not the best time for Judah to go exploring. Appreciate it."

Vic extended a hand. "It's been great to have you here. Wish you could have stayed longer. We have some pretty decent fishing spots nearby. I could have used a day off and a couple of fishing buddies."

"My name's not Buddy," Judah said, his sullen side abundantly visible.

"We all appreciate what your community has done for us, Vic," Mallory said. "Please let Ericka know too."

"I will. I'll do that. You take care now. Stay safe." He turned to go, then turned back. "Oh, and Judah, thanks for your contribution to the Village's food pantry fund. That'll go farther than you'd think to help feed the needy in our county. Very kind of you."

Connor checked on Mallory. As anticipated, she stood wide eyed and silent.

Two miles beyond the New Day Village gates, Connor pulled the rig to the side of the road. "Okay, let's get this sorted out. Mallory, would you like to go first?"

"Not right now." Her voice trembled.

"Judah? What did you do?"

"Basic rules of cinematography. The best shots are when the subject isn't aware of the camera." He looked straight ahead.

Mallory exhaled in a huff.

"But you didn't upload that video, did you? That's not your role. You didn't have the right or permission to do that."

The boy picked up his phone.

"Judah, put the phone away. I mean it."

"I need it."

"Not right now, you don't."

"I need it to prove I was trying to help."

Mallory growled. "Who did you think you were helping?"

"Well, the project." Judah's defensiveness lost its fervor. "Will you just look?"

"At what?" Connor unclicked his seatbelt and turned sideways. He took the phone Judah offered. "What am I supposed to be looking at?"

"The message from RoadRave. There. The latest text. They copied you and Mallory on it, but you must not have seen it yet, or you'd be thanking me."

Mallory reached for her phone too. She let out a pained moan.

Connor looked at the screen. "'Best response rate to date. More than 100,000 hits in the first fifteen minutes. If this keeps up, we'll have officially reached viral. Great work, all.'"

"That's good, huh?"

"Judah, what footage are they referring to?"

"Well, it's Mallory. On the hay bale."

"Can we have it taken down?" Mallory said. "Minimize the … the damage?"

"Wardrobe malfunction?" Connor said.

"No! Good grief, Connor!"

Judah folded his arms and stared out the side window. "What kind of a creep do you think I am?"

Connor scrubbed his forehead with his fingertips. "Guys, I have to see what it is that's going viral. You know I do."

Mallory turned her head toward her side window too. But she didn't say he couldn't. Connor scrolled through to find the morning's video submission. He watched what was frankly expert camera work weaving through the woods, panning the wide expanse of the field, zooming in on Mallory's climb. And her words.

He pressed his index finger to his mouth. His traveling companions expected him to say something. He scrolled through the first dozen of thousands of comments on the footage. Mallory's vulnerability—on the world stage—had struck a chord.

No wonder RoadRave was ecstatic. This single scene might have sealed the deal. This wasn't screen face. It was real and raw and exactly the kind of thing that could propel Troyer & Duncan forward.

His phone pinged a new text message from RoadRave. "Way to break the internet! Blowing up on all social media platforms. Couldn't be happier."

Everyone was talking about it. Except the one person who mattered most to him—Mallory.

She was miserable. And all he knew to do, all he wanted to do, was be miserable with her.

Oh. That's what she meant. *Marriage isn't about avoiding discomfort. It's about commitment.* Her impassioned cry played on continuous loop as Connor sat behind the wheel.

"Judah, can I trust you to stay in the Subaru and touch nothing? Mallory and I are going to walk up the road for a few minutes."

"Everybody's always walking."

Judah played sullen better than anyone Connor had met. "Judah."

"Yeah, I get it. And Mallory, I'm sorry. I thought it would help us. You know, with RoadRave, and Connor's company, and your youth center. And with you and Connor."

Help us? "Judah. Enough for now. Mallory? Walk with me?"

She opened her door and climbed out. Connor met her with his arms wide. She didn't walk into his embrace. *Stab. Stab, stab, stab, stab.*

They walked at a slow pace but farther than he thought they'd need to.

Connor eventually said, "Are you ever going to speak to me again?" Their footsteps sounded surprisingly in sync on the coarse gravel of the road's shoulder.

"It's not your fault."

"Then why do I feel so awful?"

Mallory elbowed him. "Because we're one. For now."

"About that …"

"Could we," she said, "deal with the most immediate crisis? How do we get that humiliating video taken down?"

Should I take her hand? Would she let me? Is she ready for that? Do I dare ask? He didn't need to analyze long. She took his.

"Mallory."

"I know. It's a mess. I'm a mess. Ultimately, if it's anyone's fault, it's mine. The meltdown."

"Is that what you call it?"

She dropped his hand. "What would *you* call it?"

"Wisdom." He searched her face. "What would it take for you to let us leave it online?"

"Tell me you didn't just ask me that."

"Think about it, Mallory."

She shook her head.

"Granted," he said, "Judah had no right to send it at all, much less without your permission."

"Which I never would have given."

"And he will have to pay a price for that. I don't know what, yet. But he thought he was helping."

"You believe him?"

"Mallory … the responses. We can't ignore how people are responding to the video."

Mallory flattened a hand on her chest. "You're serious? Of course they're reacting. They love having someone to mock, to laugh at. Like watching a cat trying to jump onto a bookcase unsuccessfully. Or a panicked gerbil trying to eat its way out of a box."

"That's not it. They're identifying with what you said."

"I guess I expected you to be on his side this one time," she said. "The video fits very well into your personal and professional designs."

"That's a bad thing?"

"It is, if it's at my expense."

"Can I tell you how I felt about the footage and why I think we should leave it where it is?"

They walked several feet before she spoke again. "Connor, you're opting out of the marriage. You gave up that right."

chapter thirty-one

MALLORY WATCHED A BANK OF clouds rolling toward them—a clear line between bright blue and sullen gray. "We'd better get back on the road, Connor. What that sky is threatening isn't something we'd want to get caught in."

Had he understood what she said? He hadn't moved.

"Connor? Rain's on the way."

He looked up then and nodded. "Right."

They were ten yards from the car when Connor stopped again. "Where's Judah?"

Mallory couldn't see anything, not even Judah's RoadRave or Troyer & Duncan ball cap showing through the windshield. "Probably slumped over his phone," she said. Her heart told her otherwise.

They picked up the pace, the sensation of clouds chasing them heightening the tension.

"Mallory, he's not here. And his passenger door is closed most of the way, but not latched."

"Judah!"

No answer.

She searched around and under the rig, looking for a remorseful eleven-year-old's pouting spot. He wasn't anywhere.

"Woodland rest stop?" Connor said.

Mallory shrugged her shoulders. Something about this scene didn't feel like a simple dash into the woods for an open-air bathroom break.

They both called his name while searching the grass along the sides of the road for signs that smelly sneakers had passed that way. Nothing.

"Judah, this isn't funny," Mallory said.

"And it isn't helping your cause in the forgiveness department either. Get yourself back here so we can get on the road. Judah!" Connor's voice sounded firm and loud but surprisingly calm.

"We can talk about everything in the car," she called.

Connor snorted. She didn't appreciate it but ignored his response for the sake of a united front in finding the boy.

"Your story doesn't end in a mistake, Judah," Connor called into the woods.

Exactly. Adrenalin surging, Mallory tabled a deep-dive into his statement for another time. She searched the car again.

"Connor, he took everything with him." Fear put every nerve ending on high alert. "His backpack and duffel are gone. All his electronics. He's not just out there killing time somewhere. He intended to leave."

Connor dug in the space behind the driver's seat. "Mallory, he took all three cameras."

"What?" Mallory checked under the seats, searched the storage area again.

"What was the purpose of that?" Connor said. "Sell the cameras to finance his escape?"

"Connor, that's overly dramatic, even for Judah. He's not escaping from prison."

Slamming the side door shut, he said, "He might have to if we don't get those cameras back."

Ah. His true motives finally showed themselves. He didn't want to make trouble with RoadRave and risk the account. *See, Connor? Nothing's changed.*

"Maybe Judah doesn't want anyone filming the search-and-rescue." Connor unlocked and opened the teardrop camper. No one could hide from discovery in there. And Judah wasn't.

Thunder growled, reminding them of its presence and pursuit.

"Our phones have video capabilities. What was he thinking?" Another wave of fear pulsed through her. "What if he was abducted? We would have heard something, wouldn't we?"

No place on earth seemed safe from that possibility these days.

Connor leaned his back against the side of the car. "I turned to check on him every few minutes when we first started walking. He'd smile at me and wave."

"Does that sound like the Judah we know?"

He rubbed his forehead, that tell-tale sign of his that fear was making his brain hurt. "No."

"Okay. Logic tells us he wasn't taken. If someone came along, we would have heard something, a car or truck approaching, a … a scuffle … And there's a lot more valuable stuff in here than Judah's duffel bag. Why wasn't that taken? My laptop's still here."

"This isn't the work of an abductor. This is the work of an absconder. Judah always was a flight risk. I should have known he'd react this way, especially when he was already in trouble."

Mallory leaned beside Connor. "He can't have gone far. We weren't away from the vehicle that long. And if he's hauling all three cameras plus his duffel and his backpack—"

"Until he sells off the cameras."

She stepped away from the car and peered down the road the opposite direction of where they'd walked. "Connor, you do understand that your responsibility for that equipment is not our primary concern, don't you?"

"Of course."

"A boy with his history, his emotional needs, and his—"

"Evil nature?"

"I was going to say his radar for trouble making could get himself into a world of hurt this far from home."

Connor bent forward and rested his hands on his knees. "He doesn't have a home. We're it for him right now. That's even scarier."

"We need a plan. What should we do, give it a half hour of searching this area before we call 911?"

"I suppose. We'll have to try to reach Nathan too. That won't be easy. To get a message through. Or easy to form the words."

"Should we enlist Vic on the case? He and his friends probably know this area. We're not far from New Day."

"Could Judah have gone back there?"

Hope lifted Mallory's thoughts for a moment. "No. He knows the community would contact us immediately."

"I don't like the direction our thoughts are headed," Connor said.

"I don't either, Connor. But we have to do something. Call 911 first, or search on our own for a while?"

He slapped one fist into the other palm, repeatedly, as if it held answers if he could crack it open. "I don't think there's a perfect answer to that question. It's a blueprint for possible regrets either way."

"I know."

"If he's close—"

"He has to be."

Connor stopped punching his fist into his palm. "Or if we call in the helicopters and drones and this turns into a media circus ..."

The urge to kick him in the shin, both shins, was strong. She fought it off.

"It's not what you're thinking," he said. "Judah's more important than the RoadRave account. Or my reputation. Or

Troyer & Duncan. We could lose everything, but that wouldn't be worse than losing Judah. Believe it or not," he said, "that's how I feel about losing you too."

⟵————————————⟶

They timed their "Judah!" calls to allow silence between so they could listen for responses, for rustling in the woods, for broken branches underfoot, or other auditory clues. They kept in touch with each other by text, noting direction changes. Splitting up hadn't been the first choice for either Mallory or Connor, but they knew they had to cover as much ground as possible before giving up their initial search.

They pressed on after the rain started, knowing visual clues could disappear quickly in a downpour.

Mallory unrolled the hood tucked into the zipped collar of her quilted vest to protect herself from the angry rain that dodged trees and leaves to pelt her. But the hood interfered with her ability to hear, and it blocked part of her peripheral vision, so she abandoned the protection. "Judah!"

The shivers that coursed through her—from fear and the cold—battled for dominance.

"Judah! Where are you?"

She kept an eye on the time. Desperation either made time crawl or fly, but in crisis, time never advanced at a traditional pace.

Connor's text said too little and too much. *Meet me at car.*

She heard Judah's voice in her head. *Technically it's a small sport utility vehicle.*

She hooded her phone with her arm to keep the screen drier while texting back, *Did you find him?*

No.

⟵————————————⟶

Almost an hour had passed by the time they met at their vehicle. Thunder and lightning added to their discomfort and the drama.

Connor had the engine running and the heater cranked up by the time Mallory climbed in.

"No sign?" she asked.

"None." It stung to have to say that word.

"The heat feels good. Thanks," Mallory said. "What do we do now?"

Connor slapped his cap against his pant leg to dislodge at least some of the water it had collected. He repositioned the cap on his head. Nothing would feel comfortable until they found Judah.

"I think we need to get this rig off the road, for one thing. The map app shows a farm not far ahead. A little more than a mile. We can—"

"What?"

"We can set up our base station there, if it's okay with the owners. And call the authorities."

Mallory nodded her agreement from her seat beside him. She hadn't been sitting beside him in the front seat since Judah complained of motion sickness on Day One of the trip. Connor still wondered if they'd been played on that front. Score one for the kid who pulled off a perpetual shotgun position. *No. New train of thought.*

"Sounds like a plan," she said.

Late morning, and the storm had converted it to a scene more like dusk, with bone-chattering peals of thunder and wicked lightning. A bolt of lightning struck somewhere nearby. The hairs on his arms stood to attention from the electrical charge.

They'd made an adventure out of watching water fall over rocks, seeing the evidence of how it had changed landscapes and pummeled granite, limestone, shale. What fell from the sky now—the broadest of all waterfalls—could do serious damage to an unprotected kid. They had to find him.

"Connor, if Judah is out in this …"

"Let's pray he isn't."

"I have been," she said.

The farmer and his son—not much younger than Mallory and Connor—welcomed them into the house where they too were waiting out the storm. A greasy piece of machinery lay torn apart on their kitchen table, a sign that there was no female influence in the household.

The son, Howie, made them coffee and sat with them in the comfortable but outdated living room while Mallory and Connor filled in the details they knew. Grant, the dad, glanced at his son frequently during the conversation. It happened so often, Mallory found it disconcerting. Was Grant communicating something sinister between them? Was this the wrong farmhouse to approach in the middle of a storm?

Their sympathy seemed genuine. Howie was quiet, but—

Oh, dear. That's how the eye witness news reports interviewing neighbors always start. *He seemed like such a nice boy. A quiet young man. Kept to himself …*

Mallory set aside her coffee. Did it have a curious flavor? Her imagination kept pace with her racing heart. She reeled in both and reentered the conversation.

"I'm good friends with a county deputy," Grant said, again glancing at his quiet, nice-boy son. "I recommend we get him over here and see what he says. The guidelines about when to get an official search team on the ground are changing all the time regarding runaway kids. Aren't they, Howie?"

"Yes, sir. They are."

Connor squinted Mallory's direction. Was he just now catching on to the tension that had been nagging at her?

Grant called his friend, the deputy. Or Mallory assumed that's the number he punched into his cell phone. When this was all over, she would never again watch TV crime drama.

"I drove a telescoping canoe paddle into the ground just off the road to mark the spot where we were parked," Connor said. "To mark the spot where we last saw Judah. In case the deputy wants to check things out at the site before we talk to him."

"Howie, you text that info to him, okay?" Grant said. "It looks like these people could use something dry to wait in."

Body bags are dry. Coffins are dry. *Mallory, this is not helping.*

Grant returned with what looked like hand-knit sweaters for both of them. The kind an Irish fisherman might wear. For good reason. Mallory warmed almost instantly. She could envision how the tight weave of the wool would form a barrier against biting North Atlantic winds.

"My wife knitted them for us when we were first married," Grant said. "We'd planned on getting our picture taken wearing them on our fiftieth wedding anniversary." He pressed his lips together in a half smile/half frown.

Connor's and Mallory's silent nods were so similar, Mallory would have laughed if not for the circumstances.

"We didn't have that opportunity," Grant said. A long stretch of emptiness followed.

"Pop," Howie said, "you have to tell these people what happened. They'll think you buried her in the manure pit or something. They don't know us. Lots of crazies out there in the world."

Connor reached for Mallory's hand. She gladly let him take it. Despite its welcome warmth, the wool of the sweater began to itch through her long-sleeved shirt. The skin on her back crawled with imagination.

"Yeah," Grant said. "You don't need to hear about our woes at a time like this, but she was born with a congenital heart defect that we knew would make it risky for her to bear children." He paused.

"It's okay, Pop. Go ahead."

"She insisted it was worth the risk. Eventually wore me down." He swallowed hard. "The birth went okay. We thought we were in the clear. But she was gone within a week."

"Dad's been a single parent," Howie said, "since I was a newborn. He's one of the most remarkable men I know."

Mallory's muscles relaxed to her previous state—when Judah and her marriage were her only concerns.

"I can see," Connor said, "why you would follow him into agriculture."

"He always told me," Howie said, "that I could be whatever I wanted to be, as long as it was what God wanted."

Grant's grin lit the room. "You haven't always agreed."

Howie took a deep breath and addressed Connor and Mallory. "No matter how good things are for you, no matter how much you're loved, sometimes a person turns their back on that."

Mallory felt the slightest increase in pressure from Connor's hand.

"I did," Howie said. "Until I discovered the hard way that Pop's love was never going to let up, so I might as well quit running from it. Turns out that was my smartest decision ever. Like he says—*all* the time—families fix things."

chapter thirty-two

THE RAIN HAD STARTED TO let up a little by the time the unmarked squad car pulled in the long driveway a few minutes later. The detective's height and demeanor, even seen through the streaked window of the old farmhouse, seemed familiar.

"Vic?"

"Connor? Mallory?"

"You're the deputy Grant knows?" If Connor had been drinking coffee at the moment, it would have wound up dribbled down the front of Grant's off-white sweater.

"Part time. Used to be my full-time job before I enlisted. Hey, what's going on? Did our young friend attempt another escape? Bad day for it."

Mallory snugged the sweater tighter around her.

"Vic, I can't even describe how worried we are."

Vic rested his hand on Connor's shoulder and another on Mallory's. "We'll find him. I have every confidence. We can put the whole village on alert, if you want. We'll have a hundred people or more joining the search. Take leave from their jobs, if they have to. We've got support. Sometimes that grassroots involvement can accomplish a lot more than a small law enforcement contingent. And we're not even going to think about having to get the state or National Guard involved. Good people, but I'm counting on our not needing them. We'll find your Judah."

Connor sighed.

"He's concerned," Mallory said, "about the negative publicity. And I understand."

She does? "We have to forget about all that. We have to find that kid."

"I have an idea," Howie said.

"Open to all ideas." Vic took out a small notebook and fished for a pen.

"Is he online a lot?" Howie asked. "Maybe he'd use technology to look for a place to hide out?"

Connor caught Mallory's look.

"Never mind. If he's eleven, then I already know the answer. Okay, there's a place I used to go hide out when I was … not tracking with my dad's 'rules for a productive life.'"

"Ages eleven to eighteen," Grant added.

"Yeah. So, there's a cave he could have walked to. It's tucked behind a small waterfall. It's not on any tourist destination maps."

Connor squeezed Mallory's arm. "That's it then. It has to be it."

"I'll have to lead the way," Howie said. "I know where it is."

Grant scratched his nose. "You think I don't, son?"

"You know?"

"Followed you there many a midnight. Had to be sure you were okay and your only problem was foolishness."

Vic piped up. "I know where it is too. We chased a—"

Connor tensed.

"Never mind," Vic said. "It's sure worth trying there first."

"Oh, he's there," Mallory said. "Or he attempted to get there."

"What makes you say that?" Grant said.

"The waterfall."

———————◂——————————▸———————

Vic insisted he and Howie serve as the first wave of searchers. Mallory objected. Connor objected louder. But Vic explained they didn't want to scare Judah into running before they got to him, warned by voices or the lack of stealth. Howie had apparently been an expert in stealth, and his father even better.

The final decision was for Vic and Connor to maintain a position a hundred feet away and for Howie to approach the cave.

Mallory waited with Grant at the farmhouse. At their base station.

"This isn't the fun part," Grant said. "Hoping they'll come home. Come to their senses. Not do something too stupid to repair. We're pretty sure the wanderer is okay, but not certain until you see that face and bear-hug that stiff little body."

Mallory gasped.

"I mean," Grant added, "the stiffness of a boy who knows he's put you through a lot of unnecessary worry and is probably grounded for a century or two. That kind of stiffness."

"Thanks for clarifying," she said. "I'm a little more fragile than I thought."

You're one of the least fragile people I know, Mallory, Connor had told her, not two days ago.

"Except very recently."

"What's that, Mallory?" Grant asked.

It was safer to stick with subjects like telling Grant about where they'd been on their adventures, the people they'd met, the waterfall theme. Cooking in a kitchen the size of a small desk, only with fewer drawers.

"After your boy gets found," Grant said, "do you think I could have a look-see at your rig? Sharp. A mite small for my tastes, but if it's as cozy as you say …"

Mallory hadn't remembered describing the teardrop

microcamper as cozy. It hadn't felt cozy for a minute, not even before they'd logged the first miles of their journey.

It wasn't the camper's fault. It was the campers' fault. Hers as much as anyone's. She'd told herself she could set aside their marital crisis for three weeks. Put it on hold. Hit pause. Do what had to be done for RoadRave and her husband's company and then pick up their problems after the trip.

But a conflict like theirs—grief like what she felt deep in her soul—refuses to be boxed and put on a shelf. It won't be ignored. It finds or forces a slit in a seam and slithers out, worms its way into conversations about beef sticks and fuel stops, angles of the sun and sales pitches of the hawkers at farmer stands and flea markets, blisters and burnt pancakes. Connor's, not hers.

Howie had refused his father's love. But Grant's love remained relentless. And its quiet persistence eventually drew Howie back to his father's side.

Mallory had tried that with Connor, hadn't she? She'd tried.

Not quite a year probably doesn't count as relentless.

"I don't want to pry, Grant." Mallory drew a shallow breath.

"Pry away." He handed her a bowl of soup he'd warmed up for both of them.

"Chicken dumpling." The aroma was as invigorating as the soup promised to be. "Is this homemade?"

"Howie and I always said if we had to give up farming—which we discuss about once a week—we'd both go to culinary school. Wish you'd be staying long enough to try his veggie lasagna. I'd put that up against anybody's. So, you were about to pry?"

They sat now at the dining room table for a better view of the driveway and for a surface clean enough on which to put food and utensils. The engine part occupying the kitchen table was apparently a carburetor.

Mallory laid aside her spoon and tented her hands, elbows

on the table. "Did you ever resent your wife's insistence about risking a pregnancy, with her condition?"

"All the time. I feared what might happen. And it did. I lost her. I don't know that I ever—before the fact—came to terms with how her choices about her medical condition affected us as a couple, and yes, me. And eventually Howie too."

"But you've come to terms with it now?"

"It's been more than twenty years. I couldn't grieve her right if I didn't forgive her. And forgive myself both for being stubborn and then for being what I thought was not stubborn enough." He slurped a spoonful of the soup broth. "I had to give up wondering if we'd done the right thing and start living with what I'd been dealt and with the blessing that came out of the risk."

God, how am I supposed to take that? It's time for me to stand firm or it's time to let go? Couldn't what Grant said lean either way?

"I do have a nugget of counsel for others, though. In case," he said, "you know, anyone should ever need it."

"What's that?"

"Forgive more than you think you should have to. And that includes yourself."

She smiled, a small wave of peace lapping on the shores of her pain. "Thanks, Grant."

"I have more," he said, "should, you know, anyone want it." His eyes looked as if they'd been polished.

"I can use more."

"If I'd given up loving Howie because he told me to—repeatedly—where would either of us be today?" He held Mallory's gaze. "I don't know. That was bonus material, I guess."

How could he have known that Mallory needed his "bonus material"? They hadn't given a hint that they were both miserable on any front other than their concern for Judah.

Maybe it was the same kind of inner sense Mallory felt overcome her. Judah was going to be okay.

God, please give me that same message about our marriage.

Grant's phone rang. He'd chosen an old-fashioned phone sound for his ringtone. He answered quickly, but Mallory already stood at his elbow.

"Hey, Vic. Tell me something good. I have Mallory here, can I put you on speaker? Okay. Hang on." He fussed with the touchtone screen until he found the right button. "She can hear you now. Tell us what you know."

"We found Judah," Vic said.

"Mallory isn't going to start breathing again until you tell us the boy is doing okay."

"He's good. He's just fine. And yes, he'd found the cave. Looked like he was halfway to setting up permanent residence in there, although I had the distinct honor of pointing out to him that the little piles of berries he'd seen outside the cave were bear scat, from a bear looking for a cave in which to take up hibernating any day now."

"Can I talk to him?" Mallory said.

"In a minute or two. We have the ambulance on the way."

"Ambulance?" *What happened?*

"Is that …?" Grant cleared his throat. "Is that standard procedure in these cases now, Vic?"

"It's not for Judah. It's for Connor. Think he might have broken his leg."

<hr />

No "might have" about it. She knew a broken leg when she saw one, especially the kind where part of the lower leg is pointing a direction a leg isn't supposed to bend. The video shot made it clear. Too clear.

When Judah and Howie had climbed out of the cave, Connor had taken two steps forward, then broken into a run. On wet leaves. In a dense hardwood forest. When Judah saw him, dropped what he'd been carrying and ran toward him, Connor picked up the pace, and—near as the witnesses could tell—tripped over a shelf of rock, which sent him flying. Vic gave him a 4.3 for not sticking his landing.

Mallory had insisted on talking by video while the men waited for the ambulance to arrive, including the promised first responders' all-terrain vehicle to extract Connor from his prone position deep in the woods.

"Connor, I love you."

"I … love you too." The video connection held firmer than his voice.

"Are you in much pain?"

"Only when I try to move. Or breathe. Or think. *Ah!*"

"What's wrong? What happened?"

Connor winked at her through the phone screen. "I tried to think."

She shook her head. "Help's on the way."

"I know. And I'm glad."

She blinked back tears. "Did you speak to Judah at all?"

"He's right here." Connor pointed over his shoulder. "*Ah!*"

"Don't move. I just hoped I could talk to him."

"He's"—Connor whispered—"kind of shaken up right now. Thinks, of course, that it was his fault."

"Don't we all?"

"Howie and he are having a heart-to-heart at the moment. Physically, he's fine."

"How long before you will be?"

"Good … *ahk!* … good question." Connor dropped the phone.

Vic picked it up. "Hey, Mallory. We can hear the sirens nearing. It'll take us a little time to weave our way through these woods. The path isn't wide. If only Howie had made a blacktop trail when he used to come here years ago."

"I heard that," Howie said in the distance.

"Both of your men are doing okay, Mallory. Watch for

a text from me for directions to the hospital. Depending on which ambulance service shows up, it could be one of two."

"Okay. Thanks, Vic. We appreciate this."

"Just add humans and the adventure begins, huh?"

"Something like that."

chapter thirty-three

THE DRIVE TO THE HOSPITAL had a hollow feel. No slight tug of the microcamper, which was spending the night at the Grant and Howie Ferris farm. No faint odor of Cheetos and yesterday's socks. No snarkiness coming from the passenger seat. No passengers.

Mallory's hair had time to dry at the farm during search-and-rescue, but it hadn't dried manageably. She'd piled it in a messy bun on top of her head before getting behind the wheel. The time spent outdoors over the past two weeks had given her face some color. She wore a flannel shirt, someone else's fisherman sweater, no mascara, and she didn't care. The day had finally come. Makeup was no longer a must-have.

Mallory would have detoured to pick up Judah, but Vic had already put him in his car for the trip behind the ambulance. Mallory left Grant before Howie got home, but he'd texted his dad that Judah was "more chill" and had asked for something to eat.

"That's my boy." Hungry was a good sign, for once.

The countryside left little evidence that a storm had passed. A few downed limbs. Puddles here and there. Glistening drops clung tenaciously to the tips of leaves and weeds.

But the sky had regained its deep blue status, which formed a stunning backdrop to the trees that had begun to transition from summer's green to autumn's earth tones.

She might always see the view out her window—whether in their/her/*whatever* Chicago apartment or on the road—through different eyes. She'd seen veins in a leaf that looked like the veins on the back of Slade's thin hands. She'd smelled the difference in the fragrance of pine needles when the sun is hot and not. She'd once considered water as something to drink, bathe in, cook with, or swim through. She now saw it as power and story and the birthplace of healing.

Mallory hadn't been willing to listen when Connor finally wanted to talk.

The confession consumed several of the miles that separated her from the hospital. She hadn't let him talk. Regret had a shape that plumped every cell in her body, as if she were over-hydrated with it, retaining regret water.

How long would they be off the road? Had they already experienced the last day of the RoadRave trip? If so, what a way for the journey to end. Mallory's meltdown in the hay field. Her eruption over the video footage. Connor's twisted joy that it had gone viral and his unexpressed extra reason why. Judah's disappearance. A place at Grant's table. Connor's injury.

It couldn't end this way.

She'd already texted RoadRave that they'd experienced an unexpected delay and she'd get back to them about why they hadn't responded to the company's latest instructions.

A delay. A tiny little bit of an understatement. Something similar may have sparked the original need to invent the word "understatement."

She'd report back after seeing Connor and hearing the doctor's assessment about his injury and how soon he could travel, as long as she did all the driving. And the problem solving. And the preteen discipline. And the cooking, video work, cleaning, setup, teardown, and caregiving …

Caregiving. Connor's worst fear. This could get interesting fast.

Broken legs heal. Broken legs heal.

She repeated the words all the way from the hospital parking lot to its entrance. He hadn't had a heart attack. Vic had reported he was awake and alert and hadn't been given a life-altering diagnosis. Not today, anyway.

Broken legs heal.

Mallory checked in at the emergency room desk. Waited where instructed. Moved as directed to the treatment bay to which Connor had been assigned.

Vic and Judah greeted her. Vic leaned close to say, "Judah won't leave his side. I tried. Even tried bribing with food."

"My hearing is extra," Judah said in a more subdued tone than Mallory had heard from him.

Mallory smiled at them both. "That means, in his language, very good, Vic."

"Oh. Okay. And the star of the hour …" He stepped back and gestured toward Connor's totally anti-luxurious hospital gurney.

"Connor." She rushed toward him.

He held up his "Halt!" hand signal. "Slow down, Mal. Speed kills. And I have the x-rays to prove it." Connor pointed to the lump that covered his distorted right leg somewhere under the hospital sheet.

"You've had x-rays already?" Mallory said. "I came as fast as I could. Legally."

"No," Connor said, pressing his head back into the flat pillow. "But I have a hot date with an x-ray machine any … any minute now."

"This is your brain on drugs," Judah said, then slapped his hand over his mouth and sat in one of the two plastic chairs in the cubicle. He popped to his feet and offered the chair to Mallory.

"Thanks, Judah. I'll stand for a while." *Right here. Right beside my husband.*

"Glad I had my sur-ents," Connor said, eyes closed.

Vic still stood near the entrance. "I think he means insurance. Hey, this has been real, but I have to get back home and back to pursuing hardened criminals," he said. Making a show of using two fingers to point from himself to Judah, he reminded the boy, "I have my eyes on you. I've got your personal belongings and will drop them off at Grant's place." To Mallory, he said, "The cameras too."

"Vic, thank you so much," Mallory said. "Don't know how we'll ever thank you enough."

"Feeb yerkey," Connor said, his speech more cottony than before. "Him likes feeb yerkey."

Mallory patted his shoulder and left his side long enough to give Vic a hug and promise him some beef jerky.

"Keep us informed, okay?" Vic patted his chest. "About both of them?"

"We will." Mallory stripped off the fisherman sweater that was truly *extra* in the too-warm room.

"Judah?" Vic eyed him.

"I know. Stay out of trouble."

Vic smiled. "I was going to say way to go, helping out there in the woods."

"I was the reason Connor fell, remember?" Ah, the little edge of snarky was back.

"I see it a little differently," Vic said. "If I've messed up, and as I'm making my way back, somebody can't wait and *runs* to meet me? I'd blame love, if I were you."

Judah shrugged.

Vic left, then stepped back into the room and pressed

something into Mallory's hand. "You'll have some *extra* needs, I'm sure, in addition to these two." He pointed toward the prone man and the slumped boy.

"Thanks, Vic."

A hundred dollar bill. It would help their twenty dollar a day budget significantly.

Mallory leaned close to Connor's ear. "I'm so glad you're going to be okay."

"Okey dokey," he whispered.

Their conversation traveled no farther before radiology came to get him. They assured Mallory and Judah that the two could remain there in Connor's room. It wouldn't take them long.

"He's a little loopy right now," Mallory told the radiology tech.

"We've seen that before. They come in like that, or we make them that way. Judging from what the initial exam showed his doctor, keeping him oblivious is a good idea. And don't worry. We'll be careful with your dad, young man. Back soon."

Mallory took the other plastic chair and dragged it across the now bedless room to sit next to Judah.

"I could use a hug," she said.

"So lame."

"Fine. But I could."

He leaned his head on her shoulder. "I'm, like, sorrier than I've ever been in my whole life."

"Your *whole* eleven years of life?"

"Yeeesss. And I'm almost twelve. I can't even say the words."

She could hear the tears in his voice. "But you feel the feels?" She stroked his hair.

"All the feels."

"Me too." *Joined at the heart, buddy.*

"Did you call my uncle to come get me? If he even wants me back."

"We haven't called yet. We're not sure he's done with the trial. It was expected to be a long one."

"Yeah, I know. So, you're stuck with me? In spite of everything?"

"Stuck with you. Yes. Because we want to be."

"You don't either. That's insane." Judah leaned forward, out of reach.

Mallory rubbed her eyes. It had been a long day already, and it wasn't over. "Judah, we fought for you."

"What do you mean?"

"We fought to let you come with us. Both of us." *I took the logical approach. Connor took the used car salesman approach.* She couldn't suppress the smile forming.

"Why would you do that?" He turned his head, then resumed staring at the floor. "Oh, I know. Because it would look good for the video if you were more like a real family. I was your token kid. Don't you know kids these days take on the anxieties of people around them? To pile on top of their own? Well, don't assume you did me a favor. What kind of gift is it to invite a kid into your drama? Thanks. Thanks a lot."

Our drama? Point taken. It's harder than most adults assume to hide undercurrents of emotions from young people. Connor and Mallory had a lot of repair work to do. "Judah, do you want to know the main reason we fought for you?"

"I guess."

"Because we wanted you to be in an environment where we knew you'd be—"

"What?"

"I was going to say 'safe,' but that sounds a little *sus* considering the day we've had, huh?"

"Sus?"

"Suspicious. Trying to speak your language here."

"Don't try too hard. I was safe."

"But we didn't know you were. And we were worried sick."

"Like you care."

Mallory stretched her legs in front of her. She'd thought to change out of her search-the-woods shoes into her one other pair before unhitching the camper. But the hems of her jeans were still damp and muddy. "Connor's at radiology right now because he cares so much that he couldn't wait to get to you."

"And because he tripped on a rock."

"I'll give you that."

Judah laughed. "Now what are we going to do?" he said.

"Well, we're going to take care of Connor the best we can."

"In the camper?"

"I don't see how, Judah. We'll give RoadRave a call after we know what's happening with his leg. He may need surgery."

"Oh, snap. I never thought of that."

"It's a possibility." One of many that could unnerve a person.

"Do you forgive me for posting that video without permission?"

Grant's wisdom was already at work. *Forgive more often than you think you should have to.*

"I'm working on it."

Judah sat back in his chair. Hands folded, he said, "Forgiveness takes courage, you know."

"That's literacy, Judah. The program is Literacy Takes Courage."

"I'm almost positive forgiveness does too."

"I guess you're right."

"You're one of the most courageous women I know," he said, enunciating every word slowly.

"So genuine."

"I mean it. And I know I need your forgiveness."

"Anyone else's?"

"Well, Connor's. And Vic's and Howie's."

"I like Howie," she said. She didn't mention that her first impression involved poison coffee and spontaneous grave-digging.

"I do too."

They shared a bag of beaten-up trail mix while they waited.

"I should probably tell you," Judah said, "that I gave up being an atheist."

Mallory stopped chewing. "You did?"

"It was too much work."

"It was?" *Unshockable, Mallory.*

"I kept trying not to believe. But I couldn't help it."

"I see," Mallory said. She reached for another bite of the trail mix.

"It's too obvie."

Mallory let a burst of laughter escape. "Aren't you a little young to be using a term like 'obvie'? Isn't that too yesterday or last year for you?"

"Trying to speak your language, here. Work with me."

"Okay. Yes, it seems obvious to me too. But I'd like to hear your story."

"In here," someone said. And the room quickly filled. Doctors, nurses, radiology and lab techs moved about the room as Connor was wheeled back in.

"I think," Mallory whispered to Judah, "it's *obvie* that Connor is not as comfortable as when he left."

"We'll get him more pain medication soon, Mrs. Duncan," one of the nurses said. "But we need to prep him for surgery. This young man is going to get some hardware."

chapter thirty-four

WILL YOU HELP ME WRITE my obituary, Mallory?"
Mallory looked up from the book she was re-reading, the one Slade had loaned to Judah, even though she almost knew it by heart from childhood. Judah had given it five stars. She'd wished she had an animated emoji to stick on their conversation when Judah told her that.

"Obituary? Connor, that's the anesthesia talking. It'll wear off soon. I'm not going to help you write your obituary because you're not going to die."

"Yes, I am."

"Right now? Because I could call for the zapper paddles."

Connor leaned on one elbow, then immediately laid back down and massaged his forehead with the one hand not tethered to an IV. "I feel the need to prepare my obituary."

Was he thinking of the VHL again? He hadn't mentioned it for … She couldn't remember how long it had been. Funny how crises determine which of them rides shotgun in life. Scrubbing at his forehead again—his signature move that let her know his thoughts were derailing. She opened the notes app on her phone. "What would you like to say?"

"More ice chips?"

"Got it," she said, thumbing her phone.

"Mallory, I mean …"

The last of the vitals check team had scooted the over-bed tray table just beyond his reach. She stood and spooned a gravel-sized piece of crushed ice to his lips. "I know what you mean, Connor."

"Thanks."

"You're welcome. But you don't have to thank me for every little kindness."

"Yes, I do." His eyes focused on her face and lingered.

"You're right," she said. "You do. Deal, then?" She held her hand in the air near his chest and welcomed his weak but intentional high five.

"I don't deserve you," Connor said.

"You don't have to deserve me, Connor. Just choose me." How much of this conversation would he remember when the anesthesia had fully worn off? Would the drug the nurses called the "forgetting" medication—was it fentanyl?—make him forget the important things? Or the impossible?

She moved the tray table closer and resumed her post in the vinyl chair. "How would you like your obituary to start?"

Connor answered with a soft snore.

◆————————————————◆

"I need to write my obituary, Mallory."

"You said that before, hon. Get some sleep."

"No, I really, really do." Connor squirmed in the bed.

"Are you in pain?"

"Why would I be in pain?"

Great. Mallory was about to prepare an important document for a man who wasn't alert enough to remember what they'd been through. On second thought, maybe that was the perfect time.

"How would you like it to start, Connor?"

"'Here lies ...'"

"That's an epitaph, not an obituary."

"All the fancy words are giving me a headache."

"Should we try again later? After you've had a nap?"

"'Here lies Connor Duncan Donuts.'"

Mallory's face hurt. "Good start, hon. What's next?"

"'Here lies ...'"

"Connor?"

"Yes. Yes. Connor Duncan Do— Connor Duncan. Here's the deal."

"That's it?" Mallory's thumbs hovered over her phone.

"I mean, here's the deal. I want to write an *obiturary ...*"

"Obituary, yes." *Someone should be videotaping this. Not for the world to see, but he might find it fun to watch when he's on his feet again.* "And what do you want it to say, Connor?"

"Better things about me than are true now."

"Do you need some help with the words? I could offer a few."

"That's a *eulogygy*." His eyes drifted shut.

"'Connor Duncan. It took him longer than some,'" she said aloud, "'but he finally discovered how much he was loved.' Connor?"

Snoring. She might have to write the whole thing herself.

◄─────────────►

"Where's Judah?" Connor blinked against the glare of overhead lights.

"Mom? Do you want to answer that?" the male nurse said as he raised the head of Connor's gurney another few degrees.

"He's our ... foster son," Connor said. *Temporarily.* The words tasted metallic on his tongue.

Mallory stood so Connor could see her face better. "Howie

came to get him," she said. "He spent the night on the farm. He'll probably help Grant and Howie most of the day. Vic volunteered to bring him to visit you later this afternoon unless you're discharged."

"Are you experiencing any dizziness, Mr. Duncan?" The nurse checked tubes and the IV site and raised the guardrail on his side while waiting for an answer.

"No."

"Pain level, on a scale of one to ten, ten being most severe?"

Connor considered. "Four?"

"Not bad. We like to keep it at four or lower. Let us know if that number starts to climb. It's a lot harder to come back from a ten than from a six or seven."

"I'll do that."

The nurse left with a promise that he or an aide would check on Connor in a few minutes.

"It's night?" Connor asked Mallory.

"The middle of. Yes."

"You should get some sleep." *A gentleman doesn't tell a woman how tired she looks.* Where had he heard that?

"I will if you will," she said. "That lovely chair over there folds out into a bed. But I'll be right here if you need anything."

Connor swallowed past the dryness in his throat. "I need …"Where had the words gone?

"Another ice chip?"

That would have to do. "Yes."

"Get it yourself," she said. "It's right there on the table, and your hands and arms work fine."

He laughed, which reminded him how sore his throat felt. He reached for the Styrofoam glass of ice chips and managed to get two in his mouth and one on his chest. "So, you've reached your limit of caregiving, have you?"

She leaned in awkwardly close to his face. "No, Connor. I haven't. I won't. No matter what. I will offer help when you genuinely need it and will stand back and spot you when you're capable of handling it on your own." She picked the stray ice chip from the front of his hospital gown and tossed it into an unseen wastebasket. "And that … is what love does."

She kissed him on the cheek, raised the guardrail on her side, and left him.

But she didn't. She made up the chair bed a few feet away, asked him to dim the lights with the patient remote, and slid under the comforter. "Goodnight, Connor. Don't be afraid to wake me if you need something."

Amid all the strangeness of the hospital room, the subdued noises in the hall, the confinement of his IV and his bandaged leg, the odors so distinctly "hospital," he caught a whiff of lavender.

"Good morning, sunshine," Connor said when Mallory sat up, blinking.

"Morning. What time is it?"

He watched her dig in her purse for her phone.

"Fifty percent charge. I should have brought chargers. It's seven-thirty. Nothing helps more than a good four hours of sleep. How long have you been awake?"

"Since six, when the surgeon came in."

Mallory slapped her pillow. "I missed that?"

"He said everything looked good. But—"

"But what?"

"I may need you for emotional support in a few minutes."

She stood and crossed to his bed. "What is it?"

"Physical therapy is coming within the hour. Mallory, they expect me to—get this—get out of bed and walk. Not happening."

She coughed into her hand. "I'll be all the support you need, Connor, but I have to brush my teeth first."

"Where'd you get the cool threads?"

"Your nurse took one look at the hem of my jeans and offered a spare pair of scrubs. Classy, huh? He got me a personal care packet too, apologizing for the bare necessities."

"Nice. We've been living on the bare necessities for a long time."

She paused on her way to his room's private bath. "Yes. We have."

He dug in the drawer of his wheeled tray table. Toothbrush, toothpaste, a disposable glass, a washcloth, and a kidney-shaped plastic dish. His water pitcher was full. As clumsy as he felt, Connor smeared a swipe of toothpaste on his brush and raced to beat Mallory. Mint. Much needed. Much appreciated.

He shoved the drawer closed as Mallory emerged from the bathroom, still wearing the scrubs but also sporting the sweater Grant had supplied.

"Well," she said, "aren't you all GQ?"

"Did a little personal hygiene."

She took the washcloth and dabbed at a corner of his mouth. "Minty fresh. I like."

Without another word, she removed the spit bowl, dumped and rinsed it. The one thing he couldn't do for himself. He didn't deserve her. What had she said in response to that last night? He remembered thinking it. Had he said it aloud? And she'd answered, hadn't she?

"Have we heard from RoadRave, Mallory?"

She folded the comforter and returned her bed to chair shape. "They've been wonderful, as we might have expected. Asked me to keep them informed but to worry about nothing, including medical expenses."

"What about the video blog?"

"You might find this amusing."

"I could use some amusing." He tried shifting in the bed before his leg told him that wasn't a good idea.

"Howie's involved now. Yes, I admit I checked my text messages in the bathroom. Howie and Judah are pairing up to handle the daily posts until … Well, until we know what's happening. Judah helped milk a goat this morning, which America is all over. They're posting still shots of the camper unhooked, sitting all forlorn in the barnyard, waiting for its master to return. In keeping with the 'just add humans' part."

"Clever."

"Howie's a techno-genius. Judah says he's learned a lot so it's, in his opinion, *chill* for him to skip his long-distance learning homework for a few days."

Connor shook his head. "With a little direction, that boy could go places someday."

"He already is, Connor."

"True."

She sat on the edge of the bed, lowering herself so gently he wouldn't have noticed if his eyes had been shut. "We have so much we need to discuss," she said. "Most of it can wait. But this is probably the heaviest on your mind. RoadRave says their account with Troyer & Duncan is solid. Couldn't be more impressed. They're ready to ink a five-year exclusive deal. Even if we can't finish the trip."

He'd expected to jump out of his skin if he heard news like that at the journey's end. Instead, his skin stayed where it was, and not just because he wasn't moving his right leg. The internal celebration was quieter than he'd anticipated it would be. Probably because that wasn't what weighed heaviest on his heart these days.

chapter thirty-five

MALLORY HAD WATCHED CONNOR MANEUVER up and down the physical therapy room's pretend steps as if he'd been practicing for weeks.

The rest of their trip—the last partial week of it—would, in all respects, provide a far greater challenge than three gentle, smooth steps. They'd seen few campgrounds, parking lots, scenic overlooks, or trails that were crutches-friendly.

Some were wheelchair accessible, though.

No. An insane idea. It was over.

The words stuck in a brain loop, poking at her like Connor and Judah liked to poke at a fire to stir it up. It was over. Done.

Connor would eventually heal and get back to fending for himself on all points. The need for her presence on the micro-camper adventure was done. She and Connor were tolerating each other much more comfortably. But tolerating does not a marriage make.

She could drive the rig back to Chicago. Cherise had texted that the asbestos remediation neared completion, and RoadRave had already electronically deposited their grant to the Hope Street Youth Center's bank account. One more sign of a quality company that kept its promises, beyond expectation.

Connor's hospital room boasted a RoadRave flower arrangement that frankly got in the way of traffic coming and going. Well-wishes plugged their inboxes and the comments sections on the video blog. Mallory's trending video still had a crazy life of its own, but was now linked to images of the two of them walking the hospital halls, sporting matching RoadRave tee shirts over scrub pants, Mallory with a tight grip on the back of Connor's gait belt.

The time had come for the big talk. *What now? How do we get you home, Connor? What's next?*

No, the *what's next* question would have to wait. Again.

The latest x-rays showed the titanium rod in Connor's tibia—from just under his knee to just above his ankle—was behaving as it should. Swelling was under control. No infection in the incision. All it needed was time to heal. And more physical therapy. But nothing that couldn't be accomplished off hospital premises.

"Ready to bust out of this joint, Connor?"

"Dr. Stewart, those are some of the most beautiful words in the English language," Connor said, hoisting himself higher in the bed.

"Mallory," the orthopedic surgeon said, "are you ready to have him home 24/7 for a while?"

"You know our story," she said. "We're living out of a microcamper at the moment. It's at least a couple of days' journey home. Do we need to arrange for a medi-flight for him or something?" The cost of a flight like that could cripple their finances. The pun was the only funny part about it.

Dr. Stewart pulled up Connor's x-rays on his electronic tablet. "Connor, in a significant way, that rod makes your tibia stronger than it's ever been. You don't have to be nervous about it, although you do have to be reasonably cautious and give it what it needs to heal."

"What does that mean?" Connor asked.

"Mallory, if you think you can make him comfortable in the back seat, and keep the leg elevated when it needs it … and Connor, if you'll obey doctor's orders and be diligent about the exercises to strengthen the muscles that were strained in your fall, I don't see any reason why you can't drive home."

"Do you think you could handle that, Connor?" Mallory asked.

"The driving or the … ?"

"Connor."

"I'm kidding. I feel great. Really. It was thoughtful of me, don't you think, to direct all the impact from my fall onto my lower leg? And just one of them?"

"Thoughtful," she said.

"Just take it slow," Dr. Stewart added. "Rushing home isn't as important as getting there. Take plenty of breaks. Give those crutches a workout. And"—he reached to shake Connor's hand—"enjoy a little scenery along the way."

He shook Mallory's hand and whispered, "My wife makes me watch your hay bale video every few days now. Thanks for that."

Halfway through the doorway, he turned and said, "Oh, Connor. Yeah, I almost forgot. You wanted copies of your x-rays." He set a manila envelope on Connor's tray table, tapped it twice, and left them alone.

"Judah will love to see the x-rays," Mallory said.

"So, what do you think? Can we do this?"

"What's the worst that can happen? If we get on the road and an hour later you can tell it isn't going to work, we'll stop and find a motel room and figure out something else. Maybe rent a limo for you."

"That would be a sight. A limo pulling a microcamper."

"You have to admit it would make great footage."

"And a few more memories to hold us."

What did he mean? "To hold us"? She worked to keep her expression halfway between neutral and happy, but her insides churned.

She couldn't think about "what ifs" now. She had more than enough "what it *is*" to occupy her. "Let's let Judah know he doesn't have to make Howie bring him here to visit this evening. We'll head his way."

"Are we all staying at the farm tonight?"

Something in his expression stopped her. "I had an idea but didn't know if you'd go for it."

"What?" Connor had already started packing the hospital-issue plastic garbage-sized bag she'd handed him.

"Vic and Ericka said there's a vacant rental tiny house in the Village. It has a wide deck with gentle steps, and a first-floor bedroom. No ladder or stairs you'd need to climb. They said we could use it for free, if we wanted to."

"All three of us?"

"I thought—maybe—just the two of us. Judah and Howie are working on some kind of top secret project, which scares me a little."

Connor nodded. "Remove Howie from that equation and I'd be more scared. But, there's something about that kid."

"Judah?"

"Yeah. That one."

———————————◆———————————

Connor powered down his window with the tip of his crutch. Not convenient, but it worked. "Did you remember to get gas?"

"Yes, Connor. I remembered to fill up."

"Did the check engine light come on?"

"No."

"I'll come out and look under the hood."

She poked her head through the open window, fire in her

eyes. "You will not get out of this vehicle. I will look under the hood and return momentarily with my professional assessment."

"Mallory, you—"

She reached through the window near his feet and grabbed his crutches. "I'll keep these with me as insurance that you'll stay put."

Stubborn woman. Who was almost always annoyingly right.

"It's going to be dark soon," he called, keeping his voice more helpful than dictatorial, he hoped.

"Well aware of that," she answered, her tone a fine imitation of his.

Connor would have argued longer if— "What are you doing up there?" The sound of rock on metal was not the sound of a professional mechanic.

Mallory slid behind the wheel and tried the key. The engine sprang to life. "Aha!" She revved the engine a couple of times, then left it running while she closed the hood, returned his crutches, and climbed behind the steering wheel again.

"What was it?"

"Corroded battery connection. I knocked off the corrosion, and there you go."

"How did you know to look for that?"

"My grandparents never owned a new car. Grandpa always had his head under the hood or his body under the chassis. I learned a few things. One of them was that"—she signaled to pull back onto the empty county road—"broken things offer training ground for fixing things."

He watched the back of her head. Because it was his right leg that needed support, he had to sit with his body leaning against the second seat door on the driver's side of the SUV. His view was his foot or the back of her head. The nurse's advice to load up with pain medicine before making the trip to New Day Village was good counsel. He could take up to two, per the prescription. He'd taken one. *Tough guys rule. Tough guys should have their heads examined.*

He ached every place that could ache. The leg was the least of his discomforts. He needed a pillow for his back. His arms got a workout trying to steady himself in the back seat. His left leg had cramped up from trying to decide where it belonged.

How many miles lay between here and Chicago? *Settle, dude. One chunk at a time.* They couldn't be far from New Day Village now. Someday, he'd like to return and do a little more digging into what made New Day such a unique community. Trouble and conflict and division filled the news. This place had figured out how to use their differences to everyone's advantage. Connor wanted to know how.

And if it were possible for he and Mallory to figure out the same formula.

He cranked his head to look out the left window for a change of pace. "Mallory, stop!"

"What?" She eased onto the brake until they were at a dead stop. "What's wrong?" She unlatched her seatbelt and swiveled toward the back seat.

"Can you back up a few feet?"

"Why?"

"Please?" He hadn't meant to stress her. But if that was a …

She rebuckled and backed slowly—and expertly, he had to admit—until he said, "This is it. Look at your side of the road. I mean, beyond the other lane on your side."

The telescoping canoe paddle handle. Still standing as a memorial to the spot where they'd left the rig and lost Judah. If Vic had seen it, he'd left it there for some reason.

Without Connor having to ask, Mallory retrieved it, kicked dirt off the end that had been stuck in the ground for days, and leaned it where Judah would ordinarily ride.

"Thank you," he said when they were rolling again.

She didn't respond.

"Mallory? Cat got your tongue?"

"That is so last century, Connor. And it isn't a cat." She braked again. "I think it's a dog. And I think it's injured."

"So am I." Connor squirmed. "And the dog might not be injured, it might be rapid. I mean, rabid." Pain meds. The sooner he got off them entirely, the better.

They'd never make it before dark at this pace. Connor waited, not able to position himself so he could see what she was doing. Great, she'd get mauled by a rabid dog and then he would have to get out of the car and fight off the beast, get her torn-up body loaded, and he'd have to somehow get his broken leg over the console so he could drive her to the … Hey, he could rest his broken leg on the canoe paddle in the passenger seat, and what was taking her so long?

She climbed behind the wheel and started the engine. It purred to life again, like it should.

"So, was it a dog?"

"Yes," she said. "More of a puppy, really."

"Injured?"

"It'll be okay now."

"What did you do?"

"I brought her with me."

"Mallory?"

A face poked its head over her shoulder. Tan and black and tiny. Almost … micro.

"Mallory, who is almost always right."

"Ninety-nine-point-nine percent of the time."

"What have you done?"

Mallory stroked the puppy's head. "We rescued an animal in distress."

"Is it wearing a collar?"

"Connor, it was poking its head out of a burlap bag. No collar. Or microchip, I bet. Somebody meant to leave it there."

"We need to add a dog to this … this …"

"Get your chill back on," she said. "I'll see if Vic and Ericka know anybody in the village who wants a dog. Look at that face. Somebody will want it."

chapter thirty-six

THE NO-RENT RENTAL TINY HOUSE welcomed them as if it were designed for them, as if it had been waiting. Its double front door made it even easier than expected to get Connor into the house. And it smelled like home.

Ericka had left supper warming in the teeny, tiny oven, fresh-baked molasses ginger cookies on the counter, with a carafe of hot apple cider waiting beside them.

"I didn't know what you'd be up to eating, Connor," Ericka said, moving obstacles out of his way as he headed for the L-shaped mini-couch. "So I made my fall favorite. Pumpkin pear soup."

Connor's laughter filled the tiny house, baptizing it in joy. Mallory had been holding onto peace by her fingernails. Now, she had a stronger grip.

"Did I say something funny?" Ericka asked.

"It's one of our faves too," Mallory said. "Funny that you would think to make that for us. Thank you."

"And like I said, I'd keep the pup for you, if Vic didn't have all kinds of pet allergies. But we'll spread the word. Someone in the village is bound to either take her off your hands or offer to pup-sit for the night."

The affirmation didn't feel as comforting as Mallory expected it would.

"I'll tell them to give you at least an hour to get settled before they come busting your door down for that sweet animal. Curious that there's a small kennel built into the bottom of the bookcase, isn't it?"

"Curious," Connor said, rearranging pillows.

"Oh, and I did this," Ericka said, flipping a switch. Tiny white Christmas lights outlined the window opposite the double door. "Thought it would make it homey."

"I love it, Ericka. You've thought of everything. We're indebted to you."

"Nonsense. We needed someone to test drive the rental unit since its upgrades. You're doing us a favor."

"Test drive. Nice try," Connor said. "We're still indentured. Indebted."

"The words get a little jumbled when his pain medicine kicks in," Mallory said.

"Make sure he keeps something in his stomach when he takes that stuff. And that he stays hydrated."

"Yes, ma'am. I will."

"I'll check in with you midmorning. I have a feeling you two could both use a good night's sleep without the drone of a hospital in the background."

When she was gone, Mallory took Connor's duffel bag to the bedroom. "Connor, this will work out perfectly for you. The bathroom is right here. So close, you may only need one crutch to get there."

"Mallory?"

She stepped out of the bedroom into the living area. "What do you need?"

"That silly dog is whining in her kennel."

"Whimpering a little. She'll get used to it soon."

"Bring her over here. I'll hold her."

"Are you sure?" Mallory watched his face for signs of resentment.

"Bring her here. Please."

Mallory stood over the two of them, ready to whisk the dog away at the first sign of … sign. Or aggression. Or fleas. Good grief, she hadn't checked the thing for fleas!

Connor looked as if he couldn't care less if she did have fleas. He leaned against the pillow behind his head. The pup crawled onto his chest and tucked her nose under his chin. Within a minute, both were asleep.

What were they doing? What was she doing? Pretending? Pretending she could get Connor home to Chicago? Pretending she could manage a recuperating husband on the verge of leaving her, an eleven-year-old sort-of foster son with enough issues to start his own magazine stand, an abandoned puppy, a demanding job waiting for her if the city didn't shut them down, and so many miles yet to go?

She turned off the tiny oven but poured herself a mug of apple cider and left it to cool a little on the counter while she toured the rest of the house. It wouldn't take long.

Mallory loved everything about it. The way it was decorated—modern but not cold. The flower arrangement from RoadRave would have fit perfectly from an aesthetic standpoint but would have taken up too much room. She hoped the nurses on the orthopedic surgery floor were enjoying it.

Mallory climbed to peek at the loft. The loft and its extra-large windows. If she figured right, the window above the mattress—a thick, real mattress—faced east. Dawn.

She climbed down the side of the bookcase as quietly as she could. The pup raised her head but returned to her nap on Connor's chest. *My favorite place to lay my head too, little one.*

Connor had been different in the hospital. Less stressed, weird as that sounded. It might have been the medication. Must have been the medication. It's as if the surgery had made him forget what they'd been in the middle of. She'd hoped her caregiving and his acceptance of it would have convinced him it was possible to survive being cared for. But she knew the truth and so did he. He'd coped with it only because it was temporary and every day made him stronger. Unlike …

What Connor couldn't bear hadn't changed. He couldn't imagine her having to care for a steadily deteriorating husband. It didn't matter that she was willing. It didn't matter that it might not be an issue because … 50/50.

Frustration bubbled in her. They'd come so far. But in some ways it seemed they were still at the starting line.

Forgive more often than you think you should have to. She sat at the platter-sized table under the lit window with her mug of cider and a cookie. She was adulting. Cookies could come first. While Connor and No-Name slept, Mallory caught up on her phone. Correction. She attempted to catch up. Messages still overflowed. She opened the one from Judah first.

"Miss you."

That was it.

Mallory archived the message. The crazy thing was that she missed him too. She started a new draft to tell him about No-Name but thought better of it. He'd probably highjack a cow or hotwire a tractor to come see it. She created a new message telling him she loved him. Her finger hovered over the Send button. *Send.*

RoadRave had given their blessing on the delay getting the microcamper returned and commended Judah and Howie for their recent submissions from the farm. She'd have to take a look later, maybe after she had Connor and the dog settled for the night. Mallory's infamous hay bale speech had reached over twelve-million hits. Twelve stinkin' million.

Judah messaged back. "Yeah."

Translation, *I would tell you I love you too, but then I'd have to change my name and move to a foreign country because I don't do stuff like that.*

Minnie, as in mini ha ha. That was the dog's name.

She'd let the two sleep five more minutes, then she'd pull supper out of the oven whether it woke them or not.

Connor needed to eat. *Ooh*, the dog—Minnie—was probably starving.

Mallory dug in the cupboards for plastic or disposable dishes she could use for the puppy. Had it ever eaten table scraps? Pumpkin pear soup didn't exactly make great table scraps for a dog. Where had she seen dogs in New Day Village? Who might have dog food she could purchase?

And why did nobody show up to say, "Here, I'll take the dog"?

Because it belonged to them. Connor and Mallory. That's why.

Wait a minute. The house was built with a kennel under the bookcase. She searched all the storage cubbies and then thought to check if the drawer in the main closet had another layer underneath, like the teardrop camper's kitchen storage did. Bingo. A sealed plastic tub of dog food.

Mallory filled the water dish half full and put a quarter of a cup of dog food into the other. Minnie's ears twitched. She lifted her head and bounded off Connor to head for the dishes.

"Good girl. That's my girl." She looked like a teenage small dog, like a long-haired Chihuahua with something else in her ancestry. Maybe a little bit of cocker spaniel. She didn't have a traditional narrow Chihuahua face. "How does it taste, Minnie?"

The dog didn't stop to answer.

Mallory stepped into the bathroom for a minute. When she exited, Connor stirred.

"I didn't want to wake you, Connor, but you need to eat something before it gets much later."

"Yeah. Yep. Where'd I put my crutches?"

"Right here," she said, "tucked under the couch."

"I need to get up and stretch a little."

"Go for it. You have, what, a good fourteen feet of walking path in here. One way. Do you need help standing?"

He sat on the edge of the couch and hesitated. "I could use a spotter."

"Got it."

She stood near while he maneuvered himself to a standing position, using his crutches in one hand as leverage. She waited while he got his bearings, then stepped back to give him room when he indicated he was heading for the bathroom first.

Mallory stretched her hamstrings, reached above her head, then planted her palms flat on the floor, and worked in three lunges before Minnie finished eating and Connor returned, marveling at the "sweet" bedroom.

Who but the two of them would have considered the space in a tiny house roomy?

———————————————◆———————————————

"Mini, huh?"

"Minnie ha. Ha. Two ha's. Minnehaha. Laughing waters?"

Connor took another spoonful of soup. "You're sure that's the dog's name?"

"It just came to me," she said.

"You know we can't—"

"I know it's a stupid idea to bring a dog into this mess and what was I thinking and either you'll have to keep her at the office or I'll have to move because our current … my current apartment doesn't allow pets and naming a dog you can't keep is ultra-stupid and I—"

"Mallory. Before you interrupted, I was going to say that you know we can't possibly leave her here. All her, you know, abandonment issues and everything? Who would double-abandon a dog like that?"

"You're smiling. For reals."

He looked down where Minnie curled at Mallory's feet. "Yes, it may seem like awkward timing …"

"The awkwardest."

"But awkward is kind of a theme with us, isn't it?" He wiggled his eyebrows for emphasis.

"You're serious about our keeping the dog?" Her face glowed with hope.

Connor laid a hand on top of hers. The one missing a ring. "I'm serious. As long as we agree to reconsider if the dog becomes a problem."

"No," she said.

"What?"

"I would agree to talk it through and try to problem-solve. But I won't agree to a principle I don't believe in."

"Mallory, what—?"

"I don't want to live my life giving up because things are tough or inconvenient or uncomfortable." She slid her hand out from under his and cupped it around the soup bowl. Was she searching for a warmth he couldn't give her?

"Mallory ..."

"Are you in or out, Connor?" She lifted her chin, eyes reflecting the small lights lining the window. "On the dog. Let's start with the dog."

"I'm in."

"Good. There's another thing," she said.

His leg started to slip off the small folding chair and pillow on which it was propped. He grabbed at the top of the brace near his knee. "And it is ... ?"

"Judah. Can we keep him? He's never known a forever. Don't worry. We can share custody in the divorce settlement."

The pillow slid to the floor, and so did his foot.

chapter thirty-seven

I THINK I'M OKAY," CONNOR said from his multipillowed spot on the tiny house's plush double bed.

"Should we check in with the hospital to make sure?" She knew how to do this. She was firm but not panicked. Concerned, but not demanding. Logical. So like her. But tender too.

"I have a follow-up appointment tomorrow," Connor answered, "which I thought I might skip if we were on the road home." He watched her left eye twitch at the word *home*. If he could think, they could talk. But right now ...

"Is it wise to wait for that appointment? Never mind. You know how you feel. I'll get the other ice pack."

"Did we bring it in from the car?"

"When we first arrived," she called from the kitchen a few feet away. "I don't know what made me stick it in the minifreezer as soon as we got here. It filled the freezer, but it fits." She replaced the now warm ice pack with the fresh one. "Is this the best spot for it?"

"I feel the ache in my heel. I might have bruised it. The good news is that it's on the same leg I can't use anyway."

Mallory's compassionate smile helped somehow. "Between the two of us, *you're* the look-on-the-bright-side one now, Connor?"

"I'm not the same man I was when we started this journey. I wish you knew that."

"I want to believe it," she said.

"Mallory?"

"Yes?"

"It pains me to say this, but …"

"I'm tired of our not being completely honest with each other, Connor. Whatever it is, say it. Pain and all."

"You know how you always remind Judah to use the restroom before we a) get on the road or b) turn in for the night?"

"He's eleven. He shouldn't need the reminder. But … Oh."

"I shouldn't need the reminder either. Alas …"

Grinning while she served him, Mallory removed the ice pack and pillows one by one and stood back while he left the bed into which they'd gotten him settled.

———————◆———————

Mallory did all she could to make Connor comfortable again. "Connor, do you have your phone near you? Yes, you do. Right here on the shelf. Great."

"You can probably hear me if I whisper."

She retreated to the doorway of the bedroom. "Ordinarily, yes. But I need to take the dog out. You text or call me if you need anything while I'm gone."

"I don't like you to be gone."

His last batch of pain meds for the night must be kicking in. "I won't be long. But Minnie is clawing at the door."

"I may be snoring by the time you get back. Amazing snore, how sweet the sound."

"Goodnight, Connor. Sweet dreams." Her own phone tucked in her sweater pocket, she closed the pocket door most of the way and started the search for a makeshift leash. In the end, she settled for linking a set of bungee cords from the car's tool kit. More creative than convenient. She had to stay closer to Minnie than she wanted while "exploring" the not-so-tiny yard around the tiny house.

She'd have to stop thinking of the fisherman sweater as hers. Their whole life at present depended on borrowed housing, camper, food, clothes … time. Borrowed time. All were about to come to an end.

Connor had changed, he insisted. A new man? She knew that. And loved it. Which made his one point of immovable resistance all the harder to take.

His tone may have softened regarding the possibility of a future together. But even if they remained side by side beyond that one-year marker soon approaching, at the first sign that Connor's genetic code lived on the wrong half of 50/50, he would shut her out in his twisted efforts to spare both of them from the barely-there life his parents lived. To spare her discomfort. To spare himself the need to depend on her in a way that would cost her everything.

Hadn't he paid attention during the trip? That's what families do—give everything.

A tug on the leash reminded Mallory she was outside for a reason. The dog behaved like a lady—polite, poised, and discreet. "Minnie, you're a dream dog. Let's go back in the house."

She responded to the command as if she already considered Mallory her foster mom. Small joys on a hashtag journey.

They both wiped their feet on the entry rug inside the door. "Minnie, my mini-me." The dog sipped from her water dish and headed for the kennel, waiting patiently for Mallory to close the latch. Connor couldn't afford to trip over a dog in the middle of the night.

Mallory headed for the loft but realized it would take her much longer to respond to Connor's needs if she slept up there. She made a nest for herself on the L-shaped couch.

Dawn would reveal itself through that loft window. She wouldn't be able to observe it. But dawns are persistent. Relentless. It would arrive even if she wasn't watching.

Mallory had coffee in the world's smallest coffeemaker the next morning before Connor first stirred. Minnie had already done more exploring of a personal needs nature. They had no groceries yet, and all their canned and boxed food items were in the teardrop camper on the farm. But lack of supplies proved not to be an issue.

Someone—best guess, Ericka—left a small latched cooler on the corner of the deck. A dozen eggs, two jars of Mallory's favorite yogurt, a loaf of what looked like homemade bread, and locally grown honey. They were set.

She hard-boiled half the eggs for the trip, found a serrated knife, and sliced bread for toast. She'd shower later, after Connor woke.

Light streamed in through the tiny house's large windows. Had she remembered to pull the shades in the bedroom where Connor slept? A nonissue now. He stood in the doorway, leaning on his crutches, his hair proving two things—he'd slept well, and he needed a trim.

"Good morning. Would you like a cup of coffee?"

"In a minute," he said, pointing toward the bathroom.

She popped two slices into the toaster oven/microwave combo. That appliance would take some getting used to. She'd set the table but doubted he wanted to try the leg-propped-on-a-wobbly-chair posture for eating his meals for a while.

"Something smells good," he said.

"How's your pain level?"

"Much better. I'm thinking the jolt to my heel must have helped."

Mallory pressed her lips together. *Let him think that, if he wants.* "Yogurt?"

"Love some."

"Why don't you make yourself comfortable on the couch? I'll bring breakfast to you."

"Comfortable? Is that the life goal we're looking for these days?"

She didn't answer.

"You're too good to me," he said.

"See? We can agree on *some* things."

Connor assumed the spot Mallory had recently vacated. "Oh!" he said.

"What's wrong now?"

"The pillow smells like you."

"Sorry."

"Not in a bad way. Lavender." His voice dropped below the range of human hearing.

She was working at not reading anything into any comment, so she let it go.

"How's Minnie, which again, I'm not sure is her final forever name?" Connor said.

"Love this dog. I have her kenneled now. But I hope I can find some way to let her outside more today. Wish I knew her history. I should text Judah to see if they left already and if the farm has a leash we can borrow." Living on borrowed leashes.

"And how will you do that and keep the surprise about The-Dog-Who-Shall-Temporarily-Be-Named-Minnie for when he arrives?"

"I love it when you're thinking clearly. Good point." Mallory handed him the plate of toast and honey. She set the yogurt and his coffee mug on the shelf that pulled out from the wall like a slide-out cutting board.

She started to say something, but his head was bowed. Asleep already? So much for the clear-headedness. She reached to rescue the toast plate as he lifted his head. "I thought you'd fallen asleep," she said.

He hesitated. "No. Thanking God for the food and for you."

A pickup ground to a stop in front of the house. Howie

and Judah jumped out. Judah's hat was pulled especially low over his ears. *It must be colder out there than I realized.*

She opened the door wide to let them in.

"Judah!" She didn't wait for permission to hug him. "We've missed you."

"Yeah, and …" He whipped off his cap, revealing a close-cropped haircut.

"What did you do?" Connor asked.

Judah stepped to the couch and gave Connor a guy kind of hug. "I cut it off. I'm donating it to Locks of Love." He pulled a small zippered plastic bag from his jacket pocket.

Mallory looked to Howie for further explanation.

"He kinda insisted," Howie said. "And I thought, pick your battles. Generous of him, wasn't it?"

"Yes," Mallory said. How would the Locks of Love organization explain to a bright-eyed eleven-year-old that two-inch pieces of hair are hard to make into a wig or weave?

Howie removed his own hat, revealing a similar haircut. "Then we both decided we'd go to an actual barber for professional, shall we say *corrective* measures."

"Howie, you've been such a godsend," Connor said.

"In so many ways," Mallory added.

"Judah's been a big help on the farm," Howie said, eyes a little wider than necessary for a statement like that.

"And," Judah said, "we have another surprise. Don't we, Howie?"

Mallory could hardly wait. She noticed a similar thought spilling from Connor's expression.

"Can I go get it, Howie?"

"Sure."

Judah headed back to the truck and dug under a tarp in the pickup's bed.

Mallory knew time was short. "Howie, the true scoop? How did it go?"

"It was great. Different for Pop and me. But good for both of us. Not sure we want to give him back to you."

Connor said, "We know the feeling."

"You two have made quite an impression on him," Howie said. "And he needed it."

Had God translated what she and Connor had experienced during the "adventure" into something genuinely useful for Judah? The boy had to know he was loved. He now knew more about the authenticity of God's love for him. They all had a better grasp on that.

"Okay," Judah said, breathless from his flight to the truck and back. "A brand new refurbished guitar strap! Do you like it, Connor?"

"Oh, hey, buddy. This is lit. I mean it. I … I don't know what to say. Love it. I'll put it to good use when we get back to Chicago."

"You brought your guitar. I saw it. Hundred percent."

Connor ran his fingers over the hand-tooled leather. "I was going to bring it along, but space was pretty tight, as you know, and Mallory had to leave her curling wand behind. I didn't think it would be fair to—"

"Are you kidding me?" Mallory said. "I've had to put up with this hair," she said, pulling her fingers through it for emphasis, "for nothing? You thought we left your guitar in Chicago?"

"We did," he said. "About the hair, when have you never looked great, except for that one night in the hospital? Oh, and when we got caught in the rain? And that one other time when—"

"Connor. Your guitar has been in the SUV the whole trip."

"No. I left it at the office when we were loading up."

"You tried to. I was the one who rearranged the way we were packing the vehicle, if you'll remember. You didn't discover it under all that stuff the whole trip?" Mallory didn't know whether to slug him in the arm or bust out laughing.

"Why did you do that?"

Howie looked between them. "Do Judah and I need to go for a walk or something?"

"Yes." Connor and Mallory, in unison once again.

"And take the dog with you," Mallory said, holding out the string of patched together bungee cords.

Judah swirled to face Mallory. "We have a *dog*?"

chapter thirty-eight

I T TOOK ALL OF A micro-minute for Judah to bond with Minnie and head outside with her. Howie dropped off Judah's gear and said a quick goodbye.

Exhausted from pretty much everything, Connor drank a long sip of his coffee. Mallory stood three feet away, arms crossed.

"Mallory, are we arguing because we were trying to be *kind* to the other person and it didn't work out like we'd planned?"

"Considerate. We were trying to be considerate of the other person. And that was before the journey began. When things were—"

Connor swallowed his second sip and set the cup on the pull-out shelf. "Does that strike you as the makings of a comedy routine rather than fodder for an argument?"

She pursed her lips. Refolded her arms the other way. Rocked from one foot to the other. "You don't suppose," she said, "that there's hope for us yet?"

"I'm counting on it," he said. "Would you come closer, please? I'd get up and come to you, but—" He pointed to his cumbersome black leg brace.

"What do you need? Are we supposed to change your bandage today? Was that today?"

"Not us. I have the follow-up appointment this afternoon. They said they'd take care of changing the bandage then."

"Oh. Right. Yes."

"Mallory?"

She pulled a chair near his side, as she had so often in the hospital. Sat in it with her hands in her lap.

"Mallory."

"Don't ask me to talk." Her voice quavered.

"Is it okay if I do?"

"Yes." A firm but unaccessorized yes.

"We're going to be okay. I mean," he said, "if you're willing."

Her brow furrowed. "*I* always have been."

"I know you have."

Mallory tilted her head back. Connor knew the ceiling held no answers. He'd tried that. She nodded once. Maybe she'd been looking higher than the ceiling.

"But I think—" she said. "No, it's more than think. I *deserve* more than a 50/50 commitment from you. You'd maybe, probably, likely, if the wind were blowing from the right direction, consider the possibility of our staying together if it weren't for the threat that you might be carrying—"

"Mallory, I had the genetic testing done."

"What? When?" She scraped the chair backward across the hardwood floor.

That would leave a mark. How much would it cost them to replace the flooring in a tiny house? Not the issue at hand.

"Why didn't you tell me? Connor! I'm madder now than I was a few minutes ago! No." She licked one finger and held it in the air as if testing wind direction. "Madder than I've ever been, except for the morning my deepest inner thoughts went viral and you were happy about it!"

"Please listen. I was happy," he said, "because you were

right. And I knew it. Marriage isn't about avoiding discomfort, avoiding loneliness, avoiding facing our fears. It's about commitment."

"How long have you known the results of the testing? And didn't tell me?" Hurt seemed to have replaced anger. It showed in her voice and her wildly blinking eyes.

"I don't know the results. Dr. Stewart handed them to me before my discharge. The manila envelope. He had to contact a medical facility familiar with von Hippel-Lindau syndrome to find out what they needed for bloodwork."

"What do you mean, you don't know the results? You didn't look at them?" Anger, hurt, now incredulity flashed across her face.

"And I don't plan to, Mallory. Not now, anyway."

"I thought I didn't understand you. Now, I really and most sincerely don't understand you."

"I needed to get the testing done. For your sake. For the sake of our … children. But you'd already convinced me, the trip convinced me"—he rubbed his forehead with his fingertips, then stopped—"and getting real with God convinced me that you weren't as shallow as I was. I assumed the way my parents reacted to Dad's diagnosis was a pattern we were destined to follow. Genetics. But that was wrong."

Her tears had some catching up to do to match his.

"I want you beside me no matter what. And I know what kind of woman you are. I should have known before. You're strong. You're not afraid, even if the report doesn't go the way we'd want."

"That's right."

"And I'm not my father."

"No, you're not." She pulled her chair closer again.

"But it might be very, very hard, Mallory. That is a reality."

She leaned over and rested her head on his chest. "I know. And it doesn't matter. Because … love."

He stroked her beautifully messy hair. So this was what unconditional felt like. Being leaned into and leaned on despite all the reasons she had to walk away.

"*Psst.*"

Connor looked over her head to find where the hissing sound was coming from.

"*Psst.* Can you two do that last part one more time? The audio wasn't picking up well through the door glass."

Mallory stayed where she was, her head tucked under his chin, her arms resting on his chest. "Judah," she said, "your videography days are numbered."

"Uh huh," he said. "But I'm telling you, this is good material."

She angled her head so she could see Connor's face. "What are we going to do with him?"

"I think the footage," he said, "could use this." He bent to kiss the woman who would never leave him, even if he told her to.

◆————————————————▶

Three days later, they closed up the rental tiny house with a promise to revisit someday soon and hit the road again. This time with another gift from RoadRave—an inflatable back seat mattress that filled in the foot wells and allowed Connor a more comfortable ride. He could vary his position to sit either direction. His guitar made it a tight fit, but Mallory loved hearing him play again.

The New Day Village and farmhouse goodbyes were tough to get through, but easier to take when Judah opened up and told his no-longer-an-atheist story.

"It was too hard to not believe when I saw him everywhere, in people like the Tray family, and Slade, and Vic and Ericka, and Mr. Ferris, and you, Howie. Well, and Connor and Mallory, although it took those two a while."

Mallory had whispered, "That's our boy."

"Oh, I need to give you back your book, Mr. Ferris," Judah had added. He pulled it from his backpack. A dog-eared copy from the Chronicles of Narnia.

Grant insisted it wasn't a loan, but a gift.

Mallory had to take a chair as the connection hit her. They weren't living on borrowed time, but with the *gift* of time.

Connor had crutched his way over to where Mallory sat and put his hand on her shoulder.

"And," Mallory had said, "I don't know what we would have done without these sweaters, Grant. They kept us warm in more ways than one. Thank you. They made me want to learn how to knit."

"Keep them," he'd said. "I think my wife would have wanted that. An investment in cozy nights in your future."

They'd done the no, we couldn't / yes, I insist dance until Connor said, "What if we use them this winter and return them on our second anniversary celebration road trip next year?"

Mallory pressed Connor's hand tighter to her shoulder.

"Welp," Grant had said, "we can discuss it then."

The vehicle was now pointed toward home, but in so many ways she felt they'd already arrived. Planning for the future. Reintroducing *forever* into their vocabulary.

She turned west in response to the direction of the messages that RoadRave insisted weren't complete yet. "How's the homework coming, Judah?"

"I'm learning about behavioral characteristics of the domesticated canine at the moment," he said, scratching Minnie's ears.

Judah continued petting the dog with one hand and scrolled with the other through something of interest on his phone. "Hey, did you guys know there's a county in Wisconsin that has forty waterfalls? In one county? I bet that's where we're headed next. It's the kind of thing RoadRave would love."

Connor stopped strumming. "Buddy, I think they're directing us straight home. The journey's about over."

"Yeah," he said. "My uncle Nate's done with his jury duty."

"He is?" Mallory stretched her neck muscles.

"Didn't you guys get the text?"

"I've been driving," Mallory said.

"I've been oblivious," Connor added. "I should give him a call."

"You're planning to tell him I've been an answer to your prayers, right?" Judah rested his chin on his crossed hands and batted his eyelashes so dramatically, Mallory could see the scene in her peripheral vision without having to turn her head. "That I was a GOAT?"

"A goat?" Connor asked.

"That stands for Greatest Of All Time," Mallory said. Working with at-risk teens provided her a broader education than she'd ever hope to use.

Connor laughed. "Something like that, Judah. You do know he has access to all the footage of your ... angelicness ... right?"

"Dude! I never thought about that."

"It's all there online," Connor said.

Mallory had phone calls to make too. Cherise, for one. And Charlene Tray. From what little Mallory knew about Charlene, she imagined the new mom was probably back at work already, her sweet daughter in a sling across her front.

And Mallory needed to make a phone call to Connor's mom. Mallory could have been so much more supportive, despite the distance between them. Even if Connor didn't want to know the results of his VHL tests, his mother probably did. What went through her mind when she gave birth to two sons, knowing they would have a 50/50 chance of contracting the disease? If she'd ever talked about it with Connor, Mallory had never heard the story.

Connor's mom deserved more from her daughter-in-law.

RoadRave kept them on a winding trajectory, still back roads all the way. She wasn't looking forward to another night or two of camping. Connor's leg complicated their circumstances even more than they already were. Truth be told, she was emotionally tired. Elated, but worn out. And for some reason, each mile felt like it drew them not closer to home but farther from it.

"What's that song you're playing now, Connor?"

"Do you like it? Something new."

"Does it have lyrics?"

"Maybe I'll add those tonight. Around the campfire. Still working on the melody."

The terrain revealed that in the short time they'd been gone, autumn had been tuning up. More color dotted the woods. Leaves were easily dislodged by the breeze. Fields that had once held vibrant green now were brown and crisped by the passage of time and the whim of the season.

"Mallory?"

"Yes?"

"Would you pull over, please, when you find a spot?"

"Can't it wait for the next gas station, Connor?"

"Not what you're thinking."

"There's a rustic farmers market on the right with an almost empty parking lot. Will that work?"

"Yes!" Judah said. "I can get a snack."

"That'd be great, Mallory. Thanks."

What was on his mind? Was he in pain again? As of this morning, he'd stopped taking anything except ibuprofen. Maybe it was too soon.

By necessity, she'd become adept at parking their rig, but the unoccupied parking lot made it easy. She turned off the engine, unbuckled her seatbelt, and swiveled to face Connor. "What is it?"

"First order of business," Judah said, "is the little matter of my hungry-bordering-on-hangry."

Connor dug in his pockets. "Here's my bless-somebody-with-them dollar bills and a five. Use the five to choose a healthy snack and give the twenty bucks to the proprietor. Okay, Judah? Just because. And take your time."

Judah winked. "Got it. You two want anything?"

Mallory smiled. He was learning how to think about other people's needs. "I could use a couple of apples if they have some."

"Me too," Connor added.

"I'll need more money," Judah said.

That's the Judah we know and love. Mallory fished out another five from her purse. She was back to using a purse.

chapter thirty-nine

WITH JUDAH OFF ON HIS mission, but well within sight, Connor said, "Mallory, what if we're not heading home right now, but away from it?"

Her heart jumped ahead a beat. "Did you hear me say that a few minutes ago? Or did I think it?"

"I didn't hear anything."

How was it possible they were thinking on the same wavelength for once? "Connor, we both felt that pull. What does it mean?"

He leaned forward, his face like a child on Christmas morning ten minutes before time to open presents. "What would have to happen—? No it's crazy. That's probably too much adventure, even for me."

"Say it. What are you thinking?"

Connor waited an uneasy—for her—moment. "I don't know if this would even interest you," he said, "but do you remember that night at the Gathering?"

"I can never forget it." None of it. The most authentic sense of community she'd ever felt. The camaraderie with Vic and Ericka. Seeing them cope in a graceful way with Ericka's lifelong medical need. The music. Oh, the music.

It had taken Ericka and Vic until that very morning before they finally shared the story of how they'd met. Sitting in the back of a squad car after an underage drinking bust when they were both freshmen in college. They met under the worst of circumstances. But they'd had people in their corner who gave them a chance to start making better choices. They bonded over recovery. And it was a bond that stuck.

"Vic talked about the at-risk teens in their county," Connor said, "and that there was nothing for them. Nobody knew how to connect with them, how to break through their walls. Nobody was free to invest in them the way you invest in the kids at Hope Street."

"I remember." She'd thought about it often in the last few days.

"So, there's that. And then …"

She waited for him to continue.

"What if … ?"

"Connor, come on. I'm dying here."

"What if I sold my 49% of Troyer & Duncan to Nathan and applied for a job doing something with the RoadRave company? I don't know yet what it would be. Or if they're even looking for new hires. But I don't need my name on a business. And I like how RoadRave operates. I like what it stands for. I want to be part of it."

"Connor, are you serious? No, I can tell you are."

"Does that scare you?"

"It would if I hadn't been exploring some of the same thoughts. Is there a way we can combine our passions? Has RoadRave considered sponsoring adventures like the one we've had—well, not exactly like this one."

"A little less drama, you mean?"

"That would be helpful. Would they consider your organizing or developing or leading back-roads trips with at-risk youth?"

Connor leaned against the pillow behind him. "I'd need help. But yeah. That's what's been on my mind."

"We're the ones who could do it, Connor." How long had it been since hope had soared so high? "Nothing to hold us back. Nothing telling us we can't. We can leave our jobs and invent new ones. That's one of the strengths of millennials, isn't it? That we don't feel bound to what we thought life was supposed to look like?"

"Even though we're … *ahem* … *aging out* of the millennial pool, as Judah calls it? Yeah. I think we're people who could pull this off. It wouldn't be without complications, for both of us."

Mallory rubbed her forehead with her fingertips. Connor's signature move was contagious.

"But it seems like we'd be making this move—these moves—for all the right reasons."

"It's sounding more like an answer to prayer all the time."

"And maybe more than just our prayers. Think about the youth in that county."

They hadn't been far from her mind since Vic's words, since meeting Howie, since seeing Howie strong and living with purpose because someone—his dad—was relentless.

"Did you know our rental tiny house in New Day Village is for sale?" She held her breath and pulled Minnie onto her lap while waiting for his response.

"I did hear that. Do you know how much they're asking?"

Mallory couldn't believe he was pursuing the idea. "No. It wouldn't be hard to find out. It had everything we needed."

"We're well practiced at micro-living."

"Yes. We have been living too small. And I'm not talking about the teardrop camper."

"Did you notice how much Judah loved the loft?" She watched Connor's gaze drift to the food stand.

"I realize," she said, "it's not likely Nathan wants to give up his foster parent role."

"Oh, we might be surprised." Connor chuckled.

"Probably even less likely Judah's mom would sign away parental rights. But maybe Nathan would consider ... joint custody?" She couldn't keep the excitement from her voice.

"That would be a curious arrangement. We might have just debunked the 'nothing new under the sun' expression. But if anyone could sell it to Judah's foster care advocates, you could."

She took several breaths to slow the pace of her heart. "And we'd have to sell the idea to Judah."

"Right."

"So much to consider." *But can we please keep considering, Connor?*

He lifted his braced leg into a new position an inch from where it had been. "Does the idea feel to you like an extreme sport or more like stepping onto a path carved for us?"

"A path carved for us by a creative imagination bigger than our own."

Connor laid his hand on the console. She added hers on top of his.

"What do we do now?" he said.

Mallory watched Judah chatting with the owner of the farm stand. Judah was his animated self. "I guess we talk to RoadRave. If they say no ..."

"What about the youth center? Are you concerned about what happens to it if you leave?"

Mallory faced Connor again. "We have an intern itching to step into Cherise's position. And Cherise knows the ropes. Her husband has hinted he wants to get involved more heavily than installing shelves and fixing plumbing and other maintenance issues."

She paused. A deeper truth wanted its time in the sun. It was up to her to express it. "I need to relinquish ownership, Connor. For too long, I believed it all depended on me. And it doesn't."

"I sense a theme," Connor said. "Are we both saying we're ready to take another step up in adulting?"

"Insane, isn't it?"

The joy on Connor's face was worth the whole conversation. "What do we tell Judah? Here he comes."

Mallory's heart hadn't felt this full in a long time. "He's known so much disappointment in his life. I feel we need to hold back any part of it that involves him until we know more."

"Plus, he is a wild man if you give him a video camera and news to tell."

"True."

Judah's hands were full and the farm stand owner trailed behind him with more treats. Mallory got out of the car to help.

"Here's your apples."

"Judah, caramel apples?" Mallory took two from him, leaving him with two more.

"Homemade, which means they're more nutritional."

Connor waved through the window. Mallory addressed the woman holding a box of homemade goods—jams and cookies and what looked like pumpkin bread. "Thank you so much for helping haul Judah's discoveries. I'm Mallory. That's my husband"—*my husband forever*—"Connor in the back seat."

"She's Judith," Judah said. "Get it? Judah. Judith."

"We got it, Judah."

Once Mallory had handed both of her caramel apples to Connor, the woman gave Mallory the box. "I had to come," Judith said, "and tell you folks what your gift did for my heart. My son is in track at school this year and we were forty dollars shy of his uniform fees until you drove up. Now we're halfway there because of you. Kind of restores my faith in people."

"And in a God who cares about details like that," Judah said, already dripping with caramel and apple juices.

Mallory would have dropped the box if it hadn't been full of treasures. "Do you mind holding this again for a minute, Judith?" She reached into her purse and pulled out the twenty singles that had been looking for a home for too long. "Here's the rest of what you need."

Tears welled in the woman's eyes. "I hope you don't think I was begging."

"Not at all," Mallory said, wrapping an arm around her. "You provided us with an opportunity to give. Plus supplied us with all these goodies." *Which I will have to work off next week, but it'll be worth it.*

They said their goodbyes to teary-eyed Judith and got back on the road, after pausing for a caramel apple break and time for Minnie to stretch her legs.

"I love pooling our resources," Connor said.

"Me too."

"Imagine what we could do if we pooled our resources every day."

"Imagine."

Hash marks on the highway. One after another. Inching their way back to Chicago. Back to what might turn out to be a stopover on the way to a much larger adventure. An idea. A concept. A risk. Just add humans …

"Judah," Connor said, "we'll have to discuss it with Mallory. But if my leg keeps doing this well, how would you like it if we stopped off at Niagara Falls on our way?"

Judah stayed unexpectedly quiet for a moment. "Do you have anything smaller?"

Mallory would have swallowed her gum if she'd been chewing any. "Smaller? Niagara Falls was the only thing worth seeing, you said."

"I'm older now," Judah said.

"By three weeks," Connor said. "Not that anyone's counting."

"Everybody gets to see Niagara Falls," Judah said. "Only people like us get to see what we've seen. And that's pretty lit."

"Okay then," Mallory said.

They rode in silence for several miles. With no warning, Connor interrupted the silence with, "I love technology."

"Me too," Judah said.

Mallory glanced at Connor in the rearview mirror. "In what context?"

"A text from RoadRave."

"Oh?"

"Want me to read it to you?"

"Obvie," Judah said.

"I was talking to my wife."

"Oh."

Mallory's grip on the steering wheel eased a little. She already knew that the minute they dropped him off at Nathan's, she'd miss the dynamic that Judah added to their lives. "Yes, I would appreciate hearing what RoadRave has to say."

"Random text," Connor said. "Clear blue sky."

"And … ?"

"Thanked us again for being all-in on this adventure."

"That was nice," Mallory said.

"The company prez added, and I quote, 'If you're ever looking for a job, Connor, you'd have an automatic position here with RoadRave.'"

"You made that up!" Mallory swerved but instantly corrected.

Connor handed his phone to Judah.

Judah said, "Nope. Word for word. Hey! Connor, you left out the part where they said I was cute."

"They did not."

"Probably an oversight."

chapter forty

Ohio in mid-September. Beautiful, but too far from home. Both directions. Too far from the new beginning Mallory and Connor were more than eager to start. The new day.

They'd logged so many miles. In all the ways that counted, they were miles from where they'd started.

Mallory arched her back, rubbed one shoulder at a time, and considered asking for another rest stop.

"Incoming," Judah said.

"Thank the Lord." She waited to hear RoadRave's instructions for where they'd spend what was likely their final night on the road. They had a little bit of Ohio and all of Indiana to cross the next day. If they left earlier in the morning than they normally did, they could be home by midafternoon. Judah still hadn't said anything.

Connor, too, stared at his phone screen. Her ability to check her rearview mirror without losing her focus on the highway had grown to epic proportions.

"Guys?"

"This can't be right, can it, Connor?"

"I don't know. Seems legit. But, wait … that's …"

"Guys, what does it say?"

"It's a picture of a house," Judah said.

"That's all? A house?"

"Mallory, it's my folks' house. RoadRave wants us to go to my parents' house."

◄────────────────────────────►

"It's another mile or so, Mallory." Connor ran his hands through his hair, as if it would help. Mallory was right. He needed a trim. Not as severe, maybe, as Judah's.

"I know, Connor. I've been here before."

"We haven't been here often enough."

"Connor, we don't have to do this if it's too hard for you. Especially, you know, with your leg and—"

He knew her better than that. Finally. "You don't mean that, do you, Mallory?"

"No. Not at all. You need to see your parents. For some reason, RoadRave must have thought so too. Maybe it was her comments on the blog. You need to see your parents."

"Yes, I do."

"What about me?" Judah said. "And Minnie?"

"Minnie had better stay in the car, Judah. Connor's dad is real sick. She might be a little too active."

Connor held the mellow animal in his lap. Active, she was not.

"You'll stay close to me, Judah. Okay?" Mallory said. "If you get uncomfortable, if you don't feel safe, let me know and we'll go out to the kitchen or the yard or come out here to the car."

"I'm not a baby. I've seen sick old people," he said.

Connor smoothed Minnie's fur. "Yeah, not this sick. Try to be quiet, and we'll see how things go."

He repeated the lecture to himself.

It was almost dark. The neighborhood boasted only a few weak streetlamps. The sidewalk approach to the 80s Craftsman bungalow had heaved even more since he'd last been there. Connor let Mallory and Judah run interference for him as he navigated the cracks.

"Three, no, four steps and you'll be all set, Connor. Do your parents know we're coming?" Mallory held the back of his coat as if it were a gait belt.

"I'd guess yes," Judah said. "There's a RoadRave box on the porch and a crying lady standing behind the glass door."

"Connor! Mallory!"

"Hey, Mom. I'd give you a hug, but …" he waved one crutch to emphasize his reason.

"That doesn't prevent me from hugging you." She dove at him with more strength than he knew she still had left in her thin frame. "It is so good to see you. You too, Mallory. And this must be Judah."

"She knows my name? Oh! You're @duncandonuts!"

"That's me. Young man," she said, bending to his level, which was not far, "Connor's dad and I have watched every episode. I know you better than you probably wish I did. Come on in, everyone."

"Is Dad … ?"

"He's having a good day, Connor. And your presence will make it all the better. Let's get in out of the chill."

They stepped into the foyer Connor had seen too infrequently in the past several years. Everything looked eerily the same as it always had. The same hooks in the entry for their coats. The same smell of old furniture and incessant pain.

His dad lay in a hospital bed facing the television in the living room, a gaudy afghan covering him. Every surface of the room held evidence that this was not a dad relaxing in his recliner at the end of a hard day's work. Medication. Hospital-style water jug with an accordion straw. An odd assortment of pillows tucked around his body to take pressure off of his sorest joints. A collapsed wheelchair in the corner that looked as if it hadn't been used in a dust-collecting long time.

"Dad."

His father's gray face brightened. Connor didn't think that was possible anymore.

"Connor. Oh, son. Come here, my boy."

One boy. They'd had two. The side-by-side pictures of Connor and Cody on the mantel were too much. Connor kept his attention directed elsewhere as he crossed the room.

"Dad. How are you doing? Is it okay if I hug you?"

"I'd be disappointed if you didn't. You can do better than that. Haven't you built up any muscles with those crutches?"

"We've been doing a lot more driving than walking the last day or two."

"Oh, I know," he said, his voice thin but stronger than Connor remembered. "Been watching. So proud of you. Button-busting proud of you." The string of sentences seemed to empty him of his day's supply of energy.

"You don't have to talk, Dad." Connor felt Mallory's tap on his arm as she slid a chair close for him and brought an ottoman for his leg, the navy-blue ottoman that didn't go with any of the other furniture in the room but that had been a fixture in that home for so long.

"Judah, come meet my father."

Judah inched his way from where he'd been standing on the entry rug.

"Dad, this is Judah. He's been part of our journey."

His dad reached a paper-thin hand Judah's direction. That kind of hand belonged on a man thirty years older. In his nineties, not his early sixties. Judah took his hand, his adolescent mind somehow aware that he needed to be gentle with it. "Nice to meet you, sir."

Good boy. Thank you.

It's not that conversation ever flowed freely on these visits.

Connor had come to expect the awkward silences, the moments when his dad's lungs or other organs rebelled. Or his mind shut down. Connor talked about the progress of the Cubs and the prospect for the Bears' season. His dad mostly looked at him. But they were together.

After a few minutes, Connor's mom invited the three guests into the kitchen for something to drink. She'd made hot cocoa and set a clear mixing bowl of whipped cream on the table next to their waiting mugs.

Eyes wide, Judah said, "I didn't know whipped cream comes in a bowl." He started with one spoonful, then added another to his steaming drink.

"I usually resort to the aerosol can variety," his mom said. "But this is a special night. You're here."

"We intend to be here more often from now on, Mom," Mallory said.

"We understand. You two kids are busy. Lots of adventures. Don't concern yourselves. We're doing okay."

"Is he on a new medication or something, Mom? He seems a lot better than the last time I was here."

"You think that's better?" Judah asked. "Man, I'd hate to see him on a bad day."

"Judah!" Mallory reached to hold his forearm. That's all she needed to do, and he stopped talking.

Connor's mom smiled as if remembering Connor at a similar age. And attitude. "The doctors are always looking for new combinations of treatments. Some give a little improvement. His kidneys are affected now. We expected that."

"Oh, Mom."

"Connor, it's the process. And I don't want you to keep thinking that caring for him is the burden you've always thought it was. I'm here because I want to be." Connor watched her turn her attention toward Mallory.

A shadow crossed his mom's face. "I have more than a

few regrets," she said. "But I don't regret giving birth to that husband of yours, Mallory. I don't know what your journey might hold for the two of you. But I pray for you every night."

Three weeks ago, they had no future, good or bad, sickness or health. Now they faced quests, not tests.

"We"—he glanced at Mallory—"intend to participate in *your* journey in a more involved way. We're serious about that."

"Chicago's so far away," she said. "And you're both doing important work where you are."

"We're about to change locations, Mom," Mallory said. "It won't be much closer, but the other changes we're making should enable us to offer you some hands-on help far more often."

"You're moving?"

"We're not sure about the details yet, but yes. We hope so." Connor saw the compassion on Mallory's face warm the room more effectively than the hot cocoa.

"Your dad's going into hospice soon, Connor. It would be nice if you could be here that day."

He moved his fingertips to his forehead, but thought better of the gesture and instead reached for his mother's arm. "I will, Mom. I promise."

Mallory laid her hand over Connor's. "And your son keeps his promises, Mom," she said.

◆━━━━━━━━━━━◆

"Connor, I could tell that your mom was impressed that you made her eggs Benedict for breakfast." Mallory noted they'd crossed the Ohio/Indiana state line. "The gesture blessed her."

"You don't think she was mad I wanted cereal instead, do you? Or that we let Minnie sleep in my bed?"

"No, Judah. She raised two ... two boys," Connor said.

"Hey, Judah? Why don't you listen to that book on tape I downloaded for you? With your earbuds?"

"How is that literacy, Mallory? I'm listening, not reading."

"Still counts," Connor said from the back seat.

"You want to talk to each other without me, don't you?" Judah reached for his earbuds.

"Call it Marital Literacy Takes Courage, if you want," Mallory said. *More true than I thought. Learning Connor's language. Figuring out what the words mean. Having the courage to listen to the sounds his heart makes …*

"What's on your mind, Mallory?"

"Two things. You've decided not to look at your test results until there's an overwhelmingly compelling reason, right? Symptoms. Or a need to start replenishing our baby fund someday."

"Right."

"I think your mom is a compelling reason. She's living every day not knowing if she'll lose another son."

"She might."

"Or —"

"Or she might not."

Mallory sighed. "Connor, if she's already concerned you're carrying the VHL gene, then knowing for sure won't shock her system. But if the results are negative, you have the potential to give her a gift that would mean more to her than anything in the world, don't you think?"

Connor sighed. "We could look at the results and keep them to ourselves if it's no different than what she already believes."

"Or tell her the whole truth no matter what," Mallory said. "She's stronger than she looks."

"I need some time to think about that."

"I understand."

"And the second thing?" Connor said.

"You owe me a song."

"About that …"

"Didn't want you to forget."

"I haven't forgotten."

"Me either," Judah said.

"Judah!"

"It's not my fault. I asked for noise-canceling headphones, but did I get them? No."

"Who picked up the contents of the RoadRave box?" Mallory asked as they passed yet another mile marker.

"That would be me," Connor said.

"If it was a bag of Cheetos and you didn't share …" Judah said, hands on his hips.

Connor stuck his hands through the console opening between the two front seats and turned them front to back to prove he bore no orange cheesy residue.

"I'm curious too, Connor." Mallory braked for a train. "Looks like we'll be here a while, boys." She put the SUV in park mode.

"Probably a good enough time, then, for breaking out this." Connor slid a thumb drive across the console toward Mallory.

"What's this?"

"The gift from RoadRave. And from me."

"Judah, can you … ?"

Judah opened Mallory's laptop and slipped in the USB drive.

"Open the file. It's the only one on there," Connor said.

Music. "Connor, that sounds like your guitar."

"With a little help from Joel and Janene."

"The music group from the Gathering? Connor, how did you—?"

"Dude. That is, like, extra!" Judah danced in his seat.

"Help me out here, Mallory."

"Extra," she said. "Really good."

"Ah. Right."

Mallory shushed them. "I want to hear this."

Judah slid the volume to max so the sound filled the car and overrode the clacking of the train.

Her song. The one she'd asked him to write. It was all in

there, the angst, the disappointment, the times they'd failed each other, the long crawl back to the core of who they were.

They'd come so many miles from where they'd started. And the miles ahead held the most meaningful adventures.

"Want me to play it again, Mallory?" Judah asked.

She couldn't speak.

"I'll take that for a yes." He hit Play.

The music swelled, washed over her like the healing of an endless warm waterfall.

Connor's voice. How had he gotten his voice and guitar recorded for RoadRave to send to Joel and Janene? And how had they—? It didn't matter. All that mattered was the future that lay ahead of them and Connor's song's final words:

This is not how our story ends.

←――――――――――――→

Two days later.

Mallory reached around Connor from behind and pressed her hands against his chest as he stood making one of the last batches of coffee they'd share in their Chicago apartment. Minnie politely lapped from her stainless-steel water bowl in the corner.

Connor smothered her hands with one of his. It warmed her to her toes.

She laid her head against his back. "We got a text from Judah."

"Oh? What did he say?"

"I quote: 'Next year—Europe!'"

Mallory could feel every bit of her husband's laughter with her embrace. "And …"

"More?"

"Not from Judah. From your mom."

Connor hop-turned to face her. "We talked to her last night. What was on her mind this morning?"

"Joy."

He didn't speak, but his next breath shuddered on the way in.

"We did the right thing, Connor. She hasn't been this happy in a long time." Mallory leaned her head on her favorite spot, right over his heart. A corner of the opened manila envelope peeked out of the wastebasket, as if nodding in agreement.

Connor enfolded her and said, "Neither have I, Mallory."

She heard the thunder of a thousand waterfalls resonate in his chest.

Rushing waters can't quench love;
rivers can't wash it away.

Song of Solomon 8:7 CEB

This Is Not How Our Story Ends
by Connor Duncan*

The look in your eyes when I tell you I love you,
After all the times when words came so hard,
The warmth of your hand
on the pulse of our story,
The miles tick on, and they take us far.

Far from the place where our journey started,
Far from the moment our love derailed,
Wrapped in the grace of a Love undeniable,
The miles tick on, and they take us far.

If I could erase all the tears I caused you,
If you could forget all the tears that were mine,
If all that we said and all we left unsaid
Could fade into memories we'd no longer find,

The path that we've taken,
the one we're still traveling,
Miles—steep or smooth—ahead of us now,
Would tell us the journey
of love's worth the taking.
We've come so far, but we've so far to go.

With the wind at our back,
or against it we're leaning,
When roads lead us higher,
or life twists and bends,
I promise you, love, that
though riddled, regretted,
With hope, this is not how our story ends.
No, this is not how our story ends.

* Connor Duncan's song was written by author Cynthia Ruchti

The Author's Gratitude

I've been inexpressibly grateful for every book contract it's been my privilege to sign. As I lay my fingers on the keyboard now to acknowledge those who played a part in *Miles from Where We Started*, my initial thought is gratitude for the opportunity to tell this story. This one.

Few married couples would say their first year of marriage was their best, if measured in maturity or absence of potholes and road hazards. I'm grateful to the man who didn't give up during our first year. Though we'd known each other since childhood, the journey of marriage started with that wild mix of exuberance and "Who in the name of all that is holy *are* you?" Thank you, Bill, for your tenacity and faithfulness, and for allowing God to draw us back to the song, "This is not how our story ends."

The Gilead team has had a journey of its own. It's with a deep heart of gratitude that I say *thank you* for tending this story well, for caring about it and investing in it, cover to cover, reader to reader. Thank you too, to editor Jamie Chavez, a faithful companion on my writing journey.

I'm grateful that God gave me a heart for millennials before I'd even researched their strengths and gifts, their opportunities and challenges. "Millennials. Am I right?" Yes. Aren't they amazing, fearless, unstopped by "It can't be done"?

I can still see the look on his face when I asked a twelve-year-old boy from church if I could borrow his name and parts of his personality for the Judah in this novel. I've never heard the Judah I know say an unkind word. The broad smile never leaves his face and eyes, unless he's intently focused on worship. Thank you, Judah. You've taught me much.

Once more, Wendy Lawton, my agent with Books & Such Literary Management, made this writing journey so much richer than it would have been without her. Whether sharing title discussions, cover analysis, a heartening reader letter, or artichokes and tea, the moment is meaningful and soul filling because of her.

On a spontaneous adventure afternoon, my husband and I traveled to a not-so-far-away facility that builds teardrop campers. We were generously treated to a private tour of the factory and saw teardrop campers in all stages of construction (see photographs on my *Miles from Where We Started* Pinterest page). We marveled at the efficiency ... and the smallness. Both worked their way into this book. Thank you, Camp-Inn Teardrop Travel Trailers.

Becky Melby, friend-sister-author-critique-partner, I can't imagine writing a book without your influence. Your encouragement and diligent prayers, coupled with your insights and your reminders that deadlines are not *death*lines, have kept my feet to the path.

A nephew-to-be recently asked a niece to share life with him. His social media message making the announcement to friends and family said of his fiancée, in essence, "I'm glad my faults can be filled with what Jesus has done."

That's the kind of family and extended family—long-married, soon-to-be-married, once-married, the blissful, and the blistered—I call my own, and from whom I draw inspiration. Thank you, daughters and sons, sisters and brothers, grandchildren with a long and winding road stretching ahead of you. May you know—deep in your souls—that patterning your love after the Love Undeniable will hem your journey in hope.

Readers …

Give me a moment to compose myself.

You, readers, keep me writing. Wherever you are on your journey, may you hear the whispers of my gratitude, and ultimately the Voice that calls, "Just add humans, and the Adventure with Me begins!"

Discussion Questions

1. What moment in the story *Miles from Where We Started* did you sense the first stirring of hope for Connor and Mallory? For Judah?

2. Have you found "wisdom" characters scattered along your own journey? Did they stay on the path with you for a season or a lifetime? In what way did they influence your approach to the challenges and hurdles in your life?

3. If you faced the kinds of odds Connor knew hovered over his life, how would you have handled it differently? If you have experienced something similar, did you invite others on your journey or walk the trail alone?

4. Is your normal pattern to confront and talk it out or to retreat and ponder? Does that come from your personality or your history? Which had a stronger influence on Connor? On Mallory? On Judah?

5. The author has her own ideas, but how do you think RoadRave delivered their boxes?

6. What would you have found most disturbing if asked to take the same trip Mallory was forced to take? What would you have found most exhilarating?

7. Which of the travelers Connor and Mallory met had the strongest impact on your life as a reader? Why?

8. Judah's position in the front seat held deeper meaning than merely his supposed physical issue. It guided both Mallory and Connor in not sending him to the back seat once the truth came out. What deeper meaning do you think their actions communicated?

9. Have you visited any of the locations that were destinations for Mallory and Connor? What were your impressions?

10. Is there a quote from the story that altered your thinking regarding marriage? Millennials? Foster care? Faith? Life's adventures?

11. What's your See America dream trip? Back roads or interstates? Major tourist destinations or off the beaten path?

12. How do you think Mallory and Connor's emotional journeys might have changed if their trip had led them to more heavily traveled tourist spots?

About the Author

Drawing from 33 years as writer/producer and on-air voice actor for the daily 15-minute radio broadcast The Heartbeat of the Home, Cynthia Ruchti now tells stories hemmed-in-Hope through novels, nonfiction, devotionals, and at speaking events for women. Her books have received numerous awards, including the Carol Award, Christian Retailing's BEST Award, and Inspirational Readers' Choice Award, as well as being a finalist for the Christy Awards and RT Reviews Inspirational Novel of the Year.

Cynthia serves on the worship team at her church and as the professional relations liaison for American Christian Fiction Writers (ACFW). She's a member of AWSA (Advanced

Writers and Speakers Association), WFWA (Women's Fiction Writers Association), is represented by Wendy Lawton of Books & Such Literary Management, and recently joined the Books & Such team as a literary agent.

Cynthia and her grade school sweetheart husband live in the heart of Wisconsin, not far from their three children and five (to-date) grandchildren.

Her prayer is that through her books and speaking events, readers and audiences will gain new courage to say, "I can't unravel. I'm hemmed in Hope."

Website: http://www.cynthiaruchti.com
Facebook: facebook.com/CynthiaRuchtiReaderPage/
Instagram: @cynthiaruchti1994
Twitter: @cynthiaruchti
Pinterest: @cynthiaruchti
Youtube: @hopeglows

Keep the Adventure Going
Discover exclusive content on Cynthia Ruchti's website
cynthiaruchti.com/miles-from-where-we-started-songs/